A Place to Belong

Arabella Quinn

Published by Arabella Quinn, 2024.

This is a work of fiction. Similarities to real people, places, or events are entirely coincidental.

A PLACE TO BELONG

First edition. October 6, 2024.

Copyright © 2024 Arabella Quinn.

ISBN: 979-8227623539

Written by Arabella Quinn.

Chapter 1: The Color of Change

The moment the door swung open, it felt as if a gust of fresh air had blown into my little world of soft blues and muted grays. I looked up from the colorful chaos of fabric swatches scattered across my desk, my heart stumbling at the sight of him. Jake, the owner of the café that had captured my imagination since I first wandered past it, stood there like a ray of sunshine breaking through a stormy sky. His messy dark hair framed a face that was both boyish and rugged, with laughter lines etched around his warm brown eyes. I was immediately captivated.

"Is this a bad time?" he asked, his voice a perfect blend of curiosity and charm, laced with a hint of that unmistakable barista quality—intimately familiar yet refreshingly earnest.

I felt the familiar flutter in my chest, that unexpected rush of adrenaline that always accompanied encounters with him. "No, not at all! I was just lost in thoughts about your café," I replied, trying to sound nonchalant while feeling anything but. I gestured to the kaleidoscope of colors sprawled out like a vibrant mosaic, each swatch a possibility, a dream waiting to unfold. "I'm excited about the project!"

Jake leaned against the doorframe, a playful smirk dancing on his lips. "You know, I thought my café was charming before, but it seems I've just discovered it's a canvas in need of a masterpiece."

His words wrapped around me, warming my cheeks. I busied myself with the swatches, pretending the flush was a result of the sunlight streaming through the window rather than his compliment. In the few months since I left my old job, I had dreamed of this moment—walking into a space where my creativity could flourish, where every detail could be painted with my brush. But standing there in my office, with Jake watching me, it felt like my own insecurities were on full display.

"I want to keep the essence of the café," I said, my fingers trailing over a soft sage green that reminded me of the leaves rustling in the trees outside. "It has a certain warmth, like the smell of fresh coffee and baked pastries."

He nodded, his expression turning thoughtful. "Exactly. I want people to feel at home when they come in. You know, like a cozy nook in the midst of the chaos of life."

I could see it clearly now—a blend of rustic charm and modern simplicity, where the walls would tell stories through their colors. I envisioned a space that would wrap around patrons like a comforting embrace, coaxing them to linger a little longer, to savor both their coffee and the moments spent within those walls. "How about we focus on warm neutrals paired with pops of color? Something inviting, something that reflects your personality."

"Like a warm hug with a dash of mischief?" Jake asked, his eyes twinkling with mischief that made my heart race.

"Exactly!" I exclaimed, the enthusiasm bubbling over. "Your café should be a reflection of you—a space where creativity and connection flow freely."

As we brainstormed ideas, my mind danced through textures and patterns, envisioning a café that would feel alive, where each element harmonized with the next. The light streaming through the windows could filter through sheer curtains in soft, airy whites, while the walls could boast a backdrop of creamy taupe, allowing the vivid bursts of color from art and decor to pop like confetti in the air.

I leaned forward, my excitement palpable. "What do you think about adding a community wall? A space where local artists can showcase their work? It would create an ever-changing backdrop, a living gallery that invites conversation."

Jake's smile widened, revealing a hint of mischief. "I like it. And how about a few quirky chairs? Something that invites people to sit, stay, and make memories—like those vintage armchairs at that antique store down the street?"

"Yes!" I could hardly contain my delight, my words spilling out like an overflowing cup of coffee. "They would add character, a sense of history. We could even find a mismatched table that tells a story of its own, perhaps one that was hand-painted or distressed."

Jake pushed himself off the doorframe, stepping closer, and I caught a hint of sandalwood and roasted coffee, a blend that made my pulse quicken. "You know, I really appreciate your passion for this. It's refreshing."

The sincerity in his voice ignited a fire within me, and for a moment, the world outside faded. It was just him, me, and our shared vision for something beautiful. "Thank you. This project means everything to me," I said, feeling the weight of my past choices drifting away like clouds on a summer's day. "It's more than just design; it's about creating a space where people feel welcome, where they belong."

"I can see that," Jake said, his eyes locking onto mine, and the connection between us felt electric. "You're not just transforming a café; you're breathing new life into the community."

Our conversation flowed effortlessly, as if we were two threads weaving together in a tapestry of creativity. As we discussed colors, textures, and themes, I caught glimpses of Jake's passion for his work. He spoke about the regulars who came in for their morning coffee, the way they'd linger and share stories, transforming the café into a haven of camaraderie.

Outside, the sun hung low in the sky, casting a golden hue that danced through the window, illuminating our shared dreams. In that moment, surrounded by swatches and ideas, I felt a surge of hope and excitement. I wasn't just designing a café; I was sculpting a space where memories would be made, where lives would intersect over warm cups of coffee and laughter.

I knew then, as I looked into Jake's eyes, that this project could be the catalyst for something greater. Perhaps it could be the beginning of my own story—one filled with color, connection, and the exhilarating uncertainty of new beginnings. And in that crowded office, amidst the chaos of dreams yet to be realized, I felt the promise of change tugging at the corners of my heart, urging me to take the leap into a future painted in vivid strokes of possibility.

Our conversation flowed like a well-crafted latte, rich and frothy with possibilities, and I found myself drinking in every word. As we flipped through design inspirations on my laptop—images of cozy cafes filled with greenery, mismatched furniture, and walls adorned with local art—I couldn't help but admire the twinkle in Jake's eye as he pointed out pieces that resonated with him. "What do you think about adding a reading nook?" he suggested, enthusiasm lacing his voice. "Somewhere people can grab a book and a coffee and just... escape for a while?"

I could almost see it: a small corner bathed in soft light, a pair of inviting armchairs, and shelves brimming with novels waiting to be discovered. "That's brilliant!" I exclaimed, the vision unfolding before me like a pop-up book. "We could hang a vintage sign above it that says 'Escape Here'—something playful yet inviting."

His laughter filled the room, a warm sound that danced in the air like the aroma of freshly brewed coffee. "You're making me want to spend all my time in my own café. It's dangerous, you know. I might never leave."

The flirtation hung between us, light yet tantalizing, and I felt a giddy rush as our gazes locked. He was more than just a client; he was a kindred spirit, someone who understood the magic that came from creating a space meant to welcome and embrace. I was entranced by his passion, his desire to build something that would resonate deeply with everyone who walked through the door.

In a moment of inspired spontaneity, I grabbed a notepad and jotted down ideas, my handwriting a flurry of excitement. "We should add some local plants—maybe ferns or succulents that can hang from the ceiling or sit on the tables. They'd bring life into the space," I proposed, glancing up to find him nodding in agreement, his smile widening.

"Plants are great. They really create a vibe, don't they?" He leaned closer, and I could feel the warmth radiating off him, an almost magnetic pull that made it hard to concentrate on anything else. "What about an interactive element? A community board where people can post events or share their own stories? That way, we can turn the café into a living, breathing part of the neighborhood."

The idea sent a ripple of excitement through me. "Yes! A story wall where people can pin up memories or photos. Each month, we could feature a different local artist or photographer, too." The thought of a dynamic space, one that evolved with the community, ignited something fierce within me. I envisioned laughter, connections forming over shared experiences, and conversations sparking between strangers who might one day become friends.

As we delved deeper into our brainstorming session, the hours melted away. Outside, the sun dipped lower in the sky, casting a warm golden glow through the office window. My heart raced, not just from the creative energy buzzing around us but from the realization that this was exactly where I was meant to be. I wasn't merely designing a café; I was building a haven for dreams, connection, and stories—a place where I could weave my own into the fabric of the community.

Jake's enthusiasm fueled my creativity, and I found myself swept up in a whirlwind of ideas that swirled around us like confetti in the breeze. "How about a coffee tasting event once a month?" I suggested, my voice bubbling with enthusiasm. "It could draw in more customers and create a sense of community. People love to share experiences, especially when they involve coffee."

"Now that's a plan," he replied, leaning back in his chair, his expression one of genuine intrigue. "We could even partner with local roasters to showcase different blends. I like the idea of supporting other local businesses."

His sincerity struck a chord deep within me, stirring a longing I hadn't fully acknowledged before. It was more than just designing a café; it was about breathing life into a shared vision, an opportunity to create something that transcended the ordinary. I could feel the weight of my past—a corporate life that stifled my spirit—beginning to lift as I embraced the vibrant energy of this new path.

"I can't wait to start," I said, my heart soaring at the thought of bringing our ideas to life. "There's so much potential here. Imagine the first day we open, the smell of coffee mingling with the chatter of friends. It'll be beautiful."

Jake nodded, his eyes reflecting a spark of shared ambition. "And you'll be right there with me, creating that experience. This is going to be amazing."

In that moment, I knew I had found more than just a project; I had discovered a partnership grounded in shared values, vision, and an undeniable chemistry that simmered beneath the surface. It felt like the universe had conspired to bring us together, two souls eager to make a mark in a world that often felt overwhelmingly chaotic.

The afternoon light began to fade, and as I glanced out the window, I noticed the colors of the sky shifting into hues of soft lavender and peach, mirroring the feelings blossoming inside me. I could already envision the café adorned with twinkling fairy lights, laughter spilling out onto the street, and the warmth of a community coming together in this little haven we were crafting.

"Are you free this weekend?" Jake's voice cut through my reverie, pulling me back to the moment. "I'd love for you to see the café space in person. I think it'll spark even more ideas."

My heart raced at the invitation. "I'd love that!" The thrill of stepping into the space I would help transform filled me with anticipation. I envisioned myself walking through the café, each corner whispering secrets of what it could become, how it could resonate with the lives that would intertwine within its walls.

As we wrapped up our brainstorming session, I felt lighter than I had in years. Every idea we shared wove a thread of connection between us, a tapestry of collaboration that filled the room with an almost electric energy. The scent of fresh coffee still lingered, a reminder of what lay ahead, and as I packed away the colorful swatches, my heart fluttered at the thought of this new beginning.

With Jake, I wasn't just reclaiming my dreams; I was stepping into a world bursting with potential—a world where I could transform not only a café but also my own narrative, one that celebrated change, connection, and the beauty of crafting something meaningful together.

We arranged to meet at the café on Saturday morning, and as the day approached, I could hardly contain my excitement. Friday night felt like a restless lull, every tick of the clock amplifying my anticipation. I scoured my closet, searching for the perfect outfit—a delicate balance between casual and polished, something that embodied the spirit of creativity and warmth I hoped to evoke in the café. I finally settled on a simple white blouse paired with my favorite navy jeans, a hint of color peeking from beneath a vibrant cardigan. The ensemble felt just right, a reflection of my burgeoning enthusiasm.

Saturday dawned bright and clear, the sun spilling over the rooftops of the small town like golden syrup. I made my way to the café, my heart thrumming in rhythm with each step. As I approached the charming building, I felt a swell of pride and exhilaration. It was an inviting sight, with its weathered brick façade and wide, wooden door flanked by potted plants that swayed gently in the breeze. The sign above read "Jake's Café" in elegant, swirling letters, the letters curling like tendrils of smoke rising from a steaming cup of coffee.

Pushing the door open, the gentle chime of bells greeted me, ushering me into a world that felt almost sacred. The interior was just as I had imagined—cozy and unpretentious, with worn wooden floors that creaked softly underfoot. Sunlight flooded through large windows, illuminating the mismatched furniture scattered about. A few patrons sat at tables, engrossed in their conversations or lost in their books, while the scent of freshly brewed coffee enveloped me like a warm embrace. I could already envision the vibrant atmosphere we would cultivate together.

Jake emerged from the back, apron tied around his waist and a smudge of flour dusting his cheek, instantly lighting up the space with his radiant smile. "Welcome to my kingdom!" he declared, sweeping his arms wide as if to showcase the world he had created. "What do you think?"

"It's beautiful!" I replied, my voice almost a whisper, as I absorbed the charm of the café. I felt an electric thrill run through me at the thought of what it could become. "I can see so much potential here."

He grinned, a hint of pride glowing in his eyes. "I've been waiting for someone like you to come along and help me realize it." He led me further inside, pointing out various elements that defined the café's character—an old-fashioned cash register that looked like it belonged in a museum, a coffee bar decorated with rustic shelving housing a selection of artisanal beans, and a chalkboard menu scribbled with daily specials in Jake's tidy handwriting.

As we walked, I couldn't help but notice how effortlessly Jake moved through the space, his familiarity lending a warmth to every corner. "I've always envisioned this place as a community hub," he shared, his voice tinged with passion. "I want people to come here not just for coffee but for connection."

We stood by the window, sunlight pouring in and casting a golden glow around us. "You've done an incredible job. It's inviting and intimate," I said, feeling the atmosphere hum with possibility. "We can enhance that sense of connection, make it feel like a second home."

With our ideas blossoming, we set to work. I pulled out my sketchbook, the pages blank but filled with anticipation. "What do you think about adding a communal table?" I suggested, drawing a rough outline. "Something large enough to host community events or workshops, where strangers can sit together and share stories over coffee."

Jake's eyes lit up. "That's perfect! I've been wanting to organize a weekly poetry night or open mic. It would be great to showcase local talent."

The mere thought of transforming this space into a vibrant center of creativity sent a thrill through me. We began brainstorming names for the events, tossing ideas back and forth as if they were playful confetti floating through the air. "How about 'Caffeine & Creativity' for the workshops?" I proposed, the words rolling off my tongue. "And 'Brewed Awakenings' for the open mic?"

Jake chuckled, his laughter a warm melody that danced in the air. "I love it! You really know how to capture the essence of what we're building here."

As the morning slipped into afternoon, we discussed everything from art displays to live music, envisioning a place that thrived on the energy of creativity and community. I could feel the excitement building, a heady mix of inspiration and anticipation swirling around us like steam rising from a freshly brewed cup of coffee.

"We should create a signature drink," I suggested, the idea bubbling to the surface like froth in a cappuccino. "Something that embodies the spirit of this café, something unique."

Jake's brow furrowed in thought, and I watched as a light bulb flickered to life in his eyes. "What about a 'Chai-tastic Chai'?" he said, grinning mischievously. "It could be spiced to perfection, just like you!"

I feigned indignation, my heart swelling at his compliment. "Oh, please! I'm not that spicy!" I laughed, the playful banter wrapping around us like a favorite blanket.

As the day wore on, our visions intertwined, creating a rich tapestry of ideas that felt like a shared heartbeat. I could see the café blooming in my mind, each idea a petal unfurling, ready to greet the world. The laughter, the colors, the aromas—all of it danced vividly in my imagination, and I realized this was the life I had craved: one that involved not just my passion but also connections, laughter, and a sprinkle of adventure.

We worked tirelessly, fueled by passion and the sweet aroma of coffee that filled the air. As dusk settled, the sun dipped low on the horizon, painting the sky in shades of coral and violet. We stepped outside, the evening air crisp and refreshing. The café glowed behind us, its windows shimmering like jewels against the twilight.

I turned to Jake, my heart racing with a mixture of excitement and something deeper—an undeniable connection that felt as vibrant as the world we were creating together. "Thank you for believing in this vision. I never knew how much I needed this until now."

He looked at me, sincerity etching itself into his features. "Thank you for bringing your passion. You're not just helping me design a café; you're helping me build a dream."

As we stood there, surrounded by the whispers of possibility and the hum of creativity, I felt an intoxicating sense of belonging.

It wasn't merely about the café; it was about forging connections that transcended the physical space we were crafting. It was about weaving our stories together, about the laughter that would echo off the walls and the friendships that would blossom over shared cups of coffee.

In that moment, I understood that change wasn't something to fear; it was an invitation to embrace the unknown. And with Jake by my side, the horizon ahead seemed brighter, painted with the vivid colors of hope, dreams, and the intoxicating thrill of new beginnings.

Chapter 2: A Canvas of Emotions

The café, a quaint little spot called The Willow, is a canvas waiting to be painted with life. Sunlight filters through the large bay windows, casting a golden hue over the rustic wooden tables, their surfaces smoothed by the passage of countless cups of coffee and whispered conversations. The air is rich with the aroma of freshly brewed coffee, mingling with hints of baked goods cooling on the counter. The barista, a young woman with a cascade of auburn curls, moves with an effortless grace, her laughter rising above the soft jazz playing in the background.

Seated across from Jake, I can't help but admire the way he talks about his vision for the café. He gestures animatedly, his hands painting pictures in the air that pull me into his dream. There's a spark in his eyes that captivates me—a beautiful blend of hope and worry that makes my heart ache with empathy. I find myself hanging on his every word, enchanted by the way he describes a community space, a sanctuary where creativity flourishes, where artists could gather, and where laughter could bloom like the wildflowers in spring.

As he speaks, I lean in closer, captivated by the warmth radiating from him, the way his brow furrows ever so slightly when he talks about the challenges ahead. My heart flutters, a gentle dance of anticipation and admiration. Each time he leans closer, his breath brushing against my cheek, I can feel the electricity that crackles between us, filling the air with an undeniable chemistry that makes my pulse race. It's intoxicating, this shared space, this fleeting moment where our ambitions intertwine, blending the lines between friendship and something deeper.

"Imagine," he says, a grin breaking across his face, "a wall dedicated to local art. Every month, we could host a different artist. It would be like a gallery and a café all in one." His enthusiasm is

A PLACE TO BELONG 13

infectious, sparking a fire within me. I picture the space transformed, the walls alive with color and creativity, each brushstroke telling a story, each piece a reflection of the soul that crafted it.

"What if we also had a book corner?" I suggest, the idea bubbling up like a freshly opened bottle of soda. "A cozy nook with oversized chairs and shelves filled with novels. A place where people can sip their lattes while getting lost in a good book." The thought excites me, and I can see the idea flicker in Jake's eyes, igniting another wave of conversation.

He chuckles, the sound rich and deep, a melody that wraps around me like a favorite song. "I love that! Picture it: people curled up in those chairs, lost in their stories, while the aroma of pastries fills the air." I can almost hear the soft rustle of pages turning, the comfortable hum of quiet conversations blending into the background.

The sun dips lower, painting the café in warm shades of orange and pink, creating a magical ambiance that feels like a scene from a romantic film. I catch sight of a couple in the corner, their fingers intertwined as they share a slice of cake, the warmth in their smiles radiating like the sunlight spilling through the windows. The scene makes my heart swell with longing for connection, for intimacy that goes beyond words.

Jake's gaze drifts to the window, his expression momentarily clouding with something unspoken. "I just hope I can make this happen," he murmurs, his voice barely above a whisper. The vulnerability in his tone tugs at my heartstrings, pulling me closer to him in a way I hadn't anticipated.

"Why wouldn't you?" I challenge gently, searching his eyes for the glimmer of belief I know resides there. "You have the vision, the passion. All you need is the right support." My words hang in the air, a fragile promise of solidarity, a gentle nudge towards his potential.

He looks at me then, really looks, and in that moment, the world around us fades away. I'm struck by the way his dark hair falls over his forehead, the slight dimple in his left cheek when he smiles, and the way his hands move to emphasize each point he makes. I feel a rush of warmth, a desire to be part of his journey, to help him navigate the labyrinth of obstacles that stand in his way.

"I don't want to fail," he admits, his voice thick with emotion. "This place means everything to me."

A part of me yearns to reach across the table, to take his hand in mine and reassure him that every great dream comes with its share of fears. Instead, I lean back, allowing my eyes to wander around The Willow. I envision the laughter that would echo off the walls, the community that would gather here, sharing stories over steaming mugs of coffee. It could be a place where hope reigns, where dreams are nurtured, and where every visitor leaves with a piece of joy tucked in their hearts.

"Then let's make sure it doesn't," I say, my voice steady, filled with a conviction I didn't know I possessed. "Let's build something beautiful together." I can feel the shift in the atmosphere, the air thick with possibility and the scent of adventure.

Jake's eyes widen slightly, surprise mingling with something deeper, something that makes my stomach flip in an exhilarating way. For a brief moment, I wonder if he can sense the connection we share, an invisible thread binding our hopes and dreams. It's both terrifying and exhilarating, and I can't help but smile, a warmth blooming within me.

"Together," he repeats, his lips curving into that infectious grin again. The tension eases, replaced by laughter that spills into the air, mingling with the warmth of the café. The world outside fades into a distant memory as we lose ourselves in plans and dreams, each shared idea like a brushstroke on the canvas of our future, the possibilities infinite and bright.

The sun dips below the horizon, casting a soft, golden light that envelops The Willow in an ethereal glow. It feels like the café is holding its breath, waiting for our shared dreams to burst forth and fill the space with life. As Jake talks, his voice rises and falls like a gentle tide, each wave of enthusiasm washing over me, tugging me deeper into his vision. It's as if the café itself is absorbing our energy, ready to transform into the sanctuary we're imagining.

With each new idea, I picture the vibrant greenery that could line the walls—ferns cascading from hanging pots, delicate ivy snaking its way around the wooden beams. I can almost hear the soft rustle of leaves as the breeze wafts through the open windows, carrying the laughter of friends and the soft clinking of cups. Jake speaks of an open mic night, a chance for budding musicians and poets to showcase their talents. I can already envision a small stage in the corner, adorned with twinkling fairy lights, creating a cozy atmosphere that draws people in like moths to a flame.

As he describes the menu—a fusion of local flavors and bold experimentation—my mouth waters. "Picture it: artisan sandwiches, gourmet coffee blends, and pastries that are too beautiful to eat," he says, his hands dancing in the air, painting each dish as if it were a masterpiece. I can see it now: a rustic wooden board laden with colorful salads, decadent pastries glistening with a sugary sheen, and steaming mugs of coffee, each sip a warm hug on a chilly day. My imagination ignites, and I find myself swept up in the momentum of our conversation, ideas swirling around us like confetti.

But it's the moments in between, the fleeting glances and shy smiles, that resonate with me the most. When our eyes meet, there's a spark, an unspoken understanding that hangs between us like a gossamer thread. I catch the way he runs his fingers through his hair, a nervous habit that only makes him more endearing. The world outside fades into a blur, the bustling street and honking cars reduced to a distant hum as I become enveloped in this bubble of creativity and connection.

As the café begins to empty, the atmosphere shifts subtly. The last few patrons linger, savoring their drinks, reluctant to leave this cocoon of warmth and inspiration. A couple by the window shares soft laughter, their fingers entwined, and for a moment, I feel a pang of longing—an ache for that kind of closeness, that sense of belonging. It's a reminder of why I'm here, of the dreams I've carried with me, quietly tucked away until now.

I glance back at Jake, whose brow is furrowed in concentration as he scribbles notes on a napkin, his tongue poking out slightly in concentration. It's a sight that makes me smile, a glimpse of the passion that fuels him. The way he loses himself in his thoughts, the world around him fading into insignificance, pulls me in. There's a genuine vulnerability to him that draws me closer, as if he's laid his hopes bare before me, inviting me to be part of the journey.

"Do you ever think about what it would be like to own a place like this?" I ask, the question slipping out almost instinctively. My fingers drum lightly on the table, a nervous rhythm matching the flutter of my heart. "I mean, to create something that feels like home for everyone who walks through the door?"

His eyes light up, reflecting a flicker of hope. "Every day," he admits, a hint of disbelief lacing his words. "It's more than just a café to me; it's a dream of community. Somewhere people feel safe, inspired... like they belong." His honesty strikes a chord deep within me, a resonance that feels both frightening and exhilarating.

I nod, feeling my own hopes surge to the surface. "That's exactly it. It's about creating a space where people can connect—where every corner invites conversation, laughter, and maybe even a little magic." As I speak, I picture the café alive with energy, walls echoing with the stories shared within, each person leaving a bit of their soul behind.

The sky darkens outside, stars beginning to twinkle like tiny beacons of hope against the indigo backdrop. I find myself captivated by their glow, lost in the beauty of the moment. It reminds me of late-night conversations with friends, where the world feels vast, and anything seems possible. "We could even have a star-gazing night," I muse, "an event where people can gather with blankets, sipping hot cocoa while we watch the constellations dance above."

Jake's laughter breaks through the quiet, rich and full, a sound that wraps around me like a favorite song. "You really have a knack for this, you know?" he says, his admiration evident. "Every idea you share adds to the vision. I think we make a pretty good team."

That simple compliment makes my heart swell, and I can't help but return his grin, a warmth spreading through me. I find myself leaning a little closer, encouraged by the way he looks at me—like I'm not just another person sitting across from him but an integral part of this dream we're weaving together.

We fall into a comfortable rhythm, our conversation flowing seamlessly as the minutes turn into hours. It feels as if we've known each other for years, each shared laugh and exchanged glance drawing us closer together. The clattering of dishes and the soft murmur of conversation fade into the background, creating a symphony of intimacy that is uniquely ours.

Eventually, the café begins to close for the night, the lights dimming, casting a soft glow over the remaining tables. I glance around, taking in the cozy atmosphere that seems to hum with the energy we've infused into it. The barista waves goodbye, her smile genuine as she gathers her things, leaving us in our little sanctuary.

Jake looks at me, a flicker of something unspoken dancing in his eyes. "I don't want this to end," he admits, and the sincerity in his tone sends a thrill down my spine. There's a weight in his words, a promise of something more that lingers in the air between us, drawing me in.

"Neither do I," I reply, my voice barely above a whisper. It feels monumental, this acknowledgment of the connection we've built in such a short time. The space around us, once merely an empty café, has transformed into a haven, alive with the essence of who we are and the dreams we're daring to share.

As we step outside, the cool night air greets us like an old friend, invigorating and alive with possibility. I take a deep breath, the crispness awakening my senses, grounding me in the moment. The stars shimmer above, each one a tiny reminder of the infinite dreams we're crafting together, and for the first time in a long time, I feel an overwhelming sense of hope—a belief that perhaps, just perhaps, this little café will one day become the heart of something beautiful, a vibrant tapestry woven from the threads of our shared aspirations.

The cool night air wraps around us as we step out of The Willow, transforming the warm, inviting interior into a distant memory. I take a deep breath, savoring the earthy scent of damp pavement mingling with the faint remnants of jasmine from a nearby garden. The streetlamps cast pools of soft light on the cobblestones, illuminating our path as we stroll through the sleepy neighborhood. It's late, but the streets feel alive, humming with a latent energy that mirrors the excitement swirling between Jake and me.

"What do you think it'll feel like?" he asks, his voice low and thoughtful, as we walk side by side. The way he speaks captivates me, as if he's asking about the very essence of what we hope to create, rather than merely the aesthetics of a café. I can hear the distant laughter of a group of friends celebrating on a nearby rooftop, their joy spilling into the night sky like confetti.

"Like a second home," I reply instinctively. "A place where people come not just for coffee but to find comfort—like curling up with a favorite book on a rainy day." I glance sideways at him, gauging his reaction. His expression is pensive, yet there's a flicker of joy in his eyes, as if my words resonate with a longing he shares.

We round a corner, and I spot a small park bathed in the gentle glow of the moon. The silhouette of an old oak tree stands majestically in the center, its gnarled branches reaching out like welcoming arms. "Let's sit for a moment," I suggest, my feet already gravitating toward the wooden bench that looks out over a small pond, its surface reflecting the stars above.

As we settle onto the bench, the world feels quieter, the only sounds being the gentle rustling of leaves and the soft lapping of water against the shore. I steal a glance at Jake, who's leaning back, his gaze lost in the vastness of the night sky. "What about you?" I ask, curious about the dreams tucked away behind his earnest demeanor. "What do you want from The Willow?"

His eyes remain fixed on the stars, and I can see the way his mind dances through possibilities. "I want it to be a place of connection," he finally says, his voice almost a whisper, as if sharing a sacred secret. "I want to create an atmosphere where people feel free to be themselves, to share their stories, to dream out loud." The sincerity in his tone sends a shiver down my spine, awakening a longing within me that I didn't know existed.

I nod, feeling the weight of his words settle between us. "That's exactly what we need in this world—a sanctuary for the soul." The moonlight bathes his face in silver, accentuating the intensity of his gaze as he turns to look at me. I can feel the air between us thicken, charged with a tension that is both exhilarating and terrifying.

"Do you think we can really do it?" he asks, vulnerability seeping into his voice. The question lingers, suspended in the night air like a fragile dream waiting to be grasped. I take a moment to consider it, allowing my heart to answer before my mind.

"Absolutely," I reply, my conviction unwavering. "If we're in this together, we can make it happen." My heart races at the thought of building something beautiful alongside him, each of us bringing our unique passions and talents to the table, creating a tapestry rich with texture and color.

Just then, a soft breeze dances through the trees, sending a shiver down my spine and rustling the leaves, like nature whispering its approval. The tranquility of the park wraps around us, making it feel like we're the only two souls in the universe, bound together by dreams and shared aspirations.

"Then let's start making plans," Jake declares, his enthusiasm rekindled, the earlier shadow of doubt dissipating like morning mist under the sun. "We can begin with the basics—setting up a business plan, finding the right location, even sourcing local ingredients for the menu."

As he talks, I can see the gears in his mind turning, ideas sprouting like wildflowers in spring. I catch myself grinning at the sheer fervor in his expression, the way his eyes light up when he talks about the future. It's infectious, igniting my own passion, pushing me to envision all the intricacies we could weave into the fabric of The Willow.

"I can help with the marketing," I suggest, my voice bursting with newfound excitement. "We could use social media to create buzz, maybe even host a few pop-up events before the grand opening." Each idea flows effortlessly from my lips, fueled by the exhilarating possibility of what we could create together.

"Pop-up events?" he repeats, his interest piqued. "Like mini-preview nights? I love it! We can build anticipation, draw in a crowd. It'll be a taste of what's to come." He's practically bouncing in his seat, and I can't help but laugh, the sound blending with the gentle symphony of the night.

As we brainstorm under the stars, the world around us fades further into the background. We sketch outlines of our dreams in the air, the laughter between us growing, punctuated by thoughtful pauses as we ponder logistics and themes. The park transforms into

A PLACE TO BELONG

our brainstorming haven, a sanctuary where ideas flourish under the moonlit sky.

But as the hours slip by, I sense the pull of reality creeping in. "What if we face obstacles?" I ask, a hint of concern slipping into my voice. "What if we don't have enough funding, or what if the location we choose isn't right?" The worries bubble up, threatening to dampen our enthusiasm.

Jake turns to me, his gaze steady and reassuring. "Every journey has its challenges. But if we stay focused on our vision and support each other, I believe we can overcome anything." There's a quiet strength in his words, a resolve that wraps around my heart like a warm blanket, quelling the flutter of uncertainty.

Encouraged by his confidence, I nod, ready to embrace the road ahead, wherever it may lead. As we sit together, our laughter mingling with the sounds of the night, I realize how grateful I am for this moment, for this connection that feels so much larger than either of us.

The night wears on, and reluctantly, we rise from our cozy bench, knowing that the world awaits. But as we walk back toward the café, I feel lighter, as if the weight of my dreams is now shared, a burden made bearable by the camaraderie we've forged.

We pass by a street musician playing a soulful tune, the notes floating through the air like delicate whispers. Jake stops, pulling me closer to the sound, and we sway gently to the music, lost in our own world once more. For a moment, I forget the worries and uncertainties that lie ahead, content to bask in the warmth of our shared vision.

As we finally part ways outside The Willow, I can't help but feel a sense of magic in the air, an unshakeable belief that together we can breathe life into this dream. I watch him walk away, silhouetted against the night, and a smile dances on my lips. The future, with all its twists and turns, feels vibrant and alive—a canvas awaiting the brushstrokes of our creativity, waiting for us to transform it into something beautiful. With each step I take toward home, my heart swells with excitement, anticipation swirling like the night sky above, filled with stars waiting to guide our journey.

Chapter 3: Overcoming the Shadows

The sun had dipped below the horizon, casting a warm glow that bled through the cracked windows of the old community center. Dust motes danced lazily in the fading light, swirling like tiny galaxies suspended in time. I settled into a weathered chair, the fabric worn and faded but comforting, like an old friend. Outside, the sounds of the bustling city of Asheville ebbed and flowed, the distant clinking of glasses from nearby cafes mingling with the laughter of children playing in the park. The air was thick with the smell of freshly baked bread from a nearby bakery, the aroma wrapping around me like a cozy blanket, making me forget the chill of my own uncertainties.

Jake entered with a lopsided smile, his tousled hair catching the last of the golden light. He was a vision of unrefined charm, a contradiction of bravado and fragility. I watched as he set down a stack of papers on the table, his fingers tracing the edges nervously. "I've been thinking a lot about what my mom wanted," he said, his voice low and earnest. "She dreamed of creating a place where people could come together, share ideas, and just be... you know?"

His passion for the idea radiated from him, infectious and intoxicating. I could see it in the way his eyes sparkled, like twin stars igniting in the night sky, illuminating the shadows lurking in the corners of his mind. "It was supposed to be a community hub—a sanctuary," he continued, pacing the room, his hands animatedly illustrating the vision he was sketching in the air. "Somewhere artists could display their work, families could hold gatherings, and kids could just run around without a care in the world."

I nodded, feeling the weight of his dream settle between us like an uninvited guest. "What happened?" I asked, my curiosity piqued.

Jake paused, the light in his eyes dimming slightly, replaced by an undercurrent of regret. "Life happened," he said softly. "After she passed, everything fell apart. I lost sight of it. All that's left now are shadows of what could have been. I've been scared, you know? Scared to fail, to let her down."

As he spoke, I felt an unsettling familiarity with his fear. I too had wrestled with the ghosts of my past—the suffocating weight of expectations that followed me like a shadow. Leaving my corporate life had been both a liberation and a burden. The polished suits and high-stakes meetings felt like a lifetime ago, yet I could still taste the stale coffee in the breakroom, the anxiety of quarterly reports looming over me like a dark cloud. I had traded that world for freedom, but the fear of not being enough, of not living up to my potential, lingered like a bittersweet aftertaste.

"I understand," I said, my voice surprisingly steady. "When I left my job, I thought it would be the start of something beautiful. Instead, it felt like I'd jumped off a cliff without a parachute."

A chuckle escaped his lips, the sound a balm to the raw honesty hanging in the air. "So, we're both just a couple of reckless dreamers, huh?" he teased, the familiar spark of mischief returning to his eyes.

"Exactly! Reckless and regrettably unprepared for what comes next."

Our laughter intertwined, a gentle melody that began to weave a tapestry of connection between us. In that moment, the weight of our insecurities seemed to lift, replaced by an understanding that felt almost tangible. We were both navigating the murky waters of our lives, searching for islands of hope amid the tempest of doubt.

The room around us faded into the background as we shared our vulnerabilities, our fears spilling out like water from a broken dam. I told him about the sleepless nights spent second-guessing my decisions, about the gnawing feeling that I had traded security for a whimsical chase. Jake listened intently, his expression a mix of empathy and shared pain.

"I think we're harder on ourselves than we need to be," he said after a pause, running a hand through his hair, the action both endearing and disarming. "We set these impossible standards, and when we don't meet them, we act like we've failed. But what if we redefined what success looks like?"

His words hung in the air, ripe with possibility. What if I did redefine success? What if I allowed myself the grace to stumble, to explore the messy, uncharted territory of my dreams without the chains of perfection holding me back?

"Maybe we could help each other," I suggested, my heart racing at the prospect. "You could pursue your mom's vision, and I could... I could find my own path, free from the weight of expectations."

A flicker of excitement ignited in his eyes, and I felt it mirrored in my own heart. "We could create something together," he mused, his enthusiasm returning like the sun breaking through the clouds. "A space where we can explore our dreams, invite others in, and just... be."

The idea took root between us, blossoming into something vibrant and alive. It felt like a seed of hope had been planted in the fertile soil of our shared experiences. The thought of nurturing that seed together, of transforming our fears into a shared venture, ignited a warmth that spread through me, chasing away the chill of uncertainty.

As the night deepened, the darkness outside seemed less intimidating. We continued to laugh, our insecurities unraveling like threads, revealing the richness of our aspirations woven beneath. The shadows of the past began to recede, and for the first time in a long while, I felt a glimmer of joy—a delicate light flickering in the darkness, promising new beginnings.

A soft breeze drifted through the open windows, carrying with it the sweet scent of honeysuckle from the nearby gardens. It intertwined with the rich aroma of freshly brewed coffee, filling the room with a comforting blend that wrapped around us like an embrace. As we settled into this fragile moment of camaraderie, I couldn't help but observe the transformation taking place in Jake. The lines of worry etched into his brow began to soften, his shoulders, once rigid with tension, relaxed as he allowed the warmth of vulnerability to seep in.

"What if we held a community gathering?" he suggested, a glimmer of mischief creeping into his eyes. "We could invite local artists, musicians, and even have a bake-off. Just think—a place filled with laughter, creativity, and the scent of homemade pies wafting through the air."

The image he conjured danced in my mind, vivid and enchanting. I could almost hear the strumming of guitars and the cheerful chatter of neighbors exchanging stories over warm slices of pie. "And what if we offered workshops?" I proposed, excitement bubbling within me. "Cooking classes, art sessions, maybe even a poetry night. We could create a space that celebrates what it means to be part of a community."

Jake leaned closer, his enthusiasm infectious. "Exactly! A melting pot of talents, a platform for dreams." His eyes sparkled as he envisioned the reality of our shared ambition. "And it would be a tribute to my mom. She wanted this more than anything. We could even dedicate the first event to her."

I felt a rush of warmth at his words, an undeniable sense of purpose blooming in the pit of my stomach. As we fleshed out the details, our laughter echoed off the walls, reverberating like the heartbeat of a burgeoning dream. Ideas flew between us like sparks, igniting a creative fire that felt almost palpable.

Hours slipped away unnoticed as we transformed the community center from a mere collection of tired walls into a vibrant canvas brimming with potential. Jake's sketches filled the table, a chaotic array of drawings depicting everything from stage layouts to seating arrangements, each one infused with a fervor that pulled me into his vision.

"Look at this!" he exclaimed, pointing to one particularly elaborate design that depicted a whimsical stage adorned with twinkling fairy lights. "We could string these across the ceiling. It would feel like magic!"

Magic. The word settled comfortably in my heart, evoking memories of simpler times—of backyard barbecues and sun-soaked afternoons spent laughing with friends. "And we could have a potluck!" I added, my mind racing. "Everyone brings their favorite dish. It would create a sense of belonging, like everyone is contributing to something greater."

The notion of connection pulsated between us, an invisible thread that tethered our dreams together. We could create a tapestry of experiences, a shared narrative that brought the community to life. It felt like we were not just building a project; we were crafting a haven for ourselves and others who yearned for the same sense of belonging we had been missing.

As the night wore on, the glow of the streetlights outside began to seep through the dusty windows, casting a soft, amber hue over the room. It illuminated the scattered papers, the sketches, and our animated faces as we brainstormed, lost in a world of possibilities.

But beneath the surface of our enthusiasm, a sliver of fear persisted. "What if it doesn't work?" Jake's voice broke through my thoughts, the shadow of doubt creeping back in. "What if no one shows up? What if we fail?"

The question hung heavy in the air, an unwelcome specter. I felt my heart sink for a moment, the weight of his vulnerability echoing my own fears. Yet, in the silence that followed, something remarkable happened. "What if it does work?" I countered, my voice steady. "What if we inspire someone, create connections that last a lifetime? What if we turn our fears into something beautiful?"

His eyes met mine, and in that shared gaze, a promise was forged. We weren't just two people with dreams and fears; we were a team, two souls ready to leap into the unknown together.

With renewed vigor, we resumed our planning, our laughter intertwining with the night air as we tossed around more ideas. Each suggestion felt like an act of defiance against the shadows that threatened to engulf us. We spoke of the joy we wanted to cultivate, the warmth of shared experiences that could light up even the darkest corners of our past.

As the clock ticked on, the community center transformed from a space of solitude into a lively forum of hope. With every sketch we made, we were building more than just an event; we were constructing a sanctuary where people could feel seen and celebrated.

The glow of our determination filled the room, igniting a spark that felt like it could illuminate even the darkest nights. I could see the walls of our insecurities begin to crumble, leaving behind a foundation of possibility.

And then, just as the last remnants of daylight faded into the horizon, Jake leaned back in his chair, a contented sigh escaping his lips. "You know, for the first time in a long while, I'm excited about the future. I actually feel like we can do this."

His words washed over me, and I felt a rush of gratitude. It was as if, in this moment, we had both shed our burdens—our fears, our doubts—and embraced the exhilarating uncertainty that lay ahead.

With a newfound lightness in my chest, I looked out of the window at the stars beginning to twinkle against the velvet night sky. It felt as if they were whispering promises of hope, encouraging us to reach for something more. Together, we were not just facing the shadows; we were crafting our own light, determined to chase away the darkness that had once threatened to define us.

In that sacred space, surrounded by the remnants of our shared dreams, I realized we had discovered something profound—a partnership anchored in authenticity, a promise of growth forged in the crucible of our fears. We were stepping into the unknown, hand in hand, ready to embrace whatever came next.

In the weeks that followed, the community center morphed into a flurry of activity, a vibrant hive where creativity buzzed and thrived. We transformed the dusty, neglected space into something alive—each corner painted in bold hues that reflected the spirit of the people who would soon inhabit it. Sunlight streamed through the large windows, casting playful shadows across the wooden floors, illuminating the laughter and chatter that filled the air. The old stage, once a forgotten relic, blossomed into a canvas for local musicians, its polished surface gleaming like a promise waiting to be fulfilled.

I reveled in the whirlwind of our preparations, my heart swelling with anticipation each time I set foot inside the center. We plastered the walls with vibrant murals created by local artists—each stroke of paint telling a story, infusing the space with a sense of belonging. The scent of fresh paint mingled with the aroma of baked goods as neighbors brought in their favorite dishes for our potluck, each morsel a delicious offering to the budding community we were cultivating.

But beneath the excitement, a voice of doubt lingered. As the event approached, I couldn't shake the feeling that perhaps we were just two dreamers caught in a fantasy, building something destined to crumble under the weight of our insecurities. Would anyone even show up? My thoughts spiraled into a whirlwind of uncertainty as I lay awake at night, staring at the ceiling, the rhythmic ticking of the clock mocking my fears.

Jake, however, was a beacon of optimism, tirelessly rallying the neighborhood. His infectious enthusiasm was like a warm tide, washing over me each time I began to doubt our mission. "We're creating something beautiful, and people will feel it," he'd say, his eyes gleaming with unwavering belief. "This isn't just about us; it's about bringing everyone together."

His confidence sparked a flicker of hope within me, yet the shadows of my past whispered insidiously, reminding me of every misstep, every perceived failure. I found myself at a crossroads, standing between the desire to embrace the moment and the fear of stepping onto a stage of uncertainty.

Then, the day of the gathering dawned, radiant and bright, as if the universe conspired to mirror our aspirations. The sun bathed Asheville in a golden glow, transforming the city into a picturesque backdrop for our dreams. As I approached the community center, a mix of excitement and trepidation swirled within me, threatening to unearth all my fears.

Jake was already there, directing volunteers with a contagious energy that could only be described as magnetic. He was in his element, orchestrating the flow of the event with an ease that made it seem as if he'd been doing this for years. I watched him, mesmerized by the way he moved—hands waving expressively, laughter spilling from his lips like music. He exuded warmth, drawing people in like moths to a flame.

"Come on, let's get this place ready!" he called to me, breaking my reverie. I nodded, forcing a smile, and joined him.

As the clock inched closer to the event's start, the center began to fill with people. The sound of voices mingled with the clinking of utensils and the sweet notes of a guitar strumming in the corner. I felt my heart race as I watched families enter, their faces lighting up with curiosity and joy. It was happening—people were gathering, their presence breathing life into the space we had created.

I stepped back, taking in the scene: a tapestry of diverse individuals coming together, united by the very thing we had hoped to create. Each conversation flowed effortlessly, laughter cascading over one another like a beautiful symphony. Children dashed about, their shrieks of delight weaving through the air, while older folks shared stories that danced like flickering candles, brightening the atmosphere.

Jake caught my eye from across the room, a wide grin stretching across his face as he waved me over. "Look at this! It's beautiful!" he exclaimed, gesturing to the crowd. "People are connecting, just like we envisioned!"

A swell of emotion rose within me as I joined him, the walls around my heart crumbling a little more with each passing moment. "I can't believe it's actually happening," I whispered, awe spilling from my lips.

"We did this together," he replied, his voice a soft anchor amidst the joyous chaos. "And we're just getting started."

The hours flowed like honey, rich and sweet. We danced from group to group, our laughter mingling with the music, sharing stories and smiles. I felt as though I was shedding the weight of my past, each moment of connection lifting me higher, filling the empty spaces within me with warmth and acceptance.

When the sun began to dip below the horizon, casting a breathtaking palette of oranges and purples across the sky, it felt like the universe itself was applauding our endeavor. Jake took to the stage, his silhouette framed by the soft glow of string lights, and called for attention. The room quieted, anticipation hanging thick in the air.

"Thank you all for coming today," he began, his voice steady and sincere. "This event is more than just a gathering; it's a celebration of community, of dreams, and of connection. My mother always believed in the power of people coming together, and today, I feel her spirit with us."

A hush fell over the crowd, and I could see the glistening eyes, the shared understanding of what this space meant. Jake continued, his passion palpable, igniting a fire in everyone present. "Let's keep this going. Let's support one another, share our stories, and create something lasting."

Applause erupted, resounding like thunder, and I felt a surge of pride swell within me. Together, we had transformed not only a space but ourselves, rekindling hope where darkness once lingered.

As the evening wore on, I lost myself in the magic we had crafted. We laughed, danced, and shared more than just food; we shared dreams, fears, and the kind of intimacy that blossomed from vulnerability. I watched as connections formed before my eyes—old friends reuniting, new friendships blossoming, and even a couple of shy teenagers bonding over a shared love of art.

With every heartfelt conversation, every burst of laughter, I could feel the shadows of self-doubt begin to retreat, their grip on me loosening until they were little more than a whisper. Jake's presence next to me felt like a steadying force, his laughter a reminder that I was not alone in this journey.

As the final notes of the music played, the room filled with a sense of accomplishment and hope. We had done it. We had created something beautiful out of our vulnerabilities, something that resonated deeply with everyone present. The evening concluded with a collective promise to return, to nurture this newly formed community, to embrace the stories that would unfold in the days to come.

I took a moment to step outside, breathing in the cool evening air, feeling the weight of the world shift off my shoulders. The stars twinkled above, and I realized that perhaps they weren't just distant lights in the dark—they were reminders of the dreams we had dared to chase, the connections we had forged.

And for the first time in a long while, I felt a sense of belonging settle within me, a warmth that whispered of new beginnings, inviting me to step forward and embrace the life that awaited.

Chapter 4: A Tapestry of Memories

The smell of fresh paint wafted through the air, mingling with the earthy scent of reclaimed wood and the faint remnants of varnish that clung to the walls like whispered secrets. Sunlight poured through the high windows, casting elongated shadows across the floor and illuminating the dust motes that danced in the golden glow. This was our canvas, a blank slate nestled in the heart of our quaint little town, a place where history echoed in the creak of the wooden floors and the laughter of children played outside. As I stood in the center of the room, my heart pulsed with possibilities, a symphony of colors and ideas swirling in my mind like autumn leaves caught in a gust of wind.

Jake stood across from me, his broad shoulders slightly hunched, eyes flitting between the space we were transforming and the sketches I had spread out before him. The sketches danced with vibrant hues, each one more alive than the last, brimming with the essence of what I envisioned for the community hub we were building together. It was supposed to be a place that sang with the spirit of our town, a cozy nook that invited locals to gather, create, and share their stories. I wanted it to be a sanctuary, a refuge where every corner radiated warmth and creativity.

"Picture this," I said, my voice soft yet eager, "a wall lined with photographs of local artists—each frame a testament to their journey, their craft. And over here, a cozy corner filled with mementos from community events, highlighting the heart of our town." As I spoke, I gestured toward the empty wall, envisioning it coming alive with the smiles of our neighbors, their stories woven into the fabric of this space. Jake's lips curved into a tentative smile, and I could see a flicker of hope igniting in his usually guarded demeanor.

"Yeah, that could work," he replied, his tone barely above a whisper, but the light in his eyes was unmistakable. He was beginning to see it too, the way this space could breathe and thrive with the collective heartbeat of our community.

But then I had a thought—a vision of a mural that could transform the room into a vibrant oasis, a tribute to resilience. "What if we painted a mural of a willow tree?" I proposed, my excitement bubbling over. "It could symbolize growth and healing, with its branches reaching out like open arms."

A shadow crossed Jake's face, his eyes darkening momentarily. He took a step back, as if my words had suddenly filled the room with a weight he couldn't bear. "A willow?" he echoed, his voice strained. "For me, that's... that's a symbol of loss."

The warmth of the room shifted, and I felt a chill run through me, an icy realization that this collaborative journey was also a path through his past—a past I was only beginning to understand. It was an uncharted territory, the kind that demands delicate navigation, and I suddenly felt like a ship lost in a storm. "I'm sorry," I murmured, the sincerity of my words catching in my throat. I had not intended to tread on such tender ground, to unearth memories he had buried beneath layers of paint and plaster.

For a moment, we stood in silence, the weight of unspoken emotions hanging between us like the dust motes swirling in the sunlit air. I could sense his hesitation, the way his shoulders tightened, pulling inward as if bracing for a wave of memory to crash over him. I wanted to reach out, to assure him that it was okay to share, but I also knew that some wounds required time and gentleness to heal.

"Maybe we could think of something else," I suggested gently, watching as he drew in a deep breath, his expression softening slightly. "A different tree, perhaps? Something that resonates more with hope and new beginnings."

He ran a hand through his hair, a gesture that seemed to ground him. "Yeah, I'd like that," he finally replied, his voice steadier now. "Maybe an oak? They're strong, enduring." The shift in his tone brought a flicker of relief, and I nodded, eager to explore this new avenue with him.

We began to brainstorm together, a duet of creativity melding in the air as ideas flowed like the vibrant paint we would soon splash across the walls. An oak tree, I thought, could serve as a powerful emblem of endurance, its roots deep and sprawling, connecting us to the very ground we stood on—much like the community we aimed to foster.

"Picture the oak at the center," I suggested, my excitement returning as I sketched its broad branches stretching outward. "Surrounded by wildflowers—each one representing different people in our town, each bloom unique yet part of the same tapestry."

Jake watched, a faint smile returning to his lips, and I felt a surge of warmth knowing I had found a path back into his heart. His presence seemed to fill the room, anchoring us both as we envisioned this shared dream.

As we continued to draw and discuss, I felt the atmosphere shift, each word building bridges over the chasms of uncertainty that had momentarily lingered between us. With each stroke of my pencil, I could see the future of this place blossoming—a sanctuary for the laughter of children, the gentle hum of conversations, and the gentle rustle of leaves in the breeze outside. It was a world where memories would be cherished, where we could weave together our stories into something beautiful, something that would stand the test of time, much like the oak tree itself.

Lost in our collaboration, I glanced outside, where the sun began its descent, casting a warm golden hue over the streets. The vibrant colors of autumn danced in the leaves, mirroring the palette we were about to create inside. I felt a swell of gratitude, realizing that this project was more than just a building; it was a journey—a path to healing for both of us, a step toward understanding the intricacies of love and loss. It was in these moments that I knew we would rise, together, forging a bond that could weather any storm.

As the last rays of sunlight filtered through the windows, bathing the room in a soft amber glow, I sensed the air had shifted from an earlier heaviness to a palpable excitement, the kind that felt like the promise of rain on a summer's day. The oak tree idea had taken root, and together we continued to sketch, layering our visions like the vibrant colors of a painter's palette. Each stroke of my pencil felt like an act of communion, a dance of ideas weaving us closer together.

Jake leaned over the paper, his brow furrowing in concentration, the light catching the angles of his face in a way that made my heart flutter unexpectedly. "What if we make the branches wrap around the windows?" he suggested, his enthusiasm blossoming like the wildflowers we'd imagined. "That way, it feels like the tree is part of the building, like it's embracing everything inside."

I nodded vigorously, my mind racing with the possibilities. "Yes! And we could have blossoms at different stages of blooming, each representing a different season of life—moments of joy, sadness, and everything in between." As I spoke, I could see the imagery blooming in his mind as well, the room transforming in our imaginations into a vibrant celebration of life.

The space became our own little world, an oasis where the outside clamor faded away. In our bubble, laughter and ideas spilled forth, unencumbered by past sorrows. As we delved deeper, Jake's enthusiasm ignited something in me, a flicker of inspiration that pushed aside any remnants of that earlier weight.

"Let's not just stop at the tree," I proposed, trying to capitalize on this momentum. "What if we included a path leading away from it, winding through the mural with little markers along the way? Each marker could symbolize significant moments in the community's history—like the annual fall festival or the opening of that bakery that everyone loves."

Jake's eyes lit up, and he began to scribble furiously on the paper. "We could have a little spot for the community garden that started just last year! And maybe a space dedicated to the local music scene." His voice was growing animated, each idea flowing into the next like a river gathering speed as it rushes downhill.

A warm glow filled my chest as I watched him engage with the project, the way his passion infused the room with energy. It was more than just a mural; it was a tapestry of our lives, a testament to resilience and shared experiences. "And we can feature artists, too. We could invite them to contribute their artwork to the mural—a collaborative piece that changes and evolves over time," I added, my voice bubbling with excitement.

He paused, his pencil hovering above the paper as he considered my words. "You really think they'd want to?" There was a hint of skepticism in his voice, but I could also hear the hope creeping in, like dawn breaking through a long, dark night.

"Absolutely!" I exclaimed, leaning forward, urgency coloring my tone. "Think about it: people love being part of something bigger than themselves. It's like creating a legacy."

We fell into an easy rhythm, our imaginations weaving together a vibrant narrative that made the walls around us seem to hum with life. Outside, the town was quieting down, the sounds of children's laughter fading into the warm embrace of evening. I could picture them running through the streets, the laughter of their carefree spirits echoing in the twilight.

Our conversation shifted seamlessly, touching on memories of our own experiences in the community. I shared tales of the summer fairs, the scents of caramel corn wafting through the air as kids darted from ride to ride, their squeals of delight ringing in the evening. He countered with stories of his mother, how she'd bake cookies for the school bake sale every year, turning a simple event into a cherished tradition for many.

"I used to help her," he recalled, a smile breaking through the earlier shadows. "We'd get flour everywhere, and she'd always say that a little mess was a sign of a good time." His laughter was a melodic reminder that joy could still find a place in the remnants of grief.

I could see the tenderness in his gaze as he spoke of her, a fragile light glimmering beneath the surface. "What was your favorite cookie she made?" I asked, genuinely curious.

"Chocolate chip, of course," he grinned, the fondness in his voice wrapping around me like a warm hug. "But not just any chocolate chip. She added a sprinkle of sea salt on top. It was a perfect balance of sweet and salty. Every time I taste one, I can hear her laugh."

It struck me how even in the act of remembering, there was a kind of healing in sharing. The way he opened up about his mother made my heart ache with empathy, the love he had for her palpable in the space between us. I wanted to honor that connection, to remind him that his memories were not burdens to bear alone but treasures to share.

"Maybe we could have a baking corner in our community hub," I suggested, my mind racing again. "A place for people to gather and share their recipes, a little nod to your mom's legacy."

Jake's eyes brightened at the idea, the flicker of hope now a radiant flame. "And we could have baking classes!" he added, his voice full of enthusiasm. "Teaching kids how to bake, just like she did with me. It would be like passing on her spirit."

The room seemed to vibrate with energy, the walls echoing our dreams as we sketched out plans for not just a mural, but a living, breathing space filled with laughter, memories, and the sweet scent of cookies fresh from the oven.

As we wrapped up our session for the day, I felt an unspoken bond solidifying between us. The barriers that had initially separated our histories were slowly dissolving, replaced by a shared understanding that felt profound and necessary. We were crafting something beautiful together, a testament not just to the community we cherished, but to our own intertwined journeys of healing.

Walking out into the cool evening air, I glanced back at the space we had transformed. The walls, once bare and uninviting, now seemed alive with potential, as if the very bricks were whispering secrets of love, loss, and the beauty of new beginnings. I couldn't help but smile, knowing that together we were not just building a community hub; we were laying the groundwork for a vibrant tapestry woven from the threads of our lives, rich with stories yet to be told.

The days flowed like the gentle river that wound through our town, each moment a ripple in the vibrant tapestry we were creating together. Jake and I met daily, our sketches evolving into a whirlwind of ideas. The empty walls began to fill with the heartbeat of our community, each design element meticulously chosen to reflect the stories that were often left unsaid.

One afternoon, as we sat amidst a swirl of paint swatches and discarded coffee cups, I felt a strange mix of anticipation and nostalgia wash over me. The soft hum of laughter floated in from the bustling café next door, a backdrop to our creative session that made the world outside seem both close and distant. The light filtering through the windows danced on the walls, casting playful shadows that twirled with our thoughts.

"What if we included a spot for a community garden?" I suggested, sketching the outline of a small space where flora could thrive alongside our mural. "A little oasis of color that can change with the seasons, just like us." The thought of nurturing something together felt oddly symbolic, a reflection of the growth we were both experiencing—like two seeds taking root in the same soil.

Jake's brow furrowed in concentration, and I could see his mind turning. "I love that idea," he replied, a spark igniting in his eyes. "We could have vegetables, herbs, and flowers, each with a little marker telling their story. We could involve local schools—let them plant their own rows. It could be a hands-on way for kids to learn about nature, about nurturing something."

His enthusiasm was infectious, and I couldn't help but grin at the thought of children digging their hands into the earth, their laughter mingling with the rustling leaves. "And we can host a harvest festival!" I exclaimed, my voice tinged with excitement. "Imagine families coming together to celebrate the bounty, sharing recipes, stories, and laughter."

The idea seemed to take flight between us, soaring higher and higher. It was as if we were sculptors, molding not just a physical space, but a sanctuary where community connections could deepen. Jake leaned back, his expression one of contemplation. "My mom always loved gardens," he murmured. "She'd spend hours tending to her roses. They were her pride and joy."

A comfortable silence enveloped us, the weight of his memories settling softly in the air. It was moments like this that reminded me of the delicate balance between joy and sorrow, the duality of our experiences that shaped us. I took a deep breath, letting the weight of his vulnerability settle in, allowing it to foster a sense of intimacy that felt right, necessary.

"What was your favorite flower?" I ventured, my voice gentle, inviting.

He looked up, his gaze far away as he recalled, "Sunflowers. They're so bright and cheerful, always turning to face the sun." A soft smile tugged at his lips, a tender moment that broke through the clouds of melancholy. "I remember one summer, she planted a whole row of them in our backyard. We'd wake up every morning to their golden faces."

We shared a moment of silence, a space filled with unspoken understanding and kinship. It was as if the sunflowers themselves had woven a thread between us, connecting our stories through the simple act of remembrance.

"Let's make sure sunflowers are part of our garden," I said, my voice firm with conviction. "They'll be a tribute to your mom, a reminder of the light she brought to your life."

Jake's eyes sparkled, the warmth of gratitude shining through. "I'd like that."

As we delved deeper into our brainstorming, our ideas grew more whimsical and adventurous. We decided to create a mural that not only depicted the oak tree but also integrated elements of the garden—a mosaic of vibrant flowers and vegetables that would come alive on the walls. Each bloom would represent a different aspect of our town's history, a unique story adding depth and color to our community's narrative.

I proposed we paint a winding path that meandered through the mural, lined with whimsical stones, each inscribed with the names of local families or small businesses that had been pivotal in shaping our town. Jake's eyes gleamed with excitement as he added, "And we could include local wildlife too—maybe a pair of cardinals nestled in the branches. They're the state bird, and they always remind me of home."

Our sketches soon overflowed with laughter and creativity, the ideas melding together like vibrant threads woven into a rich tapestry. We worked tirelessly, losing ourselves in the process, our lives intertwining more with each shared moment.

The day came when we finally stood before the wall that would become our mural. Armed with brushes and buckets of paint, we began the first strokes, the anticipation buzzing between us like a live wire. Each brushstroke felt like a conversation, a dialogue written in colors and textures. The oak tree took form, its branches reaching out with an eagerness that mirrored our own aspirations.

As the mural blossomed, I took a moment to step back, observing the beautiful chaos we were creating. The sunflowers burst forth in yellows and oranges, their happy faces lifting toward the sky. Beside them, the vibrant greens of tomatoes and cucumbers danced playfully, a reminder of the garden we would soon cultivate. The path twisted and turned, leading the eye on an adventure, filled with the stories of the people who called this town home.

The vibrant colors of the mural seemed to breathe life into the space, but it was the small details—the personal stories interwoven throughout—that made it extraordinary. As Jake painted a cardinal perched in the branches, I realized that this mural was more than just a piece of art; it was a living testament to the resilience of our community and the bonds we had formed through our shared experiences.

After hours of labor and laughter, we stepped back to admire our work. I was awash in the joy of creation, the vivid colors illuminating the once-bare walls. It was a kaleidoscope of memories, of laughter and loss, of roots taking hold and new shoots breaking through the earth.

"We did it," Jake breathed, a look of wonder on his face as he surveyed the mural. "It's... beautiful."

"It really is," I agreed, feeling a swell of pride.

The sun began to dip low on the horizon, casting a golden hue across the space. As the colors in the mural deepened in the fading light, it felt as though we were witnessing the birth of something truly special. The wall was now a testament not only to our creativity but also to our journey of healing.

In that moment, I realized that this mural represented more than just art; it embodied a vision for the future—a future filled with laughter, community, and love. The path we had forged together, although fraught with the shadows of our pasts, was leading us toward a vibrant horizon.

Standing beside Jake, the air thick with the fragrance of fresh paint and hope, I understood that we were not just building a community hub; we were weaving together a tapestry of memories, one brushstroke at a time.

Chapter 5: Unfolding Layers

The art fair buzzed with energy, a mosaic of colors and sounds that danced around us like fireflies in a summer dusk. Booths adorned with canvases, sculptures, and handcrafted trinkets beckoned like sirens, their beauty intoxicating. The scent of kettle corn wafted through the air, sweet and buttery, mingling with the earthy aroma of fresh paint and the warm, sun-soaked asphalt beneath my feet. As Jake and I wandered through the maze of creativity, I could feel the pulse of the community thrumming around us—a symphony of laughter, chatter, and the occasional exclamation of delight as someone uncovered a hidden treasure.

Jake was an enigma wrapped in a flannel shirt and jeans, his tousled hair catching the light like strands of spun gold. With every glance, I could see the laughter flicker in his hazel eyes, a flame ignited by the vibrant art that surrounded us. He seemed almost like a child in a candy store, his demeanor shifting with each new piece that caught his attention. I relished these moments, the way his smile widened when he found a quirky ceramic cat or an abstract painting that made his eyebrows dance with delight. In those flashes of joy, he became someone else—someone unburdened, untouched by the weight of the past.

Yet, beneath the surface, I sensed the subtle tremors of a deeper story. It was there in the way he lingered a moment too long before moving on, as if each piece had a secret it was holding back, much like him. I couldn't help but draw parallels to my own life, where the scars of a crumbled relationship clung to me like a second skin. I'd worn my heart like a fragile necklace, its chain stretched and frayed, each heartbreak a reminder to keep my distance, to tread carefully in matters of the heart.

We paused before a booth filled with vibrant paintings, each canvas a burst of emotion. An impressionistic sunset, reds and oranges melting into each other like a lover's embrace, caught my eye. I could almost feel the warmth on my skin, the cool breeze of the evening creeping in just beyond the canvas. As I admired the piece, I felt Jake's presence beside me, his shoulder brushing against mine. "It's breathtaking," I murmured, my voice barely rising above the ambient sounds.

"Yeah," he replied, his gaze fixed on the painting. "It makes me feel... hopeful. Like anything is possible." There was a flicker of something in his voice, a resonance of longing that tugged at my heart. I turned to him, curiosity piqued. "What do you mean?"

He shrugged, a gesture that seemed too casual for the depth of emotion lurking behind his words. "I guess it's just that art has this way of capturing moments we often overlook. It reminds us that there's beauty everywhere, even when we're stuck in our own heads." He paused, a shadow crossing his face. "Or our own fears."

His vulnerability surprised me, revealing a glimpse into the layers he kept tightly wrapped. I wanted to peel them away, to help him see the beauty within himself that I saw in him, but I understood all too well the fear that came with unguarded moments. Instead, I opted for lightness, a diversion from the heaviness that hung between us. "Well, if you think that piece is hopeful, wait until you see the giant metal sculpture of a chicken over there. It's utterly ridiculous but somehow works!" I pointed with a laugh, and he followed my gaze, a spark igniting in his eyes as he chuckled, the heaviness temporarily lifting.

As we meandered from booth to booth, Jake's laughter became a melody woven into the tapestry of the day, lifting my spirits like a warm breeze. The fair was alive with artists chatting passionately about their work, families sharing cotton candy, and couples lost in whispered conversations. We wandered deeper into the throng, our surroundings evolving into an abstract blur of bright colors and textured surfaces, each corner revealing new wonders.

We stumbled upon a booth that showcased local artisans' handmade jewelry. Delicate necklaces adorned with sea glass caught my eye, their translucent hues reminiscent of ocean waves. I reached out to touch a piece that shimmered like sunlight dancing on water. "This one reminds me of the shore," I said, holding it up to the light.

Jake leaned closer, his eyes narrowing in contemplation. "I can see that. There's something about it that feels... freeing. Like it's carrying a part of the ocean with it." His tone held a sincerity that wrapped around my heart.

"Would you ever want to live near the coast?" I asked, curiosity bubbling up like the fizz of a soda. I didn't know where the question came from, but it slipped out, hanging in the air between us, an invitation to reveal more.

He hesitated, his expression shifting as if he were weighing something heavy on his mind. "I used to think I wanted that, but I guess... life has a funny way of altering our dreams. I've been trying to find what really matters to me." His voice trailed off, leaving an echo of unspoken truths.

I nodded, feeling the familiar tug of my own unexamined dreams. "Sometimes, the journey to find what matters can feel more important than the destination itself," I said softly, the weight of my own experiences bleeding into my words. "It's all about discovering who we are in the process."

For a moment, our eyes locked, and the world around us faded into a distant hum. It felt as if the universe had conspired to pull us closer, weaving our narratives into a shared tapestry of understanding. I could sense the walls around him begin to crack, the sunlight of our connection spilling through the gaps.

But just as quickly as the moment had begun, it dissipated, and Jake looked away, breaking the spell. He cleared his throat, a playful grin returning. "Okay, enough of this deep talk. I want to see that chicken!"

With a laughter that rang like a bell, we moved on, chasing the lightness, yet I couldn't shake the feeling that beneath the surface, we were both navigating the same turbulent waters, yearning for something more.

We approached the chicken, a towering metal creation that stood proudly amid the chaos of the art fair, painted in hues of sunshine yellow and grass green. Its whimsicality was undeniably infectious. It was as if someone had taken the spirit of a summer picnic and forged it into a three-dimensional form. Jake's laughter bubbled up, a sound that felt like a refreshing breeze on a warm day. "Only in this town would you find a giant chicken," he exclaimed, shaking his head in amused disbelief.

I couldn't help but join in his laughter, the sound merging with the distant strumming of a street musician's guitar. This place felt like a carnival for the senses, alive with artistic expressions that pulled us in every direction. People milled about, children ran freely, their laughter echoing like a joyful chorus, while couples paused to admire the artistry, their fingers intertwined as if sharing secrets.

Jake ambled closer to the chicken, his playful side emerging as he struck a ridiculous pose beside it, pretending to be a proud farmer. I raised my phone, capturing the moment, the click of the shutter punctuating the air. "This is going straight to the café's social media," I teased, and he grinned, his eyes dancing with mischief.

"What if I become a viral sensation?" he replied, his tone mock-serious. "I could start a career in poultry modeling." The warmth of his humor enveloped me, a cozy blanket on a chilly night.

As we continued exploring, we encountered a booth showcasing paintings that were entirely different from the impressionistic flair that had captivated us earlier. The artist had combined graffiti with classical techniques, creating urban landscapes that felt both familiar and foreign. The vibrant colors pulsed with life, stories hidden in every brushstroke. "It's like a conversation between the past and the present," I mused, my fingers grazing the canvas, the texture rough and inviting.

"Exactly! It's like each piece is a postcard from a different time," Jake said, his enthusiasm palpable. I admired how he could find joy in even the most unconventional forms of art. It reminded me of the way he approached life—an open mind coupled with a cautious heart, ready to explore yet hesitant to fully engage.

As we stood there, the sun dipped lower in the sky, casting a golden glow across the fair. The shadows stretched and twisted, creating a dreamlike quality that enveloped us. I watched Jake as he leaned closer to the art, his brow furrowed in concentration. It was a look I'd seen before, one that told me he was grappling with something deeper, something that gnawed at the edges of his carefree façade.

"Do you ever feel like art reflects where you are in life?" I asked, breaking the comfortable silence. "Like, some days you see a piece and it resonates perfectly with your mood?"

His gaze shifted from the art to me, a flicker of surprise in his expression before he nodded. "Absolutely. Art has a way of making the unspoken felt. It can capture the messiness of our emotions when words just... fall short." His voice carried a weight that felt familiar, and I found myself leaning in, eager to hear more.

"I think that's why I'm drawn to it," I confessed, feeling the warmth of vulnerability wrap around me. "I've always believed art has this magical ability to heal. When I was going through a tough time, I painted to process everything—the good, the bad, the ugly. It helped me make sense of my heartache."

He studied me, the tension in his shoulders easing as he absorbed my words. "I didn't know that about you. It's brave to express yourself like that. I've always kept my art on the inside, hidden away. I guess I'm afraid of what might happen if I share it."

"Sharing can be terrifying," I said, my heart quickening at the thought of him unveiling his hidden depths. "But it can also be liberating. When you let someone in, you allow them to see the real you—the messy, complicated, beautiful you."

A silence fell between us, thick with unspoken emotions, the air heavy with possibilities. I could see the flicker of something in his eyes, a realization sparking to life. It was as if we had crossed an invisible threshold, stepping into a realm where barriers began to waver.

Just then, a group of children rushed past, giggling and squealing, their excitement echoing in the twilight. Jake chuckled, breaking the moment's intensity, his eyes sparkling with delight as they dashed toward a booth selling handmade popsicles. "Speaking of messy, I could definitely go for something sweet right about now!" he declared, his playful spirit returning as he led the way.

We made our way to the popsicle stand, the air filled with the enticing scent of fresh fruit. The vendor, a jovial older woman with a crown of wild curls, greeted us with a warm smile. "What can I get you two?" she asked, her voice smooth and inviting.

I scanned the colorful options, each more enticing than the last. "What's your favorite?" I asked the vendor, hoping for guidance in this delicious dilemma.

"Oh, you must try the watermelon basil!" she exclaimed, her eyes twinkling with enthusiasm. "It's refreshing with just a hint of something unexpected. Perfect for a warm day like today!"

I exchanged a glance with Jake, who shrugged with a grin. "Let's do it!" he said, the lightness returning to his voice.

We placed our order, and as we waited, I couldn't help but admire the joyful energy of the fair around us. The sky transformed into a canvas of pastel colors, streaks of pink and orange bleeding into the fading blue. It was beautiful and fleeting, just like the moments we were sharing.

When our popsicles arrived, I took my first bite, and the flavor burst forth like a summer day, the sweetness of the watermelon playing beautifully against the unexpected, savory notes of basil. "Wow," I said, my eyes widening in surprise. "This is incredible!"

Jake mirrored my delight, his expression a mix of wonder and happiness. "Who knew basil could be this good?" he said, and for a moment, we were simply two people enjoying a summer day, a shared experience that felt both light and profound.

As we walked through the fair, savoring our treats, I felt a flicker of hope growing between us. Each smile, each laugh, built a bridge over the invisible chasms that had kept us apart. I could sense Jake slowly unearthing the layers he'd buried so deeply, just as I was starting to peel away my own. There was something beautifully chaotic about it all—a dance of souls connecting in a world that felt brimming with possibility.

The sun dipped lower, and with it, the art fair began to take on an even more magical hue. The lights strung overhead flickered to life, twinkling like stars caught in the soft embrace of twilight. As we strolled beneath the canopy of lights, I knew we were on the precipice of something wonderful, something real.

The sky had darkened into a velvety blue, dotted with twinkling stars that seemed to nod in approval at our blossoming camaraderie. The vibrant art fair, now illuminated by strings of twinkling lights and colorful lanterns, transformed into a whimsical wonderland. Each booth glowed like a little universe, drawing us in with promises of artistry and connection. As we continued our exploration, I felt a current of excitement coursing through me, the anticipation of what lay ahead mingling with the warmth of Jake's presence.

With our popsicles in hand, we approached a booth where a potter was spinning clay with deft fingers, the wheel whirling and splattering in a dance of creativity. I stopped, entranced by the sight. There was something almost hypnotic about the way the clay transformed under the potter's guidance, morphing from a shapeless lump into a graceful bowl, delicate yet robust, waiting to cradle something precious. "Look at that!" I exclaimed, pointing to a piece taking form. "It's like watching magic happen."

Jake stepped closer, intrigued. "It's fascinating how something so raw can become so beautiful, isn't it? Like people," he added thoughtfully, casting a sidelong glance my way. "We're all a little messy on the outside, but with the right hands, we can become something extraordinary." His words hung in the air, heavy with meaning, and for a brief moment, I wondered if he was speaking about himself as much as he was about art.

I nodded, my heart racing at the intimacy of his thought. "Exactly! It takes patience and care, doesn't it? We can't rush the process or force it. The beauty lies in the journey, in the imperfections." The air around us hummed with a deeper understanding, a shared acknowledgment of the paths we were both trying to navigate.

Just then, a small boy darted past us, his tiny hands clutching a handful of clay pots, his face smeared with dirt and delight. The scene was so endearing that I couldn't help but laugh, the sound spilling forth like a sparkling brook. "Look at that little one," I said, my eyes sparkling. "He's completely unafraid of getting his hands dirty. That's the spirit of creativity!"

Jake laughed, the sound bright and free. "It's the way we all start, isn't it? Fearless, reckless, just diving in without a second thought." His gaze turned contemplative as he watched the boy scamper away, leaving behind a trail of joy. "Somewhere along the way, we forget that it's okay to embrace the mess."

As the sun fully set, a cooler breeze swept through the fair, carrying with it the faint melody of a nearby band setting up to perform. The strains of a guitar and soft percussion floated through the air, creating an atmosphere thick with promise and nostalgia.

We wandered further, drawn by the music, until we reached an open space where a small stage had been set up. The band, a mix of local musicians, was tuning their instruments, their laughter mixing with the sounds of the crowd.

"Let's grab a spot!" Jake suggested, his eyes glinting with excitement. We found a place on the grass, spreading out a picnic blanket we'd brought for the occasion. Sitting together under the shimmering lights, I felt a profound sense of belonging wash over me, as if the universe had conspired to align our paths at this very moment.

The music began, soft at first, weaving its way through the air like a comforting blanket. I closed my eyes for a moment, letting the melodies wash over me. It felt like a balm, soothing the ache of old wounds, offering hope for what lay ahead. Beside me, Jake leaned back on his elbows, a serene smile playing on his lips as he immersed himself in the sounds.

As the evening unfolded, we shared stories and laughter, our barriers gently crumbling under the weight of shared experiences. The warmth of our connection wrapped around us like the soft glow of the lanterns above. I told him about my childhood memories of painting with my grandmother, her gentle guidance igniting my passion for art. He spoke of his family's traditions, recounting tales of camping trips and late-night bonfires, the sense of adventure palpable in his voice.

But then, as the music shifted to a slower tempo, I noticed a subtle shift in Jake. The light in his eyes dimmed momentarily, and I sensed the familiar retreat behind his walls. It was as if a shadow had passed over him, a reminder of the pain that lay just beneath the surface. I wanted to reach out, to pull him back into the warmth we'd built, but I understood that this journey was his to navigate.

"Hey," I said softly, drawing his attention back to me. "You okay?"

He took a deep breath, a shadow flickering in his gaze before he offered a tentative smile. "Yeah, just... thinking."

"Thinking about what?" I pressed gently, willing him to open up, to share the weight he was carrying.

Jake hesitated, the air thick with unspoken words. "It's just... being here, surrounded by all this creativity, it makes me realize how much I've held back. How much I've kept inside." His vulnerability wrapped around us, fragile and yet undeniably powerful. "I've been so afraid of stepping out, of failing or getting hurt again."

I reached out, my fingers brushing against his hand, feeling the warmth radiating from him. "You're not alone in that. We all have our fears. But maybe it's time to start letting some of that go. To take small steps into the light, even if it feels daunting."

Jake's gaze lingered on our joined hands, the connection crackling like electricity. "You make it sound so easy."

"Maybe it isn't easy, but it can be beautiful," I replied, my heart racing as I sought to inspire him. "We can embrace the mess together. You don't have to do it alone."

His eyes met mine, a flicker of hope igniting within. "I'd like that. I think I'd like that a lot."

The music swelled around us, enveloping us in a cocoon of warmth and understanding. In that moment, surrounded by the laughter of strangers and the rhythm of life, I felt the invisible threads of connection weave tighter between us. It was a delicate dance of two souls reaching out across the expanse of their guarded hearts, willing to embrace the unknown.

As the band played on, the world around us faded, the only thing that remained was the sweet melody of potential and the soft glow of possibility. We were two artists of our own lives, each with a palette of experiences, each brushstroke adding depth to our journey. Together, we stood on the precipice of something extraordinary, ready to dive into the messiness of creation, love, and the uncharted territories of our hearts.

And in that moment, I understood that the beauty of art lay not just in its final form, but in the messy, chaotic process of bringing it to life. It was a lesson I was eager to share with Jake, and perhaps, together, we could discover the masterpiece waiting to be unveiled within us both.

Chapter 6: Whispers of Hope

The air hung thick with the scent of freshly brewed coffee and sweet pastries, weaving its way through the soft sounds of laughter and clinking ceramic cups that filled The Willow Café. Each table on the porch was a patchwork of stories, the mismatched chairs inviting friends, strangers, and lovers to gather and share fragments of their lives. My heart beat in sync with the café's rhythm, a pulse of warmth in the heart of our small town, where everyone knew everyone, and secrets were often traded like currency. It was late enough that the sky had begun to surrender to dusk, and I found myself leaning against the railing, the weathered wood cool beneath my fingertips, grounding me in the present moment.

Jake sat across from me, his vibrant blue eyes sparkling with fervor, a stark contrast to the deepening shadows of the evening. He was animated as he spoke, gesturing with his hands as if crafting the very air around him into the shape of his dreams. The way his enthusiasm radiated reminded me of summer fireflies, illuminating the corners of the café's porch, catching my imagination and sending it soaring. "Just imagine," he said, his voice rising above the hum of evening chatter, "an open mic night where locals can share their stories, their music. It could be the heartbeat of this place, something that ties us all together."

As he spoke, I could see it, too: a flickering candle on each table, the stage adorned with simple fairy lights, creating a magical atmosphere where vulnerability danced with creativity. I could almost hear the notes of a guitar strumming softly in the background, mingling with laughter and applause, each performance a thread weaving us closer together. The thought sent a delightful shiver down my spine, igniting a spark of something that had been dormant within me for far too long. I leaned in closer, my voice barely above a whisper, "What if we organize a launch event? Just a small gathering to introduce the idea, see if the community even bites."

The look on Jake's face transformed, a mixture of surprise and hope lighting up his features. "Are you serious?" His disbelief was palpable, but there was a hint of excitement lurking just beneath the surface. The kind of excitement that made the world feel alive, vibrant with possibility. I nodded, my heart racing. It was a leap of faith, a daring plunge into the unknown, but the thrill of it sent adrenaline coursing through my veins. We were both searching for something more, a deeper connection to the town we'd both grown up in, and this could be our bridge.

As the last rays of sunlight dipped below the horizon, painting the world in deep indigo and gold, I felt a rush of adrenaline. The air was electric with potential. The Willow had always been a haven for the eclectic, a space where stories were brewed as carefully as the coffee, but it lacked a heartbeat. It needed the pulse of creativity, the rhythm of voices echoing against its rustic walls. I envisioned laughter echoing through the night, words shared like currency among friends and strangers, creating a tapestry of memories that would linger long after the lights dimmed.

"Let's do it," Jake said, his voice steady and resolute. The determination in his gaze mirrored my own, and I felt an unspoken bond form between us, woven from shared aspirations and the thrill of the unknown. "We'll need to spread the word, gather talent, create a welcoming atmosphere. We can use social media, maybe put up some flyers around town."

His excitement was infectious, and I found myself swept up in his vision, each idea sparking another until the plans unfolded like origami in my mind. It was ambitious, yes, but I could almost see the café transformed under the warm glow of fairy lights, the gentle strum of a guitar inviting all to share their stories. I was ready to invest myself in this project, to see the magic that could sprout from this little corner of the world.

"Think about it," I said, my words tumbling out like confetti. "Local artists, poets, musicians—each with a piece of their heart to share. It could breathe life into this place and bring us all closer together."

A gentle breeze stirred the air, lifting a strand of hair off my shoulder and sending it dancing around my face. In that moment, I felt a sense of belonging, a warmth that wrapped around me like a cherished blanket. The café was more than just a building; it was a sanctuary, a meeting point for souls searching for connection. With every passing moment, my resolve strengthened. I wanted to help cultivate that connection, to create a space where we could all celebrate the beauty in our shared humanity.

The sun sank lower, dipping its toes into the horizon, casting a warm golden glow that danced through the café's windows. It illuminated Jake's face, framing him in a soft light, and I couldn't help but notice the way his passion ignited something deep within me. He was so alive, so magnetic in his enthusiasm. I could see the fire in his eyes, a reflection of my own hopes.

"Let's meet tomorrow to brainstorm," I suggested, feeling the weight of my own aspirations intertwining with his. The thrill of collaboration wrapped around us like a soft hug, filling the space between us with promise and excitement. I could almost taste it, the sweetness of what we could create together.

As the first stars began to twinkle above us, I realized that this venture wasn't just about the café or the event. It was about connection, about stepping outside of the shadows of our everyday lives and embracing the light of our dreams. It was a call to arms, a chance to open our hearts and share our stories.

Underneath the darkening sky, filled with whispers of hope and flickering stars, I felt ready to take that leap. I was ready to embrace the magic of possibility, to breathe life into the stories we all carried, and to foster a community bound by creativity and shared experiences. In that moment, with the promise of tomorrow looming on the horizon, I knew that together, we would find our voices in the heart of The Willow Café.

The following morning, the sun broke through the thin veil of clouds, spilling golden rays over the sleepy town, nudging it awake. I could smell the faint scent of damp earth mingling with the robust aroma of coffee wafting from The Willow. As I approached the café, the sound of my sneakers crunching against the gravel seemed to harmonize with the chirping of sparrows, each note singing of new beginnings. I pushed open the door, greeted by the comforting warmth that wrapped around me like a soft hug. The morning light danced on the worn wooden floors, casting long shadows that seemed to sway gently in time with my heartbeat.

Jake was already there, immersed in his usual ritual, brewing the day's first batch of coffee. He had a knack for turning even the mundane into something special. As the steam curled upward, it formed ephemeral shapes that dissipated into the air, much like the fleeting moments of clarity that often struck when I least expected them. I caught a glimpse of him, focused and determined, his fingers deftly maneuvering the coffee grinder, a hint of a smile playing on his lips. I felt a rush of gratitude—this was our space, and together, we were about to breathe life into it in a way that had never been attempted before.

"Good morning, bright eyes," he greeted, looking up from his task with an enthusiasm that sent a flicker of excitement through me. "I was just thinking about the flyer design. We need something that captures the spirit of this place. Something vibrant."

I slid into one of the weathered chairs at our usual corner table, the sunlight catching the edges of a ceramic mug as I cradled it in my hands. "I was thinking of a visual collage—pictures of the café, snippets of past events, and maybe even some hand-drawn elements that reflect the creativity we want to invite." My mind was already racing ahead, each idea spiraling into a series of vibrant possibilities.

Jake leaned against the counter, arms crossed, his gaze thoughtful as he considered my suggestion. "That could work, but what if we incorporated quotes from local artists or musicians? Something that speaks to the soul of our community?" His enthusiasm mirrored mine, igniting a fire within me that urged us to create something unforgettable.

With every word exchanged, a tapestry of ideas unfurled between us. We bounced thoughts back and forth, each of us shaping the vision of the launch event like sculptors molding clay. The atmosphere buzzed with creative energy, the very essence of The Willow wrapping around us, urging us onward. It felt as if the café itself was alive, each coffee bean and baked good participating in our endeavor, a silent cheerleader for our dreams.

Hours slipped away, the sun climbing higher in the sky, transforming the soft morning light into a brilliant midday glow. We sketched out plans, listing local talents we wanted to invite and discussing how to craft a schedule that would keep the energy flowing. The more we talked, the clearer the vision became: a night filled with music, laughter, and perhaps a little nervousness as people stepped up to share their hearts in front of friends and strangers alike.

"We need to get the word out," Jake said, his brow furrowing with determination. "Let's hit the farmers' market this weekend. It's the perfect opportunity to connect with the community and invite them to join us."

My heart raced at the thought. The farmers' market was the beating heart of our town, a kaleidoscope of colors and sounds where vendors proudly displayed their fresh produce and handmade crafts. It was where stories mingled with laughter, where the aroma of baked bread and fresh flowers lingered in the air. I could envision it now—us, standing side by side at a little booth, inviting locals to come share their voices, to bring their talents and heart to The Willow.

"Yes!" I exclaimed, the idea taking root in my mind. "We could create a mini performance space right there. Invite people to sign up for the open mic on the spot." I was practically vibrating with excitement, my fingers tapping a rhythm on the table as if to the beat of my heart.

Jake's face lit up, and I saw the same thrill reflected in his eyes. "And we could have a small coffee tasting to draw people in. Let them sample some of our special blends while we talk about the event." He grinned, clearly already envisioning the scene unfolding in front of us. "This is going to be amazing."

The days that followed were a whirlwind of preparation. We crafted flyers adorned with colorful designs and enticing snippets about the event, each word a beacon of warmth inviting others into our dream. The café became our haven, a headquarters where we worked tirelessly to bring our vision to life. I'd never realized how much I craved this kind of collaboration until I found myself lost in the details with Jake, the laughter and friendly banter making even the most mundane tasks feel like an adventure.

As the weekend approached, I could hardly contain my anticipation. The farmers' market was bustling, filled with the vibrant chatter of families and friends sharing their Saturday. The sun hung high in the sky, casting a golden glow over the rows of stalls. I inhaled deeply, letting the scent of fresh flowers and ripe fruits wash over me, the atmosphere buzzing with possibility.

We set up our booth, a humble affair with a bright tablecloth and our flyers prominently displayed. I felt a rush of pride as I glanced at the makeshift stage we'd assembled. It was simple, but it had potential. I could almost hear the echoes of laughter and music swirling around us.

As people began to stop by, their curiosity piqued by the inviting display, I felt a rush of excitement mixed with nerves. The first few interactions were tentative, but the warmth of our shared enthusiasm quickly drew people in. We explained our vision, our hopes for The Willow, and the opportunity for them to share their own stories. One by one, faces brightened with understanding and interest, and soon we were collecting names and contact information faster than I could keep up.

"Do you know any local musicians?" an older woman asked, her eyes sparkling with excitement. "I have a neighbor who plays the guitar beautifully."

"I'd love to hear him!" I replied, grinning. "We're looking for all kinds of talent."

As the day wore on, I realized that the stories we shared at our booth were as significant as those we aimed to showcase at the café. Each interaction, each new connection, wove us tighter into the fabric of our community. I felt a warmth unfurling within me, a sense of belonging and purpose that had eluded me for so long.

When the sun began to dip below the horizon, casting long shadows and bathing the world in a golden glow, I knew that this was only the beginning. Together, Jake and I were not just building an event; we were creating a community, a space for voices to resonate and dreams to take flight. In that moment, I realized that I wasn't just stepping into the light of my own aspirations; I was inviting others to join me in the dance, and together, we would create something truly extraordinary.

The anticipation hung in the air like the aroma of freshly baked goods, rich and intoxicating. The launch event was set for the following weekend, and preparations consumed us. As we delved into the details, a rhythm developed between us, our conversations punctuated by laughter and the occasional sigh of exasperation when we grappled with logistics. The walls of The Willow transformed into a vibrant canvas as Jake and I painted our dreams across them with splashes of creativity and energy.

Every day brought new challenges and triumphs. We enlisted the help of friends, gathering a small army of enthusiastic supporters who brought their talents to the table. Lucy, a talented graphic designer with an eye for aesthetics, offered her skills for creating promotional material that would catch the eye of passersby. She expertly blended colors that reflected the warmth of the café—a soft marigold paired with earthy browns—creating a visual invitation that felt like a warm hug.

"People want to feel something when they see our flyer," she said, her fingers dancing across her tablet screen. "Let's make it inviting, let's make it a reflection of what The Willow is all about."

Her words resonated with me, a mantra that echoed through our preparations. The Willow was not just a café; it was a sanctuary, a meeting ground where dreams intermingled with the aroma of coffee and fresh pastries.

The community buzzed with excitement as news spread about our event. It felt as if the very air around us vibrated with anticipation, drawing people in. Conversations around town shifted from mundane topics to our ambitious plans. Each encounter was a step deeper into the web of connection that Jake and I were weaving. I could see it in the smiles of the townsfolk, a flicker of curiosity ignited by the prospect of something new, something vibrant.

As the week wore on, the café began to transform. String lights were hung across the porch, casting a warm glow that promised intimacy. The small stage we'd crafted from repurposed pallets stood proudly at one end, adorned with a few potted plants that added a touch of whimsy. Jake and I spent evenings arranging the seating, trying to create a flow that would encourage mingling while

A PLACE TO BELONG 63

maintaining a sense of coziness. The soft hum of conversation and laughter began to fill the air as friends stopped by to lend a hand or simply share in the excitement.

The night before the event, I found myself at The Willow late into the evening, sitting at our usual corner table, the comforting flicker of candles illuminating the space. It was quiet, the kind of serene stillness that cradled my thoughts, allowing me to reflect on how far we had come. I had spent many nights here, dreaming and scribbling thoughts into my worn journal, but tonight felt different. Tonight, I was not merely a spectator of my life; I was a participant, a creator of something beautiful.

Jake walked in, breaking the tranquil silence with a box of last-minute supplies. "I brought the snacks! We need something to keep the energy up for the performers." He grinned, eyes sparkling with excitement, the kind of boyish charm that melted my worries away. "I figured a mix of sweet and savory would do the trick. What do you think?"

"Perfect! People love snacks," I replied, already imagining the delectable spread we could offer. The idea of people mingling over bites of homemade cookies and savory pastries while waiting for their turn to perform sent a thrill down my spine.

We spent the rest of the evening arranging tables, stacking plates, and balancing the sweet against the savory—chocolate chip cookies nestled alongside herbed crackers. With each item placed, I felt a sense of accomplishment wash over me. This was our creation, a labor of love crafted with care and attention.

As the sun dipped below the horizon on the day of the event, a sense of nervous anticipation gripped me. The air outside was crisp, and the stars began to twinkle overhead like tiny diamonds scattered against the velvet sky. I could hear the sound of laughter and music drifting through the open door as the first guests arrived, the café quickly filling with familiar faces and newcomers alike. Each smile and wave felt like a thread pulling me deeper into this vibrant tapestry we had begun to weave.

Jake stood at the entrance, welcoming guests with the charm of a seasoned host. He was in his element, radiating warmth and enthusiasm that drew people in like moths to a flame. I watched him for a moment, filled with admiration. His genuine passion had become infectious, and as I mingled through the crowd, I saw it reflected in the faces around me.

The stage was set, the atmosphere charged with anticipation as the evening progressed. One by one, performers stepped into the spotlight, their voices weaving a rich tapestry of sound. A local poet recited verses that dripped with emotion, while a guitarist strummed gentle melodies that transported us to distant shores. Each story shared was a spark, illuminating the shared humanity that connected us all.

As the night unfolded, I found myself moving through the crowd, absorbing the laughter and warmth, the whispers of encouragement exchanged among strangers. I felt a tug at my heart each time someone took the stage, their vulnerability laid bare. With every performance, I was reminded of the magic of connection, the raw power of sharing our stories.

It was during a brief intermission that I found myself outside on the porch, gazing up at the stars sprinkled across the sky. The gentle hum of conversation faded into the background, replaced by the soft rustle of leaves in the evening breeze. I could hardly believe the success of the night, the joy radiating from the café spilling out into the streets like confetti.

"Hey!" Jake called, stepping out to join me. "What do you think?"

"Honestly? This is incredible. It's everything we dreamed of and more," I replied, my heart swelling with pride.

"Just wait until the next round of performances," he said, leaning against the railing. The night was only half over, and I could see the excitement brimming in his eyes. "I think we've started something really special here."

As the night wore on, I noticed a little girl sitting quietly at the edge of the stage, her big eyes sparkling with wonder. She clutched a worn teddy bear close to her chest, the embodiment of childhood innocence. I caught her gaze and smiled, feeling a warmth bloom within me.

"Are you going to sing?" I asked her gently.

Her eyes widened, a hint of shyness washing over her. "I want to, but I'm scared," she admitted, her voice barely above a whisper.

"Everyone here is rooting for you," I said, kneeling down to meet her at eye level. "This is a safe space. Just be yourself, and you'll be amazing."

After a moment of contemplation, she nodded, her determination resurfacing. I watched her as she joined the performers, a wave of applause greeting her like a gentle embrace. With each strum of her tiny guitar, the café erupted with cheers, her voice shining like a beacon of hope and courage. In that moment, I understood the true essence of what Jake and I were creating—an opportunity for anyone, no matter their age or background, to step into the light and share their truth.

As the final notes of the night faded away, and the last guests lingered to share stories and laughter, I felt a profound sense of fulfillment. The Willow Café was no longer just a place for coffee; it was a home for the heart, a sanctuary for creativity, and a launching pad for dreams.

With Jake by my side, we had ignited something beautiful—a community bound together by the shared courage to express, to connect, and to dream. As I looked around at the smiling faces and the twinkling stars above, I realized we had planted the seeds for a vibrant future. Together, we would continue to nurture this garden of dreams, fostering connections that would blossom far beyond the walls of The Willow. In this warm cocoon of creativity, I felt truly alive, ready to embrace whatever adventure lay ahead.

Chapter 7: Fragile Foundations

The sun hung low in the sky, casting golden rays that danced across the polished wooden floors of our community center. The scent of fresh paint lingered in the air, mingling with the sharp tang of citrus from a nearby fruit stand. I moved through the space, clutching a clipboard in one hand, while the other absently smoothed the fabric of the tablecloths I had painstakingly chosen. Each fold was crisp, every shade of soft lavender contrasting beautifully against the deep emerald of the potted ferns that adorned the corners. The event was approaching, a showcase of our hard work and vision, and the thought electrified me while simultaneously weighing me down.

Jake was in the back, surrounded by boxes of flyers and banners. His brow furrowed in concentration, the faint lines on his forehead deepening as he wrestled with the logistics of setting up the sound system. There was a natural rhythm to his movements—an effortless grace that belied the tension simmering just beneath the surface. Watching him, I felt a familiar pang of admiration mixed with something else, something I couldn't quite place. Perhaps it was the way his hands, rough and calloused from years of labor, moved with such dexterity as he assembled the equipment. It was as if he was conjuring music from thin air, drawing it from the very bones of the room.

I stepped closer, attempting to inject some lightness into the atmosphere. "You know, if we don't hurry, we might end up playing 'Guess That Song' with a broken speaker. I'd like to avoid a karaoke disaster."

He looked up, momentarily distracted from his task, a faint smile breaking through his serious demeanor. "You'd be surprised at how entertaining that could be. But no, let's not go there just yet." His voice had a warmth that enveloped me, and for a moment, the weight of the world lifted from my shoulders.

The laughter faded quickly, however, as the thought of the event's significance settled back in. This wasn't just a launch; it was the culmination of dreams we both harbored in the depths of our hearts. Yet, beneath the surface, I sensed an undertow pulling at Jake—a current of unresolved sorrow that I couldn't quite navigate. I had been so absorbed in the tasks at hand, the flower arrangements and lighting schemes, that I hadn't taken the time to truly see him.

As I returned to my arrangements, the color palette swirling in my mind, I couldn't shake the feeling that Jake was still carrying the weight of his past. It was as though there were shadows lurking in the corners of his smile, whispering secrets he refused to share. I remembered our earlier conversations, snippets of his mother woven into the fabric of his life—memories that seemed like ghosts haunting him.

I turned back to him, hesitating for a moment. "Jake, do you ever think about... I mean, how are you holding up with everything? You know, about your mom?" The words tumbled out, cautious yet insistent, my heart racing in the aftermath.

His hands froze mid-movement, and the air thickened with an unspoken tension. I saw the way his eyes shifted, the light dimming as shadows fell across his features. "I don't know," he finally murmured, his voice barely above a whisper. "I've been so busy trying to build this thing that I haven't really let myself think about it."

The vulnerability in his admission struck me hard. Here we were, on the cusp of something new, yet the past lingered like a heavy fog, threatening to engulf us both. "Maybe you should," I suggested softly, feeling a rush of empathy. "Have you thought about writing her a letter? Just to say what you didn't get to say?"

He flinched at the suggestion, a rawness flickering across his face, revealing layers of pain I had never fully comprehended. "A letter? I can't even... I don't want to." His words tumbled out, heavy with the weight of unacknowledged grief.

"Why not?" I pressed gently, my heart aching for him. "It might help. You know, to get it all out. It's not just about saying goodbye; it's about holding on to the good memories, too."

Jake turned away, his posture rigid, arms crossed tightly as if warding off some invisible force. "It's not that simple, Ava. You don't understand."

The sharpness of his tone startled me, but I held my ground. "Maybe I don't understand completely, but I do know what it feels like to carry things you can't let go of." The truth of my words hung in the air between us, heavy and unyielding.

His gaze flickered back to mine, and for a heartbeat, I saw the walls he had built around his heart begin to crack. "It just feels like... like I'd be inviting all that pain back in," he said, his voice breaking, vulnerability spilling forth like a dam bursting. "It's easier to pretend it's not there."

"Is it, though?" I asked, stepping closer, my heart racing as I laid my hand gently on his arm. "Easier, yes, but what about healing? What about actually moving forward?"

He sighed deeply, the weight of the world pressing down on his shoulders. I felt a connection to him in that moment, a shared understanding of loss that tethered us together. I had learned to forge my own path after losing my father, to transform grief into something beautiful. But watching Jake, I saw the raw edges of his pain, still jagged and fresh.

We stood there, a fragile silence enveloping us, the room buzzing softly with the distant sounds of preparation. The laughter of children outside floated in through the open windows, a stark reminder of the life pulsing just beyond the walls. I longed for him to embrace that life, to find a way to blend the memories of his mother with the joy that awaited him.

"Maybe it's not about closing the door," I finally said, my voice barely above a whisper. "Maybe it's about keeping it ajar—letting the light in while still holding on to what matters. You don't have to do it alone, Jake."

His eyes met mine, and in that fleeting glance, I felt an understanding shift between us. We were both standing on the brink of something transformative, straddling the line between past and future. If only he could take that leap.

The air thickened with unsaid words and lingering emotions, the kind that clung to our skin like humidity on a July afternoon. I watched as Jake turned away from me, his profile etched against the vibrant backdrop of the community center, a living canvas that mirrored our ambition. Each color, each arrangement was a step toward something new, yet he seemed lost in the murky waters of his past. I took a breath, grounding myself amidst the chaos of chairs being set up and the distant chatter of volunteers buzzing around like busy bees.

In an attempt to shake the heaviness that threatened to envelop us both, I surveyed the room, seeking inspiration. A massive mural dominated one wall, painted by local artists, vibrant flowers spilling across the surface as if they were bursting into life. Their colors sang in harmony with the lavender and emerald theme we had chosen, but it was the way the sunlight filtered through the tall windows that captured my heart. The rays cast playful shadows, shifting like whispers, illuminating the hope that lay just beneath the surface of our concerns.

I returned my focus to Jake, still grappling with his emotions. It felt as though a chasm had opened between us, vast and unbridgeable, laden with unspoken grief. I longed to cross it, to offer him a hand and pull him back into the light, but I wasn't entirely sure how to reach him without tripping over my own fears.

"Do you remember the last time we spoke about your mom?" I ventured, my voice steady but gentle, like a soft breeze that might coax him from the depths of his silence. He turned back to me, his eyes reflecting the soft glow of the afternoon light, filled with a mix of reluctance and curiosity.

"I remember everything," he replied, his tone a complex tapestry of resignation and nostalgia. "But talking about it feels like trying to breathe underwater."

"Maybe that's because you haven't let it surface yet," I replied, emboldened by a sudden rush of empathy. "What if you gave yourself the chance to feel it? You don't have to fight against the tide alone."

A flicker of something—fear, anger, vulnerability—crossed his face. It was as if I had struck a chord within him that he had long since silenced. "It's not just about the past, Ava. It's about the guilt. The 'what ifs' that haunt me like shadows."

The admission hung in the air, a heavy weight that settled between us. I could feel the texture of his pain, palpable and raw, like a scar that refused to heal. I wanted to wrap my arms around him, to reassure him that he wasn't alone in this struggle, but I knew better than to push too hard. Instead, I leaned against the nearby table, trying to exude a calm that I wasn't sure I felt.

"What if you wrote those 'what ifs' down?" I suggested, keeping my voice soft. "You could write them all out, just to get them out of your head. It doesn't have to be a letter to her, but maybe just a way to release what's weighing you down."

Jake's expression shifted, uncertainty flickering in his eyes as he contemplated my suggestion. "And what happens after that? Do I just pretend everything is okay? Like I'm some hero who can handle it all?"

"It's not about pretending," I replied, my voice steady. "It's about confronting those feelings and letting them breathe. You're not a hero, Jake. You're human, and that's enough."

He glanced away, focusing on the intricate patterns of the tablecloth, his brow furrowed in thought. The tension in the room felt like a taut string, ready to snap, and I held my breath, hoping for a breakthrough. After a moment, he finally met my gaze, a hint of resolve flickering in his eyes.

"Maybe you're right. I guess I've been so focused on this event that I thought I could push everything aside. But it's still there, lurking," he admitted, his voice quieter now, as if he were confessing a hidden truth.

The corners of my mouth turned up at his admission, a flicker of hope igniting in my chest. "You don't have to carry it all by yourself, Jake. Let it out. You might just find it's lighter than you think."

We shared a moment of silence, the ambient sounds of the bustling community center wrapping around us like a cocoon, providing a fragile shield against the outside world. I felt a surge of warmth for him, a shared understanding blossoming between us, forging a connection that seemed to defy the barriers we had both erected.

"Okay," he said finally, the word spilling from his lips like a promise. "I'll try. Not just for me, but for her too." His eyes softened as he spoke, and I could see a hint of the weight lifting off his shoulders, the shadows retreating just a little.

With that, the tension in the room shifted. The energy buzzed around us, lighter, more hopeful, as if we had collectively taken a step toward the surface, breaking free from the grip of our pasts.

"Good," I said, relief flooding through me like a rush of cool water. "You'll see, it's a step worth taking."

We fell into a comfortable silence, the unspoken understanding lingering in the air. I turned back to the décor, adjusting a particularly stubborn flower that refused to sit straight. Jake resumed his work, the sounds of clattering equipment and the rustle of paper filling the space. The laughter of children outside faded into the background, leaving room for something new—an uncharted territory of hope and healing.

A PLACE TO BELONG 73

As the minutes passed, the bustle of the event swirled around us, each detail falling into place like the pieces of a long-awaited puzzle. The scent of blooming jasmine wafted through the open windows, mixing with the fresh paint and the lingering aroma of coffee from the refreshments table. I felt an electric thrill coursing through me, my heart beating in sync with the rhythm of the preparations.

Just then, a flash of color caught my eye as one of the volunteers bounced past, arms full of colorful balloons that bobbed in the air like cheerful whispers. The sight brought a smile to my face, and I couldn't help but laugh, my spirit lifting further. "Hey, you should help me tie these up! We need to make sure they look festive!"

Jake chuckled, a genuine laugh that seemed to echo the joy of the moment. "Alright, but I'll make sure they don't float away before we're ready!"

We moved together, laughter spilling into the space around us, the tension from earlier dissolving like mist under the morning sun. As I watched him wrestle with the balloons, I felt a surge of gratitude. This was what life was about—embracing the moments, the laughter, the connections, even when the shadows threatened to creep in.

With each balloon we secured, I felt a renewed sense of purpose settle over us. We were not just launching an event; we were launching ourselves into a future we had yet to fully define. Together, we were forging paths into the unknown, ready to navigate the fragile foundations of our lives with hope and resilience guiding our way.

As the last few minutes before the event ticked away, a flurry of activity transformed the community center into a vibrant haven. Tables were adorned with exquisite centerpieces—little jars filled with wildflowers I had gathered from the local market, each blossom a riot of color, brightening the otherwise muted palette. I flitted around, adjusting the position of one particularly stubborn sunflower that refused to face forward, its petals defiantly turned away from the light. My heart raced not only from the excitement of the launch but from the electric connection I felt with Jake, that unspoken bond growing stronger with each shared moment.

"Okay, so tell me again why we chose the middle of October for a launch event?" Jake called out, mock-seriously, as he wrestled with a banner that stubbornly adhered to the wall, threatening to rip if he pulled too hard. The banter flowed easily between us, a lightness taking hold that countered the earlier heaviness.

"Because it's the perfect season! Fall means change, and that's what we're all about," I shot back, a playful smile dancing on my lips. The autumn sunlight streamed through the large windows, casting a warm glow across the room and making the colors pop even more.

He finally managed to secure the banner, stepping back to admire his handiwork. "Well, I guess you have a point. Change does look pretty good, doesn't it?" His tone was laced with sincerity, and I appreciated the vulnerability he was willing to share, albeit in a roundabout way.

"Just like us," I replied, a soft note threading through my voice. "We're both changing, reinventing ourselves. We're like those flowers—growing stronger even when the seasons shift."

Jake's expression shifted for a moment, as if I had uncovered something deeper within him. "I never thought about it that way," he said quietly, his gaze drifting toward the window, where the branches of an oak tree swayed gently outside, its leaves turning golden as they prepared for the inevitable fall.

Before I could say anything else, a rush of guests began pouring in, laughter and chatter punctuating the air. I felt a surge of adrenaline—this was it. I busied myself, greeting familiar faces and welcoming newcomers, my heart swelling with pride. Jake stood by the entrance, charmingly disheveled, helping guests navigate the initial chaos.

The space filled quickly, vibrant with energy. Community members mingled, each conversation a melody in the symphony of our new beginning. I floated between groups, catching snippets of laughter and shared stories, the warmth of our tight-knit community wrapping around me like a cozy blanket. Yet, even amidst the joyful chaos, I could sense Jake's underlying tension. He greeted everyone with a smile, yet his eyes held a flicker of something deeper—an echo of the emotions he still struggled to articulate.

I found him later by the refreshments table, refilling cups of coffee and organizing the array of pastries. "You doing okay?" I asked, moving in closer, leaning against the table as I observed him.

"Yeah, just..." He paused, searching for the right words as he poured steaming coffee into a cup. "It's a lot, you know? Being here, seeing everyone, feeling the weight of it all."

"Do you want to talk?" I asked softly, mindful of the whirlwind around us, the laughter and chatter almost drowning out the moment.

He glanced around, taking in the scene, the faces illuminated by the golden light filtering through the windows. "I don't want to bring everyone down. They're all so happy, and I should be too."

"Your feelings are just as valid as theirs, Jake. They're not mutually exclusive. You can celebrate the moment while still acknowledging what's inside," I replied, a touch of earnestness in my tone.

He nodded slowly, his gaze drifting to a group of kids chasing one another, their laughter pure and unguarded. "You know, it's strange. Sometimes I feel like I'm stuck between two worlds—one where I can laugh and smile, and another where I feel like I'm dragging this weight behind me."

"You're not stuck, though. You're evolving. It's all part of the journey." I stepped closer, my voice barely above a whisper, as if the intimacy of our conversation needed protection from the outside world. "I've been there too, trying to balance the joy and the sorrow. It's messy, but it's also beautiful."

He turned to me, searching my eyes for sincerity. "How do you do it? How do you keep moving forward?"

I took a breath, the memories swirling in my mind like autumn leaves caught in a gust of wind. "I learned that it's okay to let those feelings wash over you. I write. I paint. I let my emotions spill onto the page or canvas, even when it's hard. It's cathartic, a release."

"Maybe I could try that," he mused, a small flicker of hope igniting in his eyes. "It sounds like a way to honor her, to let her know I'm still here, still living."

"Yes!" I exclaimed, my heart racing at the thought of him embracing his grief as a part of his identity, rather than a burden. "It doesn't have to be perfect. Just let it flow. You might be surprised at what comes out."

A genuine smile broke across his face, and for the first time, I saw a glimmer of the boy I had met all those months ago—a boy filled with dreams and laughter. "Thanks, Ava. Seriously. You always know how to put things in perspective."

Before I could respond, a volunteer dashed over, a basket of name tags in hand, interrupting the moment. "Hey, Jake! We need you to help set up the stage for the speeches!"

With a quick nod, he turned to me, his expression shifting back into the focused determination I had seen earlier. "Duty calls, right? But I'll be back. We still need to finish that conversation."

"Absolutely. I'll be right here," I promised, watching him merge back into the throng, his figure blending into the colorful tapestry of our gathering. The room buzzed with excitement, the energy palpable, but I felt a quiet satisfaction settle over me, knowing that he was willing to confront the ghosts of his past.

The event unfolded beautifully—speeches that echoed the sentiments of unity and resilience, moments of laughter shared over pastries and coffee, and connections deepening among friends and neighbors. As I mingled, I noticed a little girl, no older than seven, bouncing on her toes as she darted between tables, clutching a balloon tied to her wrist, its bright hue reflecting the joy around her. I smiled, reminded of the simple pleasures of life that often go unnoticed in the shadows of our struggles.

The sun began to set, casting a warm golden hue through the windows, and I felt a surge of gratitude for the community we had created. The event was more than just a launch; it was a testament to resilience, a celebration of both the beauty and the heartache that came with life.

Jake returned to my side, his earlier tension visibly eased, a newfound energy radiating from him. "I think I'm ready to give that writing a try," he said, his voice steady.

"Really? That's wonderful! I can't wait to see what you create," I said, my heart swelling with pride for him.

He leaned in, an impish smile lighting up his face. "You should join me. We can create our own little writing club—emotional support guaranteed."

"I'd love that," I replied, laughter bubbling between us as the vibrant chaos of the event continued to swirl around.

As the evening wore on, I felt the warmth of connection wrapping around us, a gentle reminder that we were not alone in our journeys. The fragility of life was balanced by the strength of community, the intertwining paths of our lives creating a tapestry rich with color and texture. In that moment, surrounded by laughter and hope, I knew we were both stepping into the light—together, ready to face whatever came next.

Chapter 8: The First Brushstroke

The night wrapped around us like a familiar quilt, warm and comforting, despite the uncertainty that had loomed over the last few weeks. The Willow pulsed with life; laughter mingled with the gentle strains of a jazz quartet tucked into the corner, each note weaving a tapestry of sound that embraced the heart of the evening. As I stepped further into the gallery, my senses danced with delight, overwhelmed by the vibrant spectrum of colors splashed across the walls. Each piece of artwork spoke a story—each brushstroke a testament to the local talent that thrived in our sleepy town. It felt surreal to see my vision come to life, to witness my dreams unfold before my very eyes.

A cacophony of scents wafted through the air, the buttery sweetness of pastries and the rich aroma of freshly brewed coffee forming a heady concoction that made my mouth water. I had spent countless late nights crafting the perfect menu for this event, and as I glanced at the tables adorned with delicate pastries, my heart swelled with pride. Croissants glistened under soft golden lighting, and macarons in every hue beckoned like little jewels, each one a masterpiece in its own right. The faint sound of people moving through the gallery, their shoes tapping against the wooden floor, created a rhythm that resonated deep within me.

Jake stood a few feet away, a charming whirlwind of energy. His laughter bubbled over as he greeted guests with genuine warmth, each smile radiant and infectious. I caught glimpses of his mother's spirit in the way he carried himself, the mannerisms that reminded me of her. It was as if her essence wrapped around him, guiding him through this pivotal moment. She had poured her heart into this space long before I had the honor of stepping in, and I felt her presence like a gentle whisper, urging us forward.

"Can you believe this?" Jake turned to me, his eyes sparkling like the stars that peeked through the gallery's windows. "This is really happening."

His excitement was contagious, and a wave of joy surged within me. I grinned back, unable to suppress the thrill that bubbled in my chest. "I know! It's more than I ever imagined. You've really done it, Jake."

As the night unfolded, our laughter intertwined with the soft strains of music, creating a melody of our own. I had spent countless hours dreaming of this moment, envisioning the crowd that would fill this space, the stories that would be shared among friends, and the connections that would be forged. It was more than just an art gallery; it was a sanctuary, a place where dreams could take flight, and creativity could blossom like the flowers we had planted outside.

As I stepped deeper into the gallery, I brushed my fingers against the textured canvases, feeling the roughness of the paint beneath my skin. Each artist had infused their soul into their work, and I found myself lost in the depths of a swirling abstract piece that seemed to capture the very essence of our town. The strokes of deep blue and vibrant orange danced across the canvas, telling a story of sunset evenings and tranquil lakes. It drew me in, capturing my imagination, and for a moment, I felt as if I was standing at the edge of a dream, staring into the horizon of possibility.

"Hey, you!" A familiar voice broke through my reverie. I turned to see Claire, my best friend, her dark curls bouncing as she moved towards me, a glass of sparkling cider in hand. "You look absolutely radiant tonight!"

I felt a warmth spread across my cheeks as she embraced me. Claire had always had a way of making the ordinary feel extraordinary. Her exuberance was infectious, and just being near her lifted my spirits higher. "Thanks! I'm just trying to keep up with Jake's excitement."

She laughed, a bright sound that cut through the hum of chatter around us. "Well, it's working. Look at him over there, charm personified. He's going to sweep everyone off their feet tonight."

As we watched Jake interact with our guests, I felt a swell of pride. This was his moment, a celebration not just of the gallery but of his mother's legacy, and the passion he poured into every inch of this place. I thought back to the nights we spent discussing our hopes and fears, mapping out the future while gazing at the stars. I had always believed in his dream, but seeing it come to life was something else entirely.

The evening wore on, and the space buzzed with life. Laughter erupted like firecrackers, echoing off the walls, and I reveled in the community that surrounded us. Local artists mingled with patrons, their conversations animated and alive. I poured glasses of cider, watched as people savored the pastries, and relished in the simple joys that made this evening so special. The energy was palpable, wrapping us all in a shared sense of belonging, a thread that connected each person to the other.

And then, as the clock ticked closer to the hour, Jake gathered everyone's attention. I felt a flutter of anticipation in my stomach as he stepped onto a small stage we had set up in the corner. His face, usually so animated, transformed into a picture of earnestness, and I could see the weight of his emotions in the way he clenched the edges of the podium.

"Thank you all for being here tonight," he began, his voice steady but laced with emotion. "This place means more to me than I can express, not just as a gallery but as a tribute to my mother, who taught me the beauty of creativity and community."

My heart ached with pride as I watched him speak. The room fell silent, the warmth of our shared experiences wrapping around us like a blanket. In that moment, I knew that we were all bound together by something greater than ourselves, a tapestry woven from the threads of hope, creativity, and love. And I was grateful to be a part of it all, standing beside Jake as we embraced our legacies and stepped into a new chapter, hand in hand.

A hush fell over the gallery, an electric pause that crackled with anticipation as Jake's words hung in the air like a fragile promise. His gaze roamed the crowd, catching the eyes of friends, family, and fellow artists, each face reflecting a shared history and a palpable hope for the future. I felt a swell of pride as I watched him speak, the once nervous young man transformed into a figure of authority and passion, grounded by the weight of his mother's legacy and the dreams we had dared to chase together.

"We've all faced our battles," he continued, his voice growing stronger, resonating within the hushed room. "Art has a way of bringing us together, of healing the wounds we can't see and celebrating the beauty of our shared stories. Tonight, we honor that spirit."

I could see his mother in the spark of his eyes, in the way his hands animated his speech, weaving through the air as if he were conducting an invisible orchestra. My heart raced with the rhythm of his words, each one echoing through the gallery like the soft clink of glasses in the background. The sound of laughter and conversation faded, each guest hanging on his every word, entranced. I stole glances around the room, witnessing the subtle nods and knowing smiles; we were all caught in the gravitational pull of his sincerity.

When Jake finally concluded his speech, a swell of applause erupted, reverberating through the room like a joyful wave. I felt a rush of emotion, a heady mix of elation and pride surging through my veins. He stepped down from the podium, and I rushed to meet him, throwing my arms around him in a tight embrace.

"I'm so proud of you," I whispered, my voice barely above a breath. "You were incredible."

He laughed, a genuine, heartfelt sound that made my heart leap. "I just spoke from the heart, you know? Thank you for being here with me."

As the applause faded and conversations resumed, I pulled back to take in the scene around us. The gallery felt alive, a heartbeat of its own, fueled by the passion and creativity of everyone present. I watched as guests moved from piece to piece, discussing the intricate details of the artwork, their voices blending into a symphony of appreciation. There was something intoxicating about seeing our vision come to fruition, the culmination of countless late nights and shared dreams materializing before us.

In the corner, I noticed Mrs. Thompson, a sprightly octogenarian with an eye for detail, standing with her friends. They leaned in closely, their heads together like conspirators, whispering excitedly as they studied a vibrant painting of the lake at sunset. I couldn't help but smile at the sight. Mrs. Thompson had always been the unofficial historian of our town, her stories woven into the fabric of our community. I wandered over, my heart light, eager to hear her thoughts.

"Oh, dear," she said, her eyes sparkling with delight as I approached. "This piece captures the essence of the lake perfectly! It's as if the artist bottled the sunlight and poured it onto the canvas."

I joined her, studying the painting anew through her eyes, letting her enthusiasm wash over me. "It really does," I agreed. "I think it's by Mia Sanders. She grew up by the lake and poured her heart into every stroke."

Mrs. Thompson nodded knowingly, a smile breaking across her face. "I can see it. The way she captures light is truly magical."

The room pulsed with life, a vibrant tapestry of conversations threading through the air, and I felt my spirit soar. I moved through the crowd, exchanging warm smiles and laughter with familiar faces, each interaction adding to the rich tapestry of the evening. Claire found me again, her eyes wide with excitement.

"I just overheard someone say they're thinking about hosting their next wedding here!" she exclaimed, her hands gesturing animatedly as she spoke. "Can you imagine? This place would be the perfect backdrop!"

My heart fluttered at the thought. Weddings, art, and love—a trinity of beauty that felt intertwined in the very essence of The Willow. "That would be incredible!" I replied, the idea painting my mind with vibrant strokes.

As the evening wore on, I found myself gravitating towards the small bar area where Jake had set up a selection of local wines and artisanal sodas. The soft clinking of glasses and the murmur of happy conversations created a cocoon of warmth that enveloped me. I poured myself a glass of red wine, letting the rich aroma swirl around me as I took a sip. The deep notes of berry and spice lingered on my tongue, a perfect complement to the atmosphere.

The gallery had transformed into a whirlwind of motion, and as I leaned against the bar, I couldn't help but take a moment to soak it all in. Guests mingled, laughter rang out like music, and the gallery glowed with the soft light of candles flickering in their glass holders. It was an enchanting scene, one that felt almost surreal. This was not just a launch; it was a celebration of life itself—a celebration of dreams realized, of connections formed, and of futures bright with possibility.

Suddenly, I felt a presence beside me, and I turned to find Jake, his hair slightly disheveled and a broad smile lighting up his face. "Do you have a minute?" he asked, his voice low but filled with eagerness.

"Of course!" I replied, my curiosity piqued.

He gestured toward the back of the gallery, and I followed him through the throng of people, weaving between small clusters of animated conversations until we reached a quieter corner adorned with a breathtaking mural of the town square. It depicted a vibrant summer day, children playing, and families gathered, the scene pulsing with life.

"Look at this," Jake said, his eyes sparkling with wonder. "This mural was a collaborative effort from the local high school art class. They spent weeks perfecting it, and it embodies everything we wanted to convey with this gallery—community, creativity, and the beauty of collaboration."

I marveled at the colors, the way they flowed into each other, each brushstroke a labor of love. It felt like a heartbeat, a rhythm of life woven into the fabric of our town. "It's stunning," I breathed, feeling a wave of admiration wash over me.

Jake leaned against the wall, a thoughtful expression crossing his face. "You know, I never imagined this would be my life. There were so many times I thought about giving up, but tonight... tonight feels different. It feels like the start of something bigger."

His words resonated deep within me. I glanced around at the joyous chaos of the gallery, the vibrant discussions and the laughter that echoed off the walls, and I felt a sense of belonging, of purpose, intertwining with my own dreams. "It is bigger," I said softly. "We're creating something beautiful here, something that will leave a mark on this town and on us."

Jake smiled, and in that moment, surrounded by the warmth of community and creativity, I knew we were not just artists or dreamers; we were architects of our futures, building a sanctuary of hope, connection, and love.

The air crackled with an effervescent energy as Jake and I stood in that alcove, the vibrant mural behind us capturing the essence of our town in vivid detail. Each person passing by was wrapped up in their conversations, yet the joy of the moment lingered like the sweet notes of the jazz quartet still floating through the gallery. Jake turned his gaze to the mural, the colors blending into a kaleidoscope that felt alive, much like the evening itself.

"It's funny, isn't it?" he mused, a hint of nostalgia lacing his words. "How something as simple as paint on a wall can encapsulate the spirit of a place?"

I nodded, letting the weight of his words settle over me like a soft blanket. "It's more than just paint; it's a memory, a feeling. It's laughter echoing through the streets, the scent of blooming flowers in the spring, the little quirks that make our town special." I paused, watching as a group of guests admired the mural, their faces lighting up with recognition. "Art gives voice to what we sometimes can't put into words."

As the night unfolded, the mingling voices formed a beautiful cacophony that resonated with warmth and camaraderie. I spotted Claire across the room, animatedly discussing the artwork with a couple of enthusiastic newcomers. It made my heart swell to see her so engaged, her passion for creativity mirroring my own. She had always been my partner in crime, the yin to my yang, and tonight, amidst the laughter and chatter, I was reminded of how grateful I was for her friendship.

"Let's get back to the festivities," Jake said, his eyes alight with determination. "I think people are ready for a toast."

With that, he led me back through the crowd, our hands brushing occasionally, sending a tiny thrill through me. Each step felt like a leap into the unknown, a shared journey that solidified our bond. He raised his glass high as he reached a small makeshift stage near the center of the gallery, commanding attention with an effortless grace.

"May I have everyone's attention, please!" he called out, his voice strong and clear. The chatter slowly faded as all eyes turned to him. "Thank you all for coming tonight to celebrate not just the opening of The Willow, but to honor the spirit of our community and the artistry that brings us together. Here's to new beginnings, to our shared stories, and to the art that shapes our lives!"

A chorus of cheers erupted, the clinking of glasses harmonizing with the heartfelt applause. I felt a surge of emotion swell within me. This was more than just an event; it was a collective celebration of our dreams, our history, and our hopes for the future.

As we sipped our drinks, I found myself enveloped in the joy of the moment, surrounded by laughter and animated conversations. The warmth in the room wrapped around me like a familiar embrace, the kind that felt safe and inviting. I caught snippets of dialogue, stories being shared, connections being made—all the elements of a vibrant tapestry coming together in perfect harmony.

In the far corner, I noticed a young couple, their fingers intertwined as they examined a striking piece of abstract art. Their closeness spoke volumes; they were wrapped in each other's worlds, lost in a shared reverie. It reminded me of the early days of my relationship with Jake—those tender moments when everything felt like magic. The gallery was a catalyst for that kind of intimacy, a place where dreams could flourish.

"Are you enjoying yourself?" Jake leaned in, his breath warm against my ear as he broke my reverie.

I turned to him, my heart racing slightly at his closeness. "I really am. It's everything we envisioned and more."

His smile was radiant, illuminating the dimmed light of the gallery. "And to think it all started with a wild idea and a lot of paint!" he chuckled, his eyes dancing with mirth.

The evening rolled on, and I found myself wandering the gallery, pausing to admire the pieces that adorned the walls. A landscape depicting the rolling hills of our town caught my eye, the greens and browns swirling together to create a vivid sense of place. I could almost hear the whispers of the wind as it swept through the fields, carrying stories from one generation to the next.

In a particularly cozy nook, a small group had gathered around a local sculptor, who was passionately discussing her latest creation—a striking piece that resembled a gnarled tree, its limbs reaching out as if yearning for the sky. The way she spoke about her work, the inspiration drawn from her childhood memories spent in the forest, brought a smile to my lips. Her love for her craft was infectious, and it served as a reminder that each artist infused their soul into their work, creating something truly unique.

As I continued my exploration, I found myself gravitating back towards Jake, who was now engaging a group of older guests in lively conversation. He gestured animatedly, a hand raised in enthusiasm, and I couldn't help but feel a surge of admiration for him. He had a way of connecting with people, of making them feel seen and valued, a rare gift that made him stand out even more in the warm glow of the gallery.

Just then, the band shifted into a slow, melodic tune, and I felt an impulse to dance. I approached Jake, who noticed my excitement and raised an eyebrow playfully. "Shall we?" I asked, gesturing towards the small dance floor that had formed.

He took my hand, a spark igniting between us, and together we moved to the music. The world around us faded as we lost ourselves in the rhythm, the soft melodies wrapping around us like a warm embrace. We swayed gently, the moment stretching out in sweet serenity, laughter blending seamlessly with the notes that floated through the air.

"This feels like a scene from a movie," Jake murmured, his voice low and intimate.

"Maybe we're the stars of our own story," I replied, my heart racing as I gazed into his eyes, so full of life and promise. "And this is just the beginning."

As the last notes of the song faded, a sense of contentment washed over me. It was as if all the challenges, the late nights, and the moments of doubt had led us to this perfect evening—a celebration not just of art, but of friendship, love, and shared dreams. I realized that this place, this gallery we had built together, was more than just a physical space. It was a sanctuary of creativity, a hub of connections, and a canvas on which we could paint our futures.

The night wore on, and I found myself reflecting on the incredible journey that had brought us here. Every brushstroke, every conversation, and every shared moment had woven a beautiful narrative, one that was rich with potential and hope. I felt an exhilarating sense of freedom, a belief that together, Jake and I could face whatever challenges lay ahead.

As I looked around the room, at the laughter, the camaraderie, and the art that adorned the walls, I understood that we were not just celebrating the launch of a gallery. We were igniting a spark within our community, a flame of creativity that would continue to burn brightly. This was our legacy, a testament to the beauty of human connection and the power of art to heal, inspire, and transform.

In that moment, I knew that the journey was just beginning, and I couldn't wait to see where it would lead us next.

Chapter 9: Breaking Through

The air felt electric as the last echoes of laughter faded into the cool evening breeze, leaving behind the sweet aroma of freshly baked pie mingling with the faint scent of damp earth. Under the vast expanse of the fading twilight, the remnants of the event lay scattered around us like forgotten dreams. Bright paper lanterns swayed gently in the trees, casting soft shadows over the scattered chairs and plates smeared with the remnants of sugary desserts. I busied myself with folding up chairs, my fingers grazing the warm, smooth wood, trying to anchor my thoughts in the present moment.

Jake's presence was an undeniable force, a sunbeam cutting through the twilight haze, igniting a warmth in my chest that I hadn't anticipated. He moved with a casual grace, effortlessly stacking chairs, his hands deft and strong, each motion fluid like a well-rehearsed dance. I could feel my heart quicken as he glanced my way, a playful smile teasing the corners of his lips. In that moment, the world around us faded, our laughter blending seamlessly, creating a symphony of connection. I was acutely aware of the hum of life surrounding us—the distant croaking of frogs, the gentle rustle of leaves, and the soft chirping of crickets settling into the dusk.

It was an odd feeling, this vulnerability simmering just beneath the surface. Jake's gaze lingered a heartbeat too long, and I found myself caught in the intensity of his dark eyes, which reflected something deeper, something that felt almost sacred. The world around us faded into a blur, leaving just the two of us cocooned in an intimate bubble of shared laughter and unspoken words. There was an electric charge between us, a silent understanding, and as we leaned in, the space between us shrinking, I could almost taste the promise of something more.

But the moment shattered as abruptly as it had begun, like fragile glass clattering to the ground. Leah appeared, her bright laughter cutting through the air like a knife. She breezed into our world with the kind of effortless charm that felt both enchanting and infuriating. Her hair was a cascade of golden waves, glistening in the waning light, and she wore an easy smile that seemed to belong to everyone and no one at once. The way she moved through the remnants of our gathering—confident, graceful—made the world shift under my feet.

Jake's demeanor changed instantly, the warmth in his eyes flickering as he turned his attention to her. The tension in the air thickened, curling around us like smoke. My heart sank, an unwelcome weight settling in my stomach as I sensed the unspoken history between them, a bond forged in the fires of childhood and nostalgia. I felt like an intruder in their shared space, a stranger in a familiar world, and jealousy clawed at my insides, leaving a bitter taste in my mouth.

"Leah! You made it!" Jake's voice was light, but the way he said her name was heavy, each syllable weighted with memories I could only imagine. As she drew closer, the easy banter between them revealed layers of a relationship I didn't understand, a friendship steeped in laughter and shared secrets. I stood frozen, a spectator to their reunion, acutely aware of the chasm that suddenly opened between Jake and me.

The moment stretched like a taut string, vibrating with unspoken emotions. Leah glanced at me, her bright eyes assessing, and I forced a smile that felt more like a grimace. "I'm just helping clean up," I said, my voice shaky and brittle, as if I were a porcelain doll threatened by the slightest touch. I tried to appear nonchalant, but inside, a tempest of insecurity swirled. I wanted to claw back the intimacy we had shared moments before, to reclaim that fleeting connection that felt so right.

As Leah began recounting her adventures—her voice animated, filling the air with warmth—I felt the shadows creep in, wrapping around my heart like an unwelcome embrace. Jake's laughter echoed in response, a sound that was once music to my ears now felt like a distant melody, a reminder of what I feared I was losing. My gaze flickered between them, watching their dynamic unfold, each shared glance like a punch to the gut.

"Remember that time we got lost in the woods?" Leah chirped, her laughter bright and clear. Jake chuckled, his eyes crinkling at the corners as he lost himself in the memory. "We thought we'd never find our way back!" The lightheartedness of their exchange felt like salt in a wound, and I stood there, a statue in the twilight, feeling increasingly like an outsider.

I wanted to break through this invisible barrier, to remind Jake of the promise of what could be between us, but I felt small, diminished by the weight of their shared past. With every story Leah told, I felt like I was shrinking, my heart retreating into the recesses of my mind, desperately trying to fend off the encroaching shadows of jealousy and uncertainty.

Just as Leah leaned closer to Jake, the unintentional intimacy of the moment sparking an ache deep within me, a flicker of hope surfaced. Perhaps this was a test, a moment of reckoning. I could either fold under the weight of my insecurities or stand tall, fight for what I felt was blossoming between us. The world seemed to hold its breath as I took a small step forward, the remnants of the evening swirling around me like a storm, and for a fleeting moment, I dared to believe that maybe, just maybe, I could break through the barriers that felt insurmountable.

The chill of the evening air wrapped around me, mingling with the fading warmth of the gathering as I stood caught in the crossfire of laughter and nostalgia. Leah's voice rang out, weaving a tapestry of shared experiences, her lighthearted tone lifting the atmosphere while simultaneously anchoring my heart to the ground. It was a bittersweet symphony, one I didn't know how to navigate. Each anecdote she shared seemed like a brick added to an invisible wall between me and Jake, yet there was something intoxicating about watching him—his laughter echoing like a soft melody, each grin lighting up his face, drawing me in and pushing me away all at once.

"Remember the scarecrow we made for the fair?" Leah laughed, her eyes sparkling as she reminisced. "We thought it was so brilliant until it scared away all the birds!" Jake's laughter resonated like a familiar tune, bringing warmth to the cool night. He leaned in closer to her, their shoulders brushing, and I felt my chest tighten as I fought to keep my emotions at bay. The laughter, once infectious, now felt like a distant echo of a world I could only observe.

I busied myself with folding a plastic tablecloth, focusing intently on the mundane task as if it were a lifeline. With each crease, I felt a flutter of determination bubble within me. I was more than just a spectator in this play; I had my own role, one that I needed to claim before it was rewritten by the shadows of the past. I gathered my courage and took a breath, the scent of freshly cut grass mingling with the earthy undertones of the approaching night. It was time to reclaim the narrative.

"Jake," I interrupted, my voice steady despite the tremors beneath the surface. He turned toward me, surprise flashing across his features. "How about we grab some water? I'm parched from all this..." I gestured vaguely at the chaotic remnants of the evening, the half-eaten desserts and scattered cups, my heart pounding as I pushed past my insecurities. Leah's laughter fell to a soft murmur, a flicker of uncertainty crossing her face, but Jake's eyes lit up as he nodded enthusiastically, his smile brightening the dimming world around us.

"Great idea!" he replied, and I could have sworn I saw a hint of relief in his gaze. I beckoned him toward the makeshift refreshment table, a rickety contraption pieced together with last-minute ingenuity. The air felt charged with a new energy, as if we were stepping away from the noise of Leah's stories and into a sanctuary of our own. Each step felt monumental, my heartbeat echoing in my ears like a drumroll heralding an important moment.

As we moved away from the remnants of laughter and childhood memories, the world shifted around us. The cool night air embraced me, and the distant sound of crickets became a soft backdrop to our brewing tension. I filled two cups with water, the sound of liquid splashing against plastic creating a momentary distraction from the swirling emotions in my chest. Jake stood close, his warmth radiating toward me like a gentle fire, and I turned slightly to face him, my heart racing as I prepared to take a leap into the unknown.

"Jake," I began, my voice barely above a whisper. "About what just happened..." My words hung in the air, a delicate balance between fear and hope. He met my gaze, the intensity in his eyes unwavering. The vulnerability that had passed between us before was still there, waiting to be reignited. "I know Leah is important to you," I continued, each word carefully chosen as if I were navigating a tightrope. "But I can't help feeling... I don't know, like I'm standing in the shadow of someone I can't compete with."

The weight of my admission settled between us, and I braced myself for his response, my stomach a tight knot of anticipation and dread. For a moment, he simply stared at me, a mix of surprise and something deeper flickering across his features. Then he took a step closer, lowering his voice to a conspiratorial whisper, almost as if he were afraid the night would overhear.

"Leah and I... we have history, but it's not what you think." His words flowed like a gentle stream, smoothing the jagged edges of my anxiety. "We grew up together, but what we had was never like what I feel with you. It's different—real, and I don't want you to think otherwise."

A rush of warmth flooded through me, melting away the frost of uncertainty that had encased my heart. I wanted to reach out, to bridge the gap between us and drown in the depth of his sincerity. "Really?" I managed, my voice trembling slightly as I searched his eyes for the truth, desperate for reassurance. "You mean it?"

He nodded, the weight of his gaze anchoring me in that moment. "You're the one I want to be with, not just tonight but beyond this—beyond everything. I promise you, Leah is a part of my past, and I'm ready to move forward."

As he spoke, the corners of my mouth turned upward, hope blossoming like wildflowers after a long winter. The shadows that had loomed over us began to recede, and the darkness seemed less daunting, filled with possibilities instead. I felt like I was stepping into the light for the first time, the warmth of his words wrapping around me like a soft blanket.

"Then let's move forward together," I whispered, emboldened by the sincerity in his eyes. "I want to know what this is, what we are, without any shadows." A smile broke across his face, illuminating his features, and in that instant, the world around us faded away, leaving just the two of us suspended in time.

With that promise hanging between us, we turned back toward the gathering, the lingering laughter of Leah now a distant echo. I felt lighter, as if I had shed layers of doubt and fear. Together, we were ready to carve our own path, undeterred by the shadows of yesterday. As we rejoined the remnants of our once-joyful gathering, I felt the promise of new beginnings, a chance to weave our own story into the fabric of the night.

The evening's warmth began to fade, and the crickets sang their nightly serenade as Jake and I stepped back into the realm of laughter and chatter. It was as if the universe had hit the pause button just for us, allowing a moment of clarity amid the chaos. The soft glow of the lanterns cast a golden hue over Leah's bright smile as she recounted stories from their childhood, her animated gestures punctuating the air with vibrancy. I felt the air thrum with unspoken tension, an electric current pulsing between us that made me hyper-aware of every laugh, every lingering glance Jake cast her way.

The remnants of the gathering felt like a stage set for a play I had not auditioned for, each character cast in roles I was just beginning to understand. As I picked at a half-eaten slice of pie, my gaze darted between them, my heart drumming a quick tempo of uncertainty and longing. Leah, effortlessly charming, stood as a testament to the power of nostalgia—a living relic of Jake's past that I couldn't compete with. Yet, standing beside him, I felt a flicker of resilience burning within me, urging me to stake my claim.

"Are you going to tell that story about the time we got stuck in the treehouse?" I interjected, surprising even myself with my sudden burst of confidence. The laughter around us dipped slightly, attention shifting to me. Leah's expression faltered for a moment, but then she grinned, inviting me into their shared history rather than excluding me from it.

"Oh, the infamous treehouse incident?" she chuckled, her eyes glinting with mischief. "Jake was convinced he could climb up to the roof to impress me. Instead, he got stuck and had to be rescued by my dad. It was the most embarrassing moment of his life!"

I leaned into the moment, my heart buoyed by the warmth of the memory as Jake's cheeks flushed a lovely shade of crimson. "It was not embarrassing," he protested, laughter escaping his lips. "It was a calculated risk!"

"Calculated risk?" I laughed, my heart swelling at the sight of him unguarded, his laughter infectious. "More like an uncalculated disaster."

"Okay, okay! You got me there." Jake raised his hands in mock surrender, the tension in the air beginning to dissipate like mist before the sun. I felt a shift, an unspoken agreement settling between us—a sense of camaraderie that drew us closer, allowing Leah to weave her stories without overshadowing the connection we were beginning to cultivate.

As Leah continued her stories, I leaned into Jake, our shoulders brushing, the warmth of his body grounding me amid the chaos. I caught glimpses of his smile as he exchanged banter with Leah, but now it felt different. With each laugh and shared memory, a new rhythm emerged, one that allowed me to find my place alongside him. The air thickened with the sweetness of potential, a heady concoction that made my heart race with promise.

"Remember the time we had that epic snowball fight?" Leah recalled, her laughter ringing like chimes in the wind. "You and I were unbeatable!"

Jake's eyes sparkled with delight as he leaned in, eyes gleaming. "That's because we had strategy. We formed alliances and took down the competition one snowball at a time."

"Strategy?" I quipped, eager to play my part. "More like ruthless domination! You two could start a snowball-fighting league with the way you plotted and schemed!"

Jake chuckled, and our shared laughter rang out against the backdrop of the twinkling stars, a melody of newfound connection that felt more profound than the stories we exchanged. Each shared joke and memory stitched us closer together, a tapestry woven with threads of past and present.

As the evening wore on, the air shifted, cooling as the sun dipped below the horizon, casting a twilight glow that wrapped around us like a warm blanket. The gathering began to wind down, laughter slowly giving way to yawns and sleepy murmurs. I noticed the way Leah's laughter softened, her gaze flickering to the stars, as if contemplating the shifting tides of her own emotions.

"Let's not let this be the last time we all hang out," Jake said suddenly, his voice breaking the spell of silence. The sincerity in his tone felt like an anchor amidst the current of unspoken tension. "We should do this again—maybe a bonfire or something. I can bring the marshmallows!"

I couldn't help but smile at his eagerness, a glimmer of excitement sparking within me. "I can bring the chocolate! What's a bonfire without s'mores?"

Leah chimed in, her expression brightening. "I'm in! It'll be great to have another night like this—maybe even add some music. I've got an old guitar lying around."

As plans unfolded between us, I felt an unexpected sense of relief wash over me. The bonds we were forging were strong enough to withstand the weight of the past. Leah's presence no longer felt like an adversary but rather a companion in our shared journey.

With laughter echoing through the cooling air, we began to gather our things, packing away memories like keepsakes to be treasured. Jake and I worked side by side, our movements in sync, a quiet understanding passing between us as we cleared the remnants of the night.

As I tied up the last of the trash bags, I glanced up to find him watching me, a smile tugging at his lips. "I'm really glad you're here," he said, his voice soft, almost lost amidst the sounds of the night. "Tonight was... special."

In that moment, the weight of the world felt lighter. I reached out, brushing my fingers against his, and the spark that ignited between us was electric, sending ripples of warmth coursing through me.

"I'm glad too, Jake," I replied, my heart racing as our eyes locked. "It felt like... a beginning."

As we stepped away from the remnants of the gathering, the stars twinkled above us like countless possibilities waiting to be discovered. The future loomed ahead, both uncertain and tantalizing, but one thing was clear: we would navigate this path together. The shadows of the past may have lingered, but in their wake, a vibrant world of opportunity was unfurling before us, shimmering with the promise of connection and new beginnings.

Chapter 10: A Flicker of Doubt

The sun streamed through the wide windows of the café, illuminating the eclectic mix of mismatched furniture and vibrant art that adorned the walls. It was a haven nestled in the heart of Charleston, where the aroma of freshly brewed coffee mingled with the sweet scent of pastries, and laughter danced on the air like a gentle breeze. I took a moment to appreciate the vibrant life surrounding me, but as my gaze settled on Jake, a knot formed in my stomach. His laughter, once a melody I cherished, now felt discordant.

Leah stood near the counter, a vision in a flowy sundress that caught the sunlight, accentuating the golden undertones in her hair. Her presence was magnetic, drawing people in like moths to a flame. I watched as she leaned closer to Jake, her laughter echoing across the room, a sound so bright and airy that it made my heart ache. It was a reminder of the playful bond we shared before she had entered the picture—a bond that now seemed tenuous, frayed at the edges, like an old, beloved quilt full of patches. I felt like a ghost, lingering on the periphery of their interaction, grasping for the warmth we had once shared but now felt so distant.

With every word she uttered, I could feel the distance between Jake and me grow wider, an invisible chasm that threatened to swallow our moments whole. I traced my fingers around the rim of my coffee cup, focusing on the steam that curled up into the air, as if it were whispering secrets. The café, once a sanctuary, had transformed into a stage for a performance I never wanted to be a part of. I was acutely aware of the silence that cloaked my heart, drowning out the lively sounds around us.

Later that day, I found myself in a cozy corner, my heart heavy with unresolved questions. The moment we were seated across from each other, the weight of unspoken words loomed larger than the bustling atmosphere of the café. I hesitated, watching him sip his coffee, the steam fogging up his glasses momentarily. How could someone so close feel so far away?

"Jake," I finally began, my voice barely above a whisper, thick with uncertainty. "What's going on with Leah?" The question slipped out before I could stop it, a fragile glass ornament shattering against the tiled floor. I braced myself for his response, fingers clenching around the delicate cup as if it were my only lifeline.

He shifted in his seat, the smile that danced across his lips felt rehearsed, like an actor who had forgotten his lines. "Leah? She's just... you know, someone from the past." He waved a dismissive hand, a gesture that felt practiced and hollow. I wanted to believe him, to accept that their connection was merely a distant memory, but my heart was not convinced. It raced, urging me to dig deeper, to pull back the layers of Jake's guarded heart, revealing the raw truth hidden beneath.

"I get that she's part of your history, but..." I hesitated, choosing my words carefully, "you seemed pretty... close." The last word lingered between us, charged with meaning, and I watched his expression shift, a fleeting shadow crossing his face before it was replaced by that same, frustratingly charming smile.

"She's just a friend," he insisted, but his eyes flickered with something else, a flicker that left me feeling unsteady. I couldn't help but wonder if I was merely occupying space in his heart, a placeholder until Leah returned to reclaim her spot. The thought twisted in my gut, a visceral reminder that love could be as fragile as glass, easily shattered by doubt.

As the conversation danced around us, I could feel the tension in the air, thick and suffocating. I leaned back in my chair, the fabric of the cushion cradling me while I attempted to find the right angle to view this new reality. "Do you think she wants more than friendship?" I asked, the question trembling on my lips, a daring foray into a territory I was not sure I was ready to explore.

Jake's eyes narrowed slightly, and I caught a glimpse of vulnerability behind his bravado. "It's complicated. We had our moments, but it's in the past now." His voice held a tremor that suggested he was trying to convince himself as much as me. I watched him closely, searching for any sign of sincerity, but the wall he had built around himself was formidable, and I felt like an intruder in his carefully curated life.

"Complicated how?" I pressed, my heart thumping with a mix of fear and hope. I wanted him to lay bare the truths that coiled between us, the ones wrapped tightly around his heart like a vine refusing to let go.

He sighed, leaning back and rubbing the back of his neck, a habit I recognized as a telltale sign of his frustration. "She's... we had our time together, and now it's just nostalgia for what was. You're here now, and I want to focus on that." The words tumbled from his lips, yet they felt like sand slipping through my fingers, impossible to hold onto.

"Do you?" The question was out before I could catch it, a spark igniting a flame of urgency in my chest. I needed to know if my presence in his life meant anything more than a temporary distraction.

Jake looked at me then, really looked at me, and for a heartbeat, I thought I could see the truth reflected in his deep brown eyes. It was a flicker of something raw, something that made my heart race. But as quickly as it appeared, it was gone, leaving behind the comfortable mask he wore so well. "Of course, I do," he replied, but the conviction felt rehearsed, a script he had memorized for moments just like this.

The café around us bustled with life—baristas shouting orders, couples whispering sweet nothings, and the clinking of mugs that felt like a distant echo to our conversation. I took a deep breath, allowing the rich scent of espresso to fill my lungs as I wrestled with the uncertainty swirling within me. I didn't want to drown in my insecurities, but the tendrils of doubt wrapped tighter around my heart with each passing moment.

With every fleeting smile Jake flashed my way, I felt the weight of his past pressing against the fragile threads of our present. I craved the comfort of certainty, the warm embrace of trust that I feared was slipping through my fingers. As I sipped my coffee, the warmth of the mug felt like a promise—if only I could convince myself to believe it.

The air between us crackled with unspoken tension, as though the very fabric of our connection was woven with threads of uncertainty. I tried to focus on the rich aroma of my coffee, the way it swirled in delicate patterns atop the surface, a visual balm for my fraying nerves. I watched the steam curl upwards, each tendril rising like the hopes and fears swirling within me. The café remained alive with its usual symphony of clinking mugs and soft chatter, yet my heart was locked in a solitary dance of doubt.

As Jake continued to speak, his words washed over me, but I struggled to catch them fully. He was trying to reassure me, I could tell, yet the sincerity of his intentions felt muddied. "You know how it is, right? People from our past can sometimes just... linger." He leaned forward slightly, his brow furrowing as he attempted to decipher the tumult in my expression. The sunlight streamed through the window, casting a warm glow on his features, illuminating the edges of his smile, but the flicker of anxiety in his eyes belied the ease he was trying to project.

"Linger?" I echoed, my voice carrying a hint of sarcasm, perhaps as a defense mechanism to shield the raw vulnerability bubbling just beneath the surface. "Is that what we're calling it? An unfortunate case of lingering?" The words left my mouth before I had a chance to temper their sting. I quickly bit my lip, regretting the sharpness, but the truth was, I felt as if I were fighting against a tide that threatened to pull me under.

Jake looked taken aback for a moment, surprise dancing across his features. "Come on, you know it's not like that. It's just... history," he insisted, but the tone of his voice wavered. It felt like he was pleading, as if he were the one trying to convince himself rather than me. I glanced down at my coffee, suddenly aware of how the rich brown liquid mirrored the complexity of our conversation—dark, deep, and stirring beneath the surface.

"History that you keep bringing up," I said softly, allowing the hurt to seep into my words. "You speak about her with such ease. It makes me wonder where I fit into this picture." I dared to look into his eyes, searching for the clarity I craved, hoping to catch a glimpse of the truth that seemed perpetually just out of reach.

His gaze softened, and he reached out, his hand hovering just above mine as if afraid to bridge the gap. "You fit, trust me. You're not just a chapter in my life; you're a whole new book." The sincerity in his voice was comforting, but still, the nagging doubts refused to quiet. I yearned to believe him, to feel anchored by his words, yet the shadows of Leah's presence loomed large, taunting me with reminders of what might have been.

A shiver raced down my spine at the thought of her, as if she were an unwelcome breeze sweeping through my carefully constructed facade. I imagined her golden hair cascading over her shoulders, her laughter ringing out, a melody I could no longer drown out. Jake's connection to her was palpable, like an unseen thread binding them together, and I felt like the intruder, trying to wedge myself into a story that wasn't fully mine.

"How can I be sure?" I finally asked, my voice barely above a whisper, laden with vulnerability. "How can I trust that you're not still... caught up in whatever it is you two had?" The question hung in the air, heavy and fraught with tension.

He pulled back slightly, eyes narrowing as if my words had struck a nerve. "You think I want to be here, constantly caught in memories of her? Leah was part of my life, but she's not my life. You are." The frustration in his voice melted into desperation, and in that moment, I saw a flicker of the boy I had fallen for—a boy full of dreams, laughter, and untamed passion.

I nodded slowly, feeling the weight of his words settle within me, yet uncertainty still curled around my heart. I wanted to believe him, to step into the light he offered, but Leah's shadow flickered at the edges of my mind, relentless and haunting. "What if she decides she wants you back?" The question slipped out, a trembling leaf caught in a sudden gust of wind, and I winced at my own audacity.

Jake leaned forward, the warmth of his body radiating across the table like sunlight breaking through the clouds. "I'm not interested in going back, I promise you that. I'm here, with you." His voice softened, drawing me in, and for a fleeting moment, the air shifted. It was as if the universe had conspired to align our stars, and the fragile bond we shared began to weave itself anew, strengthened by vulnerability.

But then the cloud passed, and I found myself gripped by a surge of anxiety. "You say that, but Leah's not just going to vanish because I'm here. The memories you have, they don't just disappear." The words tumbled out like rocks down a hillside, heavy and unavoidable. I could feel the walls closing in, the noise of the café fading into a dull roar as my fears took center stage.

Jake's expression shifted, his brow furrowing as he reached across the table, finally bridging the gap between us. "And neither do the memories I have of you," he countered, his grip tightening around my hand, a gesture both grounding and electrifying. "You're the one I want to build a future with. Leah is just a part of my past, a chapter I've closed."

In his eyes, I searched for reassurance, finding flickers of sincerity beneath the surface. The warmth of his skin against mine was intoxicating, a reminder that despite the past, here we were, fighting against the currents of uncertainty together. "I want you to know that what we have is real," he continued, his voice low and earnest. "It's different. It's... alive."

A part of me craved to succumb to his words, to let the warmth of his promise wrap around me like a soft blanket, warding off the chill of doubt that had nestled deep within my bones. I wanted to believe in the vibrancy of what we were building, the intricate tapestry of our lives intertwining in ways I had only dared to imagine. But still, the question lingered like a whisper on the wind: would it be enough?

In that moment, the café pulsed with life around us, the sounds of laughter and conversation weaving into a tapestry of shared human experience. I could feel the weight of the world outside pressing against the glass, a reminder that life continued, full of uncertainty and promise. Yet here we sat, in a pocket of warmth and connection, clinging to each other like lifelines in a storm.

As the sun began to dip lower in the sky, casting golden hues across the room, I allowed myself to lean into the moment. Perhaps the flicker of doubt that danced in the back of my mind could coexist with the flicker of hope blossoming in my heart. Maybe, just maybe, it was possible to forge ahead, hand in hand, even amidst the lingering shadows of the past.

The world around us seemed to pulse in rhythm with my uncertainty, a melody of laughter and clinking cups juxtaposed against the quiet thrum of my heartbeat. Jake's fingers brushed against mine, sending tendrils of warmth spiraling up my arm. It was a small gesture, yet it felt monumental, a beacon of reassurance amid the brewing storm of doubt. The barista floated by, a vision in an apron splattered with colorful paint, delivering lattes topped with delicate foam art that looked almost too good to drink. Each passing moment was an attempt to anchor me in the present, yet my mind raced with thoughts of Leah, the vibrant specter I couldn't quite shake off.

The café buzzed with life, filled with couples sharing intimate whispers and friends animatedly discussing everything from weekend plans to the latest gossip. But I felt cocooned in a bubble of uncertainty, my gaze drifting between the idyllic scene and the man sitting across from me. Jake's laughter danced with the light in the room, a sound I had cherished, but now it held an edge of something unspoken, a hint of hesitation that seeped into my bones.

"Why do you keep avoiding the question?" I probed, watching as he took a slow sip of his coffee, a slight frown furrowing his brow. "If Leah is just a friend, why does she make it feel like we're playing a game of tug-of-war? I want to understand where I stand."

His eyes darted to the window, where a couple was sharing a moment of laughter, their joy a sharp contrast to my own internal struggle. I could see him grappling with my words, caught between his past and the reality we were building. "You stand in front of me," he finally replied, his tone steady yet tinged with frustration. "I'm not looking back; I want to be here, with you."

A soft breeze filtered through the open door, carrying the scent of blooming magnolias and fresh pastries, yet it only deepened the ache in my heart. I could sense the history he carried, not just with Leah, but with his own dreams and fears, each piece a fragment of a puzzle I struggled to fit together. "But what if you're still haunted by that past? What if you're not really ready to let go?" My words hung in the air, heavy with implications.

"I can't change what's already happened," he said, his voice dropping to a whisper as if afraid the world around us might overhear. "But I can choose who I want in my life now, and that's you." He leaned closer, the intensity of his gaze igniting a spark within me, a desperate hope that maybe this moment could tether us to something more solid.

Yet, the flicker of doubt remained, a persistent little demon nestled in the back of my mind. I recalled Leah's easy laughter, the way she seemed to command the room's attention with a single smile, her confidence a blazing sun that overshadowed my own gentle glow. "You're right; I'm here now, but the question is, how do we move forward when the past refuses to fade?"

For a moment, the weight of my words settled between us like an uninvited guest. The barista returned, placing a warm croissant on our table with a bright smile, momentarily breaking the tension. "Enjoy!" she chirped, before bustling away, leaving us in our cocoon once more. I picked at the flaky pastry, my appetite suddenly diminished, the buttery layers reminding me of the complexity of the situation we faced.

Jake cleared his throat, his expression shifting to one of determination. "Let's create new memories. Why don't we plan a weekend getaway? Just the two of us." The suggestion hung in the air, a lifeline tossed into turbulent waters. "Somewhere away from the noise, where we can be just us."

A flicker of excitement sparked within me, momentarily brightening the shadows in my heart. "Where would we go?" I asked, letting my curiosity peek through the veil of doubt.

"How about the Blue Ridge Mountains?" His eyes lit up at the thought. "We could hike the trails, spend the nights under the stars. Just you and me." The image he painted was vibrant and inviting, a world where we could escape the constraints of reality and rediscover the joy we had begun to build together.

"Camping, huh?" I chuckled, picturing us snuggled under blankets, sharing stories and marshmallows by the fire. "That could be... interesting."

"I promise I'll even learn how to start a fire," he added, laughter dancing in his eyes. The warmth of his smile wrapped around me like a blanket, igniting a flicker of hope that maybe, just maybe, we could forge a path forward.

"But if Leah shows up?" I asked, the question slipping from my lips before I could censor it. "What then? What if our getaway becomes an unexpected reunion?"

Jake's smile faltered for a moment, and I could see the shadows returning, but he steadied himself quickly, his resolve evident. "I'll deal with it. I'll make it clear that what we have is different—better."

My heart swelled at his words, even as uncertainty whispered in my ear. "You promise?" I felt vulnerable asking for reassurance, but there was power in the vulnerability, a strength that came from laying bare my fears.

"I promise," he said, his tone steady, fingers entwining with mine, grounding me in the moment. I could see the sincerity in his eyes, a flame flickering against the gust of uncertainty. The sunlight poured through the window, bathing us in warmth, casting shadows that danced across our table. I wanted to believe in the promise of this moment, the fragile yet tenacious hope blooming in my chest.

As we left the café, the world outside buzzed with the vibrancy of spring, the streets alive with the hum of life. The scent of blooming jasmine filled the air, a heady mix of sweetness and nostalgia that tugged at my heartstrings. Each step we took felt laden with possibility, and I found myself contemplating the beauty of new beginnings.

We wandered along the waterfront, where the gentle lapping of the waves created a soothing backdrop to our conversation. The sunset painted the sky in hues of orange and pink, a breathtaking canvas that felt like a promise of brighter days ahead. As we strolled, Jake recounted stories from his childhood, his voice animated and full of laughter, and I felt the barriers around my heart begin to soften, melting away under the warmth of his presence.

It was easy to get lost in the rhythm of our laughter, the way our words intertwined effortlessly, creating a symphony that echoed against the backdrop of the world around us. The worries of Leah slipped away, drowned out by the vivid colors of our budding relationship. I found myself stealing glances at Jake, mesmerized by the way his eyes sparkled in the fading light, the shadows of his past momentarily eclipsed by the brilliance of our present.

As we reached a quiet spot by the water, I turned to him, my heart racing with the weight of unspoken feelings. "Jake," I began, the words feeling both heavy and exhilarating, "I want to take this leap with you. I want to believe that we can create something beautiful together, despite the shadows of the past."

He paused, looking into my eyes as if searching for something deeper. "We will," he promised, a conviction in his voice that ignited hope within me. "Together, we'll build a love that can weather any storm."

In that moment, with the world fading away around us, I realized that love is not just a singular entity but a collection of moments—fragile yet fierce, tender yet resilient. We would forge our own path, illuminated by the flicker of hope and the warmth of connection, ready to embrace whatever the future held.

Chapter 11: Threads of the Past

The air in the small town of Willow Creek was thick with the sweet scent of honeysuckle, a fragrant reminder of the lingering warmth of summer. I often found myself wandering the streets, each corner revealing snippets of the town's charm—a local diner with a flickering neon sign that read "Open 24 Hours," the kind of place where the pie was always homemade, and the coffee ran strong enough to wake the dead. The sidewalks were lined with clapboard houses, their front porches adorned with rocking chairs and potted geraniums, all bathed in the soft glow of the afternoon sun. It was a scene painted with nostalgia, a world where everyone knew each other's names and the stories intertwined like the gnarled roots of the ancient willow tree at the park's center.

As I settled into life at The Willow, the charming bed-and-breakfast that had become my temporary home, I couldn't shake the feeling that beneath the surface of this picturesque town lay untold stories, buried like treasures waiting to be unearthed. My fascination with Jake, the enigmatic owner, deepened with each passing day. I watched him interact with the guests—his laughter infectious, his smile genuine. Yet, every time Leah's name slipped from someone's lips, that brightness dimmed, replaced by a shadow that seemed to cling to him, heavier than the humid summer air.

With each mention of Leah, I noticed the flicker of pain in Jake's hazel eyes. It was a stark contrast to the warmth he radiated when he talked about the whimsical renovations he had made to The Willow or the local fishing spots he cherished. I couldn't help but feel a sense of urgency to understand this part of him that was cloaked in sorrow. Perhaps, if I peeled back the layers, I could discover the truth that haunted him.

I started my investigation at the local coffee shop, a bustling hub where the clatter of cups and the hum of conversation created an intimate atmosphere. It was here that I met Doris, a sprightly woman in her sixties with silver hair that sparkled like freshly fallen snow. She had an uncanny knack for knowing everyone's business, her knowing smile suggesting she held the secrets of the town like a cherished book.

"Ah, Jake," she said, her voice a melodic blend of warmth and wisdom. "Good boy, he is. Always looking out for others, but his heart... well, it's a bit fractured these days." She paused, her gaze drifting to the window as if she could see into the very fabric of the past. "Leah was his first love. Beautiful girl, full of dreams, but life has a way of throwing curveballs, doesn't it?"

I leaned in closer, my interest piqued. "What happened to her?"

Doris took a slow sip of her coffee, her eyes glistening with memories. "They were inseparable, those two. Sweethearts since high school. But after graduation, Leah had plans—big plans. College, traveling, a whole world ahead of her. Jake wanted to support her, to be her rock, but he had his own burdens. Family obligations, a business to run."

The conversation shifted, but I could feel the weight of her words hanging in the air like the scent of fresh-baked pastries. I left the coffee shop with a newfound understanding, piecing together the fragments of Jake's life, a jigsaw puzzle whose edges were rough and unfinished.

The following days, I continued my quest for understanding, seeking out those who might hold the key to Leah's story. I stumbled upon the local library, a quaint brick building with ivy creeping up its walls. The scent of aged paper and polished wood greeted me as I stepped inside. I was met by Carla, the librarian, a woman whose glasses perched precariously on her nose as she typed away at her computer, a fountain of information hidden behind a rather serious demeanor.

I asked about Leah, and her expression softened. "She was a bright light in this town. Always volunteering, always smiling. But when she left for college, things changed. I remember Jake coming in, looking lost. He'd ask about her, but the longer she was gone, the more he withdrew."

"Did they ever reconnect?" I pressed, desperate for any glimmer of hope.

Carla's fingers paused mid-type, her eyes clouding with sympathy. "After a while, it was like they were living in different worlds. I heard Leah had an accident. Something tragic. I think Jake never really recovered from it."

Each revelation struck me like a stone tossed into a still pond, the ripples disturbing the surface of my understanding. I felt an ache for Jake, a man carrying the weight of unfulfilled dreams, and a pang of sorrow for Leah, whose potential was cut short, leaving behind a gaping void.

Determined to uncover more, I found myself wandering to the park where the old willow tree stood, its branches swaying gently in the breeze. Sitting on a weathered bench, I closed my eyes and let the sun warm my face, imagining the lives that had unfolded beneath its sprawling canopy. It was here that I decided I would confront Jake, not with accusations or assumptions, but with compassion and understanding.

Perhaps if I could bridge the gap between his past and present, he might find solace in sharing the story that had forged the man I was growing to care for. The thought of it filled me with a sense of purpose, igniting a flicker of hope in my heart—a hope that, like the enduring roots of the willow tree, could ground him in a way he hadn't felt in years. The complexity of grief, I realized, was intertwined with love, and in the heart of Willow Creek, amid its small-town charm, I was ready to uncover the truth that had bound Jake to Leah and, in turn, bound me to him.

A PLACE TO BELONG

The sun dipped low in the sky, casting a golden hue over Willow Creek as I prepared for my first real conversation with Jake. The cozy atmosphere of The Willow hummed with the soft sounds of clinking dishes and laughter, but I could feel the weight of anticipation in the air. Each heartbeat echoed in my ears, as if the very walls of the bed-and-breakfast were urging me to step closer to the truth. Jake was setting the dining room for the evening, his fingers deftly arranging the cutlery with the kind of precision that spoke of a man who valued both beauty and order.

As I approached him, the warmth of the setting sun painted his features in soft light, momentarily dispelling the shadows that had taken residence there. I had watched him flit between guests, his genuine laughter a balm for the weary souls who sought refuge within these walls. Yet now, as I stood before him, I could sense a heaviness, a storm brewing beneath the surface of his charming exterior.

"Jake," I began, my voice barely above a whisper. "Can we talk? Just you and me?"

He paused, glancing up from the table as if weighing the gravity of my request. The brief flicker of hesitation in his eyes ignited a knot of worry in my stomach. But then he nodded, a soft smile breaking through the uncertainty. "Sure, let's step outside."

We found ourselves on the back porch, where the air was fragrant with the scent of lilacs and freshly cut grass. The sun continued its descent, draping everything in a warm glow, but the atmosphere felt charged, electric with the unsaid. I leaned against the railing, my heart thudding in time with the distant hum of cicadas. Jake leaned beside me, arms crossed, a protective posture that hinted at the walls he had built around himself.

"Is everything okay?" I ventured, my curiosity mingling with a gentle concern. "I've noticed... well, there's a sadness that lingers when Leah comes up."

He sighed, the sound rich with exhaustion. "It's just memories, I guess. She was... a part of my life that I never quite let go of." His voice cracked slightly, and I felt the air between us thicken with unspoken emotions.

"Doris and Carla told me a little about her," I said cautiously. "She sounds like she was amazing."

"She was," he replied, his eyes focusing on a point beyond the horizon, as if searching for her among the clouds. "Full of life, always dreaming big. We were supposed to take on the world together." The bitterness in his tone tugged at my heartstrings. "But dreams don't always play out like you expect."

I turned to him, wanting to reach out, to bridge the distance between his pain and the warmth of my understanding. "What happened?"

Jake hesitated, the silence stretching like an elastic band before it finally snapped. "Leah was in a car accident a few months after she left for college," he said, his words tumbling out like stones. "She was driving home for the holidays—so excited to see everyone again. She never made it."

A shiver ran through me, a chill settling deep in my bones as I processed the weight of his words. Here was the tether to his grief, the reason he seemed caught between laughter and sorrow, a vibrant man shadowed by loss. "I'm so sorry," I whispered, my voice thick with empathy. "That must have been incredibly hard for you."

"It was like losing a part of myself," he confessed, the rawness in his voice revealing a vulnerability I hadn't seen before. "I've tried to move on, but it feels like I'm living in a constant state of limbo. The Willow, this place... it's all I have left of her. I can't let it go."

His words resonated within me, echoing the struggle I had often faced in my own life. I reached out, placing my hand gently on his arm, feeling the warmth of his skin beneath my fingers. "It's okay to feel that way, Jake. It's okay to hold on to those memories. But you also deserve to find joy again, to live fully. Leah would want that for you."

He turned to me, those hazel eyes searching mine, and I saw a flicker of something—hope, perhaps. "You really think so?"

"I know so," I assured him, my voice steady. "It's not about forgetting; it's about carrying her memory with you, allowing it to inspire you rather than anchor you down. This place, it can still be a haven for you, a reminder of her love, but it can also be a place where you create new memories."

For the first time, I saw a hint of relief in his expression, as if I had offered him a lifeline in the tumultuous sea of grief. The sun dipped lower, casting elongated shadows across the porch, and for a moment, we both stood in that quiet space, wrapped in the vulnerability of our shared truths.

"I want to believe that," he said softly, his voice barely above a whisper. "I want to believe I can move forward without losing her."

I nodded, sensing the fragile threads connecting us growing stronger. "You can. You don't have to do it alone. I'm here, Jake, and I care about you." The confession hung in the air between us, a fragile promise that shimmered like the last rays of sunlight, a declaration woven into the very fabric of our surroundings.

As twilight descended, the first stars began to twinkle in the indigo sky, offering glimmers of hope against the darkening horizon. In that moment, I felt the gravity of the world shift, the heaviness in my heart lifting slightly. Together, we stood on that porch, connected not just by our words, but by the shared understanding of loss and the possibility of healing.

And as the evening settled around us, the air infused with the earthy scent of dusk, I realized that in opening ourselves to the past, we had also opened the door to new beginnings. In the heart of Willow Creek, where every whispered secret lingered in the breeze, I found not only Jake but a sense of belonging that promised to mend the frayed edges of my own heart.

A cool breeze rustled the leaves of the willow tree, whispering secrets only the ancients could know, as I stepped back inside The Willow, leaving behind the weight of our conversation. The air was thick with the scent of freshly baked bread and the distant clinks of glasses being set upon tables. The comforting ambiance welcomed me back, wrapping me in its warmth like a soft, worn blanket. Jake was busy in the kitchen, the rhythmic chopping of vegetables punctuating the hum of the old ceiling fan.

I perched on a barstool, watching him with a mixture of admiration and concern. There was something almost poetic about his movements, the way he danced around the kitchen, his hands a blur as he prepared dinner for the guests. Yet beneath that grace, I sensed the remnants of the pain we had just shared, lingering in the corners of his smile.

"Need a sous-chef?" I ventured, attempting to inject a lighthearted note into the atmosphere.

He chuckled, but it was tinged with a melancholy that tugged at my heart. "Unless you're good at chopping onions, I think I've got this." His eyes sparkled for a moment, a flicker of the man I had come to know—a man who poured himself into his work, trying to fill the void that Leah had left.

"I can slice and dice with the best of them," I declared with mock bravado, hopping off the stool and grabbing a knife. The kitchen was a sanctuary of aromas—sautéing garlic, the sharp bite of herbs, and the sweetness of caramelizing onions—all blending into a symphony that resonated within me.

As we worked side by side, the rhythm of our movements began to forge an unspoken connection. Each chop of the knife seemed to echo the conversations of the past, melding with our present, creating a tapestry woven with laughter and shared sorrow. I couldn't help but steal glances at him, marveling at how he seemed to find solace in the act of creation, even if it was only a meal.

"Tell me about Leah," I said, the question flowing out as easily as the olive oil I poured into the pan. "What were her dreams? What did she want?"

Jake paused, his hands stilling as he considered my words. "She wanted to be an artist. She had this incredible gift with a paintbrush, transforming blank canvases into worlds filled with color. She saw beauty everywhere—more than I ever did." He chuckled softly, a hint of pride in his tone. "She could turn the simplest moment into a masterpiece, whether it was a sunrise over the lake or the smile of a child. She had this way of capturing life in its rawest form."

His voice carried the weight of admiration, and I could picture Leah vividly in my mind's eye—a free spirit, unbound and unfiltered, weaving magic into the mundane. "Did she ever finish her degree?" I asked, my heart aching at the thought of unrealized potential.

"She was on her way, but..." His voice trailed off, the unspoken words hanging heavily in the air between us. "She was only a few credits away. She had big plans for her final project, an exhibition she was so excited about. I can still see the sketches she'd drawn on napkins at the diner." He shook his head, as if trying to dispel the memories that were threatening to take hold.

I could feel the quiet frustration emanating from him. The notion of dreams thwarted, like leaves caught in a gust of wind, made my heart clench. "Do you think she would have succeeded?" I ventured, wanting to pry open the door to his memories, hoping to guide him toward the light.

He considered this for a moment, his brow furrowing in thought. "Leah didn't just have talent; she had passion. I have no doubt she would have taken the art world by storm. But her spirit..." His voice broke, and he looked away, swallowing hard. "Her spirit was bigger than any canvas could contain."

The kitchen fell silent, the clattering of pots and pans replaced by the quiet hum of our unearthing. I wanted to reach out, to pull him back from the depths of despair, but I also knew he needed to feel this. Grief had its own timeline, and sometimes, the only way to navigate through it was to walk alongside it.

"I wish I could have met her," I said, my voice softening. "I would have loved to see her art."

Jake turned to me, a glimmer of surprise flashing in his eyes. "She would have liked you," he said, a small smile breaking through. "You have this light about you, a warmth that draws people in. I can imagine the two of you getting along like old friends."

The compliment lingered in the air like a fine wine, rich and intoxicating. It was a fleeting moment of joy, a reprieve from the sorrow that often consumed him. "You know," I continued, eager to sustain this newfound connection, "if you ever want to honor her memory, you could hold that exhibition yourself. Showcase her sketches, her work. Let the world see her through your eyes."

His brow furrowed as he mulled over the idea. "That's a beautiful thought, but I don't think I could do it without falling apart." The vulnerability in his voice shattered my heart.

"Maybe that's exactly what you need," I encouraged, my voice steady. "To let it out, to share her with the world instead of keeping her locked away. It might be hard, but think of the joy it could bring. For you and for everyone who loved her."

Jake nodded slowly, and I could see the wheels turning in his mind, the ember of inspiration igniting amidst the ashes of his grief. "You might be onto something there," he said quietly, the spark of hope flickering in his eyes.

As the evening wore on, we served dinner to the guests, laughter and chatter filling the air. The comforting ambiance of The Willow wrapped around us, a cocoon where moments were forged and memories made. I watched Jake as he moved through the room, his demeanor lighter, the burden of the past no longer as heavy.

After the guests retired to their rooms, he lingered in the dining area, a soft smile dancing on his lips as he caught my gaze. "Thank you for today," he said, his voice low, almost reverent. "For listening. I didn't realize how much I needed to talk about her."

"I'm glad you did," I replied, feeling a warmth blossom within me. "You don't have to carry that alone, you know. It's okay to lean on someone."

"I think I'm starting to believe that," he said, his expression softening. "Maybe there's a way to keep her alive without being lost in the shadows."

As we locked eyes, the space between us pulsed with an unspoken understanding, a promise that we would navigate this journey together. And in that shared moment, I felt the tapestry of our lives intertwining, threads of laughter and sorrow weaving together into something uniquely ours.

The night deepened, and the world outside The Willow faded into a gentle hush. In the cocoon of that beautiful space, I began to realize that healing didn't mean forgetting; it meant allowing the past to coexist with the present. With each breath, I felt the richness of Willow Creek wrap around us, the beauty of life still very much alive within its embrace. We were not just two souls wandering through the shadows; we were two hearts, ready to find light in each other's company.

Chapter 12: A Creative Collision

The café stood like a beloved old friend at the edge of Main Street, its faded blue façade hugging the charm of a bygone era. Sunlight filtered through the leaves of the gnarled oak tree outside, casting dappled shadows across the weathered wooden tables. I took a deep breath, the aroma of freshly brewed coffee swirling around me like a comforting blanket, and my heart swelled at the thought of transforming this place into something vibrant and alive.

"Imagine a splash of color," I said to Jake, my voice barely above the rustling leaves. He leaned against the café's counter, a playful smirk tugging at the corners of his mouth. The way he stood there, arms crossed and brow furrowed in thought, was a sight I had grown fond of—a blend of mischief and deep contemplation that made my pulse quicken.

"A community garden event?" His eyes lit up, and I could see the wheels of his mind turning, intertwining with my vision like the vines I wanted to plant. "We could have a Saturday market! Local vendors could set up stalls. Maybe even live music!"

The idea spiraled into something beyond the two of us, blooming into a colorful vision that danced in my mind—a vibrant tapestry of sounds, scents, and laughter that wrapped around the café like a warm hug. I pictured blooming marigolds, basil leaves swaying in the breeze, and hand-painted signs directing customers to artisanal bread and homemade jams. Each detail flickered to life as I sketched out plans on a napkin—my heart racing with the possibility of it all.

"Imagine it," I murmured, nearly lost in the daydream. "Families could come, children would laugh as they dig in the dirt. The café would become a community hub, a heartbeat in this sleepy town."

Jake nodded, his enthusiasm palpable as he leaned closer, his eyes shimmering with inspiration. "We could partner with local schools for the kids to plant flowers and herbs. They would love that! And what if we set up a little area for them to learn about gardening?"

Each idea he tossed into the air was like tossing a handful of seeds into fertile soil, and I watched as they took root in my mind. Yet, even amid this burgeoning excitement, I felt a shadow creeping in—Leah's memory loomed like a specter, casting a cool shade over the warmth of our brainstorming. It was impossible not to think of her, of how Jake's gaze sometimes drifted toward the door as if waiting for her to walk back in. That specter of their past lingered, and I wrestled with the tug-of-war in my heart, caught between joy and jealousy.

"Let's get the word out," I said, trying to shake off the unease. "We could post flyers, maybe use social media. Everyone loves a good garden party!"

As I spoke, I noticed the little things—the way Jake's hair caught the sunlight, the warmth of his laughter, the ease with which our conversation flowed. It was as if we were two musicians finding harmony in an unexpected duet. The café, with its rustic charm and fading paint, became our canvas, and I felt my spirit lifting as we shared the same vision.

"Okay, so we have a theme," he said, bouncing on the balls of his feet. "What about the name? It needs to be catchy, something that screams summer."

"'Blooming in the Heart of Town'?" I suggested, the words tasting sweet on my tongue. "It has a nice ring to it, don't you think?"

He chuckled, a deep sound that sent ripples of warmth through me. "I like it, but maybe something simpler? How about 'Garden Glow'?"

"Short and sweet," I nodded, feeling the energy of the moment pulse between us. "I love it."

Our laughter floated in the warm air, mingling with the sound of distant chatter and the clinking of dishes. The world outside continued on, oblivious to the small revolution brewing within the café's walls. With each passing minute, the heaviness of Leah's memory began to lift, replaced by the sweet thrill of collaboration, the magnetic pull of ideas sparking between us.

But just as the warmth of the sun enveloped us, I felt a chill. What would happen when the dust settled? When the blooms faded? I was dancing with the ghost of our shared ambitions, and the thought tugged at the corner of my mind like an unfinished symphony.

As if sensing my momentary lapse, Jake placed his hand over mine, grounding me in the present. His touch was electric, igniting a warmth that spread through my veins. "We can make this happen, you know. Together."

I looked into his eyes, searching for assurance, and found a kindred spirit staring back. This was a man who believed in possibilities, in blooming even when roots were tangled and buried in shadows.

We spent the rest of the afternoon immersed in plans and laughter, sketching out ideas for our garden. I could see the future unfolding, a collage of colors and scents, life and laughter blossoming in the very space that once felt like a stagnant pool. We could breathe new life into this café, and perhaps into our lives as well.

Each hour slipped by in a blur of creativity, our imaginations painting a vibrant world where the past and present could coexist. As the sun dipped lower in the sky, spilling molten gold across the café's rustic tables, I felt a sense of hope rising within me—an echo of what could be.

I realized then that I wasn't just competing against a memory. I was forging something new, a connection that felt as real and invigorating as the garden we dreamed of creating. And maybe, just maybe, the ghosts of our pasts could be woven into the fabric of this new beginning.

As the sun dipped below the horizon, a symphony of orange and pink splashed across the sky, illuminating our surroundings in a warm glow. The café began to settle into its evening rhythm, with a gentle hum of patrons and the comforting clinks of cups and saucers creating a cozy backdrop. The promise of our garden event hung in the air, each idea swirling between us like fragrant petals caught in a breeze. I couldn't shake the feeling that each thoughtful suggestion we exchanged was an unspoken bond forming—one that was both thrilling and daunting.

With every laugh we shared, every shared glance, I felt the weight of Leah's memory shift slightly. It was as if we were weaving a new tapestry, one thread at a time, against the tapestry of their past. Yet, there were moments when I sensed that Jake's laughter echoed in my ears, mingled with a hint of nostalgia, reminding me of the unseen shadow lingering just behind his smile.

"Okay," he said, tapping his fingers on the counter as if conducting a symphony of plans. "Let's outline our vision. I think we should start by clearing out that corner where the old chairs are stacked. It's just collecting dust."

I nodded enthusiastically, envisioning the area transformed into a vibrant display of greenery. "We could install a rustic wooden bench there, maybe painted in a soft pastel color. Something that invites people to sit, linger, and enjoy their coffee surrounded by flowers."

His eyes sparkled at the idea. "And we could create a little herb spiral too! Fresh herbs, right outside the café? Talk about farm-to-table."

I pictured it clearly—a spiral garden, lush with basil, rosemary, and mint, perfuming the air with their heady scents. "Customers could pick their herbs while they wait for their coffee. Talk about adding a personal touch!" The thought of our vision materializing felt electrifying, like the first stirrings of spring after a long winter.

As we continued to toss ideas back and forth, my heart raced with the excitement of collaboration. We bounced between concepts, letting our imaginations unfurl like the petals of the flowers we dreamed of planting. Jake suggested fairy lights strung overhead, glimmering like stars against the twilight sky. The idea struck a chord, and I could already hear the laughter and music mingling in the air, a soundtrack to our community's blossoming spirit.

The sun sank lower, casting long shadows across the wooden floor, the café bathed in a golden hue. I felt an urge to capture the moment—this energy, this budding friendship. I grabbed my phone and snapped a candid picture of Jake mid-laugh, a moment suspended in time, where the worries of the world melted away. The warmth of our shared excitement wrapped around me like a cozy scarf, warding off any lingering doubts.

Yet, even in this cocoon of creativity, Leah's specter reared its head again, uninvited. It was not just her memory that weighed on me but the very essence of what she represented. The love, the laughter, and the moments they had shared echoed in the corners of my mind. I pushed the thoughts aside, reminding myself that this was not a competition; this was a new beginning. Jake was not Leah's—he was his own person, and this connection was ours.

"Okay," he said, breaking the reverie, "how about we create a little sign for the garden, something playful? Maybe something like 'Pick a Posy, Make a Memory.'"

A smile spread across my face at his suggestion. "I love that! It embodies everything we want to create—a space for connection and joy. And we could have an art station where kids can paint their pots for herbs!"

The thought of children laughing, their small hands covered in paint, created a vivid picture in my mind. We could teach them about plants, about nurturing life, and in doing so, perhaps nurture a community spirit that had been dormant for too long.

I leaned back, envisioning the vibrant scene—families gathered, exchanging stories over cups of coffee, the air rich with laughter, and the enticing scents of fresh pastries and herbs swirling together. "What if we incorporate some local artisans? We could invite them to sell their crafts, maybe have a spot for a local baker to showcase their treats!"

Jake's eyes widened, excitement blooming like the flowers we planned to plant. "Yes! Imagine the buzz of the market—like a little fair every weekend!" He was practically vibrating with energy, his passion sparking mine further. It felt intoxicating, invigorating, and I realized then that this project wasn't just about beautifying the café; it was about breathing new life into the entire community.

As twilight enveloped us, I glanced around the café, taking in the vibrant energy that pulsed through it. The soft sounds of conversation, the clattering of dishes, and the warm laughter wrapped around us like a familiar embrace. It was a reminder that we were part of something bigger, a thread woven into the fabric of this town.

Our planning sessions continued late into the evening, and with every shared idea, every plan solidified, the bond between us deepened. Yet the thought of Leah flickered in the back of my mind like an errant candle flame, unpredictable and unsettling.

"Let's do this," I said suddenly, my resolve firming. "Let's make our dreams for this garden a reality. I want to see the café come alive again."

Jake met my gaze, the intensity of his blue eyes reflecting a shared determination. "Absolutely. Together."

The weight of his promise felt like a spark igniting in the cool evening air.

As we wrapped up our brainstorming session, a sense of anticipation thrummed beneath the surface, the excitement crackling like electricity. With plans forming and laughter echoing, I couldn't help but feel that perhaps this was the beginning of something profound, a journey filled with potential and possibilities.

And just like that, in the heart of the café with the last remnants of daylight slipping away, I decided to embrace the adventure, one bloom at a time.

The following days unfolded like the petals of a flower awakening to the morning sun. Jake and I dove headfirst into planning our community garden event, the rhythm of our collaboration seamlessly intertwining our ideas. Each day brought with it the scent of possibility, mingling with the aroma of fresh coffee wafting through the air of the café. Our initial sketches on napkins evolved into a sprawling plan, an intricate tapestry woven with threads of color, texture, and vibrancy that I could almost feel pulsating with life.

One crisp morning, as the sun cast a golden light over the sleepy town, I decided to visit the local farmers' market, a perfect place to gather inspiration and perhaps some partnerships. Strolling through the market was like stepping into a painting, where the colors of fresh produce burst forth in an explosion of hues. Bright red tomatoes, golden squash, and leafy greens created a riot of colors, each stall radiating its own charm and inviting customers to taste the essence of the season.

"Look at these!" I exclaimed, stopping in front of a stall piled high with fragrant herbs. The vendor, a cheerful woman with a sun-kissed complexion, grinned at me, her hands dusty from a morning spent tending to her plants.

"Fresh from my garden! You can't get more local than this." Her passion was palpable, and I could feel my own excitement bubbling over.

I browsed through the varieties—basil, mint, cilantro, each bunch lush and fragrant. I imagined how they would flourish in our café garden, mingling their scents with the rich aroma of coffee. "We're starting a community garden event at the café," I shared, my words tumbling out in a rush. "Would you be interested in participating? Maybe you could sell some of your herbs or offer a workshop?"

Her eyes twinkled, the offer clearly sparking her interest. "Absolutely! I'd love to teach folks how to grow their own herbs. It's a simple joy that everyone should experience." We exchanged contact information, and I felt a warm glow of triumph. This was the first step in creating the community connection we had envisioned.

As I continued to explore the market, my mind danced with ideas, each new vendor adding another layer to the dream we were building. A local baker offered samples of her exquisite pastries, each bite a buttery revelation, and I could almost hear the laughter of children echoing as they savored the sweet treats. A couple of artists displayed their handcrafted jewelry, the delicate pieces gleaming in the sunlight like tiny stars waiting to be discovered.

"Jake!" I called, spotting him across the way, engrossed in conversation with a vendor. He turned at the sound of my voice, and I couldn't help but grin at the sight of him, animated and engaged, a man in his element. As he approached, the warmth of his presence wrapped around me, making the bustling market feel even more inviting.

"Hey! I was just talking to this guy about offering a live music set during the event," he said, his enthusiasm infectious. "He's a local musician—plays folk tunes that would be perfect for a sunny afternoon."

The thought of melodies intertwining with laughter, the gentle rustle of leaves overhead, felt like the final piece of a beautiful puzzle sliding into place. "That's brilliant! Music would create such a welcoming atmosphere," I replied, excitement bubbling within me.

We continued wandering through the market, discussing ideas and possibilities, the conversation flowing as easily as the river that wound its way through town. As we stopped at a stall selling vibrant flower seedlings, I felt a warmth spread through me at the sight of Jake carefully inspecting the blooms, his brow furrowed in concentration.

"What do you think?" he asked, holding up a pot of sunflowers that towered over the other plants, their bright yellow petals a beacon of joy.

"They're perfect," I replied, unable to suppress my smile. "Sunflowers are the epitome of happiness. We should definitely include them in the garden!"

Jake's grin mirrored mine, a shared understanding dancing between us. We spent hours at the market, gathering ideas, and solidifying connections, our energy weaving a rich tapestry of community spirit that enveloped us like the sweetest summer breeze.

With each vendor we met, each new plan we solidified, I could feel the specter of Leah begin to fade, a softening of the edges that had previously clouded my heart. It was as if I was stepping into my own light, embracing the warmth of newfound possibilities instead of being overshadowed by memories that felt distant yet persistent.

By the time we returned to the café, the sun hung low in the sky, casting long shadows across the rustic tables. I looked around, my heart swelling at the sight of our little haven, the promise of our garden blooming in my mind. The café felt alive with potential, ready to host laughter and joy, and the excitement between us crackled like fireflies in the dusky evening.

Over the next few weeks, we poured ourselves into the planning process. Every detail we coordinated felt like an intricate brushstroke on a canvas, adding depth and color to our vision. Flyers adorned the café walls, the designs bursting with life, inviting the community to join us in this endeavor. Social media buzzed with anticipation, and soon enough, the townsfolk were talking, excited whispers and eager questions lighting up the atmosphere.

As the event day approached, anticipation swirled in the air like the heady aroma of coffee, and I felt a mix of nerves and excitement building within me. I could hardly sleep, my mind racing with thoughts of what we were creating, but it was also laced with a twinge of anxiety. What if the event didn't live up to the expectations we had built?

The morning of the event dawned bright and clear, the sky a brilliant blue, unmarred by clouds. I arrived early, the crisp air invigorating, my heart pounding with a blend of hope and fear. As I set up tables for vendors and arranged colorful pots of flowers around the café's outdoor space, I could feel the community spirit swirling around me.

Jake arrived shortly after, his arms laden with supplies and a wide smile on his face. "Are you ready for this?" he asked, his excitement infectious.

"I think so," I replied, returning his smile, though a flicker of doubt crept into my heart. "What if nobody shows up?"

"Trust me, they will. This is our moment," he reassured me, placing a comforting hand on my shoulder. His presence grounded me, and I felt the tension begin to ebb away.

As the clock ticked closer to the event's start, people began to trickle in, first a few curious faces, then a steady stream of familiar townsfolk, their smiles bright and welcoming. I breathed a sigh of relief as laughter and chatter filled the air, mingling with the melodies of the local musicians setting up in the corner.

I watched as children rushed toward the flower pots, their excitement bubbling over as they picked up colorful blooms to plant in the garden we had envisioned together. The vibrant scene unfolded around me like a joyful painting, the very essence of community blooming before my eyes. I felt the tension in my chest release entirely as I realized that we had done this—created something beautiful and meaningful.

In that moment, standing amidst the laughter and the colors, I glanced at Jake, who was laughing with a group of children over a particularly cheeky sunflower. The sunlight highlighted his features, and for the first time in what felt like ages, I allowed myself to simply be. The worries, the comparisons, the shadows of the past faded into the background, leaving space for the warmth of the present.

As the sun began to set, casting a warm glow over the café and the community we had built, I realized that while Leah's memory may linger in some corners, it no longer held power over me. Instead, I was creating new memories, hand in hand with Jake, our laughter merging with the music and the joy swirling around us.

And in that moment, I understood that life, much like a garden, was about growth. We were nurturing something beautiful together, our connection blossoming into something vibrant and real. I felt an exhilarating sense of freedom, ready to embrace whatever lay ahead—an adventure unfurling like the petals of a flower, and I was right where I was meant to be.

Chapter 13: An Unexpected Visitor

The sun was just beginning to peek over the horizon, casting a warm, golden hue across the quaint town of Maplewood. The scent of freshly brewed coffee wafted through the air, mingling with the floral notes of blooming marigolds and daisies that decorated the garden I had spent weeks preparing. Today was the day of the annual garden event, a cherished tradition in our community, where residents showcased their floral artistry and culinary delights amidst the backdrop of the towering maple trees that had given the town its name. The anticipation crackled in the air, vibrant and electric, but beneath that excitement lay a simmering anxiety that I couldn't shake.

As I flitted between tables, adjusting the brightly colored tablecloths and arranging the potted plants, I felt a twinge of pride swell within me. This year, I was determined to outdo myself. The colors seemed to pop against the emerald green of the grass, each petal whispering promises of warmth and joy. The sun glinted off the small ceramic pots I had painted, each one adorned with a quirky little face, giving them personality and charm. I had envisioned this day as a celebration of community and growth, but the moment I spotted Leah's familiar figure approaching, clipboard in hand, my heart sank.

Leah had an uncanny ability to command attention without even trying. With her tousled chestnut hair cascading in waves down her back and her expressive hazel eyes, she was effortlessly enchanting. I had always admired her flair for creativity, but today, she felt like an unexpected storm rolling in, threatening to unravel everything I had worked so hard to create. As she approached, her presence loomed larger than the golden sun hanging in the sky.

"Hey there!" she called, her voice dripping with cheerfulness that made my stomach churn. "Need any help?" She flashed a smile that could light up the darkest corners of my worries, yet I felt that familiar knot tightening in my chest.

I forced a smile, a feeble attempt to mask the turmoil churning within me. "I think I've got it covered, Leah. Just adding the final touches." I gestured to the tables, hoping my enthusiasm would drown out the unease.

"Oh, come on! I'm here now. Let me pitch in!" Without waiting for a response, she slipped into my personal space, clipboard in hand, eyes scanning the chaos I had orchestrated. The warmth of her proximity sent an involuntary shiver down my spine. With each glance she threw in Jake's direction—a casual flick of her gaze, a light laugh shared between them—I felt the walls I had built around my heart begin to crack.

Jake was over by the drink station, his easy smile as bright as the sun shining down. His sandy blonde hair glinted like spun gold, and the way he casually leaned against the table, chatting with the local baker, sent my heart racing and my stomach tumbling. He had been my rock, the person I leaned on during my darker days, and while Leah's presence threatened to eclipse that light, I refused to let it dim completely.

With Leah now entrenched in the preparations, I focused on my breathing, trying to channel the excitement of the event instead of the discomfort brewing beneath the surface. "Let's see," she mused, scribbling furiously on her clipboard. "How about we arrange the potted plants by color? It'll create a vibrant rainbow effect!"

Her suggestions danced through the air like butterflies, fluttering dangerously close to the edge of my composure. I nodded, attempting to mask the resentment swelling within me. "Sure, that could work." My voice felt foreign, strained under the weight of the afternoon's potential heartache.

As Leah buzzed about, I caught snippets of her conversation with Jake, snippets that made my heart ache with an intensity I hadn't anticipated. Laughter echoed like a familiar song, sweet yet tinged with bitterness as I fought against the urge to turn and leave, to hide away from the joyous chaos that had morphed into a battle of wills and feelings.

"Did you see the way the sun hits the roses over there?" Jake's voice floated over to me, rich and inviting. "It's like they're glowing!"

"Yes!" Leah's laughter chimed back, light and carefree, the very sound wrapping around me like a cozy blanket I couldn't quite snuggle into. "It's so magical. You're right, Jake!"

I busied myself with a particularly stubborn geranium, its roots stubbornly tangled, as if they too sensed my unease. The prickly texture of the leaves beneath my fingertips became a focal point, grounding me amidst the storm brewing inside. I forced my mind to shift away from their laughter, from the lingering touches and shared glances, and instead to the work at hand. The vibrant colors and lively chatter around me became a distracting symphony, a gentle reminder that this was still my event, my moment to shine.

Hours slipped by in a whirl of laughter, chatter, and the clinking of glasses as guests began to trickle in. The garden transformed into a tapestry of colors and scents, with vibrant sunflowers swaying to the rhythm of the soft breeze, while the air buzzed with friendly banter and the occasional burst of laughter. Yet, amid the celebration, Leah's presence felt like a shadow, hovering at the edges of my happiness, darkening the brilliance of the day.

As the sun reached its zenith, casting a warm, golden glow across the gathering, I caught sight of Leah and Jake again, this time sharing a moment by the rose garden. Leah leaned in closer, her laughter ringing out like the sweet chime of a bell, and I felt an all-too-familiar feeling surge within me—an unwelcome blend of envy and sadness. My heart twisted painfully, a tangible ache that settled in my chest, and I couldn't help but wonder if I would ever escape this feeling of inadequacy that had wrapped around me tighter than the vines climbing the trellises.

In that moment, standing amidst a sea of blooming beauty, I felt smaller than ever. The laughter continued to dance around me, but all I could hear was the deafening silence of my own insecurities, echoing louder than any joy shared in the garden.

With the sun now dipping lower in the sky, the garden transformed under the warm embrace of twilight. Strings of twinkling fairy lights adorned the trees, casting a soft, ethereal glow across the tables. The laughter of children playing nearby mingled with the distant sound of a guitar strumming, creating a gentle symphony that wrapped around the event like a comforting shawl. Yet, beneath this picturesque scene, the thrum of my heart raced in a dissonant rhythm, each pulse reminding me of the tension simmering just beneath the surface.

Leah flitted around the garden like a playful breeze, her clipboard now seemingly a prop more than a necessity as she reveled in the ambience. She greeted guests with a vibrant smile, her energy infectious, drawing people into her orbit. I stood on the periphery, arranging the last of the wildflower bouquets, my fingers deftly intertwining the delicate petals as if weaving together my own frail defense against the chaos within. Each stem was a silent prayer, a hope that I could push through this day without completely losing myself.

"Can you believe how many people came?" Leah exclaimed, her voice rising above the hum of chatter. She leaned close to Jake, her laughter ringing out like the chime of a delicate bell. Each giggle felt like a stab to my chest, a reminder of the easy connection they shared. I caught Jake's gaze as he turned toward me, his expression warm and inviting, but the moment was eclipsed as Leah playfully nudged him. It was a simple gesture, yet it seemed to tether them closer together, and I felt the familiar wave of frustration wash over me.

As the event flowed like a gentle river, guests meandered through the garden, stopping to admire the colorful arrangements and indulge in the assortment of baked goods spread across a long wooden table. The tantalizing aroma of freshly baked pie mingled with the sweetness of lemonade, creating a comforting atmosphere that should have felt inviting. Instead, it felt like a masquerade, one in which I was not entirely sure of my role.

"Your setup looks incredible," Jake said, his eyes sparkling with admiration as he approached me, leaving Leah momentarily behind. The warmth of his compliment wrapped around me like a cashmere blanket on a chilly evening, a small comfort amidst my internal tempest. "You really outdid yourself this year."

"Thanks, Jake. I just wanted it to be special." I tried to sound lighthearted, but I could feel the tremor in my voice, betraying the turbulence roiling within. The way he looked at me, genuinely impressed, sent a rush of heat to my cheeks, yet the knot in my stomach refused to loosen. I couldn't help but glance at Leah, who was now charming a small group of guests, her laughter dancing through the air like fireflies at dusk.

"So what's your secret?" Jake continued, a playful smile on his lips as he leaned in closer, his warmth radiating like the summer sun. "Care to share how you pulled all of this together?" His eyes held mine, and in that moment, I felt a flicker of hope that maybe, just maybe, this day could turn around.

"Lots of late nights, coffee, and a few well-timed panic attacks," I replied, attempting to infuse humor into my response. Jake laughed, the sound rich and melodious, and for a moment, the weight of Leah's presence faded into the background.

"I think it paid off. You've made this place feel magical." He gestured broadly, encompassing the entire garden, and my heart soared for a brief moment before reality crashed back in.

"Can you help me with those chairs?" Leah's voice sliced through the air, summoning Jake back to her side. The disappointment felt like a cold draft, snatching the warmth of our brief connection. He nodded and walked away, the space between us widening with each step he took toward her. I watched them move together, their ease evident as they collaborated on shifting tables and arranging chairs, Leah directing with all the authority of a conductor leading an orchestra.

The golden hour painted everything in soft hues, yet the glow felt distant to me as I busied myself with the last remnants of my arrangements. A gentle breeze rustled the leaves overhead, a soothing reminder of nature's embrace, but my heart was tethered to the unease that had taken root inside. Guests continued to filter in, their laughter mingling with the rustle of leaves, a soothing melody I tried desperately to tune into.

As dusk began to wrap its arms around the garden, the colors of the day faded into deep purples and blues, the glow from the fairy lights casting an enchanting shimmer across the petals. My initial excitement had morphed into a quiet dread, a feeling that maybe, just maybe, I was not meant to be the star of this particular show. Leah's laughter with Jake echoed in my ears, a sound that tugged at the edges of my heart like a distant, haunting song.

"Let's grab some lemonade!" I announced to myself, needing to step away from the spectacle for just a moment, to breathe and gather my thoughts. As I made my way toward the refreshment table, the vibrant chatter and laughter faded into a dull roar, my mind clouded with uncertainty. I poured a glass, the cold liquid refreshing against my fingertips, but it did little to soothe the turmoil brewing inside.

Just then, a soft voice interrupted my thoughts. "You okay?"

I turned to find Clara, a longtime friend, her brown curls bouncing with each step. She had a way of cutting through the noise, her sincerity grounding me in moments when I felt adrift.

"I'm fine," I replied too quickly, offering a smile that didn't quite reach my eyes. "Just a bit... overwhelmed."

"Leah, right?" Clara gestured subtly toward the duo, now deep in conversation, her brow furrowing slightly. "I saw the way she was with Jake earlier. You don't need to compete with that. You're amazing in your own right."

"I know, but it feels like I'm invisible sometimes," I admitted, my voice barely above a whisper. "She just has this way of captivating everyone, and I... I just feel like I'm fading into the background."

Clara's expression softened, empathy radiating from her like sunlight breaking through clouds. "You've created something beautiful today. Don't let anyone take that away from you, especially not Leah. You have something that she can't replicate."

Her words struck a chord within me, reverberating through the layers of self-doubt that had settled around my heart. Maybe Clara was right; perhaps I didn't need to compete. Maybe I just needed to be myself, to embrace the moments that made me who I was.

"Thanks, Clara. I needed to hear that." I took a deep breath, the cool lemonade refreshing against my lips as I found a renewed sense of determination swelling within me.

As I turned back toward the festivities, I felt a spark of resilience ignite in my chest. The evening stretched before me like an unwritten story, and I was determined to shape it into something worth telling. With the garden glowing softly around me and laughter ringing out like a promise, I stepped forward into the thrumming heart of the event, ready to reclaim my place amidst the colors and camaraderie that defined Maplewood.

The night air cooled gently, wrapping the garden in a soothing embrace as laughter bubbled and swirled like the fireflies beginning to awaken in the twilight. The ambiance shifted, taking on a whimsical charm, a feeling of hope and celebration mingling with the lingering remnants of unease. I wove my way through clusters of guests, their smiles and cheers igniting something within me that had dimmed under the weight of insecurity. Each face I encountered—familiar, friendly—added a stroke of color to my canvas, pushing the darker hues of doubt further into the background.

A local artist had set up a small booth in the corner of the garden, showcasing vibrant paintings that captured the essence of Maplewood in hues so vivid they seemed to pulse with life. I paused, captivated by a piece that depicted the very garden we stood in, bathed in golden sunlight with children playing among the flowers. It was a moment frozen in time, a reminder of the beauty that existed beyond my current turmoil. I let my fingers brush against the textured surface of the painting, and for a fleeting moment, I lost myself in the artistry, the vibrant strokes a silent affirmation that life—much like art—was meant to be lived boldly.

"Isn't it amazing?" Clara's voice broke through my reverie as she joined me, her eyes sparkling with enthusiasm. "The artist really captured the spirit of this place. It's like I can feel the warmth of the sun and hear the laughter just by looking at it."

I nodded, trying to absorb the radiance of the moment, feeling the warmth of camaraderie seep into my bones. "It's stunning. I love how art can transport us, isn't it?"

"Just like this garden," she replied, gesturing to the scene unfolding around us. "Look at everyone! They're here to celebrate you and what you've created. Don't let Leah's presence dull your shine."

Clara's encouragement wrapped around me like a cozy blanket, but the sight of Leah with Jake again snagged my attention. They were now leaning against a table, engaged in a deep discussion about the garden's layout, their heads bent close together, laughter spilling freely between them like champagne bubbling over. I felt that familiar pang of inadequacy, but Clara's words echoed in my mind.

They reminded me that I had cultivated this space and the joy it offered.

With a newfound determination, I set my sights on the crowd. I began to mingle, engaging in light-hearted conversations, sharing stories about the plants and the inspiration behind each arrangement. Laughter flowed freely, and with each exchange, I felt a flicker of the confidence that had initially fueled my vision for the event.

"Have you tried the lemon bars?" I called to a group of friends from the book club, their chatter a comforting hum in the air. "They're a secret family recipe!"

"Only if you promise to share the secret!" one of them teased, laughter echoing through the garden like the gentle chime of bells.

As the evening progressed, I lost myself in the rhythm of the event. The vibrant hues of the flowers began to feel like old friends, their presence grounding me amidst the chaos of emotions swirling inside. A soft breeze whispered through the leaves, the faint scent of lilac perfuming the air and mingling with the sweetness of the treats on display.

Then, just as I thought I'd managed to push past the encroaching shadows, a voice called out from behind me. "Hey! What's the secret?" It was Leah, her smile bright and her eyes glinting with playful mischief.

I turned, instinctively bracing myself for whatever came next, yet there was a curiosity in her tone that was hard to ignore. "What secret are you referring to?"

"The lemon bars, of course!" she said, her laughter infectious as she stepped closer. "I heard you've got the family recipe hidden away. You've got to share it with me!"

Her enthusiasm was palpable, and for a moment, I hesitated. This was the Leah I had known before the anxiety of today had seeped into every corner of my mind. The part of her that brought joy to the table, the part that reminded me of the playful friendship we once had. I could see Jake watching from a distance, his brow slightly furrowed, as if trying to decipher the dynamics between us.

"Alright, but only if you promise to share some of your gardening tips in return," I said, surprising myself with my willingness to engage. It was like stepping into the light, a gesture of goodwill against the tempest brewing inside.

"I'll gladly share all my secrets!" Leah replied, her smile widening, genuine this time. "The trick to the perfect garden is in the love you pour into it. Kind of like baking, I guess."

"Then we both have that covered," I said, a lightness spreading through me. "Especially today."

Just then, a burst of laughter erupted from Jake and the group he had been mingling with, and I felt a rush of warmth bloom in my chest. Leah followed my gaze and laughed along with them, her earlier competitiveness fading for a moment as she joined in the camaraderie of the evening. The tension between us began to dissipate, giving way to a sense of shared enjoyment.

"Let's grab some of those lemon bars and bring them over," Leah suggested, her eyes sparkling with a sense of mischief. "Show them what they've been missing!"

Together, we walked to the dessert table, laughter bubbling between us like effervescent soda. As I prepared to serve the lemon bars, I noticed Jake watching us with an expression that was difficult to read. There was warmth there, but also an undertone of uncertainty that made me wonder if he sensed the shift between Leah and me.

Once we returned, I presented the dessert with a flourish. "Behold! The famous lemon bars!"

The group erupted into cheers, and I found myself laughing, genuinely enjoying the moment. I was no longer just a backdrop to Leah's charm; I was a part of the tapestry woven through this evening, contributing my own vibrant threads.

The warmth of the gathering enveloped me, a testament to the connections we forged within this enchanting garden. As the evening wore on, I joined in the laughter, the stories flowing like the refreshments. I could see Jake chatting with the artist, gesturing toward a painting, his smile unguarded.

"Do you ever wonder what stories these flowers could tell if they could speak?" I mused aloud, catching the attention of a few nearby guests.

"Oh, absolutely! They'd share secrets of the sunlight and whispers of the wind," one of them replied, a twinkle in their eye.

"And the tales of love and heartbreak they've witnessed," Clara added, leaning in as if conspiring with me.

The night deepened, and beneath the fairy lights, we shared dreams, laughter, and even a few tender moments of vulnerability. I felt a renewed sense of belonging, a reminder that despite the tension and jealousy that had threatened to consume me, there was still beauty in connection.

As the final strains of music floated through the air and the last bites of dessert were savored, I caught Leah's eye from across the table. The earlier tension had melted away, replaced with an understanding that perhaps we could coexist, each holding our own place in this vibrant tapestry of life.

The evening wound down with hugs and promises of future gatherings. As I looked around at the glowing faces illuminated by the soft light, I felt a sense of fulfillment wash over me. I was not just a gardener of plants, but of relationships, weaving together the moments that mattered, nurturing connections that would continue to bloom long after the sun had set.

In that magical garden, amidst the laughter and warmth, I realized I was ready to embrace whatever came next.

Chapter 14: Blooming Connections

The sun dipped low in the sky, casting a warm golden hue over the sprawling community garden, its vibrant colors clashing deliciously with the deep greens of the foliage surrounding us. Each plant seemed to pulse with life, and the scent of damp earth mingled with the sweet perfume of blossoming flowers, wrapping around me like a comforting embrace. Children giggled nearby, their laughter ringing out like chimes in the gentle breeze, as families clustered together in joyful anticipation of what the evening would bring. This garden, once merely a backdrop to our lives, was now a canvas painted with the potential for connection, and I felt it stirring in the air like the onset of spring.

With every flower we planted, I felt a flicker of hope igniting within me. I watched as Jake knelt beside me, the muscles in his arms taut and defined as he dug into the soil, laughter bubbling to the surface with each mischievous quip. His dark hair fell across his forehead, framing those striking blue eyes that danced with mischief and warmth. For a moment, I could forget Leah's presence hovering just beyond our circle. She was an enigma—beautiful and daunting, like a vine that threatened to entwine everything I held dear. But here, with Jake by my side, I felt an intoxicating rush of confidence; the kind that had eluded me for far too long.

As I picked up a delicate marigold, its petals like little suns, I turned to him, our shoulders brushing, and the electric warmth surged through me like a wildfire. His fingers brushed against mine, light as a whisper, and in that heartbeat, I felt the world around us fade. The distant sound of kids playing, the soft rustling of leaves—everything melted into the background. I focused solely on the gentle rise and fall of his breath, on the way his laughter made my insides twist deliciously. It was as if I were standing on the precipice of something monumental, teetering on the edge of discovery.

"Have you ever thought about how each flower tells a story?" I asked, my voice barely above the din of activity around us. "Like marigolds, they symbolize warmth and creativity. I read somewhere that they attract butterflies, which, honestly, is a pretty good metaphor for us, don't you think?"

Jake chuckled, tilting his head to meet my gaze. "You're telling me you think we're butterflies?" There was a teasing lilt in his voice that sent my heart racing.

"Well, why not? We're certainly flitting around this garden like we own the place." I gestured to the array of colors before us—pinks, yellows, and purples intertwining in a riot of beauty.

His smile widened, and in that moment, I could see the walls around him starting to crumble, piece by piece. I longed to dive deeper into his laughter, to explore the hidden recesses of his mind, where thoughts danced just out of reach. The way he responded to my words felt like a secret shared between us, something precious that no one else could touch.

But just as I began to believe in our little world, Leah's laughter pierced through the air like a sharp note in a beautiful melody. She approached with an effortless grace, the sunlight catching her golden hair, making it shine like spun gold. She leaned down to whisper something in Jake's ear, and I felt my heart plummet like a stone into the depths of uncertainty. It was as if a shadow had fallen over my bright little bubble, dimming the colors around me. Jake's expression shifted; the light in his eyes dulled momentarily as he turned toward her, his smile faltering.

I stood there, clutching the marigold like a lifeline, feeling like an overgrown weed amidst a garden of flawless blooms. Their shared laughter wrapped around me like ivy, choking my budding confidence. The warmth that had surged between Jake and me dissipated, leaving only an uncomfortable chill. Leah's beauty was intoxicating, a reminder of the ease with which she moved through the world, while I felt like an interloper in my own narrative.

Desperately trying to recapture that fleeting connection, I forced myself to refocus on the task at hand. I dug my fingers into the cool earth, the texture grounding me as I planted the flower, its roots nestled snugly in the soil. With each handful of dirt, I imagined planting a piece of my heart, hoping to cultivate something beautiful despite the uncertainty hovering above me.

Yet, as I glanced over at Jake and Leah, I realized how effortlessly she pulled him into her orbit, her laughter ringing out like a siren song. There was a magnetism between them that I couldn't deny, a pull that felt far more substantial than anything I had begun to build. It stung like the prick of a thorn, a harsh reminder of how easily I could be overshadowed by her brilliance.

I shook my head, trying to dispel the darkness creeping in. I wanted to believe that my connection with Jake was genuine, that there was something real between us, but the shadows loomed larger with every passing moment. I longed to call him back, to bridge the distance Leah had woven between us, but doubt clenched my throat. The ground beneath my feet felt unsteady, and I found myself wishing desperately for the courage to pull him back into the light.

As the sun continued its descent, the sky blazed with colors that mirrored the chaos within me. The laughter around me grew louder, echoing with the vibrant energy of life, but I felt more like a ghost, lingering just beyond the edges of what I yearned for.

The sun, now a fiery orb sinking toward the horizon, cast long shadows across the garden, wrapping everything in a soft, golden glow. I could almost convince myself that the evening's magic could lift the weight pressing on my chest, that I could drown out the specter of Leah's laughter and reclaim the flickering connection I had with Jake. But as I looked across the expanse of blooms, my heart twisted painfully at the sight of them.

Jake stood a few feet away, his back turned to me as Leah leaned in closer, whispering something that caused him to chuckle, that delightful sound echoing in the stillness, drawing attention as effectively as a firework bursting in the night sky. Each laugh seemed like a needle, pricking at my resolve, stitching together an intricate tapestry of insecurity and longing. I ached to be the one eliciting that laughter, to be the one wrapped in the warmth of his attention.

Desperation crept in, gnawing at me as I forced myself to join in the merry chaos. I sought out a patch of earth devoid of flowers, feeling a wild urge to plant my own mark, something bold and unmistakable. With every shovel of dirt I tossed aside, I imagined digging deeper into my own desires, pulling out roots of insecurity and replacing them with blooms of hope. As I worked, my hands dirtied and my heart racing, I turned my focus toward the vibrant blossoms around me—their brilliant colors almost mocking the grayness I felt inside.

The mingling scents of marigolds, petunias, and zinnias filled my senses, grounding me. Each flower seemed to whisper its own secret, urging me to take a chance, to dive headfirst into the unknown. And so, I planted, envisioning a garden bursting with colors that reflected the wildness of my dreams.

In my peripheral vision, I caught sight of Jake, now entirely under Leah's spell. They were laughing together, the space between them charged with an energy I couldn't quite decipher. For a fleeting moment, I entertained the notion that perhaps Leah was merely a distraction, an ephemeral presence that would soon fade like a wilting flower. But reality's grip tightened around me, and I felt the very air grow thick with doubt.

Just as I finished arranging the last flower in my small patch, I heard a soft, measured voice behind me. "Those look lovely." It was Mrs. Donovan, our neighbor, who had cultivated her own garden of wildflowers that danced in the breeze like they were sharing secrets.

She wore a sun hat, its wide brim casting a protective shadow over her lined face, but her smile shone brightly as if it could light up the dimmest of days.

"Thanks," I replied, my voice cracking slightly as I wiped my dirt-streaked hands on my jeans. "I'm hoping they'll grow into something beautiful."

She tilted her head, her eyes gleaming with a knowing kindness. "Beauty is often born from persistence. Don't be afraid to dig deep." Her words struck a chord, reverberating within me, and I caught her gaze drifting toward Jake and Leah. There was a moment of silence, a palpable understanding exchanged between us as we both watched them.

"Love can be like a garden," she continued, pulling me from my reverie. "Sometimes, it needs nurturing and care, while other times, it requires patience as it grows on its own."

I nodded, though the knot in my stomach tightened. What if my garden was doomed to wilt? What if I was simply a weed, one that was never meant to bloom in the first place? The shadows from the setting sun stretched long, intertwining with the light of hope that flickered within me.

With a gentle pat on my shoulder, Mrs. Donovan turned to join her family. I stood there for a moment, trying to reconcile her wisdom with the whirlwind of feelings in my heart. The world around me pulsed with life—the sounds of laughter, children playing, and the faint strumming of a guitar somewhere in the distance. But my focus remained fixed on Jake and Leah, whose joyous energy felt like a distant melody I could no longer hear.

Gathering my resolve, I decided to approach them, to reclaim my footing in this beautiful chaos. As I drew nearer, the laughter faded into a hushed conversation, and I felt an unwelcome shyness seep into my skin. Leah's gaze flickered toward me, a curious spark igniting in her eyes, as if she were assessing a threat.

"Hey! You did an amazing job with those flowers," Jake said, his voice warm, igniting a flutter in my chest. "I was just telling Leah how incredible they looked."

"Thanks," I managed, forcing a smile despite the tremor in my voice. The warmth of his compliment washed over me, but Leah stepped in smoothly, her voice like honey, sweet yet sticky.

"You know, we were just discussing our plans for the fall festival," she said, her tone light yet veiled with something I couldn't quite place. "Jake has some great ideas about decorating the space."

I felt the air thicken around me as Jake's eyes sparkled with excitement. "Yeah, I thought we could do something with pumpkins and hay bales. Maybe a scarecrow contest?"

"Sounds fun!" I said, trying to inject my enthusiasm into the conversation, but Leah's expression hardened for a brief moment. I sensed the unspoken challenge in her gaze, and the flutter in my stomach morphed into a turbulent storm.

"Well, let's not let your flowers go to waste. How about you join us?" Leah asked, her voice friendly, yet I could hear the underlying intent.

"Of course," I said, forcing myself to sound more assured than I felt. I stepped into their circle, acutely aware of the way Leah's presence loomed, casting a shadow over my light. I could feel Jake's warmth beside me, and yet the air crackled with tension, as if I were navigating a minefield littered with unspoken words.

As we began brainstorming ideas for the festival, I let my imagination spill forth, weaving together strands of creativity and joy. The words flowed as I painted vivid images of what could be, trying to carve out a space where I belonged in this blooming connection. But as the laughter erupted again, I couldn't shake the feeling that I was still a flower struggling to unfurl in the shade, hoping for the sun to find me and illuminate my path.

The conversations swirled around me like the autumn leaves beginning to scatter across the ground. My heart raced in tandem with the excitement in the air, yet an unsettling weight lingered in my chest. The laughter of children echoed against the backdrop of rustling leaves and the occasional call of a distant bird. I could almost hear the symphony of the garden—its rhythms vibrant and alive, yet it felt as if I were standing just offstage, watching the show unfold without being part of it.

Jake's enthusiasm filled the space between us, his words spilling forth like petals from a blossoming flower. "What if we had a scavenger hunt?" he suggested, his eyes gleaming with possibilities. "We could include all sorts of activities, like a pie-eating contest and a pumpkin carving station." The vision in his mind was palpable, as if I could almost see the festival bursting forth from the soil beneath our feet.

Leah chimed in, her voice smooth, "Oh, I love that! But let's make it a little more upscale. Perhaps we can pair each station with themed decorations? Think harvest chic—string lights, burlap, and maybe some handcrafted signs." Her tone was cheerful, but I could sense the underlying intention; she was steering the conversation, as if laying claim to our shared ideas.

While Jake's face lit up at Leah's suggestion, I felt a small flicker of irritation ignite within me, mingling uneasily with my earlier optimism. It was as though I were painting a mural only to have someone else come in with a roller, smoothing over my colors. I took a breath, steadied myself, and began to weave my own ideas back into the tapestry.

"Maybe we could incorporate a 'gratitude wall' where everyone can pin up their thankful notes? It would add a personal touch," I ventured, hopeful that my words would bloom like the flowers I had just planted.

"Great idea!" Jake replied, his enthusiasm buoying me momentarily. But Leah's smile flickered, and I sensed her tightening grip on the narrative. "Perhaps it could be a small addition," she interjected smoothly. "But let's not lose sight of the grand design, shall we?"

Her words hung in the air, and I felt the air grow heavier, stifling the warmth that had sparked moments earlier. Yet, in Jake's gaze, I saw a flicker of awareness; it was almost imperceptible, but there was a shift, a realization that perhaps Leah wasn't the only one with brilliant ideas.

The festival plans unfolded over the next hour, yet my enthusiasm began to wane as Leah reigned supreme over our ideas, molding them into her vision. I could almost hear the laughter of the families around us morphing into a distant echo, a reminder that I was somehow both part of this community and also apart from it. With each suggestion, I felt the fabric of my budding connection with Jake fraying at the edges, as if Leah were carefully unraveling the threads that bound us together.

As the sun dipped lower, casting shadows that danced across the garden, a new wave of determination washed over me. I could almost feel the evening air whispering promises of change, urging me to dig deeper within myself. I didn't want to be just a spectator, waiting for my moment to shine while Leah overshadowed me like a cloud blocking the sun.

Taking a deep breath, I stepped forward again, this time planting my feet firmly. "What if we added a storytelling corner?" I proposed, my voice more resolute. "We could invite community members to share their favorite fall memories or local legends. It would create a warm, inviting atmosphere and connect everyone in a meaningful way."

Jake's eyes sparkled, and a smile broke across his face. "That's fantastic! We could even have local musicians play softly in the background."

Leah's expression soured slightly, but she masked it quickly. "That could work," she conceded, her voice tinged with reluctant agreement. But it was Jake's reaction that bolstered my confidence; he leaned closer, his excitement palpable. "It could become a tradition!" he said, turning to Leah with a look that urged her to join us, to embrace the idea as a collective vision rather than a solo endeavor.

The laughter and chatter of families began to merge into a warm blanket around us, wrapping us in the fabric of community spirit. I felt a flicker of triumph ignite within me, and for a moment, I believed that maybe—just maybe—I could carve out my own space amidst the blooming chaos.

As dusk descended, the garden transformed. String lights began to twinkle like stars, illuminating the faces of children darting around, their giggles and shouts merging with the crisp rustle of leaves. The scent of woodsmoke wafted through the air as families began to gather around a fire pit, marshmallows and laughter colliding in a sweet symphony.

Jake and I moved closer, joining in the fun, the festival's spirit enveloping us like a cozy blanket. I reveled in the small interactions—our fingers brushing as we reached for the same bag of marshmallows, the gentle hum of conversation punctuated by bursts of laughter. Each moment seemed to weave us together, creating a tapestry of shared experiences that threatened to spill over into something deeper.

Just as I allowed myself to lean fully into the joy of the evening, Leah swept back into our orbit, her presence commanding as always. "Jake, let's take a quick photo for social media! We need to capture this moment." She leaned in, her arm wrapping around him as she pulled him close, posing for the camera.

I stood on the periphery, the warmth of the fire a stark contrast to the chill that gripped my heart. I felt like an intruder in a moment meant for them, a solitary flower struggling against the encroaching weeds. Yet, as I watched them pose, something shifted within me. I realized I could choose to be part of this narrative, not merely a supporting character but a force in my own right.

Determined, I stepped forward, breaking into their frame with a smile. "Don't forget about me!" I exclaimed, throwing my arms around them, my voice full of playful defiance. Jake's surprised laughter rang out, and Leah's startled expression morphed into a reluctant smile, the tension momentarily forgotten.

The camera clicked, capturing a moment suspended in time—three individuals, each holding a piece of this garden's heart, entwined in the budding connections around us. As the flash faded, I felt something blossom within me. It was the realization that I had a voice, that my ideas mattered, and that I belonged here amidst the laughter and life, no matter how many shadows lurked at the edges.

That night, as the stars began to twinkle above, I embraced the magic of the garden, the warmth of the fire, and the potential for connections yet to bloom. I was no longer a weed amongst the flowers; I was part of this vibrant tapestry, my colors vibrant and alive, intertwined with those around me. And with that realization, I knew I was ready to grow.

Chapter 15: Shadows and Whispers

The sun dipped low over the horizon, casting a golden glow over the quaint streets of our little town, a place where gossip travels faster than the evening breeze. The café, with its worn wooden tables and mismatched chairs, stood as a sanctuary against the weight of the outside world, a refuge where laughter mingled with the rich aroma of freshly brewed coffee and the tantalizing scent of cinnamon rolls. Each corner was alive with memories, the walls adorned with art from local artists, their vibrant colors reflecting the heartbeat of our community.

As I leaned against the counter, my hands cradling a steaming mug of chamomile tea, I watched Jake from across the room. He was animated, lost in conversation with Leah, his laughter a melodic counterpoint to the soft hum of the café. Yet, beneath the surface of his charm, I sensed an undercurrent of something darker, an unspoken struggle that haunted his every gesture. The moment he caught my eye, his laughter faltered, replaced by a fleeting shadow that passed over his face. It was a look I had come to recognize—a reminder of the weight he carried from the past, a weight that often felt heavier than the world could bear.

Later that evening, after the last stragglers had left and the café was wrapped in the soft embrace of twilight, I found Jake standing by the window, staring into the dimming light. I approached him cautiously, feeling the charged air between us. The weight of the day seemed to linger in his posture, the way his shoulders hunched slightly as if he were bracing himself against an invisible storm. I wanted to reach out, to remind him that he wasn't alone in this, but the words caught in my throat, entangled in my own fears of saying the wrong thing.

"Hey," I said softly, letting the warmth of my voice weave through the silence.

He turned, and for a moment, the light from the window framed him in a halo of gold. It was a beautiful, heartbreaking image that made my heart flutter, but the sadness in his eyes anchored me back to reality. "I'm okay," he replied, though his voice trembled slightly, betraying the facade he wore like a well-tailored suit. "Just... thinking."

I stepped closer, feeling the warmth radiate from him. "Thinking about your mom?"

He nodded, his gaze drifting to the floor, as if it held the answers to questions he had yet to articulate. "It's just... I feel like I'm betraying her by moving on. Like I'm leaving her behind." The vulnerability in his voice broke something inside me, a dam of empathy that flooded my heart with understanding.

The café's quiet hum was punctuated by the distant clatter of dishes being washed in the back, a soothing rhythm that contrasted sharply with the chaos I sensed within him. "You're not betraying her, Jake," I whispered, stepping even closer until I could feel the warmth radiating from him, comforting and familiar. "You're honoring her by living your life fully. She would want that for you."

He looked up, his eyes glistening in the fading light. I could see the battle raging behind them, the conflict between his past and the present we were trying to build. I wanted to take away the pain that clung to him like a second skin, to pull him into the light and away from the shadows that threatened to engulf him.

Just as I leaned in, preparing to bridge the gap between us with words of comfort, Leah burst through the door, a whirlwind of energy and excitement. "You won't believe what I just thought of for our next event!" she exclaimed, her voice bubbling over with enthusiasm.

My heart sank as I watched Jake's expression shift, the warmth in his eyes retreating like a tide pulling away from the shore. The vulnerability we had shared moments ago slipped through our fingers, dissipating like steam from my forgotten cup of tea. Leah's interruption had cast a long shadow over our moment, reminding me of how easily the past could intrude upon the present.

"Uh, yeah? What is it?" Jake asked, feigning interest, but I could see the flicker of annoyance in his eyes. He was back to that familiar pattern of deflection, slipping away from the rawness we had begun to explore.

Leah launched into a passionate description of her idea—a poetry night combined with open mic performances, a chance for local talent to shine and for the community to come together. "We could call it 'Voices Under the Stars,'" she suggested, her excitement infectious, but I could see Jake's expression harden, a wall going up that I desperately wished I could tear down.

As Leah's words washed over us, I felt like a spectator in my own life, standing on the sidelines of their conversation. The laughter echoed in the café, but it felt hollow, each note bouncing off the walls like a ghost, leaving behind the bitterness of unaddressed feelings. I wanted to scream, to shake him and say, "Don't you see? You're slipping away!" But the fear of pushing him further into his shell held me back, leaving me to stew in my own frustration.

Jake's gaze drifted back to the window, the last remnants of sunlight fading into the horizon. The shadows began to creep in, filling the café with an air of melancholy that seemed to cling to his very essence. "Sounds great," he said, though his voice lacked conviction, as if he were simply going through the motions, his mind a million miles away.

The tension hung in the air, thick and suffocating. I could see the flicker of a thought in his eyes, a glimpse of the man he could be if only he would allow himself to embrace the present. As Leah continued to speak, her enthusiasm contrasting sharply with Jake's retreat, I made a silent promise to myself: I would not let him slip away again. Whatever shadows loomed over him, I would stand firm, ready to battle against the whispers of the past.

The café's familiar hum turned into a gentle background murmur, with Leah's excitement painting a cheerful facade over the palpable tension. I could see the way Jake's expression shifted again, the flicker of interest sparking briefly before extinguishing under the weight of expectation. It was as if he had donned a mask, the friendly barista façade he wore to greet customers now becoming an armor against the vulnerability we had almost shared.

"Imagine, a night filled with poetry and music, just as the stars come out," Leah continued, her voice rising with enthusiasm. "We could set up fairy lights outside, make it magical! What do you think, Jake?" She spun around to face him, her smile bright enough to rival the sun setting beyond the café's windows.

"Yeah, sounds cool," he replied, but his eyes remained distant, reflecting the cool indifference of a late autumn sky. He turned away, a slight frown forming as he stared out at the night creeping in, the streetlights flickering to life like hesitant fireflies.

I couldn't help but feel the ache inside me grow, a sense of urgency to reach him, to pull him back from the brink of this emotional abyss he had stepped toward. "What if we included a theme?" I interjected, my voice softer, trying to draw him back into our orbit. "Something that resonates with the community, like... healing or new beginnings?"

Jake's head turned slightly, curiosity flickering in his eyes, but it was a fragile flame. "That could work," he said, a hint of hesitation lacing his words, as if he were weighing the idea against a mental ledger of potential outcomes. Leah, ever the optimist, seized the moment.

"Perfect! We could get local poets to read pieces about hope and resilience. Maybe even invite a few musicians!" She clapped her hands together, eyes sparkling as though she could see the whole event unfold in front of her.

I watched Jake closely, the way his brow furrowed slightly as Leah spoke. Each word seemed to stack onto the emotional weight he carried, the guilt still lingering in the corners of his heart like stubborn autumn leaves clinging to branches before the first winter frost. There was a brief flicker of something deeper behind his eyes, a glimmer of hope perhaps, or maybe it was just the reflection of the fairy lights Leah had conjured in her mind.

"Yeah, it could be something," he said finally, though the inflection in his voice made it clear he was still struggling to commit. I could see the tumult within him, a swirling storm of past grief and present fears, colliding and dancing like errant leaves in the wind.

"I'll help with the planning!" I said quickly, eager to bridge the gap that had formed once again. "We could brainstorm ideas together, create a schedule, maybe even practice our own pieces."

"Practice? You want me to read something?" Jake's eyes widened in surprise, his facade cracking just a bit. I could see the corners of his mouth twitch, a ghost of a smile that might've bloomed had the weight of his emotions not pressed down so firmly.

"Why not? Everyone has a story to share. I think you'd be amazing," I replied, feeling my own heart race at the thought of encouraging him to step out from behind his carefully constructed walls. There was something intimate in sharing our stories, a way to connect threads that otherwise lay frayed and unacknowledged.

"Maybe," he muttered, uncertainty still swirling around him like a thick fog. "I don't know if I can... I mean, how do you even begin to share something like that?"

I could feel the shift in the air, a heavy silence descending as I contemplated how to articulate the jumble of thoughts racing through my mind. "You just start where you are. There's beauty in vulnerability. It's not about perfection; it's about honesty. Besides,"

I added, trying to inject some humor, "the worst thing that could happen is that you'll fumble a line or two. But isn't that part of being human?"

He chuckled softly, the sound a welcome melody amidst the weight of the moment. "Yeah, and maybe I'll end up being the next big thing. 'Jake, the Poetry Sensation.'"

"Exactly! You can tour the world, read your heart out, and then retire to a beach somewhere—if you do, don't forget to send me a postcard." The image danced in my mind, a vibrant tapestry of laughter and freedom, pulling him into the warmth of hope and away from the chill of the past.

As Leah excitedly returned to her notes, scribbling ideas furiously, I watched Jake's expression soften ever so slightly. It was as if I could see the weight begin to lift, a hesitant shift towards acceptance. The café, alive with the chatter and clinking of mugs, faded into a backdrop as I focused solely on him.

"Jake," I said gently, drawing his attention back to me. "You don't have to carry that guilt alone. You can let it go, even just a little. There's so much life ahead of you, and I want to be there for it, alongside you."

He held my gaze, the vulnerability reflected in his eyes a mirror of my own desire to connect. It was a moment suspended in time, a fragile thread weaving us closer, allowing us to share our burdens without the fear of judgment.

"I don't know if I can," he finally admitted, his voice barely above a whisper. "It feels like if I let go of the past, I'll forget her."

"You won't forget her," I reassured him, stepping closer, driven by an impulse I couldn't quite explain. "Remembering is different from holding on. It's about cherishing the love, not the pain. We can create new memories together, ones that honor her and celebrate your journey."

His breath caught, and for a fleeting moment, I thought I saw the spark of understanding flicker in his gaze. The shadows still loomed large, but perhaps, just perhaps, he was beginning to see a glimmer of light shining through them.

Leah looked up from her notes, her excitement palpable. "You two are going to be the stars of this event!"

Jake turned to her, his mask slipping slightly, revealing a tentative smile. "Maybe I'll give it a shot," he said, and my heart soared at the words, the promise of growth and connection unfurling before us like petals blooming in the spring sun.

As the night deepened outside, the café transformed into our little world, an oasis where stories could be shared, burdens lifted, and dreams ignited. The journey ahead was uncertain, but it felt like we were finally taking steps toward something meaningful—a tapestry of hope woven from the threads of our lives. And in that moment, with laughter mingling with the aroma of coffee and the soft glow of fairy lights illuminating our path, I felt a sense of belonging that wrapped around me like a warm embrace, anchoring me in the present.

The café buzzed with an easy warmth, the kind that seeps into your bones and makes you forget the chill of the outside world. The lingering scent of vanilla and brewed coffee danced in the air, wrapping around us like a cozy blanket. Leah, overflowing with ideas, jotted down details with a fervor that seemed to ignite the very walls. The cheerful chatter of the remaining patrons served as a reminder of the life surrounding us, a stark contrast to the heaviness that still clung to Jake.

"Let's start brainstorming a list of poets," Leah chirped, her pencil flying across the paper, almost defying gravity with its speed. "We should reach out to everyone—high school students, local artists, anyone who has a story to tell. This can really bring our community together!"

"Yeah, that sounds great," Jake replied, his voice carefully measured, as if he were weighing each word before releasing it into the ether. I could sense the tension in his shoulders, the way they remained rigid, as though he were bracing for a storm. It was an all-too-familiar dance—one where his heart wavered between longing and fear, the thrill of possibility countered by the weight of grief.

I leaned in closer, determined to keep the momentum alive. "Jake, think about the last time you felt truly connected to someone, sharing a piece of yourself. It can be electrifying, can't it? Sharing your truth, knowing it resonates with others?"

He turned his gaze to me, the weight of his unspoken thoughts shimmering like heat haze over asphalt. "Yeah, but sharing your truth can also expose your vulnerabilities," he said quietly, almost as if he were reminding himself rather than me.

"True," I nodded, wanting to bridge the gap between our perspectives. "But isn't it that vulnerability that makes us human? That connects us to one another?" The words hung between us, a delicate thread waiting to be pulled tighter or severed altogether.

Leah, blissfully unaware of the emotional turmoil, chirped away, already mapping out logistics and potential themes. "We can even have an open mic section for anyone brave enough to step up! Imagine the variety—different voices and stories filling the air! It'll be transformative!"

The fire of Leah's enthusiasm reignited something in Jake, a flicker of curiosity that hadn't been present moments earlier. "I suppose it could be cool to hear what people have to say," he said, his voice betraying the slightest hint of interest. The storm clouds above his head seemed to part just a bit, letting in slivers of light.

"Exactly! And it'll help you see you're not alone in your feelings," I added, trying to harness that glimmer of hope. "Others will be sharing their stories, their shadows too. You might find that it's easier to face your own when you see how beautifully imperfect everyone else is."

As the conversation flowed around us, I couldn't help but admire Leah's boundless energy. She had this innate ability to pull people into her orbit, wrapping them in warmth and positivity that felt almost magnetic. I wondered if I could learn a thing or two from her. The way she lit up the room reminded me that joy could coexist with sorrow; they were not mutually exclusive.

Jake caught my eye again, and for a brief moment, we exchanged a silent understanding. There was a tentative acknowledgment of the emotional landscape we were navigating together. It was daunting, yes, but perhaps it was also necessary—a climb we had to tackle to reach the summit of healing and growth.

"Okay," he said finally, a half-smile breaking through the shadows on his face. "I'll think about it. Maybe I'll even write something. No promises, though."

"Just take it one step at a time," I encouraged, my heart racing with the prospect of him stepping beyond his comfort zone. The journey to acceptance would be long and winding, but perhaps we could walk it together. The idea felt like a seed being planted, needing nurturing and patience to blossom.

The café slowly emptied, the chairs scraping against the hardwood floors, a soft reminder that the night was drawing to a close. Leah packed up her notes, her eyes sparkling with excitement. "I'll handle the flyers, and we can start promoting it next week!"

As we prepared to leave, I noticed a shift in Jake. He lingered by the window, looking out at the street where shadows mingled with the flickering streetlights. I stepped beside him, letting the silence settle around us like an embrace.

"What are you thinking about?" I ventured, my curiosity piqued.

He sighed, the sound heavy yet liberating. "Just... everything. How do you even begin to move forward when you're constantly looking back?"

"Sometimes, you don't," I replied gently. "Sometimes, you just allow yourself to exist in that space for a while. It's okay to feel lost, Jake. It's okay to take your time."

He turned to me, and for the first time that evening, I saw a glimmer of hope in his eyes, mingled with a deep appreciation. "Thank you," he murmured, the sincerity of his gratitude washing over me like a warm tide.

As we stepped outside, the crisp night air kissed our faces, a reminder of the world beyond our little café bubble. The stars twinkled above us, an endless canvas of possibilities stretched out against the inky sky. I felt invigorated, as if the very essence of the universe was whispering promises of change and growth.

We walked together down the quiet street, our footsteps echoing softly on the pavement, punctuated by the distant laughter of a couple walking hand in hand. The world felt alive, vibrant, and pulsing with potential. I stole glances at Jake, the way the moonlight played upon his features, illuminating the deep lines of thought etched across his brow.

"Do you think people will actually show up to the event?" he asked, his voice a mix of hope and doubt.

"Absolutely," I replied, a smile tugging at my lips. "People crave connection. They want to be heard and understood. We all do."

As we reached the corner where our paths would soon diverge, a sense of anticipation swirled in the air. "Let me know if you want to work on your piece together," I offered, not wanting to let this moment slip away like grains of sand through my fingers.

"I just might take you up on that," he replied, the vulnerability still present but now intertwined with a budding confidence. "I'll think about it."

"Good," I said, feeling a surge of warmth at his willingness to consider it. "Remember, the only way out is through."

He nodded, the faintest hint of a smile playing at the corners of his lips. "I'll remember that."

As we parted ways, I felt the weight of the evening shift. Each step I took felt lighter, infused with the promise of tomorrow. The café's warm glow faded into the distance, but its essence lingered, a reminder of the conversations yet to come, the stories waiting to be shared. The shadows and whispers of the past would always be a part of us, but they needn't dictate our future. In that moment, as I walked beneath the vast, starry sky, I felt a sense of belonging and connection blossom within me, intertwining our narratives in ways that might just lead us both toward healing.

Chapter 16: Cracks in the Facade

The bell above the café door jingles softly as I step inside, the familiar scent of roasted coffee beans and warm pastries wrapping around me like a comforting shawl. This quaint little haven, nestled between a bookstore and a flower shop in our small Midwestern town, has always been my refuge. It's the place where I found solace during the long days of high school, where I savored moments of blissful solitude or shared laughter with friends over steaming mugs. Today, however, the air is thick with tension, a fragile barrier between Leah and me that I can no longer ignore.

Leah sits at a corner table, her long fingers tracing patterns on the edge of her coffee cup, her gaze averted as if the swirling foam holds the answers to questions neither of us dares to ask. I've known Leah long enough to recognize the signs; she's in a mood that could either ignite a playful banter or escalate into an emotional standoff. My heart beats a steady rhythm of resolve, bolstered by the image of Jake's smile. There's a warmth that blossoms in my chest whenever I think of him, and I'm not willing to let anything—or anyone—snuff it out.

I approach with a cautious step, bracing myself for the impact of our inevitable confrontation. "Leah," I say, my voice steadier than I feel. "We need to talk." Her head lifts, and our eyes meet; hers are a stormy gray, mirroring the unease that churns within me. There's a flicker of surprise, then something more—an understanding, perhaps, that echoes in the air between us.

"What's there to talk about?" she replies, a touch of defensiveness creeping into her tone. "You know I'm here for the coffee."

"Right, but it's not just about the coffee, is it?" I take a seat across from her, the small table feeling like a fragile bridge between two worlds. "It's about Jake." The name hangs in the air, heavy with implications, a thread woven into the fabric of our shared history.

Her expression hardens for a fleeting moment, a flicker of something—fear? Jealousy?—crossing her face before she quickly masks it with a neutral facade. "What about him?" she asks, her voice cool, yet I catch the subtle tremor in her words.

"I can't shake the feeling that you're... lingering," I say, my throat tightening around the words. "I mean, it's like every time I turn around, you're there, hovering. It's unsettling."

Leah leans back, her arms crossing over her chest, a barrier I can almost see materialize between us. "And what about that? You think I'm just going to disappear because you've decided to be with him? It's not like that, you know."

"Then what is it like?" I challenge, the heat of my emotions rising. "You've been a part of his life for so long, and now that I'm in the picture, it feels like you're reluctant to let go."

Her eyes narrow, the storm brewing behind them intensifying. "You don't get it, do you? Jake and I have history. We've shared things that you can't just erase with a few flirty texts or late-night drives."

"I'm not trying to erase anything!" I protest, feeling my pulse quicken. "But I'm starting to feel like an outsider in my own story." The vulnerability in my admission hangs in the air, a delicate thread connecting us momentarily.

For a heartbeat, Leah's guard falters, and I see a glimpse of something raw in her expression—fear, perhaps, or the reflection of her own insecurities. "I didn't mean to make you feel that way," she says softly, her bravado crumbling like stale bread. "I'm just... I'm scared, okay? Scared of losing him. Losing what we had."

Her confession resonates within me, a deep chord struck in the silence. I can see it now, the ghost of their past intertwined with the present, and suddenly, I understand the weight of her presence. Leah isn't just a shadow in our love story; she's a lingering echo, a reminder of the person Jake used to be before I stumbled into his life, flipping everything upside down.

"I don't want to take him away from you," I admit, the words spilling out before I can rein them in. "I just want a chance to be with him too, to make new memories."

Leah's gaze softens, and for a moment, I feel as though we're two young girls again, sharing secrets under the stars. "He talks about you," she says quietly. "He's different with you. Lighter. Happier."

The corners of my mouth tug upwards, warmth spreading through me at the thought of Jake. "He makes me feel like I can breathe again."

The vulnerability hangs between us, an unspoken agreement to drop the defenses we've both built. It's a delicate truce, yet it fills the air with an undeniable energy. "Maybe we both want to protect him in our own ways," I whisper, realizing the truth in my words.

Leah nods slowly, her expression a mixture of resignation and acceptance. "I just don't want to be the one who gets left behind," she murmurs, her voice laced with a sincerity that breaks my heart a little. The atmosphere shifts, the tension loosening as we forge a connection grounded in empathy, our struggles interwoven like threads in a tapestry of friendship and love.

"None of us want to be left behind," I reply softly, feeling the fragile bond between us strengthen. "But maybe it's not about choosing one over the other. Maybe there's room for all of us in this story."

The bell above the café door chimes again, and as I glance toward the entrance, I spot Jake standing there, his presence like a beacon amidst the haze of uncertainty. He meets my gaze, a smile breaking across his face, and I can't help but feel that spark of hope igniting in my chest once more. This moment, however fragile, has carved a space for understanding where once there was only rivalry.

The air shifts as Jake strides into the café, a natural light flooding the space around him, as if he carries his own sun. His smile broadens when he sees me, and the little cocoon of tension that had enveloped Leah and me bursts like a soap bubble under a soft breath. The aroma of coffee and pastries fades into the background, replaced by the magnetic pull of his presence. There's an effortless charm about him, a way he fills the room without even trying, and my heart does a familiar little dance at the sight of him.

"Hey, there you are!" he exclaims, his voice warm, sending a pleasant shiver down my spine. "I thought I'd find you here." His eyes flicker to Leah, and I can't help but notice the way her posture shifts—she leans back slightly, a defensive gesture, her smile more polite than genuine. In that moment, the fragile alliance Leah and I forged feels like a gossamer thread, precariously woven but not yet severed.

"Just having a chat," I say, injecting as much nonchalance into my voice as I can muster, my heart racing as I gauge Leah's reaction. She offers a tight-lipped smile that barely reaches her eyes, and I silently urge her to play along. This isn't the time for old wounds to reopen.

Jake pulls out a chair and sinks into it, blissfully unaware of the simmering tension beneath our surface. "What did I miss?" he asks, oblivious, his attention wholly on me. It's moments like these that remind me of the power of his gaze—the way it seems to tune out everything else, drawing me in like a moth to a flame.

"Just some girl talk," Leah chimes in, her tone light, but the flicker of her eyes suggests there's more simmering below. "Nothing you'd want to hear about."

"Oh, I don't know about that," Jake teases, leaning back and crossing his arms. "I could use a little gossip in my life. Make it more exciting."

A giggle escapes my lips despite the tension. "You'd be surprised how exciting girl talk can get," I shoot back, giving Leah a pointed look that silently reminds her to keep it friendly. For a moment, we share a fleeting smile, a pact sealed over steaming cups of coffee, until Leah looks away, her fingers fiddling with her ring as though it holds the secrets of the universe.

"So, what's new with you?" Jake asks, a genuine interest lacing his voice. I can see the way he studies me, taking in every detail—my hair tucked behind my ear, the way my fingers trace the rim of my cup. There's an earnestness in his expression that pulls at my heart, a quiet reassurance that makes me feel anchored.

"I was just telling Leah about how the fall festival is coming up," I say, leaning forward, hoping to steer the conversation toward something lighter. "I thought it might be fun to check it out together. You know, the corn maze, pumpkin carving, maybe even a hayride?"

His eyes light up, the corners of his mouth curving into a smile that could rival the sun breaking through storm clouds. "That sounds awesome! I've always wanted to try the haunted house they set up in the old barn."

I can't help but laugh at his enthusiasm. "Haunted houses? You're braver than I am. I'll be the one hiding behind you the entire time."

"Then I guess I better start practicing my bravery!" he quips, and Leah's soft laugh breaks the tension again, though I can still feel the current of uncertainty buzzing beneath the surface. It's a delicate balancing act, each of us walking a tightrope strung between friendship and something deeper, something undefined yet palpably real.

As we discuss plans for the festival, I can feel Leah's presence like an added weight on my chest. The laughter rings true, but beneath the surface lies a sense of unease that makes my stomach twist. I can't shake the feeling that her acceptance is only a veneer, a fragile mask that could shatter at any moment. Still, I push through the discomfort, focusing on Jake, on the way his eyes crinkle when he smiles, the warmth radiating from his laughter.

After a few more minutes, Leah excuses herself, citing an early class, but I can't shake the feeling that she's retreating into the shadows again, leaving me to bask in the sunlight of Jake's affection. As she slips out of the café, a bittersweet pang shoots through me, an uninvited reminder of the complex web we're all tangled in.

"I'm glad you're here," Jake says, pulling me back to the present. "I've been wanting to talk to you about something."

I lean in closer, curiosity piquing my interest. "What's up?"

His gaze flickers toward the window, where the autumn leaves dance in the breeze, golden and crisp. "You know how I told you about the band I'm trying to put together? Well, we've finally nailed down a practice schedule, and I was wondering if you'd want to come watch us play sometime. I think it'd be fun."

A thrill runs through me, a mixture of excitement and a dash of anxiety. "You really think I'd enjoy that?"

"Of course! You can give me pointers," he teases, his eyes twinkling with mischief. "And, you know, keep me from making a fool of myself."

My heart swells at his words, the earnestness of his invitation wrapping around me like a warm blanket. "I'd love to! Just promise me you won't play anything too embarrassing."

He chuckles, and for a moment, it feels as though the weight of Leah's earlier presence has lifted. "No promises! But I'll definitely make sure you're having fun."

We continue to chat about the band, my worries about Leah fading into the background, replaced by dreams of music and laughter. The café buzzes around us, but in this moment, it feels like we're the only two people in the world. It's intoxicating, the way he makes me feel alive, like a melody I've been waiting to hear all my life.

As we share stories, I can't help but wonder if Leah's fears will ever truly fade, if the cracks in our fragile facade will deepen or mend. The path ahead is uncertain, and though I know there will be bumps along the way, the warmth of Jake's laughter wraps around me like a promise—a whisper of hope in a world painted with shades of gray. For now, I'll savor this moment, allowing myself to believe in the possibilities, even as the echoes of our tangled past linger softly in the background.

The afternoon sun pours through the café windows, illuminating the corners where shadows gather, and the aroma of coffee and cinnamon fills the air. As Jake and I settle into our easy banter, the warmth of the moment envelops me, a stark contrast to the tempest of emotions swirling beneath the surface. I can still feel the echoes of my earlier conversation with Leah, her vulnerability an unwelcome reminder of the delicate web of relationships we're all weaving.

"Have you thought any more about the festival?" Jake asks, leaning forward, his eyes sparkling with excitement. "I heard there's going to be a pumpkin cannon this year. I mean, how cool is that? We have to see it!"

I laugh, picturing the spectacle of pumpkins flying through the air, each one a burst of color against the crisp blue sky. "I've seen videos! I can't believe they're doing it this year. It sounds like an absolute blast." The joy in his voice pulls me deeper into the moment, and I momentarily forget about the complexities that linger just beyond our laughter.

As we discuss the festival's activities, I let the conversation flow freely, allowing myself to bask in the ease of our connection. With every shared laugh and playful jab, the world around us recedes until it feels like we're encased in our own little bubble, safe from the outside chaos. But as my thoughts drift back to Leah, the edges of that bubble begin to fray. I wonder how much longer we can dance around the truth of our entangled lives without addressing the underlying tension that's taken root.

"Let's make a pact," Jake says, his voice cutting through my musings. "No matter how crazy things get, we promise to have fun. No pressure, no drama—just us enjoying every moment."

I nod, feeling the weight of his words settle in my chest. "I like that. Let's make it a rule."

The way he looks at me, a mix of sincerity and mischief, sends warmth spiraling through my veins. I can see the spark of excitement in his eyes, a light that draws me closer to him. There's something intoxicating about this—his laughter, his passion, the way he effortlessly makes the mundane feel like an adventure. But as much as I want to lose myself in this moment, the nagging fear of Leah's lingering presence refuses to let go.

The café begins to fill with the familiar rhythm of life; friends chatter animatedly, a barista yells out orders, and the sound of milk frothing punctuates the air. It's the soundtrack of our small town, a backdrop I've always loved. Yet today, the harmony feels discordant, a reminder that while I am here, caught up in the joy of Jake's company, another piece of my heart is still tangled in the complexities of my relationship with Leah.

"Are you okay?" Jake's question pulls me back, his brow furrowed with concern. "You seem a bit... distant."

"I'm fine!" I say too quickly, forcing a smile that doesn't quite reach my eyes. "Just thinking about the festival and everything we could do."

He studies me, and for a moment, I can see the shadows of doubt in his gaze. "You sure? You can talk to me about anything, you know that, right?"

His words flutter around me like butterflies, each one reminding me of the trust I've begun to build with him. But even as I feel the urge to confide in him, I hesitate. I can't bring the weight of my insecurities into this space we've created. I want to protect the joy between us, to shield it from the storm brewing in the distance.

"Really, I'm good," I assure him, but the tightness in my chest gives me away. As we finish our drinks and rise from the table, I can't help but glance out the window, my mind spinning with the possibilities of the festival, yet still tethered to the questions swirling around Leah.

As we step outside, the brisk autumn air wraps around us, invigorating and crisp, laced with the scent of fallen leaves and the promise of impending change. "Shall we take a walk?" Jake suggests, his hand brushing against mine, sending a spark of electricity that momentarily drowns out my anxieties. "I want to show you something."

Curiosity piqued, I follow him down the sidewalk, the golden afternoon light spilling over the quaint shops that line the street. Each storefront bursts with character—an antique shop brimming with forgotten treasures, a vibrant bakery with the enticing aroma of freshly baked bread wafting through the door, and a cozy bookstore with windows filled with the promise of stories waiting to be discovered.

Jake leads me toward the edge of town, where the vibrant colors of autumn transform the landscape into a tapestry of golds, oranges, and reds. We arrive at a park I haven't visited in years, its sprawling lawn dotted with trees shedding their leaves like confetti. A small pond sits at its center, mirroring the cobalt sky, where a few ducks paddle leisurely, oblivious to the chaos of human emotions just a stone's throw away.

"I used to come here all the time as a kid," he reminisces, a fond smile tugging at his lips. "We'd have picnics and play games. I always thought it was magical, you know?"

I look around, taking in the scene. The place does have a certain charm, a whimsical air that captures the heart. "It's beautiful," I reply, my voice almost a whisper. "I can see why you loved it here."

As we walk, our footsteps crunching on the fallen leaves, he stops to pick one up, holding it between his fingers. "Do you believe in magic?" he asks, his tone playful yet earnest.

"Depends on what kind of magic you're talking about," I respond, half-smiling, half-curious. "Are we talking about card tricks or fairy-tale magic?"

He chuckles, tossing the leaf back to the ground. "I'm talking about the kind of magic that happens when you find someone who makes the world seem a little brighter, even on the gloomiest days."

My breath catches at his words, a warmth blooming in my chest. "I think I know what you mean," I say softly, feeling the weight of his gaze upon me, an unspoken bond weaving its way through the space between us.

We continue walking, the sun dipping lower in the sky, casting long shadows that dance like spirits along the path. But just as I feel the delicate thread of connection tightening between us, my mind drifts back to Leah. What would she think of this moment? Would she feel the same pang of uncertainty I do, or has she already settled into a sense of peace regarding her own feelings for Jake?

The shadows lengthen as we reach a wooden bench overlooking the pond. Jake gestures for me to sit, and as we settle beside each other, the air hums with unspoken words. The quiet is comfortable yet heavy, each heartbeat echoing the thoughts swirling in my mind.

"What's on your mind?" he finally asks, his voice breaking through the silence like a lifeline.

I hesitate, torn between the urge to confide in him and the need to protect the delicate balance we've struck. "It's just..." I start, my voice faltering. "Things feel complicated. With Leah, with everything."

He turns to face me, his expression serious, concern etched across his features. "You can tell me. I want to understand."

I take a deep breath, feeling the weight of my thoughts press against my chest. "I guess I'm just worried about what it means for all of us. I care about you, Jake, but I don't want to step on Leah's feelings. It's not easy to navigate."

For a moment, he is silent, his gaze drifting toward the pond, where the water reflects the shifting colors of the sky. "You shouldn't have to worry about that," he says finally, his voice low and steady. "I want to be with you, but I don't want to hurt her either."

His words hang in the air, heavy with the weight of truth. "It's just... I never intended for this to be messy. I just want to enjoy what we have."

"I know," he replies, reaching out to squeeze my hand gently. "I want that too. We'll figure it out together."

I glance down at our hands, entwined like the branches of the trees surrounding us, and for a moment, the world feels right. The breeze rustles the leaves, whispering promises of change, and I take a deep breath, allowing myself to believe that maybe, just maybe, we can find a way to navigate this tangled web without losing ourselves in the process.

As the sun dips below the horizon, casting hues of orange and purple across the sky, I realize that life's complexities are not just obstacles to overcome but opportunities for growth, connections to deepen, and love to flourish. And even in the midst of uncertainty, I know one thing to be true: this moment, this feeling, is a kind of magic worth holding on to.

Chapter 17: A Serendipitous Encounter

The air hummed with a playful energy, the kind that wraps around you like a cozy blanket on a brisk fall afternoon. I meandered through the bustling artisan market, its lively chaos weaving a vibrant tapestry of sights and sounds. Vendors called out with friendly exuberance, their voices mingling with the soft laughter of children darting between stalls, while the intoxicating aroma of fresh pastries and spiced cider danced in the air. Each booth brimmed with unique treasures, from hand-knit scarves boasting colors that seemed plucked from a sunset, to glistening jewelry crafted from the heart of the earth. It felt like stepping into a kaleidoscope where every turn offered a new delight.

I was on a mission, of course, my list of café supplies clutched in one hand and a worn leather tote bag slung over my shoulder, ready to be filled with anything that might add a dash of charm to my little corner of the world. My café, nestled on a quaint street in the heart of the town, had become a sanctuary for those seeking refuge from the mundane. Each table cradled stories—conversations spilling into the air, laughter punctuating the quiet corners, and moments of solitude wrapped in the warmth of a steaming cup of coffee.

As I navigated the labyrinth of stalls, I was struck by the playful choreography of the market—an elderly couple perusing handmade quilts, a mother helping her daughter select the perfect caramel apple, and a group of artists passionately discussing the merits of different glaze techniques. The atmosphere thrummed with life, but it was the bright, sun-kissed pottery that truly captured my attention. A booth lined with colorful bowls and plates beckoned me closer, each piece a testament to the artisan's meticulous craft. I felt drawn to a particular bowl, its surface painted with swirling designs that danced like flames in the sun. It was a riot of colors—deep blues and bright yellows intertwining with hints of crimson and sage—each stroke telling a story of its own.

Just as I reached out to admire the delicate curves, I felt a familiar presence behind me. My heart fluttered, an unexpected rush of warmth flooding my veins. I turned slowly, and there he was—Jake. The world around me faded into a soft blur, the vibrant market transforming into a mere backdrop to the magnetic pull I felt toward him. He stood there, as effortlessly handsome as I remembered, his dark hair tousled just enough to seem charming rather than careless. His eyes, an electrifying blue, sparkled with a mix of surprise and delight.

"Hey! Fancy seeing you here," he said, his voice warm like the first sip of coffee on a chilly morning.

"Jake!" I replied, perhaps a little too enthusiastically, a shy smile spreading across my face. "What are you doing at the market?"

"Just wandering, looking for some inspiration for a new piece," he gestured vaguely to his sketchbook peeking out of his messenger bag. "What about you? Stocking up for the café?"

I nodded, trying to suppress the thrill bubbling within me. We fell into easy conversation, our words flowing like the river nearby, each bend revealing something new about the other. I discovered that he had recently been experimenting with a different style of painting—abstract landscapes that captured the spirit of the changing seasons. It was refreshing to see the world through his artistic lens, a perspective that was both enchanting and grounding.

As we explored the market together, I felt the rhythm of our footsteps sync in an unspoken dance. We wandered past stalls filled with handcrafted soaps, their scents bursting forth like blooming flowers, then paused at a display of local honey that glimmered under the afternoon sun. It was during this casual stroll that I found myself laughing freely, the weight of the world feeling lighter with each shared joke and story. But beneath that laughter lay a flicker of unease, a reminder of Leah's presence in Jake's life. The thought hovered like a shadow, tainting the sunlit moment with a hint of melancholy.

We soon found ourselves back at the pottery booth, the bowl I had admired still perched enticingly on the table. I leaned closer, tracing the intricate designs with my fingertips, the cool ceramic grounding me amidst the whirlwind of emotions. I caught a glimpse of Jake out of the corner of my eye, watching me intently. The way he looked at me, with that blend of curiosity and warmth, made my heart race in a way I hadn't expected.

Then, in a surprising twist, Jake stepped forward and asked the vendor about the bowl. "How much for this one?" he inquired, his voice steady and confident. I felt a flush of warmth spread through me, the kind that blooms when you know you're being seen, truly seen.

The vendor's price sent a small gasp escaping my lips—it was more than I had anticipated, certainly more than I could justify spending that day. But Jake, with an ease that took me by surprise, reached into his pocket and handed over the cash before I could protest.

"This is for you," he said, a playful smile dancing on his lips as he handed me the bowl, its vibrant colors now shining even brighter in my hands. My heart swelled, but a pang of guilt tugged at me—what would Leah think of this? What was I even allowing myself to feel?

"Jake, you really didn't have to," I protested, my fingers clenching the bowl as if it were a lifeline.

"I wanted to," he replied softly, stepping closer, our eyes locking in a moment that felt electric. "You bring a lot of joy to people. This is just a small token."

As I stood there, cradling the gift and grappling with the whirlpool of emotions swirling within me, I realized that life, in all its chaotic unpredictability, had a way of leading us to unexpected places—places where connections could blossom, where joy could overshadow the shadows of doubt. And as I looked into Jake's eyes, I felt a flicker of hope igniting in the recesses of my heart, a chance to redefine what happiness could look like amidst the complexities of life and love.

The warmth of the market lingered in the air as I cradled the bowl, its glossy surface catching the afternoon sun and reflecting a kaleidoscope of colors. I could hardly fathom the generous gesture, the way Jake had effortlessly reached into his pocket to offer me this beautiful piece of art. Yet, the weight of Leah's presence loomed larger than ever, a shadow that darkened the corners of my joy. I cast a sideways glance at Jake, who was now animatedly discussing the artisan's techniques with the vendor. His enthusiasm lit up his face, illuminating the vulnerability that was often hidden beneath his easygoing demeanor.

"How do you find the time to create something so intricate?" he asked, genuinely curious as the vendor explained the painstaking process behind each brushstroke. I watched him, captivated by the way he engaged with the world around him. It was as if he could see the beauty in everything—a quality I had longed to possess, to observe life through a lens of wonder rather than worry.

While Jake was engrossed in conversation, I stole a moment to admire the bowl in my hands. The swirling patterns reminded me of the eddies of a river, vibrant and unpredictable. It was more than just a bowl; it was a reminder that beauty could exist even amidst the chaos. I imagined it holding a rich, steaming soup on a cold winter's night or cradling a colorful salad during a sunlit picnic. In that moment, it felt like a promise, a tangible token of something brighter that could bloom in the space between us.

After Jake wrapped up his conversation, he turned to me, his eyes sparkling with excitement. "What do you think? Are you going to give it a special place in your café?"

"I think it deserves a spot right in the center of my counter," I replied, laughter bubbling up as I imagined it drawing in customers like moths to a flame. "It'll be the first thing they see, and I want them to know that they're walking into a place that values art as much as coffee."

Jake's smile widened, a warm, genuine beam that lit up the entire market. It was in moments like these that I found myself forgetting about Leah, about the complexities weaved into our lives, allowing me to revel in the sheer delight of the moment. We continued exploring the market together, wandering hand in hand through a maze of stalls. Each turn brought new surprises: a vibrant display of hand-painted canvases, delicate jewelry that sparkled like starlight, and fragrant herb sachets that smelled like a summer garden.

Jake seemed to have a knack for discovering hidden gems, nudging me toward booths that piqued my interest. "You have to see this!" he exclaimed, tugging me toward a stall draped in colorful textiles. The vendor, a cheerful woman with a wild mane of curls, showcased an array of scarves, each woven with intricate patterns that whispered of distant lands. I held one up, a soft piece dyed in shades of deep purple and gold, and let it cascade through my fingers like silk.

"I think it would look great with that outfit you wore last week," Jake said, his voice teasing yet sincere. "You know, the one that made you look like you just stepped off a Parisian runway?"

My cheeks flushed at the compliment, and I couldn't help but chuckle. "Oh please, I barely manage to put on matching socks most days! But I appreciate the boost to my ego." The playful banter between us felt like an electric current, lifting me higher and higher as we ventured from stall to stall.

As the afternoon light began to soften into a warm glow, we stumbled upon a booth filled with baked goods. The aroma wafting from it was intoxicating—freshly baked bread, buttery pastries, and rich, chocolatey desserts danced in the air, teasing my senses. We approached, and I watched as Jake's eyes lit up at the sight of a towering chocolate cake, its layers gleaming with rich frosting.

"Can we share a slice?" he asked, looking at me with a mischievous glint that made my heart skip.

I nodded, excitement bubbling in my chest. "Only if we can get a piece of that lemon tart too! I need something refreshing to balance out all this chocolate."

We exchanged money with the vendor, who smiled brightly at our eagerness, and soon we were balancing two plates stacked high with desserts, our laughter mingling with the sounds of the market around us. Finding a nearby bench, we settled down to indulge in our treats.

The first bite of chocolate cake was pure ecstasy, the flavors melting together like a sweet embrace. I closed my eyes, savoring the richness. "This is amazing! I think I might just want to swim in this cake," I said, exaggerating my delight, causing Jake to erupt in laughter.

"Maybe that's the secret to life—find what makes you happy and dive into it headfirst," he replied, his eyes twinkling with warmth. "What would your life be if you could do just that? No limits, just pure bliss?"

I contemplated his question, my thoughts swirling like the colors in the bowl I held. "I think I'd want to travel," I admitted, the words spilling out before I could second-guess them. "I'd explore quaint little towns, sip coffee in tiny cafes, and gather stories like souvenirs."

"Let's do it," Jake said suddenly, his expression earnest. "We could plan a little road trip—just you and me, the open road, and all the pastries we can eat."

The idea sparked something within me—a flicker of adventure I had long since buried under the weight of responsibilities and unfulfilled dreams. My heart raced at the thought of stepping outside my comfort zone, of embracing spontaneity.

"Are you serious?" I asked, my voice barely a whisper, as if saying it too loudly might shatter the delicate possibility of it all.

"Absolutely," he replied, and the sincerity in his voice sent warmth cascading through me. "Life is too short to stay in one place, to let fear dictate our choices. Besides, how often do we get to explore the world with someone who makes it feel a little brighter?"

As I gazed into Jake's eyes, the shadow of Leah momentarily faded, replaced by a vibrant tapestry of hope and possibility. In that instant, I realized that perhaps it was time to embrace the unknown, to allow joy to weave its way back into my life, even if it came with complications and uncertainty. The journey ahead shimmered with potential, and I felt an exhilarating thrill at the thought of sharing it with someone who understood the beauty of adventure.

The sun dipped lower in the sky, casting a golden hue over the market as Jake and I finished the last bites of our dessert. I could feel the excitement simmering between us, a palpable connection that seemed to spark and crackle in the air. Jake leaned back on the bench, stretching his arms above his head, a carefree gesture that made me want to reach out and brush my fingers against his warm skin. It was an innocent thought, yet it sent a thrill coursing through me, one I hadn't felt in far too long.

"Are you ready for this adventure?" he asked, breaking my reverie. His voice was playful, laced with the promise of spontaneity that seemed to hang in the air like the scent of cinnamon from the nearby bakery.

I smiled, the possibility of road trips and new experiences swirling around my mind like the colorful patterns on the bowl he had gifted me. "I've always wanted to explore the coast," I replied, my heart racing at the thought. "From little seaside towns to hidden coves, there's something magical about the ocean, isn't there?"

Jake's eyes lit up, his enthusiasm infectious. "Absolutely! Imagine us standing on the edge of a cliff, the wind whipping through our hair, waves crashing below. I can see it now—us, living our best lives!"

His vivid imagery ignited a fire within me. I could almost feel the salty breeze and hear the seagulls calling above. The idea of shedding the weight of expectations and simply enjoying the journey felt intoxicating. "Let's do it. Let's plan a weekend trip," I declared, surprised by my own daring.

"Perfect! We can map out a route, stopping at every quirky roadside diner and art gallery we find along the way. And we have to take pictures—so many pictures!" Jake's excitement was palpable, and for the first time in what felt like ages, I was swept up in a wave of hope and adventure.

As we talked, the sun began its descent, casting long shadows across the market. A nearby band struck up a cheerful tune, the lively music wrapping around us like a warm embrace. We watched as couples danced awkwardly, laughter spilling into the twilight, and I couldn't help but feel a sense of belonging swell within me. It was in moments like these, surrounded by people reveling in the simple joys of life, that the world felt ripe with possibility.

"We should probably head back soon," I said reluctantly, glancing at the vendors who were beginning to pack up their goods. "I have to get everything ready for the café tomorrow." The thought of returning to my little haven felt bittersweet, yet the allure of the café offered comfort, a tangible reminder of my passion.

"Right, we don't want to keep your customers waiting," Jake replied, his expression shifting momentarily to one of seriousness. "But how about this? Let's finalize our plans tomorrow over coffee. I want to hear all about your ideas for the café and how I can help."

His offer struck a chord deep within me. The prospect of spending more time with Jake felt exhilarating, yet the reality of

Leah's shadow loomed like a specter. I swallowed hard, pushing the thoughts aside. "That sounds great. I'd love that," I said, trying to infuse my words with a confidence I didn't entirely feel.

As we walked together through the market's exit, the vibrant colors fading into dusk, I felt a mixture of exhilaration and anxiety. The night air cooled against my skin, and I shivered slightly, pulling my jacket tighter around me. Jake noticed and immediately shrugged off his own jacket, draping it over my shoulders. "Here, take this. You'll catch a chill."

The warmth of his jacket enveloped me, not just from the fabric, but from the thoughtfulness behind the gesture. I turned to thank him, my heart fluttering in my chest, but before I could speak, our eyes locked. In that moment, everything else faded—the market, the lingering thoughts of Leah, the pressures of running a café. It was just us, suspended in a bubble of possibility, and I could see the unspoken connection blooming between us.

"Can I ask you something?" he said, his voice softer now, almost hesitant.

"Of course," I replied, my pulse quickening.

"What's holding you back from fully embracing this? From diving into all the things you want to do, the adventures you want to have?"

The question hung in the air, heavy with significance. I opened my mouth to respond, but the truth felt tangled within me—an intricate web woven from past hurts, insecurities, and the fear of stepping beyond the familiar. "It's just... I've been so focused on running the café and maintaining a sense of normalcy," I finally managed, my voice barely above a whisper. "I don't know if I can just... let go."

Jake nodded, his expression understanding yet determined. "You deserve to let go. Life isn't just about responsibilities; it's also about creating memories and embracing joy. You've built this incredible café, but it's just one part of who you are. You're more than that—you're an adventurer waiting to happen."

His words resonated deep within me, echoing against the walls I had built around myself. Perhaps I had been so busy curating a sense of stability that I had forgotten to make space for spontaneity and joy. "I think I'm scared," I admitted, my voice trembling slightly. "Scared of stepping out of my comfort zone and facing the unknown."

"Scared is okay," he said gently, a warmth radiating from his gaze. "But don't let it stop you. If you fall, I promise I'll be there to catch you."

There was something reassuring in his promise, a tether that felt both comforting and thrilling. I swallowed hard, the weight of my fears feeling a little lighter in the face of his unwavering support.

As we approached my car, I could feel the air shifting around us, charged with the possibilities of the future. "Let's make a pact," Jake suggested, a playful glint in his eyes. "No backing out on this trip. We'll hold each other accountable."

I couldn't help but smile, the warmth of the moment washing over me. "Deal," I said, extending my hand toward him. He took it firmly, a jolt of electricity coursing between us.

We stood there for a moment, the stars beginning to twinkle overhead, our laughter echoing through the quieting market. In that instant, I felt the walls I had built around my heart begin to crumble, replaced by the vibrant possibility of what lay ahead. The night was just beginning, and with it came the promise of adventure—of taking chances, embracing the unknown, and perhaps, just perhaps, opening my heart to something new.

As I slid into my car, the warmth of his jacket lingering against my skin, I realized that I wasn't just driving home; I was steering toward a future filled with color, light, and the thrilling uncertainty of what might come next. And that thought, buoyed by hope and excitement, felt like a breath of fresh air, clearing away the cobwebs of doubt and fear. It was a chance to rediscover myself, to dive headfirst into the adventures that awaited us, and to embrace the beauty of serendipity in every moment.

Chapter 18: The Weight of Choices

The kitchen exuded warmth, the kind that clung to the air and settled comfortably into the corners of the room. I placed the bowl on the counter, its surface gleaming under the soft glow of the pendant lights that hung overhead like eager fireflies. The rich scent of rosemary and garlic lingered from my earlier preparations, wrapping around me like a cherished memory. As I pulled back the curtain to let in the dusky evening light, the golden hour bathed everything in a mellow hue, painting the walls with strokes of warmth that invited peace. It was a contrast to the brewing storm within me, a tension so palpable it felt like I could reach out and touch it.

I had long come to love this little corner of the world—the Willow, as we fondly called it. Nestled in a cozy pocket of Americana, it felt like a sanctuary from the chaos beyond its front door. The wooden beams, aged and sturdy, whispered stories of laughter and sorrow, echoing the lives that had come and gone through these very walls. Here, I was learning to weave my own narrative, a patchwork of experiences stitched together by the threads of love, loss, and hope. I felt a warmth in my chest as I thought of Jake. His presence had become a comfort, a soft blanket on chilly nights, and I yearned for another evening wrapped in the simplicity of his company.

Just as I allowed myself to sink into the promise of the evening, my phone buzzed, breaking the spell. The sound was jarring against the backdrop of serenity, a shrill reminder of the outside world and its unrelenting demands. Leah's name lit up the screen, and a pang of dread twisted in my stomach. An invitation to her gathering, yet another attempt to pull me back into the chaotic orbit of her life. My fingers hovered over the screen, the choice weighing heavily on my conscience. Should I go? Should I confront the whirlwind that was Leah, the storm I had so desperately tried to avoid?

I could almost see Leah's vibrant smile and hear her infectious laughter, yet it was tinged with a familiar edge of possessiveness. She had a knack for intruding, for turning moments of quiet into battles of will. I recalled the last time she'd barged into my life, her presence bursting through the door like a confetti cannon, colorful and loud, shattering the stillness I had fought so hard to build. But the chaos had a charm, didn't it? The way she embraced life with a gusto that was both exhilarating and exhausting. It tugged at me like a siren's call, pulling me away from the steady current I had begun to navigate with Jake.

Standing there, my heart a tumultuous sea of uncertainty, I could see the two paths diverging in front of me. One was the bright, chaotic path of Leah, filled with spontaneous laughter and tumultuous emotions that would sweep me up like autumn leaves in a windstorm. The other was a quieter, steadier route, one that promised solace, healing, and the growing intimacy I was forging with Jake. I could almost hear the whispers of my heart urging me toward the latter, the call of a safe harbor where love could flourish unchallenged by the storms of external chaos.

Yet, as I bit my lip, I wondered if it was possible to hold both paths in balance. My friendship with Leah had always felt like walking a tightrope, the danger exhilarating and terrifying in equal measure. I envisioned Jake, his warm brown eyes glimmering with curiosity as we shared a bowl of homemade pasta, laughter echoing softly against the walls, creating a cocoon of intimacy that I had long craved. But could I truly build this sanctuary if I kept ignoring the chaos that Leah represented?

The thought of Jake's gentle smile made my heart flutter, a reminder of the warmth that had begun to replace the emptiness I had felt for so long. He was a steady force, a calm amidst the turbulence, encouraging me to explore the depths of my emotions while giving me the space to navigate my own fears. Each moment spent with him felt like unwrapping a present, layers peeling away to reveal something precious beneath. With every shared glance, every gentle touch, I felt pieces of myself being stitched together, memories crafted from laughter and quiet conversations under the stars.

Yet Leah's invitation loomed large, a specter that reminded me of the unfinished business I had with my past. The allure of chaos and nostalgia danced tantalizingly on the edges of my mind. It would be easy to slip back into the familiarity of old routines, the kind that thrived on unpredictability and unfiltered joy. I could already hear Leah's voice, her spirited laughter ringing in my ears, promising adventure and companionship. It felt like a gravitational pull, one that I had resisted for far too long.

But did I want to lose the beautiful connection I was nurturing with Jake? Did I want to risk the delicate balance we had created in this small sanctuary, just for a taste of nostalgia wrapped in the guise of friendship? My heart whispered no, yet my mind hesitated, each beat echoing the fear of missing out on a vibrant piece of life that Leah represented. It was a tangled web of choices, each thread representing the complexity of relationships, the weight of decisions that could either uplift or unravel me.

As I looked around the room, taking in the cozy ambiance I had created, the flickering candles casting playful shadows on the walls, I felt a resolve crystallizing within me. Perhaps it was time to confront this head-on. To not allow the specter of Leah to dictate my choices but rather to step into the light of my own decisions. Maybe, just maybe, it was possible to find a way to navigate both paths—one foot in the vibrant chaos of Leah's world and the other firmly planted in the grounding presence of Jake. I took a deep breath, allowing the warm scents and soft light to envelop me, a silent promise that whatever I chose, it would be with intention, and above all, with love.

I stared at my phone, the screen glowing ominously, casting a harsh light on my face. Leah's invitation dangled before me like a wobbly fruit on a branch, ripe for picking yet fraught with the risk of falling. Should I respond, adding a layer of complexity to the evening, or should I let it wither on the vine? A thousand thoughts swirled in my mind as I wrestled with the decision, each scenario unfurling like a movie reel, complete with dramatic music and colorful characters.

My fingers trembled slightly as I contemplated my options, but then I inhaled deeply, the aroma of rosemary bringing me back to the present. I reminded myself that I had cultivated this space for a reason. It was not merely a backdrop for Jake and me; it was a sanctuary, a canvas upon which I was painting my newfound self, brush strokes laden with vibrant colors of hope and resilience. The world outside was wild and unpredictable, but here, in the cozy embrace of The Willow, I had the freedom to breathe, to discover, and to redefine my relationships.

I could picture Jake arriving, his face lighting up with that charming grin that melted the edges of my anxiety. He had a way of transforming even the most mundane evenings into delightful escapades. He loved the rustic charm of our home, the way the light flickered through the stained glass windows, casting colorful patterns that danced like fireflies across the walls. It was easy to forget about the chaos of the outside world when we were cocooned in our bubble, sharing pasta and stolen glances over candlelight.

But Leah was a tempest. Each time she entered my life, it was like inviting a whirlwind to tea, stirring up emotions I had thought buried. Her spirit was infectious, her laughter a clarion call that could cut through the soft murmur of my new reality. I could imagine her voice echoing in my mind, a potent mix of excitement and spontaneity that both thrilled and terrified me. Did I want to rekindle that vibrant chaos tonight, at the expense of the peace I was beginning to cherish with Jake?

With my heart pounding in my chest, I let the phone slip from my fingers, its potential rejection landing softly on the counter. It could wait. I could feel the warmth radiating from the kitchen, a gentle reminder of the love I was nurturing here. Leaning against the counter, I let the weight of my choices settle around me, swirling like autumn leaves in a brisk wind. I could forge ahead into the unknown or hunker down in the security of the familiar.

The kettle whistled in the distance, piercing the silence and anchoring me further in the moment. I moved to pour a cup of tea, the steam curling upward like soft whispers, comforting in their familiarity. As I cradled the warm mug in my hands, I recalled the times Jake and I had shared simple pleasures. We had explored the cobblestone streets of our little town, walking hand in hand, while the world blurred into a colorful backdrop.

Each sip of tea felt like a hug, warming me from the inside out. I closed my eyes, picturing Jake's laughter mingling with the clinking of our mugs, the way he would lean in closer, whispering some playful nonsense that made me giggle uncontrollably. There was a sweet intimacy in those moments, a budding connection that felt electric, raw, and genuine. I had longed for this simplicity, the kind that made life feel significant without demanding much at all.

But Leah's presence could throw all of that into disarray. The thought of her unexpected arrival and the chaos that would inevitably follow sent a shiver down my spine. I envisioned her breezy confidence taking over our carefully curated space, her laughter drowning out the subtle rhythms we had created together. Did I want to trade the tender, heartfelt moments with Jake for the uncertainty of Leah's world? It felt like a choice between a cozy fireplace and a raging bonfire—both warm but one much more manageable than the other.

I returned to the counter and turned my phone over, the notification still glowing, the text waiting like an impatient child. With a small sigh, I sat back down, letting the warmth of the mug seep into my palms. I envisioned Jake's understanding eyes, the way he looked at me with that blend of admiration and curiosity. I could feel the edges of my anxiety begin to soften at the mere thought of him. He was my anchor in this storm of choices, the steady current in a sea of indecision.

As I took another sip of tea, a wave of determination washed over me. I could invite Leah into our lives on my own terms. I didn't have to dive headfirst into the chaos; I could navigate it, ensuring that my connection with Jake remained intact. I could handle the storm while still cherishing the peace I had found. Perhaps this was the growth I had been seeking—the ability to assert myself in relationships without losing sight of what mattered most.

With a newfound clarity, I picked up my phone, the screen shining brightly under the warm light. I hesitated only briefly before typing out a response, careful to balance honesty with tact. I knew I had to confront the dynamics of my friendship with Leah without letting it overshadow the magic Jake and I were creating.

I set the phone down, a weight lifted from my shoulders. As I stepped back into the kitchen, the flickering light cast playful shadows on the walls, almost as if celebrating my decision. I turned my attention to the dinner preparations, the clinking of dishes a symphony against the backdrop of my thoughts. I began to hum softly, a familiar tune drifting through the air, as I poured the pasta into a bowl and arranged it with care. The clatter of utensils seemed to echo my heartbeat, each thud affirming my resolve.

I could already imagine the conversation that would unfold, the banter and the laughter, the warmth of companionship mingling with the tantalizing aromas that filled the kitchen. I was ready to embrace both worlds, to navigate the delicate balance between friendship and romance, chaos and calm.

As the door creaked open, I heard Jake's footsteps echoing in the hallway, a melody of comfort and familiarity. I turned, ready to embrace the evening, knowing that whatever happened, I would stand firm in my choices, navigating the tangled web of relationships with grace and love.

The moment Jake stepped through the door, the world outside seemed to fade away, leaving only the warmth of his smile and the familiarity of our shared space. He was a burst of sunshine on an otherwise gray day, his presence illuminating the corners of The Willow that I had grown to cherish. With tousled hair and a playful glint in his eyes, he stepped closer, the soft fragrance of cedar and fresh linen trailing behind him, mingling perfectly with the aroma of the pasta simmering on the stove. My heart swelled as I took in the sight of him, the embodiment of everything I wanted and needed at that moment.

"Hey there, chef," he said, leaning against the counter, arms crossed casually as he surveyed the kitchen with an appreciative grin. "What's on the menu tonight? It smells incredible."

I beamed, reveling in the way he made me feel—like the center of the universe, if only for a fleeting moment. "Just a little something to warm the soul," I replied, a teasing lilt in my voice. "Nothing too fancy, but it's definitely better than the takeout you always suggest."

He chuckled, the sound deep and rich, reverberating through the air like a comfortable melody. "What can I say? I have an adventurous palate, even if it leans heavily on the side of convenience." He stepped closer, reaching for the steaming bowl of pasta, and I instinctively pulled it back, feigning offense.

"Oh, so you're saying my culinary skills aren't adventurous enough?" I shot back, pretending to pout, the laughter bubbling up inside me. His teasing was a playful dance, one I had come to look forward to, an unspoken language woven between us that held more weight than words alone.

"No, no! I would never imply that," he replied, raising his hands in mock surrender. "You could make a Michelin star meal and I'd still find a way to suggest pizza."

We fell into an easy rhythm as we moved around the kitchen, each of us gravitating toward the tasks that felt natural. I found myself stealing glances at him, his easy smile a balm to my fraying nerves. The phone buzzed again on the counter, a stark reminder of the tempest brewing just beyond our cozy cocoon. I thought of Leah's invitation, the tantalizing chaos she represented, and struggled to keep my thoughts focused on the man before me.

As I set the table, I could feel the weight of my decision looming like a shadow, yet Jake's laughter filled the room, distracting me from my worries. We talked effortlessly, the conversation flowing like the wine I poured into our glasses, rich and full-bodied. Every shared joke, every knowing glance reminded me of how right it felt to be here, nurturing something beautiful that had the potential to flourish.

Jake leaned back in his chair, his expression turning thoughtful as he took a sip of wine. "You know, I've been thinking," he began, his tone shifting into a more serious cadence. "About how important it is to surround ourselves with the right people. The ones who lift us up, not pull us down."

I held my breath, feeling the subtle tremor of anticipation. He was dipping into waters that felt too close to the shoreline of my anxiety. "What do you mean?" I asked, feigning casualness, though I was acutely aware of the storm cloud brewing behind my own eyes.

He shrugged, but the intensity in his gaze didn't waver. "Just that sometimes we have to make tough choices about who we allow into our lives. It's easy to get swept up in the excitement of friendships that might not be good for us. You know?"

I nodded slowly, the words wrapping around me like a warm embrace, yet leaving an unsettling chill at my core. "Yeah, I get that," I said, aware of the implications lingering beneath the surface of his casual observation. "Sometimes it's hard to let go of people, even if they're not the best for us."

He leaned in, his voice low and sincere. "I just want you to know that whatever choice you make, I'm here for you. You don't have to navigate this alone." The sincerity in his eyes melted the heaviness in my chest, offering a flicker of hope amidst the turmoil.

I felt my defenses begin to crumble, a wave of gratitude washing over me. Jake's support was the anchor I desperately needed, grounding me amidst the uncertainty. And yet, the phone buzzed again, breaking through the moment with a jarring reminder of the outside world. I glanced at the screen, half-expecting Leah's name to light up once more, but this time it was just a message from a friend, innocuous and mundane.

Jake, noticing my distraction, raised an eyebrow. "You okay?" he asked, concern etched across his handsome features.

"Just a text," I replied, dismissing it with a wave of my hand. "Nothing important." But deep down, I knew the truth: the battle within me was far from over. It was a delicate dance of balancing my history with Leah against the tender threads of my burgeoning relationship with Jake.

With the tension still thick in the air, I decided it was time to confront the issue head-on. "You mentioned surrounding ourselves with the right people," I started, my voice steadier than I felt. "What do you think about Leah?"

Jake's expression shifted slightly, a flicker of something—recognition, perhaps—crossing his features. "Leah? She's... well, she's a force, isn't she?" He leaned back, his gaze thoughtful. "I can see why you're conflicted. She's charismatic and fun, but I also see how her energy can sometimes overshadow things. You have to decide what's more important to you."

His words hung in the air, heavy with unspoken implications. "And what if I'm not sure?" I whispered, the vulnerability slipping through the cracks I had so carefully sealed.

He reached across the table, his fingers brushing mine, a spark igniting in the contact. "Then you take your time. No rush. Just remember, it's your life, your happiness. You deserve to choose what brings you joy."

The sincerity in his words filled the room with a warmth that chased away the last remnants of doubt. I could feel the knot in my stomach begin to loosen, a gentle reminder that navigating the complexities of relationships didn't have to be an isolating journey. With Jake by my side, I could explore the possibilities without losing sight of myself.

As we finished dinner, laughter echoing through the cozy confines of The Willow, I felt a renewed sense of clarity settle over me. The phone buzzed one last time, but this time, I didn't look. I was here, in this moment, savoring every shared glance, every soft smile that spoke volumes. Leah could wait. The choices before me, daunting as they were, no longer felt insurmountable.

In this sacred space, with Jake's warm gaze locked onto mine, I knew I could embrace whatever came next—both the chaos and the calm—fully aware that I was not alone in this journey. The evening wore on, each moment a precious thread weaving the tapestry of our lives, rich with complexity yet beautifully simple. The world outside could do its worst; inside, I was finally learning to dance to my own rhythm.

Chapter 19: Under the Stars

The evening air carried a subtle chill, just enough to tease the edges of my consciousness, reminding me that autumn was well on its way. As I stepped into Leah's backyard, I was greeted by a scene that felt almost like a page ripped from a magazine dedicated to idyllic small-town life. String lights hung like fireflies suspended in midair, casting a warm glow over the gathering, illuminating smiling faces and echoing laughter. I could smell the sweet aroma of grilled vegetables and the unmistakable sizzle of burgers on the barbecue, mingling with the fresh scent of grass and the faintest hint of smoke curling lazily from a fire pit in the corner. It was a picturesque setting, designed to soothe the heart and warm the soul. But all I felt was a tightness in my chest, an unwelcome reminder that not every beauty was without its shadows.

Leah stood at the center of it all, radiating warmth as she juggled drinks and snacks with an effortless charm that made her the perfect hostess. Her laughter bubbled up, clear and melodic, as she chatted with friends, effortlessly weaving in and out of conversations. I wanted to be pulled into that joyous flow, to feel the same lightness that seemed to buoy everyone else around me. Instead, I felt anchored to the ground, burdened by the weight of unsaid words and unacknowledged feelings swirling in the pit of my stomach.

Among the crowd, I spotted Jake, and my heart performed an odd little dance at the sight of him. He stood across the yard, leaning against the railing with his hands shoved deep into the pockets of his jeans, his head tilted back in laughter as Leah animatedly recounted a story. His tousled hair caught the light, framing his face in a halo of soft warmth, while his eyes sparkled with a mix of mischief and sincerity. There was something inherently captivating about him, something that made the world fade into the background whenever he smiled. My fingers fidgeted with the hem of my shirt, and I felt a blush creep up my neck, as though I were caught in a private moment, an unseen observer in a play that was not mine to direct.

It had always been this way with Jake—a strange gravitational pull that both exhilarated and terrified me. He was the embodiment of everything I found appealing yet unattainable. I wanted to stride over and join the lively conversation, to throw myself into the warmth of their camaraderie, yet I remained frozen in place, battling the fear that had crept in like a thief in the night, ready to snatch away any semblance of normalcy.

In this little bubble of friendship, the laughter swirled around me like a gentle wind, taunting my unease. I felt like an outsider looking in, as though the more I tried to fit into this idyllic scene, the more I was reminded of the storm brewing within me. The stars above twinkled with an almost mocking brilliance, their beauty juxtaposed against the turmoil roiling in my heart. They seemed to whisper secrets of the universe, urging me to unearth the truth that lay buried beneath layers of uncertainty.

As the evening deepened, the conversation flowed effortlessly, moving from mundane topics to the deeper currents of dreams and aspirations. I listened to the ebb and flow, watching as Leah leaned in closer to Jake, their laughter entwining like the strands of fairy lights overhead. A pang of longing surged through me, an ache so profound I almost couldn't breathe. I wanted to share in their joy, to be part of the light they created, yet the shadows of doubt and hesitation loomed large. Would my presence be welcomed, or would it disrupt the delicate balance of this perfect gathering?

Leah caught my eye, and for a fleeting moment, her expression shifted from mirth to concern. She raised her glass in a silent toast, urging me to join them, to cast aside my worries and embrace the moment. I smiled back, trying to convey my gratitude and uncertainty in a single gesture. The smile felt like a fragile mask, one that could shatter at the slightest tremor. I took a deep breath, summoning every ounce of courage I had, and moved toward them, the weight of hesitation still clinging to me like a heavy cloak.

As I approached, I was enveloped in the familiar warmth of their conversation. "You finally made it!" Jake exclaimed, his voice a rich baritone that vibrated through me like a gentle wave. "We were just talking about the best camping spots in the area. You know, the ones where the stars look like they're painted across the sky?" His eyes shone with a fervor that sent a shiver of excitement coursing through my veins.

"Yes! I love camping!" I replied, injecting as much enthusiasm into my voice as I could muster. My heart raced, propelled by the adrenaline of stepping into the light. As we chatted, the laughter flowed freely, and for a moment, the doubts that clung to me began to melt away like the ice in my drink.

But as the night deepened, I couldn't shake the feeling that the very air around me was charged with something unspoken. There was a current beneath the laughter, a tension that I couldn't quite identify, lurking just out of reach like a shadow slipping through the trees. The conversation danced around a familiar theme—friendship, love, and the complexities that came with them. I couldn't help but wonder where I fit into this tapestry woven from the threads of shared experiences and mutual admiration.

The stars above glittered like a promise, and in that moment, I felt the stirrings of hope. Maybe I was meant to be here, standing among friends, even if uncertainty loomed in the background. Maybe facing the unknown wasn't about banishing fear but rather embracing it as part of the journey. As I looked around at the faces illuminated by the gentle glow of the lights, I realized that sometimes, it's the very things that unsettle us that lead us to the greatest discoveries about ourselves and the world around us.

The chatter around me swelled and ebbed like a gentle tide, the warm light of the string bulbs flickering in time with the soft laughter that floated through the air. With each moment, I felt myself being pulled deeper into this swirling current of camaraderie, the tension in my chest easing, albeit reluctantly. Leah's energy was infectious, and it felt as though the very essence of her spirit wrapped around me like a comforting blanket, urging me to let go of the shadows.

Jake caught my eye again, his expression shifting as he noticed me standing slightly apart from the crowd. He raised an eyebrow, an amused smile playing on his lips, as if inviting me into a secret he was not yet ready to share. I felt the familiar blush creep up my neck, a traitorous heat that betrayed my composed facade. There was an unspoken understanding between us, an uncharted territory laden with both hope and fear, and as he turned his attention back to Leah, I found myself caught in the web of possibilities.

A particularly boisterous group of friends huddled around the fire pit, their faces illuminated by flickering flames that danced in the cool evening air. Stories were exchanged, embellished with the kind of zest that only late-night gatherings can inspire. I could hear snippets of laughter rising like smoke, each note mingling with the crackle of burning wood. The night felt alive, a vibrant tapestry woven from shared memories and burgeoning aspirations, yet I felt like a thread pulled too tightly, on the verge of snapping.

I wandered toward the fire, drawn by its warmth and the radiant glow that made everyone's faces seem like they were painted with gold. I settled onto a nearby log, the rough bark scratching against my legs, grounding me in the moment. I listened as a friend recounted a tale of their disastrous camping trip—tent poles that refused to stay upright and a raccoon that had expertly snatched away their snacks. The hilarity of the mishap sent ripples of laughter through the group, and for a fleeting second, I felt a part of it all, a contributor to this lively discourse.

Yet, even amidst the laughter, my gaze kept wandering back to Jake. His presence was magnetic, and despite the distance, it was as though an invisible thread tethered us together, pulsing with the electric tension of unexpressed feelings. Leah leaned closer to him, and I felt a pang of something sharp, something like jealousy mixed with longing. I wondered if they had shared moments like this before, creating a secret language with their laughter, and whether I was merely an intruder in their world.

As the evening wore on, the laughter grew softer, the stories winding down as the stars above twinkled like distant guardians of our secrets. A cool breeze swept through the backyard, rustling the leaves and carrying with it a hint of nostalgia. I wrapped my arms around myself, as if trying to capture the warmth that was slowly ebbing away, leaving behind a chill that burrowed deep into my bones.

"Hey, you!" Leah's voice broke through my reverie, a cheerful beacon cutting through my introspection. "Come over here! We're playing a game!" She waved me over, and I couldn't help but grin at her enthusiasm, even as my heart raced at the prospect of joining in. I hopped off the log, shaking off the remnants of my earlier thoughts, and made my way toward the group.

The game turned out to be a raucous rendition of "Never Have I Ever," and as the statements bounced from one person to the next, the air crackled with revelations and laughter. Each confession was met with cheers or teasing laughter, a collective sharing that felt like peeling away layers of pretense. As I took my turn, my heart thumped in my chest, both excited and nervous to share a piece of myself with this vibrant crowd.

"Never have I ever..." I began, glancing around the circle, "gotten lost in a grocery store." The laughter that erupted felt like a balm, easing my nerves. Hands shot up, and I couldn't help but chuckle at the shared absurdity of our childhood escapades. Each turn unveiled another layer of our personalities, connecting us in ways I hadn't anticipated.

When it was Jake's turn, I felt the air shift, an electric buzz that seemed to pass through everyone present. He leaned forward, a glimmer of mischief in his eye. "Never have I ever... confessed to someone I liked them." The group erupted into laughter, but my stomach twisted in knots, and I felt the world tilt slightly on its axis. The truth of his statement lingered in the air, thick with unspoken implications.

Leah, quick-witted as ever, elbowed Jake playfully. "Well, that's a little too vague, don't you think?" She shot him a teasing smile, and the conversation flowed on, yet I couldn't shake the weight of his words. I felt the blush creep back into my cheeks, an unwelcome reminder of my own uncertainty, a stark contrast to the playful banter that surrounded me.

The game continued, and as the night deepened, I found solace in the laughter of my friends, even as my thoughts drifted toward the space between Jake and me. I could sense a shift in the atmosphere, a subtle undercurrent that whispered of unacknowledged feelings swirling just beneath the surface, waiting for the right moment to burst forth.

As the final round wrapped up, I caught Jake's eye across the flickering firelight. There was something there, a spark of understanding that seemed to transcend words, a silent acknowledgment of our shared tension. The space between us felt charged, a thin veil of possibility ready to be pierced. I held my breath, waiting for him to break the distance, to say something that would untangle the knots in my heart.

But before he could, Leah bounded over, her face flushed with excitement. "Who wants s'mores?" she exclaimed, breaking the spell. The moment evaporated, slipping through my fingers like sand, and I couldn't help but wonder if I'd ever have the courage to voice the thoughts dancing on the tip of my tongue. As the sweet scent of roasting marshmallows filled the air, I reminded myself that sometimes, the most profound connections begin in the quietest moments—those fleeting, fragile sparks that flicker under the stars, waiting for a chance to ignite.

The air grew richer with the scent of melting chocolate and toasted marshmallows, creating an olfactory symphony that beckoned me back into the present. Leah's enthusiasm was contagious as she orchestrated the chaos around the fire pit, urging everyone to gather closer. The flames flickered with a playful intensity, casting long shadows that danced across the grass, illuminating the faces of my friends in a warm embrace.

With a wooden skewer in hand, I expertly pierced a marshmallow, watching it swell and turn golden brown under the careful gaze of the fire. I let myself sink into the simplicity of the moment—the laughter, the warmth, the camaraderie—each element a reminder of why I had come. Yet, even as I joined the fun, a part of me remained acutely aware of Jake's lingering presence. I could feel him watching, his eyes a quiet anchor that both steadied and unsettled me.

"Who's brave enough to make the biggest s'more?" Leah declared, her voice ringing with mischief, and the challenge electrified the air. Hands shot up eagerly, ready to construct culinary masterpieces that could rival the towering buildings in the city skyline. I grinned, buoyed by the collective excitement, but my heart raced with the underlying tension that seemed to thrum in my veins.

As I built my s'more, layering chocolate, marshmallow, and graham crackers with exaggerated care, I couldn't shake the sense that every moment was a delicate balancing act. The night felt charged with the weight of unsaid words, of emotions tucked away like the marshmallows in their bag. I could almost hear the unspoken conversations swirling between us, a symphony of what-ifs and maybes that echoed through the laughter.

Finally, with a triumphant flourish, I presented my creation—a towering monstrosity that seemed to defy the laws of physics. "Behold!" I proclaimed, eliciting cheers and laughter from the group. The playful spirit of competition wrapped around us like a cozy blanket, and for the briefest moment, I allowed myself to forget the tension that lurked just beneath the surface.

Jake stepped forward, a mischievous glint in his eye. "I think I can do better," he challenged, and as he began constructing his own towering s'more, I couldn't help but admire his confidence. He expertly balanced the ingredients, his fingers deft and sure, and I found myself mesmerized by the way he moved—fluid and focused, as if the world around us had faded into a soft blur.

Our eyes met for a heartbeat, and in that fleeting moment, I felt an electric connection, a pull that set my skin alight. It was a glance heavy with the weight of unspoken words, of emotions that had lingered just out of reach, and I was certain he felt it too. The laughter around us faded into a gentle murmur, the night feeling infinitely vast, the stars bearing witness to our tentative connection.

The laughter returned as Leah declared a winner, but the moment lingered like a half-remembered dream, just out of reach. As we devoured our creations, the sticky sweetness clinging to my fingers and mouth, I caught glimpses of Jake joining in the revelry, sharing stories and laughter with our friends. I watched him, my heart thrumming to an unsteady beat, wondering if the night would culminate in some form of revelation or remain a beautiful, ephemeral memory wrapped in layers of uncertainty.

As the laughter died down and the remnants of our feast were cleared away, the group began to drift, some retreating to the cozy confines of the house, while others settled back around the fire, letting the warmth seep into their bones. I lingered, lost in thought, watching the embers float into the night sky like tiny wishes escaping into the universe.

Suddenly, I found myself standing shoulder to shoulder with Jake as he reclined against the railing, the golden light of the fire casting soft shadows on his face. The space between us felt charged with anticipation, each heartbeat echoing with possibilities. The air was thick with the scent of smoke and sweetness, and I was acutely aware of the warmth radiating from him, a gentle heat that pulled me closer.

"Can I ask you something?" Jake's voice broke through the stillness, rich and inviting, and I nodded, my heart pounding in my chest. The night seemed to hold its breath, as if the world had shrunk down to just the two of us, the cacophony of voices fading into the background.

"Why do you seem so distant tonight?" His gaze was steady, penetrating, and I felt exposed, stripped of the layers I had carefully wrapped around myself. I hesitated, searching for the right words that could capture the maelstrom of thoughts swirling inside my head. "It's not that I'm distant," I finally admitted, "I'm just... unsure."

"Unsure about what?" He leaned in closer, his expression softening as if he truly wanted to understand. The moment felt monumental, as though we were standing on the precipice of something transformative.

"About everything," I confessed, my voice barely above a whisper. "About us, about what it means to put myself out there. I feel like I'm balancing on this tightrope, and one wrong move could send me tumbling." My words poured out like a dam had broken, the truths I had hidden from myself cascading into the open air.

Jake studied me for a long moment, his gaze unwavering. "You're not alone in that, you know," he said, his voice low and steady. "We all have our insecurities, our fears. I've been feeling the same way. But maybe we don't have to walk this path alone."

His words wrapped around me like a gentle embrace, soothing the frayed edges of my uncertainty. For the first time, I felt seen, understood—not just as a friend but as someone worth taking a chance on. The idea of not being alone, of sharing the weight of our fears, ignited a flicker of hope within me, warming the corners of my heart that had grown cold with doubt.

Just then, a few friends burst into laughter, their voices bright and carefree, momentarily breaking the spell between us. I glanced toward them, laughter spilling from my lips as I watched Leah trip over a fallen branch, her exuberance drawing everyone in. But when I turned back to Jake, I noticed something different in his expression—an earnestness that made my pulse quicken.

"I've been wanting to say something," he began, his voice hushed, laden with sincerity. "I think there's something real between us, something worth exploring. I know it's scary, and I don't want to rush anything, but I can't shake the feeling that we're meant to figure this out together."

The words hung in the air, suspended in the stillness of the night, and I felt a rush of emotion surge within me—fear, excitement, vulnerability all tangled together. I opened my mouth to respond, my heart pounding as the reality of what he was saying settled in.

Before I could speak, the stars above blinked, and for a moment, the world felt impossibly bright, as if the universe were affirming his words. My heart swelled, each beat a whisper of courage urging me to take a leap of faith. The tightrope didn't seem so daunting anymore; perhaps it was just a path waiting to be walked, together.

With that thought lighting a fire in my chest, I took a step forward, letting the warmth of his gaze envelop me as I prepared to embrace the unknown. The night stretched ahead, filled with infinite possibilities and the promise of new beginnings, waiting patiently for us to uncover them, one cautious step at a time.

Chapter 20: Heartstrings

The sun spills through the café windows, drenching the wood-paneled interior of The Willow in a warm golden hue, dancing over the mismatched chairs and the freshly polished tables. The familiar scent of coffee, rich and earthy, swirls around me, enveloping my senses like a soft embrace. It feels like home, this place, where the chatter of regulars and the occasional clink of cups create a comforting symphony. I breathe in deeply, grounding myself, but the echoes of last night's gathering cling to me like the remnants of a dream, sweet yet suffocating.

As I rearrange the layout, moving a potted fern from one corner to another, I can't help but think about Jake. His laughter had rolled through the air, a melody that seemed to play just for me, even amid the joyful chaos of friends. But then there was Leah, her presence a vivid burst of color, effortlessly drawing attention with her vivacious spirit. I had watched the two of them share stories, their eyes glimmering with a spark that made my heart lurch, both thrilling and painful. I shove the feeling down as I shift the coffee station slightly to the left, willing my heart to follow suit.

The bell above the door jingles, drawing my attention. In walks Jake, a vision in a faded denim jacket that hints at countless adventures and a white T-shirt that clings just right. His hair is tousled, as if he's just rolled out of bed, and his smile—oh, that smile—carries a warmth that could melt even the frostiest of mornings. I greet him, trying to sound nonchalant, but the flutter in my stomach betrays my excitement.

"Hey, you," he says, sliding onto a stool at the counter. "I thought I'd come by and see how my favorite barista is holding up."

The warmth of his gaze steadies my racing heart, and I lean against the counter, resisting the urge to fidget with my apron. "Just trying to make sense of this chaotic little corner of the world. You know how it is." I attempt to inject lightness into my tone, but the weight of last night hovers over us like a cloud.

He nods, taking a sip of the dark roast I've just brewed, and the rich aroma wafts around us. "Perfect as always." There's an ease to our banter, a rhythm built over countless conversations, but today, there's an underlying tension I can't ignore. The moment hangs in the air, thick with unsaid words, so I plunge ahead, heart pounding in my chest. "So, about last night... Did you have fun?"

His gaze drops to the half-full mug in front of him, and the silence stretches uncomfortably. "Yeah, it was good. Just a friendly gathering," he replies, but there's a hint of uncertainty lacing his words, as if he's searching for the right thing to say and coming up short.

I hold my breath, biting my lip as I feel my heart begin to race. "Just friends, huh? I couldn't help but notice you and Leah seemed to have a moment." My voice is steadier than I feel, though a tremor dances beneath the surface.

He meets my gaze, his brow furrowing. "Leah's great, but it's nothing like that." There's a sincerity in his tone, but the fire in my chest stokes itself with each word. I want to believe him, but the image of them laughing together, leaning closer, lingers stubbornly in my mind.

I lean in, lowering my voice, "Then what was that spark? Because it felt... charged, you know?" The vulnerability in my tone surprises even me, but I push through, desperate for clarity.

Jake rubs the back of his neck, a habit I've come to recognize as a sign of his own discomfort. "Honestly? I think she likes me. I mean, who wouldn't? But I don't see her like that. Not really. You know me, right? I'm not the guy to jump into something like that." His eyes meet mine, a flicker of something deeper hiding beneath the surface.

Relief floods through me, warming the chill of doubt. Yet, something still gnaws at me. "You don't see her as more than a friend?" I ask, tilting my head, trying to read the depths of his expression.

"Not like that," he insists, leaning forward, his voice dropping to a conspiratorial whisper. "It's you I think about. You're the one I want to hang out with, the one who makes me laugh."

His admission feels like a beacon of light cutting through my uncertainty, illuminating the shadows that have loomed over my thoughts. The air between us crackles with something electric, a tension both thrilling and terrifying. I can't help but smile, a warmth spreading through my chest. "You mean it?"

Jake nods, and the sincerity in his gaze makes my heart skip. "Absolutely. We have a connection, and I'm not just saying that to make you feel better."

We share a moment, the café bustling around us fading into the background, a cocoon of warmth enveloping us. But as the seconds stretch on, the moment begins to shift, and the questions I've been suppressing start to push their way to the forefront. "So, what does that mean for us?" I ask, the vulnerability in my voice hanging between us like a fragile thread.

He leans back, contemplating, and I feel the weight of his thoughts pressing against me. "I think we should explore it. I mean, if you're open to it. It's just..." he trails off, a flash of uncertainty flickering in his eyes. "There's always the risk, right? What if it doesn't work?"

I can't help but chuckle softly, the absurdity of the situation lightening my heart. "Oh, believe me, I know all about risks. My life feels like a tightrope walk half the time."

Jake's laugh breaks through the tension, and the sound is like a balm to my frayed nerves. "Exactly. But maybe we could be each other's safety net."

The thought ignites a spark of hope, and for the first time that morning, I allow myself to envision a future colored by possibilities.

I lean in closer, wanting to absorb every detail—the warmth of his skin, the faint hint of sandalwood in his cologne, and the way his laughter can weave through my soul like music.

Our eyes lock, and in that shared gaze, I sense the potential for something beautiful blooming amidst the uncertainty. Perhaps it was time to embrace the chaos, to leap, knowing that sometimes the net appears only when we take the plunge.

The sunlight streams through the windows of The Willow, illuminating the small café like a scene from a sun-drenched painting, each ray highlighting the gentle dust motes swirling in the air. The sounds of clinking cups and low conversations create a comforting background hum, but my thoughts swirl in chaotic patterns, tethered to Jake and the unexpected warmth of our conversation. There's an undeniable thrill in the air, a fragile connection that has begun to weave itself between us like the intricate latticework of an old fence, both charming and precarious.

As the day unfolds, the scent of freshly baked pastries fills the café, beckoning customers inside. My fingers dance over the espresso machine, each movement becoming more fluid, more instinctual, as I lose myself in the rhythm of the moment. The hum of the frothing milk, the rich aroma of ground coffee beans, and the familiar banter with regulars help to anchor my racing thoughts. Yet, even amid the comforting chaos, Jake's words resonate like a melody, teasing the corners of my mind.

Lunchtime arrives with a burst of activity, patrons flowing in and out like a tide, their laughter mixing with the clatter of dishes. Just as I begin to feel overwhelmed by the influx, I spot Jake again, his silhouette framed in the doorway, a beacon amid the bustling crowd. He walks in with a casual grace, his presence instantly grounding.

"Need an extra hand?" he asks, his playful smile disarming, as he leans against the counter, glancing at the chaos around us.

I chuckle, grateful for the distraction he offers. "It would help, but I might just put you to work behind the bar."

"Sounds like a deal. Just don't let me burn anything." He rolls up his sleeves, and I can't help but admire how effortlessly he transforms into a partner in this little world of ours. Together, we navigate the lunch rush, serving lattes and pastries, the conversation flowing as easily as the espresso shots we pull.

With every shared laugh and banter, the tension from earlier begins to dissipate. I feel lighter, the weight of uncertainty lifting like fog under the sun. Yet, the undercurrent of our earlier discussion still hums between us, sparking in the little glances we exchange when we think the other isn't looking. There's something electric in the air, a potential that vibrates like the strings of a guitar just waiting for the right hands to play it.

After the rush settles, we find a moment of reprieve in the small courtyard behind The Willow, a hidden gem lined with potted herbs and string lights that twinkle like stars. I lean against the cool brick wall, taking a deep breath as I let the peace of the moment wash over me. Jake joins me, the warmth of his presence radiating in the small space.

"You know," he begins, his voice low and thoughtful, "I was thinking about what you said earlier. About risks."

I look up at him, intrigued. "Oh? And what conclusion did you come to, oh wise one?" I tease, nudging him playfully.

He smirks, his eyes dancing with amusement. "Well, I realized that life is just a series of calculated risks, isn't it? We can stay comfortable, tucked away in our safe little boxes, or we can jump, not knowing if there's a safety net or not."

I nod, contemplating his words. The simplicity of his statement resonates deeply within me. "So, what's it going to be? Are we jumping or just talking about it?"

His expression shifts slightly, seriousness creeping in. "I think we should jump. Together."

There's a heaviness in his voice that makes my heart race. This isn't just playful banter anymore; it's a leap into the unknown, and the thought both thrills and terrifies me. "But what if we fall?" I ask, testing the waters of our newfound understanding.

He takes a step closer, the distance between us shrinking until I can feel the warmth radiating off him. "What if we soar?" he counters, his gaze steady and unwavering.

His words wrap around me, igniting a spark of courage I didn't know I possessed. It's intoxicating, this idea of leaping into something that feels so right, yet carries with it the potential for heartbreak. "Okay," I whisper, the decision hanging in the air like a promise, and the sound feels both monumental and terrifying.

A grin spreads across his face, brightening his features and making my heart flutter in response. "Okay," he echoes, as if sealing our pact.

As we linger in the moment, the world around us fades. The distant sounds of the café, the rustling leaves, the laughter of customers—all of it blurs into a soft background hum. It's just Jake and me, standing on the precipice of something new and exciting, the air crackling with possibilities.

"Let's not overthink this," he suggests, breaking the silence, his eyes sparkling with mischief. "How about we start with coffee? A real date, just us."

I can't help but laugh at the simple brilliance of his suggestion. "Coffee sounds perfect. But just so you know, I will judge you on your coffee order."

"Oh, bring it on!" he replies, throwing his hands up in mock surrender. "I'll have you know I'm a coffee aficionado."

We both dissolve into laughter, the lightness of the moment a stark contrast to the weight of our earlier conversation. There's an undeniable shift, a lightness settling over us as we transition from uncertainty to excitement, and I feel as if I'm floating, buoyed by this newfound connection.

As we make our way back inside, the anticipation of our first official outing sends a thrill through me, mingling with the warmth of the afternoon sun. I catch Jake glancing my way, a soft smile playing on his lips. In that brief moment, I see a glimpse of something deeper, a flicker of hope that perhaps this leap we're taking could lead us to a place where our hearts can soar together.

I'm not naive enough to believe that everything will be perfect; life rarely grants such luxury. But with Jake by my side, the uncertainty transforms into an exhilarating challenge, a dance between risk and reward that I'm eager to embrace. In that instant, the café, the customers, and even the world outside fade away, leaving just the two of us—two hearts ready to explore the beauty of what could be.

The days following that pivotal conversation with Jake drift into a soft blur, each moment threading together like the delicate lace curtains fluttering in the late afternoon breeze at The Willow. The café has become a sanctuary, a place where the world outside recedes into a gentle hum of distant traffic and laughter. I lose myself in the warmth of freshly baked scones and the aromatic pull of espresso, each day feeling like a new opportunity, a fresh start with Jake woven into its fabric.

As the sun climbs higher in the sky, casting a dappled light through the windows, I find myself taking more chances—testing the waters of what we've tentatively defined as "us." A week has passed since we agreed to explore this connection, and each shared glance between us feels charged, electric with possibility. Our playful banter flows freely, effortlessly, like the steam rising from the milk frother, and I often catch him looking at me with an intensity that sends ripples of excitement through my heart.

One particularly warm afternoon, we find ourselves alone in the café as the last of the lunchtime rush fades. The scent of vanilla and cinnamon lingers in the air, mixing with the sweet notes of fresh pastries. The soft music playing in the background enhances the cozy atmosphere, creating a perfect little bubble where nothing exists beyond these four walls. I wipe down the counter, my movements steady and rhythmic, when Jake leans over, resting his elbows against the polished wood, his expression playful.

"You know, I think you're trying to keep me away from the pastry case," he teases, pointing at the array of baked goods displayed behind the glass.

I raise an eyebrow, a smirk forming on my lips. "What? You think I'd deny you a chocolate croissant? Hardly. You just need to earn it first."

His eyes light up with mischief, and he straightens, feigning offense. "Earn it? Do you know how many times I've come here just to see you? I think I've paid my dues!"

"Oh really? And how much would you say that amounts to in croissants?" I challenge, leaning forward, the playful dance of our conversation igniting a warmth within me.

"A lot," he replies, matching my tone. "Let's say, an entire bakery's worth."

His laughter is infectious, and I can't help but join in, the tension from earlier in the week dissolving with each shared moment. The flirtation between us is unmistakable now, a delightful game that feels both thrilling and terrifying, as if we're tiptoeing along the edge of a cliff, peering down into the abyss of something wonderful, and yet so unknown.

As I finally relent and reach for a perfectly flaky chocolate croissant, handing it to him with a flourish, our hands brush. The contact sends a jolt through me, and for a fleeting second, I'm aware of the world slipping away, leaving just the two of us suspended in that moment. He takes a bite, closing his eyes in exaggerated bliss, and I watch him, utterly captivated.

"Mmm, worth every penny," he declares, voice muffled by pastry. I lean back against the counter, laughing, feeling the warmth in my cheeks, and the simple joy of the moment makes my heart swell.

"So, are we actually going to go on this coffee date, or are you just going to keep flirting with me behind the counter?" I ask, my tone teasing yet laced with genuine curiosity.

Jake wipes a crumb from his lips, leaning closer as if to share a secret. "I thought we were already on one. But if you want to make it official, I'm all for it."

The breath catches in my throat, and I nod slowly, excitement bubbling within me. "Okay, then. Let's make it official. Saturday? Breakfast?"

He grins, a genuine smile that crinkles the corners of his eyes, and I feel a rush of warmth that settles in my chest like a cozy blanket. "Saturday it is. Prepare yourself for the best pancakes of your life."

"Only if you're making them," I shoot back, feeling the playful edge of our conversation build the anticipation of the weekend.

As the week progresses, our banter transforms into something more profound, laced with glimpses of vulnerability that make my heart race. We exchange stories and dreams, our laughter often punctuated by moments of quiet reflection. Each conversation peels back layers, revealing the complexities of our lives, the challenges we've faced, and the hopes we hold dear.

Jake speaks of his passion for photography, sharing tales of capturing the world through his lens, how he finds beauty in the mundane—a raindrop on a petal, the shadow of a tree against a sunlit sidewalk. His words paint vivid pictures in my mind, allowing me to see the world through his eyes, and I'm captivated. I share my own dreams, my aspirations to expand The Willow's offerings, perhaps introducing art nights or music events.

The more we talk, the more I realize how much he understands me. There's an ease in our connection, a mutual understanding that makes me feel seen in a way I've never experienced before. By the time Saturday rolls around, anticipation buzzes in the air, making the morning feel electric.

The café is quieter than usual, the calm before the storm, and I use the time to prepare for my day with Jake. I dress carefully, selecting a sundress that flows around my knees, the fabric catching the light with every movement. I pair it with my favorite sandals, the kind that are comfortable yet cute, and take a moment to admire myself in the mirror, the reflection beaming back at me, a mixture of nerves and excitement.

When the clock ticks closer to our meeting time, I feel butterflies dance in my stomach. Each minute stretches like taffy, pulling out my anticipation. Finally, just as the sun begins to cast a warm glow over the city, I spot Jake approaching, his easy stride a familiar comfort. He looks effortlessly handsome, wearing a light blue button-down that complements his eyes and adds a splash of summer cheer.

"Hey there, gorgeous," he greets, a playful smirk on his lips as he takes in my outfit.

"Careful, flattery will get you everywhere," I reply, the playful banter already weaving us into a comfortable rhythm.

He laughs, his gaze lingering for a moment before he gestures toward a quaint breakfast spot across the street, a hidden gem known for its pancake stack that rivals the height of a small building. "Shall we? I'm starving."

We walk side by side, the chatter of the city swirling around us, blending into a symphony of life that feels rich and vibrant. As we approach the restaurant, I steal a glance at Jake, who seems to radiate an infectious enthusiasm that brightens even the sunniest of days.

We settle into a small booth, the kind with plush cushions that make you feel like you're enveloped in a warm hug. The menu is filled with mouthwatering options, and as we peruse it, I steal sideways glances at him, reveling in the way his brow furrows in concentration.

"I think I'll go for the lemon ricotta pancakes," I declare, finally settling on a choice, my taste buds already tingling at the thought.

"Bold choice," he replies, his eyes sparkling with delight. "I'm sticking with the classic buttermilk. You can't go wrong with the classics."

As our order is placed, our conversation flows effortlessly, shifting from playful teasing to more profound topics—our families, our dreams, and what we hope to achieve in the future. I find myself revealing pieces of my past, the struggles I've faced, and how they've shaped who I am today.

In return, Jake shares stories of his childhood, the pressures of pursuing his passion in a world that often values security over creativity. His openness captivates me, weaving a tapestry of trust between us that feels both rare and precious. I admire his tenacity, the way he pursues his dreams with unyielding determination, and it ignites a fire within me to chase my own ambitions with equal fervor.

The pancakes arrive in a glorious stack, drizzled with syrup that glistens like liquid gold. We dive into our meals, the flavors dancing on our tongues, and as we share bites and laughter, I can't help but marvel at how natural this all feels. Each bite pulls me deeper into this moment, and I relish the way he looks at me when I laugh, his gaze filled with something profound, something that goes beyond mere attraction.

"Okay, I have to ask," he says between bites, his expression turning serious yet playful. "On a scale from one to ten, how would you rate these pancakes?"

I pause dramatically, contemplating my response as if it were a weighty decision. "I'd say... a solid ten. They're fluffy enough to float away, and the lemon ricotta is a game changer."

He grins, and I catch a glimpse of mischief in his eyes. "Good to know. I'll hold you to that. If you ever open a pancake place, I expect you to include these."

"Oh, you know it. I'll call it 'Willow's Wonder Pancakes' or something equally cheesy."

His laughter fills the space, a melodic sound that wraps around me like a warm blanket. "I'd dine there every weekend. Just don't make me a waiter—I'll burn the pancakes."

As the meal winds down, we find ourselves drifting toward more serious topics, discussing the complexities of relationships, the intricacies of love, and the risks we take when we allow ourselves to feel. Each moment spent together feels charged, and I can't shake the sensation that something beautiful is unfolding between us, a tapestry being woven from our shared laughter and heartfelt conversations

Chapter 21: Cracks in the Armor

The sun hung low in the sky, casting a warm golden hue across the living room as I paced the hardwood floor, my mind racing. The scent of fresh coffee lingered in the air, mingling with the faint, briny hints of the ocean that teased from the open window. Jake was silent on the couch, a deep furrow etched across his brow, the weight of unspoken thoughts pressing heavily against the casual ambiance of our home. It was a Saturday, a day meant for relaxation, but the tension between us felt palpable, a thick fog that muted the usual sounds of laughter and lighthearted banter.

I paused, stealing a glance at him, his fingers splayed across his knees as if they were anchoring him to the earth. The way he stared into the distance, his eyes clouded and far away, made my heart twist. I reached for his hand, but he flinched slightly, a subtle withdrawal that spoke louder than words. My pulse quickened, not from anger but a profound concern. I wondered how it had come to this, how the man I adored could seem so far away, trapped behind an invisible barrier he constructed around himself.

"Jake," I said softly, the name slipping from my lips like a prayer. "What are you thinking about?"

He turned to me slowly, as if my voice had pulled him from a dream, and for a fleeting moment, I saw a flicker of something—vulnerability, perhaps. But just as quickly, it vanished behind the familiar mask he wore so well.

"I'm fine," he replied, his voice a gravelly whisper, devoid of conviction. I knew better than to accept that simple dismissal; we had shared too much of our lives to pretend otherwise.

It was in these moments, when his walls seemed impenetrable, that I felt most alive, a sense of purpose igniting within me. I refused to let him drown in silence. "Let's go to the beach," I proposed, my voice laced with an excitement I hoped would be contagious. "A weekend away, just us. Fresh air, the sound of the waves... It could be good for us."

He shifted slightly, the weight of my suggestion clearly settling in. I watched as a fleeting guilt crossed his features, a telltale sign that he wasn't entirely on board with the idea. But there was something in the way he hesitated that suggested he was more afraid of the shore than of the ocean itself.

"I don't know, it's a lot of driving," he replied, his tone careful, each word a cautious step away from commitment. But I pressed on, my heart racing as I envisioned our feet buried in the sand, laughter filling the spaces between us, erasing the misunderstandings that hung in the air like storm clouds.

"Come on, it'll be fun! Just imagine it—waking up to the sound of waves crashing outside our window, the salty breeze ruffling the curtains. We can walk along the shore at sunset, just like we used to."

There was a flicker in his eyes, a momentary spark of memory as he recalled those carefree days. I could almost see the wheels turning in his mind, the nostalgia mixing with his internal conflict, battling for supremacy. "I guess... I could use a break," he conceded, his voice softer now, almost hesitant.

I felt a rush of triumph, a tide of hope that surged through me, threatening to wash away the doubts that had settled like sand in my heart. But I couldn't shake the feeling that his compliance was just that—an agreement made out of obligation rather than desire.

The drive the next morning was filled with a palpable tension, the silence between us punctuated only by the rhythmic hum of the tires against the asphalt. I stole glances at Jake, studying the contours of his face, the way his jaw tightened every time he turned his gaze toward the passing scenery. We drove through towns that wore their history like a badge—dilapidated motels with faded neon signs, diners where time stood still, and sprawling fields that rippled like a green sea under the morning sun.

A PLACE TO BELONG

As we crossed over into the coastal town, the air changed—tinged with salt and freedom, bursting with the promise of adventure. I could almost taste it, a zest that sparked excitement in my veins. But beside me, Jake remained a stone statue, his mind clearly elsewhere.

Arriving at the beach, I felt a rush of exhilaration. The sprawling shoreline beckoned, a vast canvas painted with shades of blue and gold. I jumped out of the car, inhaling deeply, allowing the salty air to fill my lungs. This was what we needed—a respite from the world, a moment to rediscover each other beneath the expansive sky.

"Let's go," I urged, grabbing his hand with a fervor that belied my earlier doubts. His fingers felt stiff against mine, but I tugged him forward, leading him to the shore.

The sand was warm beneath my feet, a comforting embrace, and I let out a laugh, a sound that echoed across the beach. I glanced back at Jake, whose lips quirked into a reluctant smile, but his eyes remained clouded, shrouded in an unshakeable weight.

As I danced toward the water, I turned to see him standing a few paces behind, a giant among sandcastles, his shadow stretching long against the setting sun. It was as if the ocean itself was trying to call him back, to pull him into its depths, but I refused to let him remain anchored in his doubts.

"Come on!" I called out, my voice bright against the backdrop of crashing waves. "The water is perfect!"

He hesitated for a moment longer, and just when I thought he would retreat into his shell, he took a step forward, his eyes finally meeting mine with a flicker of something akin to determination. In that brief exchange, I felt the tide shifting.

The sun dipped lower in the sky, casting a fiery glow across the horizon as I stood at the water's edge, the waves curling around my ankles in playful caresses. I turned back to Jake, his tall frame silhouetted against the fading light, the lines of his body tense and coiled, like a spring waiting to be released. I could see that the ocean, with its vastness and unpredictability, echoed the tumult within him—a reflection of the storm that seemed to churn beneath his surface.

"Just one step," I coaxed, my voice bright against the low roar of the sea. "Just feel the water, I promise it won't bite."

He moved cautiously, the soft sand shifting beneath his feet as he approached. Each step seemed deliberate, as though he were weighing the decision against all the unspoken words that lingered between us. Finally, the cool water lapped at his toes, and he let out a small gasp, the chill igniting a flicker of surprise in his eyes.

"See? Not so bad, right?" I laughed, the sound carrying over the waves, light and airy, desperate to pierce through the heaviness surrounding him.

His lips curved slightly, but it was fleeting—a delicate smile that vanished as quickly as it appeared. Instead, he stepped back, retreating from the water as if it held the answers to questions he wasn't ready to ask. I felt a familiar pang of frustration but pushed it aside, focusing instead on the beauty of the moment—the sunset painting the sky with strokes of orange and pink, as if the world itself was urging us to let go, to breathe.

"Let's walk," I suggested, taking his hand again, this time more firmly. His fingers wrapped around mine, the warmth of his skin grounding me amidst the rising tide of uncertainty.

We wandered along the shoreline, the sand a fine grain that clung to our feet. The rhythmic sound of the ocean became a soft symphony, each wave crashing like a heartbeat against the shore. With each step, I felt the weight of our troubles lifting, but I could sense Jake's thoughts swirling like the foam on the waves—unsettled and tumultuous.

"I used to come here every summer as a kid," I shared, hoping to draw him out. "My family would rent a little cabin, and we'd spend hours in the water, making sandcastles and searching for shells."

He glanced at me, his expression a mixture of curiosity and guardedness. "Did you enjoy it?"

"Enjoy? It was magical," I replied, my voice rising with enthusiasm. "The way the sun glistened on the waves, like diamonds scattered across a blue blanket. It felt like the world was ours, untouched and full of possibilities."

A brief silence fell between us, the kind that invited intimacy but felt weighted with expectation. Jake stopped walking, his gaze focused on the horizon, where the sun was sinking into the ocean, a slow surrender to the night. "I never really did things like that," he murmured, almost to himself.

"What do you mean?" I pressed, my heart quickening.

He sighed, a deep, soul-baring sound that seemed to echo with his unspoken fears. "I was always the responsible one. The one who stayed home while everyone else went out to play. I had to help my family... it just never felt right to want more."

"Jake," I said softly, stepping closer. "Wanting more isn't wrong. It doesn't mean you're abandoning anyone. It's okay to live for yourself."

He met my eyes then, and for a moment, I thought I glimpsed a crack in the armor he wore so well—a hint of vulnerability beneath the stoic facade. "What if I don't know how?"

I could feel my heart cracking open for him. "Then let's learn together," I suggested. "Right now, all you have to do is be here, with me."

He looked at me, uncertainty flickering in his gaze, but there was something else—a spark of recognition, as if he were beginning to realize the truth of my words. I squeezed his hand, an unspoken promise that we would navigate this journey together, that he didn't have to face his demons alone.

As the last sliver of the sun dipped beneath the waves, I pulled him toward a cluster of weathered driftwood, the remnants of storms past. We sat together, the cool evening air wrapping around us like a comforting blanket. I leaned back, gazing up at the stars beginning to twinkle against the velvet sky. "Look at that," I whispered, pointing toward the constellations starting to emerge, brilliant and breathtaking.

Jake followed my gaze, and for the first time that day, I saw his shoulders relax slightly. "It's beautiful," he admitted, his voice barely above a whisper.

"Just like you," I teased, nudging him gently with my shoulder. "And you deserve to feel it."

We settled into a comfortable silence, the sounds of the ocean filling the spaces between our thoughts. I watched as he shifted slightly, glancing at me from the corner of his eye. "Do you really think I can change?"

"Of course," I replied, the conviction in my voice surprising even me. "You're not trapped, Jake. You're allowed to break free from the expectations others have placed on you. You just need to believe that you can."

A breeze picked up, tousling my hair and carrying the faint scent of salt and adventure. I felt alive, buoyed by the beauty around us and the tender connection beginning to unfurl between us.

"You know," I continued, "every person we meet is a chapter in our lives. Some will teach us lessons, others will break our hearts, but you get to choose who stays in your story."

Jake turned to me, a flicker of understanding illuminating his expression. "And what if I want to rewrite mine?"

"Then do it," I urged, my heart racing at the thought. "Take this moment, this weekend—make it a part of your new beginning."

With the ocean as our witness, I felt the space between us begin to dissolve, each wave pulling away the debris of unspoken fears, allowing something fresh and hopeful to take root. In that moment, under the vast expanse of stars and the soothing rhythm of the sea, I believed with all my heart that we were on the cusp of something beautiful, something transformative, where love could flourish amid the cracks that had once threatened to divide us.

The night settled around us like a shroud, the stars twinkling like scattered diamonds across an indigo canvas. The air was crisp and fragrant, filled with the mingling scents of salt and earth. I sat cross-legged on the sand, feeling its coolness seep through my skin, grounding me in this moment where everything felt possible. Jake sat beside me, his presence solid yet distant, as though he were caught between two worlds—one of familiarity, where he was my partner, and the other, an unfathomable abyss pulling at the corners of his mind.

The rhythmic crash of waves against the shore played a soothing melody, each roll echoing the rise and fall of my heart as I searched for words that could pierce through the haze enveloping him. "Tell me about your childhood," I said suddenly, feeling a spark of inspiration. "What was it like growing up in your house?"

He turned to me, his brow furrowed as he contemplated the question. "It was... complicated," he began, his voice a mixture of hesitation and raw honesty. "My parents were always busy, you know? My mom worked two jobs, and my dad... well, he was around but not really present."

The moonlight danced across his face, illuminating the shadows etched in his skin—the lines of worry that marred his otherwise handsome features. I could see the weight of his memories resting heavily on his shoulders, and I yearned to reach out and help carry the burden. "What did you do when they were gone?" I probed gently.

"I took care of my little brother, Ethan," he replied, his eyes clouded with nostalgia. "I was supposed to be the responsible one. We spent countless hours outside, playing soccer in the backyard, building forts out of old boxes, pretending we were explorers. But I always felt this pressure... like I couldn't just be a kid."

The ache in his voice struck a chord deep within me. "Jake, you had to grow up so fast," I whispered, imagining the weight of responsibility pressing down on him even as a child. "That's not fair."

"It wasn't," he admitted, a hint of bitterness seeping into his tone. "But it taught me how to take care of others. I never wanted to be like my dad, who was always gone. I wanted to be there for Ethan."

As he spoke, I could see the flicker of pain and pride in his eyes. The tumult of his childhood echoed the struggles we faced as adults, where the lines between love and responsibility blurred, leaving a trail of confusion. I wanted to bridge that gap for him, to show him that it was okay to let go of the past. "You can still be a protector without carrying all the weight alone," I said softly. "You don't have to be responsible for everyone's happiness."

He turned toward me fully, the intensity of his gaze igniting something within me. "But what if I fail?" His voice trembled slightly, as if the very notion of inadequacy threatened to unravel him.

"Failure is part of being human," I reassured him, my heart swelling with emotion. "It's how we learn. Look at us—we're here, trying to figure this out together. That's what matters."

For a moment, the tension between us shifted, allowing a glimmer of hope to seep through the cracks in his armor. The ocean breathed its own rhythm, and I felt the undeniable connection that had tethered us for so long spark back to life, electric and bright. I reached for his hand, intertwining my fingers with his, offering warmth and understanding.

We sat in comfortable silence for a few moments, listening to the symphony of the sea and the distant call of seagulls, lingering like a memory. The chill of the night air was tempered by the warmth of our connection, and as I stole glances at him, I could see the barriers beginning to crumble, piece by piece.

"Why did you choose the beach?" he asked suddenly, his voice laced with curiosity. "Why not somewhere else?"

"It felt like the right place," I replied, a smile breaking across my face. "There's something magical about the ocean—the way it ebbs and flows, like life. It reminds me that there's always something new waiting just beyond the horizon. I wanted us to feel that."

His gaze softened, and I saw a flicker of understanding in his eyes. "You're pretty wise," he teased, a gentle smirk breaking through the shadows.

"Only when it comes to you," I shot back, grinning. "Besides, wisdom is often just a fancy term for learning the hard way."

He chuckled, the sound rich and warm, and for a moment, I reveled in the simplicity of the moment. It felt as though we were the only two people in the world, the rest fading away beneath the blanket of stars. But just as quickly as it had come, that sense of intimacy was broken by the intrusion of his thoughts.

"Do you ever worry?" he asked, the lightness dissipating like mist in the morning sun.

"Worry about what?" I asked, genuinely curious.

"About us," he confessed, his eyes locking onto mine with a seriousness that sent a shiver down my spine. "About this connection we have... about whether it's enough."

The weight of his words hung heavy in the air, and I could feel the gravity of our relationship pressing down on both of us. "Of course, I worry," I admitted, my heart racing as I spoke. "But I also believe that we can work through anything, as long as we're honest with each other."

He nodded slowly, the shadows in his eyes shifting as he considered my words. "I guess that's the hardest part for me," he said, almost to himself. "Being honest about what I want and who I am."

"You don't have to have it all figured out," I reassured him, reaching out to cup his cheek. "You just have to be brave enough to take that first step."

In that moment, the barrier between us seemed to dissolve completely. The vulnerability in his gaze matched the tenderness of my touch, and I felt an undeniable urge to draw him closer. "Let's promise to be honest, no matter how hard it gets," I said softly.

He leaned into my hand, the warmth of his skin igniting a fire within me. "I promise," he whispered, his voice steady and sure, and I felt a surge of hope ripple through me, illuminating the dark corners of uncertainty that had clouded our relationship.

As the stars continued to twinkle above us, I knew that we stood on the precipice of something beautiful. Our journey wasn't without its challenges, but as long as we faced them together, hand in hand, we would navigate the waves of life, finding our way back to the shore of understanding and love. The ocean roared in the background, a reminder of the storms we had weathered, but tonight, under the canopy of stars, we were simply two souls entwined, daring to dream of a future unfettered by the past.

Chapter 22: Waves of Emotion

The beach stretches out like a golden ribbon, weaving through the tapestry of my thoughts, each grain of sand a memory caught between the shifting tides of time. I can hear the gentle roar of the ocean, its waves rolling in with a rhythmic grace that contrasts sharply with the tumult inside me. The salty air tingles against my skin, each breath filling my lungs with the scent of freedom and sun-drenched adventure. I glance sideways at Jake, his silhouette a stark outline against the canvas of dusk. He stands there, his hair tousled by the sea breeze, laughter spilling from his lips like warm honey, yet somehow it feels as if I'm listening to a distant melody played on an out-of-tune guitar.

The sun dips lower, and the horizon ignites in a dance of vibrant oranges and deep purples, the colors reflecting off the gentle ripples of the water. I can almost taste the sweet tang of the ocean mixed with the bittersweet pangs of uncertainty that gnaw at me. We've spent countless evenings like this, lost in the simplicity of sandcastles and playful splashes, but today feels different. The laughter feels rehearsed, a mask that conceals the complexities brewing beneath the surface. I bury my toes deeper into the warm sand, seeking solace in its embrace, but it offers little relief.

As we build our castle, I meticulously craft towers that seem to reach for the sky, each grain of sand molded by my hands. I can't help but think of the walls we erect around ourselves, sturdy yet fragile, built to withstand the world but ultimately susceptible to the tides of life. I steal a glance at Jake, who is focused on sculpting a moat, his brow furrowed in concentration. He's enchanting in his dedication, but the shadows behind his eyes tell a different story, one that I am desperate to uncover.

"Jake," I say, my voice barely above the sound of the waves. I hesitate, my heart racing like the seagulls soaring overhead. The moment stretches, the weight of unspoken words pressing heavily on my chest. I take a breath, summoning the courage that feels like it's draped in fog. "Can we talk about Leah?"

His hands freeze mid-sculpture, and the air around us shifts, heavy with an unspoken tension. I watch as the light in his eyes flickers, shadows playing across his face. For a fleeting moment, I see the boy who bravely faced the world, but that glimmer is quickly eclipsed by the weight of his past. He exhales slowly, a sound that seems to carry the weight of the ocean itself, and I can feel my heart constricting with anticipation.

"I didn't think you'd want to know," he replies, his voice low and gravelly, tinged with vulnerability that catches me off guard. There's a rawness to his honesty, an unpolished truth that makes me ache for him. I nod, urging him silently to continue. He runs a hand through his hair, the golden strands catching the last rays of the sun.

"Leah and I... we had something real. It felt like a dream, but dreams have a way of unraveling, don't they?" The corners of his mouth twitch, an attempt at humor that feels as fragile as the sand beneath our feet. I can see him searching for the right words, the hesitation in his voice mirroring the uncertainty that resides in my heart.

"Her past is... complicated," he continues, eyes fixed on the horizon where the sun dips into the embrace of the sea. "We were each other's first love, but life isn't as simple as fairytales, is it?"

His words cut through the air like a knife, leaving behind a raw ache. I can feel the tides of emotion swirling within me, crashing against the shores of my heart. Each wave brings memories of my own past—fragments of pain intermingling with flickers of joy. As he speaks, I imagine Leah, a phantom from his memories, dancing like a mirage on the water's edge, and jealousy coils around my heart, tight and unforgiving.

"She's always been there, you know?" His voice falters, and I can hear the struggle in his tone. "It's like a pendulum, swinging between loyalty to her and the fear of what moving on might mean."

I take a step closer, the sand shifting beneath my feet, grounding me in the moment. "You don't have to carry that burden alone, Jake. I'm here." The sincerity of my words hangs between us, a bridge spanning the chasm of uncertainty that threatens to divide us.

For the first time, he turns to face me fully, the vulnerability in his gaze piercing through the walls I thought I'd carefully constructed. There's a tremor in his voice as he responds, "I want to move on. I really do. But it feels like leaving her behind would mean erasing a part of me."

In that instant, I understand. His heart is a battlefield, caught in the crossfire of past loyalties and present desires. The laughter that once echoed around us fades, replaced by the poignant silence of shared vulnerability. I reach out, brushing my fingers against his, and the contact sends a jolt of electricity through me. His warmth envelops me, an anchor amidst the tumultuous waves of our emotions.

The sunset deepens into a cascade of color, casting a golden hue over our shared moment. I can almost hear the heartbeat of the world, a gentle reminder that we are part of something larger, bound by the complexities of love and loss. The ocean swells and recedes, a constant reminder of life's ebb and flow, and as I stand beside Jake, I realize that amidst the chaos, we are forging our own path through the sand, one step at a time.

His laughter, once distant, now resonates within me like a cherished song, and I know that this moment, raw and unfiltered, is just the beginning of a journey that neither of us can navigate alone. The waves crash behind us, their rhythm a testament to the resilience of the heart, and for the first time, I feel the promise of new beginnings lapping at our feet, waiting to be embraced.

The sun sinks lower, and the hues of twilight blend together like the brushstrokes of an artist desperate to capture the last moments of a fading day. The sound of the waves crashing against the shore echoes the tumult of my heart, each swell and retreat a reminder of the unsteady rhythm of our conversation. I steal glances at Jake, his features illuminated by the dying light, and I feel an overwhelming urge to reach out, to pull him closer as if the simple act could somehow erase the shadows of his past. But the air between us hums with a fragile tension, as if the ocean itself holds its breath, waiting for our next move.

"Jake," I say softly, my voice a thread weaving through the cool breeze, "what if you let yourself feel what's right in front of you?" The question hangs in the air, heavy with implications. I see a flicker of conflict in his eyes, the battle between the comfort of the familiar and the exhilarating uncertainty of the new. His gaze wanders out to the horizon, where the last rays of sunlight flirt with the water, casting a shimmering path that seems to beckon us forward.

"It's not that simple," he replies, his voice low, gravelly with the weight of truth. "Leah is a part of my story, a chapter that won't easily close. We shared so much—dreams, secrets, even fears." He pauses, and I can feel the tension coiling tighter, like a wave preparing to crash. "Letting go of that feels like erasing a part of myself."

His words hit me like a rogue wave, crashing through the fragile façade I had built around my heart. I take a deep breath, grounding myself in the moment, the cool grains of sand pressing against my skin. "But what if holding on to that part keeps you from experiencing something beautiful?" I challenge, my heart racing with the vulnerability of my question. It feels like a gamble, a roll of the dice that could either bring us closer or shatter what fragile connection we've forged.

He turns to me, and for a moment, I see the storm behind his eyes. It's a whirlwind of emotions—regret, nostalgia, longing. "I don't want to hurt you," he admits, the raw honesty of his admission wrapping around my heart like a delicate vine. "You deserve someone who's not caught between two worlds."

"Maybe I don't need someone who's perfect," I counter, my voice firm yet gentle. "Maybe I just need someone who's real. And right now, that feels like you."

The moment stretches, an eternity suspended between the crashing waves and the whispering wind. I can almost feel the universe shifting, as if it's bending to accommodate the truth of our shared existence. Jake's gaze softens, and in that instant, I can see the flicker of possibility—a spark igniting amidst the uncertainty.

"Sometimes, I wish I could just... forget," he murmurs, his eyes searching mine for understanding. "But how do you forget someone who shaped who you are?"

"Maybe you don't forget," I reply, my heart swelling with empathy. "Maybe you carry those memories with you, like seashells collected on the shore. They become a part of you, but they don't have to weigh you down. You can still make space for new memories."

The breeze picks up, tousling our hair, and I feel as if the ocean itself is encouraging us, pushing us to explore this uncharted territory. There's a tension in the air, electric and vibrant, as we stand at the crossroads of possibility, our hearts entwined like the tendrils of seaweed caught in the surf.

"I don't want to lose what we have," Jake finally says, the sincerity in his voice wrapping around me like a warm embrace. "I just... I don't know how to navigate this."

"Neither do I," I admit, a nervous laugh escaping my lips. "But maybe we can figure it out together."

His smile, tentative at first, transforms into something brighter, and the corners of his eyes crinkle with warmth. The setting sun seems to recognize our newfound connection, casting a golden glow around us as if to bless this moment. The ocean continues its rhythmic song, a soothing backdrop to our unfolding narrative.

"Okay," he replies, a newfound determination lacing his words. "Let's take it one step at a time."

We stand together, two souls intertwined, as the tide rolls in, and I can't help but think of how beautiful it is to share this vulnerability with him. The weight of the past is still there, a shadow lurking just beyond the horizon, but it no longer feels insurmountable. It feels like a bridge we can cross together, one foot in front of the other, guided by the gentle lapping of the waves at our feet.

As the sky darkens and the stars begin to peek through the velvet canopy of night, I feel a warmth blossoming in my chest, the kind that hints at new beginnings. The laughter that once felt forced now flows freely between us, buoyed by the promise of honesty and openness. Each chuckle and playful tease seems to dissolve the remnants of hesitation that lingered like a morning fog.

Jake and I begin to gather our things, our sandcastle a testament to our afternoon together, a beautiful, albeit slightly lopsided, representation of our journey thus far. "Maybe we should have built a lighthouse instead," he jokes, his laughter bright against the backdrop of the twinkling stars.

"Or a bridge," I counter playfully, nudging him with my shoulder as we walk back along the shoreline. "To connect all the stories we hold inside us."

The beach feels alive with possibilities, each whisper of the wind carrying secrets of the past while promising hope for the future. The gentle pull of the tide mirrors the tug in my heart, a reminder that both love and loss are as fluid as the ocean itself. As we walk, the sand shifting beneath our feet, I realize that the path ahead may not always be clear, but with Jake by my side, it feels like an adventure waiting to unfold.

With the moon casting a silvery glow over the water, we leave our footprints in the sand, a mark of this moment—this fragile yet beautiful connection forged amidst the waves of emotion. In the quiet intimacy of the night, I can feel the warmth of his presence beside me, and for the first time in a long time, I dare to hope that we might navigate this tangled web together, embracing the ebb and flow of what lies ahead.

The moon hangs low in the sky, its silver glow reflecting on the water like scattered diamonds, illuminating the path ahead. Jake and I walk side by side, the cool sand beneath our feet grounding me as the weight of our conversation lingers in the air like the scent of salt. I glance at him, his expression softened by the gentle light, and I feel a swell of affection that rushes through me like the tide reclaiming the shore. There's an unspoken understanding between us now, a shared acknowledgment of the complexities we both carry.

As we leave the remnants of our sandcastle behind, I can't shake the feeling that the shoreline is a metaphor for our lives—ever-changing, marked by the ebbs and flows of our experiences. I can almost see the waves of our past crashing against the present, each one carving out new shapes in the sand, leaving behind an imprint that will fade but never fully disappear. The juxtaposition of the steadfast ocean against the shifting sands reflects the delicate balance we must strike between honoring our pasts and embracing the future.

"Do you think we can really navigate this?" Jake's voice breaks the serene silence, pulling me from my reverie. I sense the vulnerability behind his question, and it draws me in closer, like a moth to a flame.

"Together," I reply, the word hanging between us like a promise, fragile yet potent. "I believe we can."

The evening air wraps around us, warm and inviting, yet tinged with the tension of possibilities. The waves crash rhythmically in the background, a soothing symphony that echoes our own heartbeat. I glance up at the night sky, a canvas splattered with stars that seem to twinkle in agreement, as if the universe itself is cheering us on.

Jake watches me, his brow slightly furrowed, a hint of uncertainty clouding his eyes. "It's just... I don't want to drag you into my mess," he admits, his voice barely above a whisper, as if speaking too loudly might shatter this fragile moment. "You deserve someone who isn't weighed down by their past."

"Maybe we're all a little messy," I counter, my heart pounding in my chest. "What if we embrace that mess together?"

He smiles, the corners of his lips turning up slowly as if testing the waters. The moonlight catches the flecks of gold in his eyes, illuminating a depth that resonates with my own tumultuous emotions. I take a step closer, our shoulders brushing together, and I feel a spark of connection—one that transcends the fears we both harbor.

As we continue down the beach, we come across a bonfire flickering in the distance, the glow inviting and warm against the cool night. Laughter and music float through the air, drawing us closer to a group of friends gathered around the flames, their faces aglow with joy and camaraderie. I feel a pull to join them, a desire to be swept up in the carefree atmosphere, but a part of me hesitates. I know that Jake and I are on the cusp of something profound, yet the lure of shared laughter is hard to resist.

"Shall we?" I ask, gesturing toward the fire. Jake's gaze lingers on the flames, a flicker of hesitation clouding his expression.

"Yeah, let's go," he finally replies, a hint of determination behind his words, as if he's decided to push through his apprehensions. As we approach the gathering, I can feel the warmth of the fire washing over us, wrapping us in a cocoon of light and laughter.

The moment we step closer, we're greeted by a cacophony of voices, familiar faces lighting up as they notice us. "There you are!"

one of our friends exclaims, waving us over with enthusiasm. "We thought you two got lost in the sand!"

Laughter erupts around us, the sound infectious, and I can't help but smile as we join the circle. The fire crackles and pops, sending sparks dancing into the night sky, and for a moment, I forget the turmoil swirling within me. I lose myself in the joy of shared stories and lighthearted banter, the worries about Jake's past slipping away like smoke dissipating into the air.

As the night deepens, I find myself seated beside Jake, the warmth of the fire reflected in his eyes. We share soft smiles, comfortable in our proximity, and I feel the distance between us shrinking with each shared glance. The flickering flames cast playful shadows across his face, illuminating the contours of his jaw and the softness in his gaze. I feel a flutter in my chest, a delicate thread of hope weaving through the remnants of uncertainty.

At some point, the conversation shifts, and we find ourselves discussing dreams, those shimmering illusions we chase with a relentless fervor. Jake leans closer, his voice low and conspiratorial. "What's your dream?" he asks, genuine curiosity etched across his features.

I take a moment to reflect, the question resonating within me like a wave washing over the shore. "I want to travel," I admit, the desire spilling from my lips with an unfiltered honesty. "I want to see the world—the hidden corners and the bustling streets, the untouched landscapes and the heart of each culture. I want to collect stories, experiences, and memories like seashells, one trip at a time."

Jake's eyes widen, a spark igniting within him. "That's beautiful. Where's the first place you'd go?"

"Maybe Paris," I reply, a wistful smile creeping onto my lips. "There's something so magical about the thought of wandering through cobblestone streets, sipping coffee at a café, and watching the world go by. I want to feel that sense of wonder."

He nods, his gaze thoughtful. "I've always wanted to see the Grand Canyon. Just to stand on the edge and feel that rush of insignificance. To realize how small we are in the grand scheme of things."

As we share our dreams, the laughter and light of the bonfire fade into a distant hum, and it feels as though we've created our own little world—a sanctuary where the outside chaos can't touch us. With every word exchanged, I sense a deeper connection growing between us, intertwining our pasts and futures in ways I never anticipated.

"Maybe we should make a pact," I suggest, the idea bubbling to the surface. "A promise to chase our dreams together. If you want to see the Grand Canyon, I'll go with you, and when you're ready to explore Paris, I'll be there."

His smile broadens, illuminating his face with a warmth that sends butterflies fluttering in my stomach. "Deal," he says, and as we shake on it, I feel a sense of solidarity wash over us. This promise, simple yet profound, binds us together in ways that go beyond words.

As the fire begins to dwindle, casting long shadows across the sand, I realize that this night is more than just a collection of moments; it's the beginning of something beautiful. The worries of the past linger like distant echoes, but in this moment, surrounded by laughter and light, I feel a glimmer of hope. Jake and I are embarking on a journey, navigating the murky waters of our emotions, and while the path may be rocky, I am confident that together we can find our way.

In the heart of that night, as the stars twinkled like dreams waiting to be chased, I leaned in closer to Jake, feeling the warmth of his presence beside me. The world around us faded, and for a fleeting moment, it felt as if nothing else mattered. In the depths of uncertainty, we were building our own foundation, one laughter, one shared secret, and one promise at a time, ready to face whatever the tides may bring.

Chapter 23: Beneath the Surface

The night enveloped us like a thick velvet cloak, deepening the indigo sky, speckled with pinpricks of starlight that twinkled like distant promises. We sat on the weathered driftwood logs that served as benches along the sandy beach, their salty scent mingling with the faint sweetness of the bonfire crackling before us. The flames leaped and twisted in a frantic dance, casting flickering shadows that played across our faces, illuminating the worn lines of worry etched around Jake's eyes and the freckles dotting my sun-kissed skin.

The rhythmic sound of the waves lapping against the shore created a symphony, punctuated by the occasional caw of a distant seagull, their cries echoing like the last remnants of summer before it succumbed to the encroaching chill of fall. I could feel the grains of sand shifting beneath my toes, each tiny particle a memory, a fragment of time, whispering stories of sun-soaked days and starry nights spent on this very stretch of coast.

Leaning closer to the fire, I let the warmth seep into my bones, trying to chase away the remnants of a lingering chill that seemed to creep under my skin. The firelight danced in Jake's eyes, revealing a depth of emotion I hadn't noticed before. Tonight, something felt different—an invisible tether, perhaps, binding us in our shared vulnerability. With a deep breath, I decided to share a piece of my history, the jagged edges of which still left scars.

"I lost my father when I was thirteen," I began, my voice barely rising above the crackling flames. The words felt like stones in my throat, heavy and unwieldy. Jake's gaze was unwavering, his brow furrowed with empathy, and I knew he was ready to listen. "He was everything to me—my hero, my compass. The day he died, the world tilted on its axis, and I was left to navigate the chaos without him." I felt the heat of the fire as it danced around us, but an even deeper warmth radiated from Jake as he shifted closer, as if he could absorb some of the sorrow spilling from my lips.

His presence was steady, a stark contrast to the turbulent emotions roiling within me. I painted the picture of that day, vivid and haunting—the scent of freshly cut grass mingling with the tang of impending rain, the somber faces of family members blurring in my memory like the watercolor paintings I once created in art class. "I remember standing in the backyard, watching the storm roll in, thinking it was somehow symbolic, a reflection of the turmoil inside me." I closed my eyes, letting the memories wash over me like the tide reclaiming the shore.

As I spoke, I glanced at Jake, and for a fleeting moment, I could see a glimmer of understanding pass through his eyes. "The weight of it all shaped who I became," I continued, my voice gaining strength. "I built walls to keep others out, afraid that if I let them in, they would see how broken I truly was." Each confession peeled back a layer of armor I had so carefully constructed over the years, exposing the tender vulnerability beneath.

His expression shifted, and I sensed a shift in the atmosphere around us, an electric charge that hung in the air, urging us to share more, to strip away the façades we both wore. "What about you?" I asked softly, inviting him to reveal the shadows that lingered behind his bravado. "What has shaped you?"

He hesitated, the shadows dancing across his face reflecting the turmoil within. "I guess I always thought I had to be the strong one," he finally said, his voice thick with emotion. "My dad was gone before I was even born, and my mom had to bear the weight of it all alone. I wanted to be her rock, to be everything she needed." The vulnerability in his words struck me; it was a weight I recognized, one that had become so familiar to me in my own life.

As he spoke, I could see the flicker of pain in his eyes, the way his shoulders tensed with the unspoken burden he carried. I reached out, my fingers brushing against his arm, an instinctual gesture of solidarity. "You're not alone, you know," I said gently. "It's okay to lean on someone else for a change." The honesty in my words seemed to hang in the air, weaving a fragile connection between us that both frightened and exhilarated me.

Just as I thought we were breaking through the invisible barrier that separated our hearts, my phone buzzed, shattering the moment like glass. Leah's name flashed on the screen, and a pang of disappointment settled in my chest. I glanced at Jake, who wore an expression of understanding mingled with frustration, and reluctantly picked up the call.

"Hey, Leah," I said, trying to mask the irritation in my tone. "What's up?" Her voice crackled through the speaker, lighthearted and bubbly, a stark contrast to the weighty emotions I had just shared with Jake. As we spoke, I felt the warmth of our conversation fade, the firelight dimming in comparison to the bright distraction of my friend's laughter.

Yet, even as I smiled and responded to Leah, my gaze drifted back to Jake, who sat quietly, his expression thoughtful. I couldn't help but feel a deep yearning for the moment we had just shared, a fleeting glimpse of something deeper than friendship. The connection we forged felt tangible, a thread woven through the fabric of our lives, and as I hung up the call, the emptiness in its wake felt like a wound, fresh and aching.

The laughter and chatter faded into the background as I returned my attention to the crackling fire. The embers glowed softly, casting a warm light over Jake's face. In that moment, I realized that while the call had interrupted our fragile connection, it had also solidified something undeniable between us. We were bound by our pasts, by the weight of loss and the quiet hope of healing. I didn't know what the future held, but I was beginning to believe that perhaps together we could navigate the darkness and find a way to the light.

A PLACE TO BELONG 241

As the final echoes of Leah's laughter faded into the salty air, I felt the cool bite of reality settle around us, thicker than the mist rolling in from the ocean. The fire flickered defiantly, throwing shadows that danced upon our faces, but the warmth of our earlier conversation seemed to slip away, replaced by an awkward silence that lingered like the taste of burnt marshmallows on my tongue. I shifted on the log, the wood rough against my skin, and caught Jake's gaze. The unspoken words hung between us, begging to be released from their captivity.

He cleared his throat, the sound heavy with unshared thoughts. "You know, it's funny how life takes you places you never expected," he said, his voice low, barely rising above the crackling fire. I nodded, sensing a shift in his demeanor as he leaned back slightly, arms crossed, the flame's glow highlighting the contours of his jaw. "I used to think I had everything figured out—until I didn't."

The air thickened with his words, and I could see in his expression that he was recalling a deeper narrative, one layered with experiences that had sculpted him into the man sitting beside me now. I leaned forward, instinctively drawn into the orbit of his presence, urging him silently to continue.

"After my mom lost her job, everything changed," he said, his eyes reflecting a distant memory, a landscape painted with both hardship and resilience. "We went from a cozy apartment in the city to a tiny house on the outskirts. I was supposed to be her support, but I was just a kid. I wanted to make things right, to be the hero, but I felt more like a sidekick, always in the shadows." He chuckled, but it was devoid of humor. "I guess I've been trying to figure out how to step into the light ever since."

I could sense the bitterness threading through his bravado, and I was struck by the sincerity etched on his face. The bravado he wore like armor had cracks in it, revealing the vulnerability beneath. In this moment, I saw not just Jake, the handsome guy with the easy smile, but a young boy burdened by expectations, navigating a world that had taken too much from him too soon. "You don't have to carry it alone," I whispered, as if speaking louder would shatter the fragile atmosphere we had begun to build.

He turned to me, his brow slightly furrowed, as if weighing my words against his reality. The warmth of the fire flickered in his eyes, casting a soft glow that made them appear almost golden. "I guess that's the thing, isn't it?" he said, a hint of uncertainty threading through his voice. "I've always felt like I needed to be strong, but what if I don't even know how to be vulnerable?"

The question hung in the air, heavy yet poignant. I contemplated the fragility of vulnerability, how it could simultaneously make one feel alive and exposed. "Maybe vulnerability isn't about knowing how to be strong," I suggested, my heart racing slightly. "Maybe it's about letting go of the need to be anything other than what you are."

He considered this, his gaze drifting to the horizon where the dark sea met the star-specked sky, and for a brief moment, I could see the internal struggle playing out on his face, like waves crashing against a rocky shore. "I think I've been so afraid of failure that I forgot what it felt like to just be," he murmured, almost to himself.

The warmth of the fire did little to chase away the chill of the night air, and as the wind picked up, I wrapped my arms around my knees, feeling the embrace of my own memories. The past clung to me like a ghost, whispering reminders of loss and heartache, but as I looked at Jake, I found an unexpected comfort in the shared weight of our stories. Perhaps we were both searching for redemption in the dark, fumbling toward each other like moths drawn to a flame.

"You know," I began, my voice softening, "sometimes I think our pasts are like waves. They come crashing in, pulling us under, but they also shape the shore. They create a beautiful, albeit jagged, landscape of who we are." I smiled, trying to lighten the heaviness in the air. "I guess we're both just trying to carve out our own piece of the coastline."

He smiled back, a fleeting expression that lit up his features, revealing the boyish charm that had first caught my attention. "That's a poetic way to put it. I like it," he said, and I felt a flutter of warmth in my chest. There was something undeniably comforting in the way we spoke, as if the fire had sparked not just flames, but a connection, a bond that was beginning to weave itself into the fabric of our shared experience.

As we exchanged stories, the world around us faded into a soft blur—the sound of the ocean became a soothing lullaby, the stars above twinkled like diamonds scattered across a dark velvet canvas, and for a moment, time seemed to stand still. I felt seen, unguarded, and inexplicably drawn to this man who had been nothing but a stranger just days before.

Jake's laughter broke through my reverie, rich and warm, wrapping around me like the arms of an old friend. "You know, I always thought I'd be the one giving comfort to someone else, not sitting here spilling my guts out," he admitted, shaking his head as if in disbelief.

I couldn't help but chuckle at the irony. "Life has a funny way of flipping the script on us, doesn't it?" I replied, my heart swelling with a sense of camaraderie. "One minute, we're the ones offering the advice, and the next, we're the ones needing it."

He met my gaze, his expression softening as he allowed the weight of our conversation to settle between us, a palpable force that both frightened and thrilled me. "Maybe this is what it means to let someone in," he said quietly, and the sincerity in his voice sent a thrill coursing through me.

Just as the embers crackled in the fire, igniting the air with their warmth, I felt a flicker of hope within myself, a longing to see where this fragile connection might lead. It was a journey into the unknown, filled with the potential for both beauty and pain, but perhaps that was what made it worth pursuing.

As the night deepened, I couldn't shake the feeling that something profound was unfolding between us—a shared reckoning, a gentle unraveling of our tightly held defenses. We were two souls, navigating the tumultuous waters of life, seeking solace in the company of one another, and I couldn't help but wonder what awaited us beneath the surface.

The fire crackled softly, as if in protest against the cool air that wrapped around us like an unwelcome guest. I could still feel the warmth of our shared moment lingering, a bittersweet reminder of the vulnerability that had surged between Jake and me. As I sat there, cradling my knees against my chest, I watched the flames flicker, each blaze casting a myriad of shadows that danced across the sand. It was a mesmerizing display, yet the soft whisper of the ocean waves provided a far more compelling backdrop, a gentle reminder that life ebbed and flowed just as rhythmically as the tide.

Jake was lost in thought, his brow furrowed and his gaze distant, as if he were peering into the depths of his own mind, searching for the words he had yet to say. I wanted to reach out, to bridge the gap that had reappeared in the wake of Leah's interruption, but there was something magical about allowing silence to envelop us too—a tranquil cocoon spun from threads of shared pain and budding hope.

"What do you think it is about the ocean that draws us in?" I mused, breaking the silence. "It feels both calming and chaotic, doesn't it?" My words hung in the air, a gentle nudge to bring him back from the depths of his contemplation. He turned to me, a hint of a smile tugging at the corners of his mouth, the kind of smile that hinted at both mischief and warmth.

"I think it's the duality of it," he replied thoughtfully, leaning back slightly and running a hand through his tousled hair. "It can be soothing, like a lullaby, but it can also rip everything apart if you let it." The gravity of his statement hung heavy in the air, punctuated by the distant sound of a fishing boat's engine cutting through the night, a reminder of the life that existed beyond our own small world.

I nodded, feeling the truth of his words resonate within me. The ocean was an endless expanse, one that could both cradle you in its embrace and drown you beneath its waves. "Kind of like us," I said softly, half-joking yet fully aware of the deeper implications. "Trying to find a balance between our pasts and our present."

He chuckled, the sound warm and inviting. "Exactly. Sometimes, I wonder if I'll ever really find that balance. It feels like I'm constantly teetering on the edge." I sensed a flicker of apprehension beneath his bravado, an echo of the uncertainty that mirrored my own feelings. The truth was, I had spent so much time trying to build walls around my heart that I had forgotten how to let anyone inside.

The fire crackled again, sending a shower of sparks into the night sky, and I felt a surge of warmth that chased away the cool night air. "Maybe it's okay to be a little unsteady sometimes," I offered, my voice imbued with a sudden confidence. "Life isn't about perfect equilibrium; it's about the moments that catch us off guard—the ones that challenge us to grow."

Jake regarded me, his expression shifting, an understanding blooming in his eyes. "You're wiser than you look," he teased gently, and I couldn't help but smile, a blush creeping across my cheeks. There was something thrilling about our exchange, an electric charge that seemed to spark between us with each shared thought, each subtle compliment.

We fell into an easy conversation, the topics shifting like the tide. We spoke of dreams and aspirations, of mundane moments that defined us, the laughter that punctuated our stories lending a much-needed levity to the heavier topics we had broached. I told him about my plans to travel after graduation, the places I longed to visit—sun-drenched beaches in far-off lands, bustling cities alive with culture, and the whispering forests that held ancient secrets. He shared snippets of his own dreams, the desire to write, to capture the world on paper and transform it into something more—something beautiful.

"Isn't it funny," he mused, "how we often feel like we're alone in our struggles, yet here we are, two people sitting on the beach sharing our dreams?"

"Not so funny," I countered, a teasing lilt to my voice. "More like a cosmic joke, a reminder that the universe has a sense of humor." The banter flowed easily between us, each exchange a building block, fortifying the fragile structure of our connection.

As the fire began to dwindle, I found myself stealing glances at Jake, the way the firelight danced across his features, illuminating the softness in his gaze. It was a moment that felt suspended in time, the world around us fading into a blur as we lost ourselves in each other's stories. The air crackled with an energy that felt both exhilarating and terrifying, a palpable tension that hinted at something unspoken simmering beneath the surface.

Eventually, the sky deepened into a velvet black, the stars now casting a silvery glow over the world. I glanced up, momentarily lost in their brilliance, and then turned back to Jake, who was now gazing at the horizon, lost in thought. The waves whispered secrets to the shore, their rhythm steady, a reminder of the ebb and flow of our own lives.

"What do you think happens after this?" he asked suddenly, his voice low and contemplative. "After tonight? After this moment?"

I pondered his question, feeling a mix of hope and uncertainty swirling within me. "I think we choose," I replied slowly, searching for the right words. "We can either let this moment fade into a memory, or we can take the risk to explore what it means for us. It's about making choices, isn't it?"

His gaze met mine, a flicker of something deeper passing between us, an acknowledgment of the vulnerability inherent in taking that leap. "And what if we fall?" he asked, his voice barely above a whisper.

"Then we pick ourselves up, brush off the sand, and keep going," I answered, my heart racing at the weight of the moment. "Life is too short to live in fear of falling."

Jake smiled then, a genuine smile that reached his eyes and crinkled the corners. "You know, I think you're right," he said, his voice steady now, infused with a newfound determination. "Maybe it's time I stop worrying about what could go wrong and start embracing what could go right."

The words hung in the air, filling the space between us with promise. In that instant, I realized that we were not just two souls adrift in a vast ocean; we were fellow travelers, learning to navigate the waters together, buoyed by the hope of shared experiences and the thrill of the unknown.

As the last embers of the fire faded into a soft glow, I felt a profound sense of gratitude wash over me—a deep appreciation for the connection we had forged amidst our respective storms. Together, we were more than our pasts; we were dreamers, explorers, and perhaps, in some small way, we were beginning to carve our own paths through the darkness.

With the sound of the waves as our soundtrack, we lingered in the magic of that night, knowing that whatever the future held, we would face it together—one step, one breath, and one moment at a time.

Chapter 24: The Ripple Effect

The sun had already dipped beneath the horizon by the time I returned home from the beach, leaving behind a swath of indigo sky, punctuated by the first daring stars. I parked my old Volkswagen Beetle, its vibrant yellow paint chipped and faded like a long-lost memory, beside the sprawling oak tree that stood sentinel at the edge of my front yard. The air was thick with the scent of saltwater mingling with the sweet aroma of blooming honeysuckle. I stepped out, my sandals sinking slightly into the warm, cracked asphalt, and took a deep breath, trying to chase away the heaviness that clung to me.

Home was a small, two-story cottage nestled in the heart of the town, its weathered clapboard siding a testament to years gone by. I pushed open the creaky wooden door, greeted by the familiar scent of lavender from the air freshener I kept in the kitchen. My walls were adorned with pieces that spoke of my journey, each one telling a story. A vibrant canvas of swirling colors hung above the couch, the embodiment of a summer's day I had spent painting in the park. It glimmered with the joy I longed to feel again.

Yet, tonight, the laughter of the ocean waves seemed a cruel reminder of the tumult within me. Jake's words replayed in my mind, his promise to be better, to try harder. Hope sparkled momentarily, only to be dulled by the shadow of Leah that loomed ever closer, as if waiting to snatch away the happiness I dared to reclaim. With a sigh, I stepped into the kitchen, determined to push the gnawing sense of inadequacy aside. I flicked on the lights, illuminating the space, and pulled out a bag of flour, envisioning the soft, warm dough I could shape into something comforting.

Baking was a ritual, one that wrapped around me like a warm hug. I measured each ingredient with care, letting the familiar motions guide me. The rhythmic sound of the mixer filled the room, creating a symphony that drowned out my chaotic thoughts. I added vanilla and cinnamon, scents that reminded me of childhood afternoons spent helping my mother, her laughter ringing like a bell as we flour-dusted the countertops. The memory was both a balm and a weight, bittersweet, but still precious. As the dough began to form, my heart swelled with anticipation, imagining how I could share this warmth with Jake when he arrived.

But as the dough rested, I found myself wandering to the canvas draped in the corner of the living room. It was waiting for me, an empty promise. The art exhibit at The Willow loomed on the horizon like an approaching storm, both exhilarating and terrifying. The community center was a heartbeat of our town, a place where artists gathered and dreams took flight. My mind raced with ideas for the new design, colors and shapes tumbling together in a chaotic dance. With each brushstroke, I could transform not only the canvas but perhaps my own life, reclaiming a sense of purpose that felt so distant.

I set up my easel by the large window, the dim glow of the streetlights illuminating my workspace. The cool evening breeze drifted through, rustling the leaves outside, whispering secrets I longed to understand. I squeezed the tubes of paint, bright hues pooling on my palette, vibrant against the stark white of the canvas. Each stroke was deliberate, a catharsis of sorts, as I allowed my emotions to spill out, losing myself in the colors. The blues were calming, soothing like the waves, while the fiery reds and oranges ignited a sense of passion I had thought lost.

Hours melted away as I painted, the world outside fading into a blur. I lost track of time, lost in the colors and the feelings that flowed through me. It was an escape, a way to push aside the uncertainty that wrapped around my heart like an unwelcome guest. But the bliss was punctured when the familiar sound of Jake's truck rumbled into the driveway. My heart fluttered, a mix of excitement and apprehension. I glanced at the clock. It was late, later than I had anticipated.

As I cleaned my brushes, I felt a flutter of nervous energy. Would he see the progress I was making, or would the specter of Leah's memory overshadow everything? The door swung open, and Jake stepped inside, his tall frame silhouetted against the twilight. He looked tired, his curls tousled, but the moment his gaze found me, a smile broke across his face that sent warmth flooding through me.

"What are you up to?" he asked, leaning against the doorframe, his eyes sparkling with genuine curiosity.

"Just working on something for The Willow," I replied, trying to keep my voice steady. I gestured to the canvas, feeling a mix of pride and vulnerability. "What do you think?"

He stepped closer, the scent of the ocean still lingering on him, a reminder of our day at the beach. As he examined my work, I held my breath, waiting for his reaction. "This is beautiful," he said, his voice low and sincere. "It captures so much light. It's like you've poured your soul into it."

His words wrapped around me like a warm embrace, igniting a flicker of joy that pushed back against the lingering shadows. "Thanks," I murmured, warmth flooding my cheeks. "I was hoping to evoke a sense of community, of connection."

"Can I help?" he asked, his enthusiasm contagious.

The offer ignited a spark within me, a mix of excitement and trepidation. Collaborating with him felt like opening a door to possibilities, yet the shadow of Leah lingered, an unwelcome ghost haunting the edges of my thoughts.

The afternoon light slipped through the window like a gentle whisper, casting soft shadows across the canvas, and I couldn't help but feel the tension in my chest begin to ease as Jake grabbed a brush, his fingers delicate yet assured. He turned to me, a playful smirk dancing at the corners of his lips. "Okay, what's the plan? Are we making a masterpiece or an abstract disaster?"

I chuckled, the sound freeing me from the chains of worry that had wound too tightly around my heart. "Let's aim for a masterpiece, shall we?" The excitement in my voice was unmasked, a contrast to the anxiety I had been harboring. I handed him a brush, and our fingers brushed ever so slightly. The electric spark was undeniable, sending a fluttering sensation through my stomach.

As we painted, our conversations flowed easily, punctuated by laughter and the occasional playful jab. I could feel the walls I had built around my heart starting to crumble as the weight of Leah's presence became less suffocating. We dipped our brushes into vibrant colors, mixing them on the palette like kids in a candy store, each hue radiating the essence of our intertwined lives. Jake was a natural, his strokes bold and confident, complementing my more whimsical approach. The canvas transformed under our hands, bursting with life, mirroring the connection blooming between us.

I watched him, the way his brow furrowed in concentration, a dimple appearing on his cheek when he focused too hard. It made me want to capture that moment in paint, to immortalize the look of determination on his face. I admired how effortlessly he immersed himself in the process, his passion igniting a similar fervor in me. Each time our shoulders brushed, a jolt of warmth raced through me, and I found myself stealing glances, savoring the moment like the last bite of dessert.

"Why did you want to do this exhibit?" he asked suddenly, breaking the comfortable silence that had settled over us. The question was simple, yet it echoed with unspoken layers.

I paused, considering my response. "It's... it's my way of connecting with the community," I began, the words spilling out before I could overthink them. "I want to show that art can bring people together, spark conversations. In a world that can feel so disconnected, I want to create a space where people can see themselves reflected, you know?"

Jake nodded, his eyes locked onto mine, the sincerity in his gaze drawing me in. "I get that. There's something powerful about sharing a piece of yourself. It's like leaving a part of your heart out there for the world to see."

His understanding made my heart swell. I hadn't realized how much I needed that affirmation until now, how important it was to feel seen, especially by someone I cared for so deeply. "Exactly," I replied, the warmth spreading through me again. "Art can be vulnerable, and yet it's so liberating. I want to create something that speaks to people, makes them feel less alone."

As we painted, the colors began to intertwine like the threads of our conversation, vibrant yellows dancing alongside deep blues, the juxtaposition of warmth and coolness creating an interplay that was almost mesmerizing. I felt invigorated, the creative energy between us tangible.

Yet, just as the canvas blossomed into something beautiful, a fleeting thought of Leah flitted through my mind. I could almost hear her laughter, a cruel reminder of the uncertainty that still loomed. The laughter of the ocean waves, once comforting, now seemed to echo her name, a shadow stretching across my heart. I fought against the creeping doubt, reminding myself that I was deserving of this moment, of joy and connection.

As the sun began to set, casting a golden glow through the window, I stepped back to admire our creation. The canvas was alive, each stroke a testament to our collaboration, a blend of our two spirits captured in the hues of paint. I turned to Jake, my heart racing at the thought of sharing this piece with the world. "We did this," I said, my voice laced with wonder.

"Yeah, we did," he replied, a smile spreading across his face that lit up his entire being. "I think we make a pretty good team."

The moment felt significant, a turning point that offered a glimpse of what was possible. But before I could dwell on it, he took a step closer, his expression shifting to something more serious. "You know, about Leah... I don't want to bring it up if it's too much, but I want you to know I'm here for you. Whatever you need."

The sincerity in his voice cut through the haze of uncertainty. "I appreciate that," I murmured, my heart both heavy and light at once. "It's just... hard sometimes."

He nodded, understanding evident in his eyes. "I can't imagine what you're going through, but I promise I'll do my best to help you navigate it. You don't have to carry it alone."

Jake's kindness washed over me like the ocean waves, soothing and refreshing. In that moment, I realized that despite the shadows that lingered, there was a light shining through, and it came from the connections I was building.

As we resumed painting, the atmosphere shifted, filled with renewed energy. I found myself humming a tune softly, letting the rhythm guide my strokes. Jake joined in, his voice deep and melodic, creating a symphony of colors and sounds that enveloped us. The worries that had weighed so heavily on my heart began to dissipate, replaced by the simple joy of creating something meaningful alongside someone who cared.

The light outside deepened, the sky transitioning from gold to the deep navy of twilight. The world beyond the window faded, and for a moment, it felt as if we existed in our little bubble of color and creativity. I caught his eye, and for a heartbeat, everything else faded—the shadows of Leah, the weight of expectations, the looming doubt. In that instant, it was just us, two artists bound together by paint and passion, weaving our own tapestry in a world that often felt overwhelming.

As the last brushstrokes found their place on the canvas, a sense of accomplishment washed over me, a reminder that amidst the chaos, beauty could emerge. This exhibit, this journey, was ours to share. And for the first time in a long while, I felt like I was standing on the edge of something beautiful, ready to leap into the unknown.

The smell of paint mingled with the lingering aroma of cinnamon in the air, a symphony of senses that wrapped around us like an old quilt. Jake stepped back to assess our masterpiece, the fading sunlight filtering through the window, casting a warm glow that danced across the canvas. The painting stood proudly, a riot of color that seemed to pulse with life. It was as if we had captured the very essence of the town—the vibrant spirit of The Willow and the voices of the community, each brushstroke echoing the laughter and stories shared beneath its roof.

"Okay, what's next?" he asked, leaning against the wall with an ease that made my heart flutter. "Do we need to add anything? Maybe a splash of neon?" His playful suggestion drew a chuckle from me, the sound feeling foreign yet welcome. The burden of Leah's memory felt lighter, floating away with the brush of his laughter.

I tilted my head, inspecting the work with newfound perspective. "Maybe a bit more green," I replied, my fingers itching to add depth. "The trees, the park—there's so much life out there."

Without waiting for a response, I began mixing a rich emerald shade, allowing the colors to blend together in a whirl of inspiration. As I worked, I could feel Jake's presence beside me, a quiet encouragement that nudged my creative spirit forward. I glanced at him from the corner of my eye, watching as he added his own strokes with surprising finesse, bringing a touch of boldness to the piece.

"Who knew you had an artist hidden in there?" I teased, unable to suppress my smile. "Maybe we should enter this in the exhibit together. 'The Two Artists' or something equally dramatic."

Jake feigned a dramatic gasp, placing a hand over his heart. "Oh, the pressure! What if I embarrass you with my abstract disaster?"

"The beauty of art is that it's subjective," I shot back playfully. "Besides, disaster is just another form of expression."

Our laughter filled the room, mingling with the vibrant colors that enveloped us. As the sun dipped below the horizon, casting deep shadows that seemed to dance along the walls, I could feel a palpable shift within me. The insecurities that had nagged at my mind were replaced by a bubbling excitement, the kind that made my pulse race and my heart sing.

With the night creeping in, we took a break, leaning back to admire our work, which had transformed from a blank canvas into a vibrant tapestry of our shared energy and creativity. It felt as if we had not only painted a piece for the exhibit but had created a bond that transcended words.

"Can I get you anything? Water? A snack?" Jake offered, breaking the comfortable silence that had settled over us.

"Maybe a cookie?" I replied, glancing at the kitchen, where my earlier baking project had been left to cool. The aroma was intoxicating, a gentle reminder of the warmth I had tried to create amidst the turmoil in my heart.

"I'll be right back!" he declared, and with a playful skip, he dashed into the kitchen, leaving me alone with our creation.

I stepped closer to the canvas, my fingers itching to add those final touches of green. The painting seemed to breathe with potential, a portal into a world where dreams took shape and connections blossomed. As I dipped the brush into the paint, I couldn't shake the feeling that this was just the beginning of something significant, a ripple effect that would change the course of our lives.

When Jake returned, balancing a plate piled high with cookies, I couldn't help but laugh. "I think you've brought back the entire batch!"

He shrugged, his grin infectious. "Art requires fuel! Besides, I figured you could use some sweetness."

"Now you're just trying to butter me up for our future collaboration." I raised an eyebrow, taking a bite of the warm cookie, the chocolate melting in my mouth.

"Guilty as charged," he said, and we both burst into laughter again. There was something inherently delightful about sharing this moment with him, the camaraderie easing the remnants of my worry.

As we settled down on the floor, leaning against the couch with our painting between us, I couldn't help but steal glances at Jake, soaking in his presence. The way his hair caught the fading light, the gentle curve of his smile—it was all too perfect. I felt as if I were holding onto a fragile moment, one that could slip away if I blinked too hard.

"Have you ever thought about what it would be like if this town didn't exist?" Jake asked suddenly, the thought hanging in the air.

I considered his question. "What do you mean?"

"Like, if everything we know—the beach, The Willow, the little diner down the road—just disappeared. Would we still find each other in some other place? Some alternate universe where art and cookies still exist?"

I chuckled, the notion both absurd and strangely endearing. "I'd like to think we would. Maybe in a parallel universe, we're both famous artists, living in a penthouse overlooking the Eiffel Tower."

Jake laughed, the sound rich and warm. "I can see it now. You, painting masterpieces, and me... probably trying to paint a cat that looks more like a potato."

"Art is subjective, remember?" I teased, nudging him playfully.

In that moment, our laughter faded into a comfortable silence, the kind that envelops you like a favorite blanket. I leaned back against the couch, the weight of my worries lifting with every shared glance and smile. The shadows of Leah's presence felt distant, fading into the background like an old film reel.

As the night deepened, the soft glow of the lamp illuminated our artwork, and I felt a swell of gratitude for this moment. The warmth of Jake beside me felt safe, as if he were a tether anchoring me to this reality. I had poured my heart into this painting, and somehow, it had become a reflection of the journey we were on together.

With each passing second, I realized how much I longed for this—connection, creativity, and the freedom to express myself without fear of judgment. The ripple effect was real, unfolding beautifully before me. I turned to Jake, a smile breaking across my face, and in that instant, I knew this was just the beginning of a new chapter, a bright and colorful path that awaited us, woven together by art, laughter, and perhaps a sprinkle of love.

Chapter 25: Shifting Currents

The evening air in Larkspur was thick with anticipation, a palpable energy that crackled like electricity. The Willow, our town's beloved art gallery, glowed with a warm, inviting light that spilled from its wide windows, casting long shadows on the cobblestone streets. Inside, the scent of fresh paint mingled with the sharp aroma of brewed coffee, while the walls were adorned with vibrant pieces that danced with color and emotion. This was more than just an art exhibit; it was a celebration of creativity, an outpouring of local talent that had everyone buzzing with excitement.

As I moved through the throng, my heart fluttered with pride. I'd helped organize this event, a small victory in my ever-evolving role within the community. The laughter and chatter swirled around me like a comforting blanket, wrapping me in the warmth of shared enthusiasm. The locals were dressed to the nines, their outfits ranging from bohemian chic to polished elegance, each person a reflection of their own unique story. I could see them point and admire, their eyes lighting up at the striking pieces that adorned the walls, as if each stroke of the brush whispered secrets of its creator.

Jake stood nearby, animated and passionate as he discussed the nuances of one particularly bold piece—a canvas splashed with hues of crimson and gold that seemed to leap off the wall. His enthusiasm was infectious, and I felt a rush of admiration as I watched him interact with our guests. He was a natural, effortlessly charming everyone with his easy smile and quick wit. When he caught my eye, he winked, and my heart skipped a beat. In that moment, we were not just colleagues; we were allies in this creative endeavor, bound by a shared vision and a spark that made every task feel effortless.

Yet, as I stepped away to check on the refreshments, my gaze wandered. That's when I saw her. Leah, standing in the corner with her perfectly tousled hair and radiant smile, was engrossed in conversation with Jake. My stomach twisted in knots, an unsettling sensation tightening around my heart. The two of them appeared so at ease, their laughter ringing out like a melody that drowned out the rest of the world. The vibrant hues of the gallery faded slightly in my periphery, replaced by the sharp pang of jealousy that tugged at my insides. I knew I shouldn't feel this way; after all, Leah was a friend, and Jake was just being friendly. Yet, the way they leaned into each other's words made me feel like an outsider in my own celebration.

I forced myself to shake off the unease, reminding myself of the importance of this night. I was here to support local artists, to bask in the glow of our community's creativity. I immersed myself in conversations, engaging with familiar faces and new acquaintances alike, all while the tension simmered just below the surface. Each laugh, each clink of glasses, and every compliment about the artwork felt like a temporary distraction from the knot in my stomach.

As I moved deeper into the gallery, I found solace in a group discussing a piece by an up-and-coming artist, a young woman whose talent was only just beginning to be recognized. The painting—a swirling mass of blues and greens, evoking the turbulent depths of the ocean—captured the room's attention, drawing admiration and contemplation. The discussion unfolded with layers of insight, each comment adding to the vibrant tapestry of interpretation. It was moments like these that reminded me why I loved this town so fiercely; we were a collective of dreamers, each one bringing their own brush to the canvas of life.

Yet, no matter how engrossed I became, the sight of Leah's laughter would drift back into my thoughts like a stubborn ghost, haunting my mind. I could feel the heat of the gallery, the hum of conversation, and the pulse of music echoing in the background, yet all of it felt distant. The air grew thicker around me, the laughter and excitement morphing into a muffled sound, like a radio tuning out. I shifted my gaze, trying to find an anchor in the swirling chaos of my emotions.

Finally, I spotted my best friend, Mia, weaving her way through the crowd, her auburn hair glowing under the gallery lights. She had a gift for reading people, and I felt an immediate sense of relief as she approached. "You look like you need a distraction," she said, her voice laced with mischief. I laughed, the sound feeling foreign in the midst of my spiraling thoughts.

"Is it that obvious?" I replied, trying to mask the tumult within me.

"Just a bit," she said, her eyes darting towards Jake and Leah, the corner of her mouth twitching upwards. "What's the scoop?"

I sighed, leaning closer, my voice a hushed whisper. "It's silly. I shouldn't even care, but..." My words trailed off, lost in the sea of noise around us.

"Jealousy is never silly, especially when it's aimed at someone who seems to swoop in at the most inconvenient times," she said, her tone light yet understanding. "Want me to help you plot a distraction?"

I smiled at her unwavering support, the kind that only a best friend could provide. We began to strategize, forming a plan to steal Jake's attention back, but the truth lingered in the back of my mind. No matter how much I tried to push those feelings aside, the reality remained: this was about more than just an art exhibit; it was about the shifting currents of my own heart, tangled in the vibrant fabric of our small town's artistic tapestry.

Mia's presence felt like a lifeline thrown into turbulent waters. Her mischievous grin, coupled with her uncanny ability to lighten the mood, grounded me in the chaos of my swirling thoughts. "Okay, let's do this," she said, her voice laced with excitement as she led me toward the snack table, which had become a focal point of activity. The spread was impressive: artisanal cheeses, freshly baked bread, and an array of colorful fruits. Each item seemed meticulously curated, like the artwork hanging on the walls, meant to complement the evening's artistic theme.

"Let's start with a cheese wheel," she suggested, her eyes twinkling with mischief as she picked up a large wedge of aged cheddar. "This will give us some serious power in our distraction efforts." I laughed, appreciating her knack for turning even the simplest moments into a lively affair. As we indulged in the delightful assortment, I could feel the warm hum of the exhibit wrapping around us again, a reminder that we were amidst friends, art, and shared dreams.

With a mouthful of cheese, I tried to push aside my earlier thoughts. "You know," I said, wiping my mouth with the back of my hand, "it's hard not to feel a bit overshadowed right now. Leah is so... effortless." I gestured toward her, still animatedly chatting with Jake. The light caught her hair, turning it into a halo that accentuated her radiant smile. I admired her from a distance, wondering if she even realized the effect she had on those around her.

Mia followed my gaze, her brow furrowing slightly. "Effortless, yes, but you know what? It's her charm. You have your own, you just need to remember it. You're the one bringing this entire event together. You are not just a supporting player; you're the star of this show, and Jake knows it."

I bit into a slice of pear, savoring its sweetness as I processed Mia's words. "Maybe I just need to show it a bit more," I mused, my mind beginning to shift away from jealousy and toward empowerment. "I mean, I love what we've created here. Everyone seems to be enjoying themselves."

With renewed energy, I turned back to the gallery, allowing the vibrant atmosphere to wash over me once more. The laughter, the animated conversations, the strokes of color on the walls—it was intoxicating. Each corner of The Willow was alive, filled with artists mingling, patrons critiquing, and friends bonding over shared admiration for the creativity that surrounded us.

"Let's grab Jake," I said, a mischievous smile creeping across my face. "I have a brilliant idea that will put us back in the spotlight."

"Lead the way, Captain," Mia said, her playful salute making me chuckle.

As we approached Jake and Leah, I could see them in a moment of effortless camaraderie. Their conversation seemed easy, their laughter a comforting backdrop. But beneath that, I felt the urgency to reclaim my space. I cleared my throat, feeling the excitement build within me like a well-tuned piano ready to burst forth in song.

"Hey, you two!" I called out, a blend of enthusiasm and feigned nonchalance in my voice. "What do you think about starting an impromptu art critique? I've heard some opinions are just waiting to be shared!"

Leah turned to me, her smile radiant but with an edge of surprise. "That sounds fun! I'd love to hear what you think about some of the pieces. You've got an eye for this."

Jake's expression lit up as well, his eyes glimmering with intrigue. "Absolutely! Let's make it official. Lead the way."

As we moved toward the first piece, a striking installation of twisted metal and vibrant acrylics, I felt the previous tensions dissipate. The exhibit was indeed a celebration, and I was determined to infuse it with my own energy.

"This piece," I began, gesturing toward the installation, "makes me think of the beauty of chaos. It feels like a representation of our town—layered, multifaceted, and sometimes a bit jumbled. But within that chaos, there's artistry."

Jake nodded, his gaze sharp as he examined the piece. "I can see that. It's almost like a metaphor for life, don't you think? Beautifully messy and unpredictable."

Leah chimed in, her voice flowing effortlessly. "And yet, it's those very messes that make us who we are. I love how the artist captured that tension."

The conversation danced around us, each thought building upon the last. The trio of us moved from piece to piece, my earlier insecurities fading like the shadows in the gallery. We analyzed colors, styles, and techniques, sharing laughter and thoughtful nods as we unraveled the intricacies of each work.

I caught Jake's eye, the playful glint returning, and I felt a warmth blossom in my chest. "This one is striking, isn't it?" I pointed to a canvas awash in deep blues and stark whites, evoking the depths of the ocean and the expanse of the sky. "It's like looking into a mirror of our souls."

"Very poetic," Jake said, leaning closer, his voice dropping to a conspiratorial whisper. "Maybe you should start writing art critiques professionally."

"I'll think about it," I replied, the flirtation simmering in the air between us like a summer breeze.

As we continued our critique, I felt a shift. Leah's laughter blended seamlessly with ours, and the competitive edge I had initially felt began to dissolve into camaraderie. We shared insights, poked fun at pretentious interpretations, and marveled at the sheer talent that flourished in our town. It was exhilarating, a tangible reminder that art was meant to bring people together, not pull them apart.

I glanced at Leah, who seemed genuinely engaged, her warmth radiating throughout our discussions. In that moment, I realized that my earlier feelings of jealousy were misplaced. She was not a rival; she was a part of the tapestry of our community, just like I was. Each of us brought our own colors, our own flair, adding depth and richness to the canvas of Larkspur.

As we gathered around the final piece, an abstract work that evoked a swirling galaxy, I felt a sense of contentment settle over me. The night was not just about the art but about connection, understanding, and the beautiful chaos that life had to offer. The three of us stood together, laughter echoing like a symphony, as the gallery buzzed around us—a beautiful reflection of the moment, a memory woven into the fabric of who we were.

As the evening unfolded, the vibrancy of The Willow enveloped us in a kaleidoscope of creativity. The hum of animated conversations formed a comforting backdrop, resonating through the gallery like a heartbeat, matching the rhythm of my own thoughts. Each laughter felt like a brushstroke on the canvas of the night, weaving together the stories and aspirations of those gathered. My earlier insecurities began to fade, replaced by a sense of belonging that permeated the atmosphere.

Mia leaned in closer as we huddled around the last piece, the galaxy-inspired canvas shimmering under the soft glow of the gallery lights. "What do you think the artist was trying to convey with this one?" she asked, her eyes sparkling with curiosity.

"Possibly the vastness of dreams," I mused, squinting slightly as I examined the swirling colors. "It's like the artist is inviting us to lose ourselves within the infinite possibilities. Each swirl could represent a different journey."

Leah nodded, her expression thoughtful as she considered my words. "It's almost as if the artist is suggesting that while the universe may seem chaotic, there is an underlying order to the madness. Each star has its place, just waiting to be discovered."

"Now you're both getting too deep for me," Jake interjected, feigning a gasp of dramatic surprise. "You're going to make me feel inadequate in my understanding of the cosmos!"

We erupted in laughter, the camaraderie solidifying the bond between us. In that moment, the earlier tension I had felt towards

Leah evaporated completely, replaced by a genuine sense of partnership. This was no longer about competing for attention or validation; it was about celebrating the artistry and stories that had drawn us together in the first place.

As the night wore on, I found myself wandering the gallery with renewed enthusiasm. The ebb and flow of conversation created a tapestry of voices around me, each thread vibrant and unique. The local artists mingled with patrons, sharing tales of inspiration and passion, their voices echoing off the polished wood floors like the faint echo of a symphony. Each corner of the room held a distinct energy, a pulsating heart that resonated with the spirit of our community.

I drifted over to a large mural dominating one wall, a breathtaking explosion of color depicting the landscape of our town. Each brushstroke told a story, capturing the rolling hills that cradled Larkspur and the glistening river that wound its way through the heart of the town. The artist had skillfully woven in glimpses of local life—children playing, couples strolling hand in hand, and the town's beloved historic buildings standing proudly against the skyline.

"Isn't it beautiful?" I murmured, captivated by the mural's lifelike details.

Jake stepped beside me, his eyes sparkling with admiration. "It feels like looking into a living memory, doesn't it? The artist truly captured the essence of this place."

Leah joined us, her expression softening as she took in the mural. "It's like the past and present are colliding in such a perfect way. You can almost hear the laughter and feel the warmth of the sun."

As we stood in front of the mural, I couldn't help but think of the countless memories woven into its fabric. Larkspur was more than just a town; it was a tapestry of experiences, filled with laughter, heartaches, and triumphs. The mural was a reminder that we were all interconnected, our stories blending into a greater narrative.

With renewed energy, I suggested, "Why don't we gather everyone around and share some favorite Larkspur memories? It could be a fun way to celebrate the town and its spirit."

Jake grinned, clearly on board with the idea. "That's a fantastic notion! Let's do it."

As we made our way through the gallery, I felt a growing sense of excitement. We called for attention, and soon a small crowd gathered around us, curiosity sparkling in their eyes. I introduced the idea, my voice laced with enthusiasm. "We want to hear your stories! What makes Larkspur special to you?"

A ripple of laughter and chatter erupted as one brave soul stepped forward. A middle-aged woman with silver hair and a warm smile shared a tale of her childhood adventures by the river, where she and her friends would spend long summer days building rafts and exploring the winding banks. Her words painted vivid imagery, bringing the crowd into her world, and soon, others began to share their own stories, weaving a rich tapestry of nostalgia.

As the memories flowed, I felt the power of connection enveloping us all. Each tale resonated deeply, reflecting the unique spirit of Larkspur. A man shared how he proposed to his wife at the very spot where the town's annual festival was held, while a young artist described her journey of finding inspiration among the historical architecture that dotted our streets. Laughter and tears mingled as we celebrated the essence of our community, each story a brushstroke adding to the mural of our lives.

Mia stood beside me, her eyes shining with joy as she listened to the stories unfold. "This is what it's all about," she said, her voice barely above a whisper. "These moments of connection remind us why we love this place."

A PLACE TO BELONG

As the stories continued, I glanced over at Jake and Leah, their laughter ringing out like music against the backdrop of heartfelt anecdotes. A warmth spread through me, a realization settling in. We weren't just individuals competing for attention; we were part of something much larger—a community bound by shared experiences and dreams.

After the last story was shared, applause erupted, filling the gallery with an atmosphere of warmth and celebration. I felt a surge of gratitude for everyone who had gathered, for the connections we were building, and for the art that had brought us together.

As the evening began to wind down, I glanced around the gallery, taking in the vibrant faces illuminated by the soft glow of the lights. The warmth of shared laughter hung in the air like a cherished memory. The unease that had once plagued me was replaced by a profound sense of belonging.

Leah approached me, her smile genuine and bright. "Thank you for inviting us to share our stories. It made the night feel even more special."

I smiled back, feeling the earlier tension between us dissolve completely. "Thank you for being a part of it. This wouldn't have been the same without your energy."

As the last remnants of the exhibit faded into memory, I felt a renewed sense of purpose igniting within me. Art had the power to connect, to heal, and to inspire. And in that moment, surrounded by friends and shared stories, I knew that I was exactly where I was meant to be—part of a vibrant community, woven together like the threads of a beautiful tapestry, celebrating the art of life itself.

Chapter 26: Fractured Reflections

The air was thick with the scent of fresh paint, a concoction of linseed oil and something sweetly pungent, as I stepped into The Willow. The gallery had always been a sanctuary for me, a place where colors and shapes twisted into stories, narratives that danced on canvases like fireflies at dusk. But now, it felt like a theater with the curtain drawn, the audience whispering in hushed tones about what once was. I was enveloped by a lingering melancholy that mirrored the muted hues of the latest exhibit: a collection of photographs that captured the fleeting essence of life's most vibrant moments—kaleidoscopic sunsets, children playing under the spray of a summer fountain, couples laughing as they twirled through city streets. But none of those images felt like my reality anymore.

Jake was no longer the sun in my sky; he was a fleeting shadow, a silhouette that darted away before I could catch up. It was disheartening to watch him become a ghost of his former self, slipping through my fingers like sand, his laughter now more of an echo than a melody. I often found myself at the café across the street, nursing a cup of bitter coffee, watching the world bustling by, unaware of the storm brewing in my heart. The clink of spoons against porcelain and the rich aroma of roasted beans did little to distract me from the gnawing worry that Jake was slipping away. I had seen Leah's familiar silhouette in the gallery on more than one occasion, her presence a chilling reminder of past wounds that seemed to fester just beneath the surface of our fragile relationship.

It was on a particularly gray afternoon, the sky heavy with the promise of rain, that I decided enough was enough. I could no longer stand idly by as our love flickered like a candle in the wind. The warmth that once enveloped us felt distant, like the remnants of a fire long extinguished. My heart raced as I made my way to his apartment, each step heavy with dread and determination. The world outside mirrored my inner turmoil; drops of rain began to splatter against the pavement, creating a symphony of sound that echoed my heart's chaotic rhythm.

As I reached the door, my knuckles hovered for a moment, hesitating before I rapped on the wood. It opened slowly, revealing Jake's tired eyes, the light within them dimmed as if someone had drawn the curtains on the brightness we once shared. He stepped back, allowing me to enter, but the space between us felt vast, filled with unspoken words and unresolved feelings. I took a deep breath, inhaling the scent of his cologne mingled with the faint trace of oil paints and turpentine. The familiarity of it all tugged at my heart, reminding me of who we were, of the magic that had once flowed effortlessly between us.

"Hey," I said, my voice softer than I intended, laced with a mixture of hope and anxiety. "Can we talk?"

He nodded, his expression a blend of concern and reluctance, as he led me to the living room, where light streamed in through the large windows, illuminating the chaos of canvases and half-finished paintings that lay scattered around. It was a beautiful mess, a reflection of his artistic mind, yet I felt the weight of his distraction pressing down on us.

"Is it about Leah?" I ventured, my heart pounding as I watched his gaze drift to the window, where rain began to streak down in earnest, blurring the outside world into a watercolor dream.

He hesitated, a flicker of guilt passing across his face before he nodded. "I don't know how to let her go," he confessed, his voice barely above a whisper. The admission hung in the air, heavy and suffocating. It was as if he had unwittingly laid a bare wound between us, a chasm I feared we might never cross.

I took a step closer, my resolve hardening despite the heartache swelling within me. "You can't keep holding on to the past, Jake. It's eating you alive, and it's pushing us apart."

His eyes met mine, a storm of emotions swirling within their depths. "I'm trying," he replied, frustration creeping into his tone. "But it's hard to just forget. She was... she was my everything."

"Then let me be your everything," I implored, desperation creeping into my voice as I reached out, my fingers brushing against his. The contact sent a jolt of warmth through me, a reminder of the connection we shared, yet the barrier of his unresolved feelings felt insurmountable.

"Do you really think it's that simple?" he challenged, pulling his hand away, and the loss felt like a dagger to my heart. "I wish it were. But every time I look at you, I see her. I hear her laugh echoing in the back of my mind. It's not fair to you."

My heart sank, the words he spoke like stones tossed into the depths of my soul, creating ripples of despair. "But I'm here, Jake. I'm standing right in front of you. I love you. Isn't that worth fighting for?"

The rain outside intensified, drumming against the windows as if the world itself was urging him to make a choice. I could see the struggle etched across his features, a battle between love and grief that left me feeling both helpless and fiercely protective.

In that moment, I realized the truth: love, in all its complexities, was never meant to be easy. It was a tumultuous journey, filled with bumps and detours that tested the strength of even the most vibrant connections. I was prepared to weather the storm, to fight for the flickering light that remained between us, even if it meant confronting the shadows of his past.

The silence between us expanded like the space between the stars, both infinite and suffocating, while the rain continued its rhythmic percussion against the glass. Jake's eyes, typically a vibrant green, now seemed clouded with uncertainty, flickering between anger and vulnerability as he battled the remnants of his memories. I wanted to bridge the chasm that had formed, to weave our lives together like the vivid strokes of his paintbrush across the canvas, but I felt a deep-rooted fear, an insidious whisper that told me I might be fighting a losing battle.

With a deep breath, I stepped further into his world, hoping to fill the void with warmth. "I don't want to be a shadow in your life, Jake. You have to know that." My voice cracked, betraying the strength I tried to project. I needed him to understand that my feelings weren't a mere flicker but a blazing fire willing to burn away the darkness of his past.

He turned away, his gaze lost in the chaos of his studio, where half-finished canvases loomed like ghosts of dreams unfulfilled. Each piece told a story, yet there was a certain hollowness to them now, as if they too were waiting for Jake to reclaim the vibrancy he had once poured into his art. The colors seemed muted, and for a moment, I felt like I was peering into a distorted reflection of our relationship—beautiful yet unrecognizable.

"Sometimes," he began, his voice barely above a whisper, "I don't know how to separate my past from my present. Leah... she was my muse, my reason to paint. Losing her felt like losing the very essence of who I am." He turned back to face me, and the raw pain in his eyes nearly shattered me. "And I don't want to keep hurting you."

The weight of his honesty wrapped around us, thick and palpable. It was both a blessing and a curse, the truth that illuminated our fractured connection while simultaneously dimming the hope I clung to. I could see the battle raging within him, a tempest of love and loss that kept him bound to memories he could not shake.

"Jake," I said, stepping closer, my heart racing with the urgency of my next words. "You're not losing yourself by moving forward. You're allowing room for something new, something beautiful." My fingers brushed against the back of his hand, and I could feel the heat radiating from his skin. I craved that warmth, the connection that had always felt like home. "I'm here, right here, ready to be your muse if you'll let me."

He shook his head slowly, a defeated smile gracing his lips, though it didn't reach his eyes. "You deserve more than to be someone's rebound. I can't promise that I won't think of her, that I won't see her when I look at you. It's not fair to you."

I swallowed hard, the lump in my throat threatening to choke me. "What if I want to be here anyway? What if I want to help you rediscover the joy in your art, in life? I'm not asking you to forget her, Jake. I just want you to let me in."

There was a beat of silence, a heartbeat suspended in time, before his expression shifted, the walls he'd built around himself beginning to crack. "You really mean that?" he asked, uncertainty mingling with something more hopeful in his voice.

"Absolutely," I replied, my own heart daring to rise from the ashes of despair. "I believe in us. I believe in your art, in the love we can create together. I'm willing to face the shadows with you."

He hesitated, his internal conflict playing out like a tragic ballet. The weight of the world was etched into the lines of his face, yet beneath it all was the glimmer of something that made my heart race—a flicker of hope. It was a small spark, but in that moment, it felt like the dawn after an interminable night.

"Okay," he whispered, and the word lingered in the air, heavy with possibility. "Let's try."

As the rain continued to cascade down the window, I felt a warmth blossom in my chest. It was a fragile connection, yet somehow more real than any feeling I'd ever known. We stood together, caught in a moment that felt both precarious and exhilarating, like the first breath of spring after a long, bitter winter.

Days turned into weeks, and I watched as Jake began to paint again, the brush gliding across the canvas as if it had a life of its own. Each stroke seemed to breathe life back into his art, pulling vibrant colors from the depths of his heart and soul. With each visit to his studio, I felt a renewed sense of purpose, as though I was witnessing the rebirth of not just his creativity, but of us.

It became our ritual; I would bring coffee and pastries from the café down the street, and together, we would transform the stark white walls of his studio into a gallery of our shared experiences, a testament to the moments we dared to embrace amidst the lingering shadows of the past.

I would sit cross-legged on the floor, watching him work, the way his brow furrowed in concentration, the delicate way his fingers danced over the canvas as if coaxing the colors into existence. The world outside faded, the clatter of the city diminishing into a gentle hum as our laughter filled the space between us. I reveled in the simplicity of those moments, relishing the way his eyes would light up when he unveiled a new creation, the joy palpable in the air as he shared it with me.

But even in those moments of bliss, the specter of Leah lingered like a stubborn shadow, and I knew I couldn't entirely escape her ghost. I sensed the occasional flicker of sorrow in Jake's eyes when he spoke of her, a reminder of the depths of his loss. Yet I remained steadfast, offering him my support, my love, as he navigated the delicate terrain of his emotions.

One afternoon, as we shared an impromptu picnic in his studio, surrounded by scattered sketches and splatters of paint, he turned to me with an earnest expression. "I've been thinking about her again," he confessed, his voice a mixture of vulnerability and strength. "And it doesn't hurt as much as it used to. It's like she's become a part of who I am, not something that defines me anymore."

My heart soared at his words, the admission a testament to the journey we were embarking on together. "That's a good thing, Jake," I replied, reaching for his hand, intertwining our fingers. "You're allowing yourself to heal, to grow. You're painting your own path now."

He smiled, a genuine smile that brightened the room like the sun breaking through the clouds. In that moment, I realized that love wasn't just about erasing the past; it was about embracing it, allowing it to shape us while also carving out space for new memories, new experiences.

And as we sat there, the world outside alive with the vibrant sounds of city life, I felt an overwhelming sense of hope surge within me. The journey ahead would undoubtedly have its trials, but we were no longer two solitary souls adrift in the tide. Together, we were a masterpiece in the making, colors blending and swirling, creating something uniquely ours—a testament to resilience, love, and the courage to face the future.

The weeks flowed like a gently winding river, filled with currents of emotion, hope, and the occasional rock that threatened to capsize us. Each day, I found myself sinking deeper into the vibrant tapestry we were weaving, the colors bold and brash against the faded memories of what once was. Jake had become more than just a man battling his ghosts; he was a canvas alive with potential, and I was determined to help him realize that potential, to paint a new picture together.

As autumn unfurled its golden tendrils, the air turned crisp and fresh, carrying the scents of cinnamon and burnt sugar from nearby cafés. The streets of our neighborhood transformed into a mosaic of amber and ochre leaves, crunching beneath our feet as we wandered hand in hand, exchanging stories and laughter like treasures waiting to be unearthed. The city felt alive, buzzing with the hum of life, and for the first time in a long while, I felt as if we were part of something larger than ourselves, like threads in a vast tapestry, weaving together tales of love, loss, and redemption.

It was during one of these walks that Jake paused beneath a gnarled oak, its branches sprawling like a wise old sage. He turned to me, his expression suddenly serious, the shadows of his past momentarily eclipsing the sunlight that danced in his eyes. "I've been thinking a lot about Leah," he admitted, the vulnerability in his voice echoing the rustling leaves around us. "I need to visit her grave. I need to say goodbye, to truly let go."

His words struck me like lightning, illuminating the dark corners of my heart where I had tried to bury my fears. Part of me felt the instinctive urge to recoil, to protect our fragile connection from the inevitable pain of his memories, but I also recognized the importance of this step for him. It was a necessary journey, a rite of passage that he needed to undertake if we were ever to find solace together.

"I'll go with you," I offered, trying to inject a sense of reassurance into the air thick with anticipation. He looked at me, surprised yet grateful, the corners of his lips quirking upward in a small, genuine smile. "Are you sure? It might be... difficult."

I nodded, meeting his gaze with unwavering resolve. "You're worth it, Jake. We're worth it."

The day we chose to visit the cemetery, the sky wore a somber gray, as if the universe itself understood the weight of our task. I dressed in layers, my heart a chaotic blend of apprehension and determination, and together we made our way to the hallowed grounds where memories rested beneath the earth. The air grew colder with each step, and I could sense Jake's growing tension, his shoulders tight and his hands fidgeting as we approached.

The cemetery was serene, a sanctuary adorned with weathered gravestones and flowers that whispered tales of lives well-lived. We walked in silence, the crunch of gravel underfoot harmonizing with the distant chirping of birds and the rustle of leaves. I squeezed his hand, hoping to lend him strength as we neared Leah's resting place, marked by a simple stone adorned with her name and a few delicate blooms.

Jake stopped before the grave, and I felt him draw in a deep breath, the weight of his memories pressing down on him like a shroud. I stood slightly behind him, granting him the space he needed while remaining close enough to lend my support. He knelt, placing a trembling hand on the cool stone, and I watched as a single tear rolled down his cheek, a testament to the pain he had long bottled up inside.

"Hey, Leah," he whispered, his voice cracking. "I know it's been a while, and I'm sorry I haven't come sooner. I've been lost, tangled in memories and grief."

The wind seemed to carry his words, wrapping them in a gentle embrace, as if the very earth beneath us acknowledged his struggle. I could feel the heaviness in the air begin to shift, the tension slowly easing as he poured out his heart, sharing not just his regrets but also the gratitude he felt for her presence in his life.

"I'll always love you," he said, his voice growing steadier. "But I can't keep living in the past. I want to move forward, to find joy again, to create a new life."

With those words, it was as if a dam broke within him. He released a shaky breath, and I felt the air shift, the weight of the past slipping away like a leaf carried off by the wind. It was a poignant moment, filled with both sorrow and liberation, and I silently thanked Leah for the part she had played in Jake's life, for the lessons she had taught him, and for the love that would always remain.

As he stood, brushing the dirt from his knees, I stepped forward, wrapping my arms around him, feeling the tension in his body slowly dissolve against me. "You did it," I whispered, reveling in the warmth of his embrace, the barriers he had erected beginning to crumble, if only for a moment. "You took the first step."

He pulled back slightly, searching my eyes, and I could see the uncertainty that still lingered there. "But what if it's not enough?" he asked, the vulnerability in his voice pulling at my heartstrings. "What if I'm still not ready?"

I cupped his face in my hands, grounding him with my gaze. "This isn't a race, Jake. Healing takes time, and it's okay to have days when you stumble. What matters is that you're trying, that you're willing to confront what you've lost so you can embrace what lies ahead."

His lips curled into a tentative smile, and in that moment, I felt the warmth of hope blooming once more. We walked back through the cemetery, hand in hand, the weight of unspoken fears lifting as we ventured into the world beyond the gates, the air tinged with the fresh scent of possibility.

The weeks that followed were a tapestry of shared moments, laughter echoing in the corners of our lives as we ventured into new experiences together. We explored local art galleries, finding inspiration in the creative expressions of others, our discussions deepening as we challenged one another's perspectives. I watched as Jake began to embrace the beauty around him, his art transforming into vibrant reflections of his journey—each stroke a celebration of life, love, and the lessons learned through heartache.

One evening, as the sun dipped low in the horizon, painting the sky in hues of coral and lavender, Jake surprised me with a picnic in the park. We settled on a blanket, surrounded by the gentle sounds of laughter and music, the warm breeze weaving through the trees. He pulled out a sketchpad, flipping it open to reveal a series of paintings he had created, each one infused with raw emotion and vivid color.

"I wanted to show you what I've been working on," he said, his eyes glinting with excitement and a hint of vulnerability. "It's inspired by us, by everything we've shared since… since Leah."

As he revealed each piece, I marveled at how he captured our moments—the way the sunlight spilled through the leaves, the laughter we shared over coffee, the tender glances that spoke volumes. It was as if he had taken the essence of our journey and woven it into a vibrant tapestry, one that reflected not just his healing but the deepening of our connection.

"Jake, these are incredible," I breathed, my heart swelling with pride and love. "You've captured so much beauty. It's as if you've turned your pain into art."

He smiled, a look of relief washing over his features. "It feels good to finally express what's inside me, to let go of the burdens I've been carrying."

As we sat beneath the expansive sky, a sense of peace enveloped us, the colors of the sunset merging with the warmth of our hands intertwined. I realized that this was more than just a relationship; it was a journey of rediscovery, a testament to the power of love to mend broken hearts. Together, we were building a new foundation, one colored by laughter, healing, and the beautiful complexity of two souls choosing to embrace each other fully.

And in that moment, surrounded by the whispers of the wind and the fading light, I knew that the path ahead would not always be smooth. Yet, I felt an unshakable certainty that we were ready to navigate it together, two artists painting our lives with the vivid colors of hope and resilience, creating a masterpiece that would forever tell the story of love reborn.

Chapter 27: Choices in the Dark

The familiar chime of the bell above the door marked my entrance into the coffee shop, a cozy haven tucked away on a sunlit street in Austin, Texas. The air inside was warm and fragrant, infused with the earthy aroma of roasted coffee beans and the sweet scent of baked goods. I closed my eyes for a moment, allowing the atmosphere to wash over me like a comforting embrace. The gentle hum of conversations mingled with the sound of espresso machines hissing, creating a backdrop that felt both bustling and intimate.

As I settled into my usual corner seat, the sun streaming through the large windows illuminated the mismatched wooden tables and eclectic decor—vintage posters plastered on the walls and bookshelves filled with dog-eared novels. It was a place where time seemed to slow, where laughter danced alongside the clinking of ceramic mugs, and where secrets could be whispered over steaming cups. Today, however, the beauty of it all felt muted, a soft filter against the backdrop of my anxiety.

I wrapped my fingers around the warm ceramic mug, the heat seeping into my palms, and took a sip of my rich mocha. The chocolatey sweetness coated my tongue, but it failed to lift the weight that pressed against my chest. Jake and Leah—two names that had become like a pair of anchors in my life, dragging me down into a sea of uncertainty. Their faces flashed through my mind, a collage of memories both sweet and bitter.

Jake, with his easy smile and mischievous eyes, had always been my north star, guiding me through the twists and turns of life. But lately, that guiding light felt more like a flickering candle, threatened by the winds of doubt that swirled around us. And Leah—my confidante turned adversary—her laughter had once been a melody that danced in the air, but now it felt like a dissonant note in an otherwise harmonious song. The thought of our friendship unraveling made my stomach churn, a sickening knot tightening with each passing moment.

Just as I was lost in this mental fog, the door swung open again, and the bell chimed, bringing in a rush of cool air. I looked up, and there she was—Mia. Her entrance was like a gust of fresh wind, revitalizing the atmosphere. With her long chestnut hair cascading over her shoulders and a grin that could rival the sun, she exuded warmth. We hadn't seen each other since graduation, life pulling us in different directions, but here she was, brightening my gloomy afternoon.

"Mia!" I exclaimed, the smile on my face genuine and wide. I waved her over, and she glided across the room with the grace of a dancer, her presence a balm to my frayed nerves.

"Hey, stranger!" She slid into the seat across from me, her eyes sparkling with curiosity. "What's going on? You look like you just lost a battle with a tornado."

I chuckled, though it felt strained, and stirred my drink absentmindedly. "More like I'm caught in the eye of one," I replied, letting out a sigh that carried the weight of my worries. I found solace in her company, the way her presence instantly made the chaos in my head quieter, like the calm after the storm.

We exchanged pleasantries, reminiscing about shared memories of late-night study sessions and spontaneous road trips that had defined our teenage years. Yet, as the laughter faded, I felt the familiar heaviness return. I leaned in closer, my voice barely above a whisper. "It's Jake and Leah," I confessed, feeling vulnerable as I laid my soul bare. "Things are... complicated. I don't know what to do."

Mia's expression softened, her brow furrowing slightly as she took in my words. "Complicated how?" she asked, her tone inviting yet probing.

"Jake is... he's everything I thought I wanted, but now I'm not so sure. And Leah, she's not just my friend anymore; she's become something else—someone I'm afraid to lose." My voice trembled as I spoke, the tension building within me like a storm ready to unleash its fury.

Mia leaned back, her fingers wrapped around her own steaming mug. "You're letting fear guide your choices," she said, her voice steady yet filled with a gentle urgency. "You need to take control of your own narrative. You can't let the opinions and feelings of others dictate what you want."

Her words struck a chord deep within me, resonating like the first clear notes of a song I had forgotten. The realization that I had been living in a state of reaction, allowing circumstances to dictate my choices, was unsettling. "But what if I make the wrong choice?" I countered, a thread of anxiety lacing my words.

"What if you don't?" Mia's gaze was unwavering, fierce yet compassionate. "Life isn't about making the perfect choice; it's about making choices that align with who you are. Embrace the uncertainty—it's where growth happens."

I mulled over her words, feeling a flicker of determination ignite within me. Perhaps it was time to reclaim my story, to step into the unknown with courage rather than fear. The thought filled me with a strange mix of excitement and trepidation. As I looked around the coffee shop, the patrons around me—lost in their own worlds, wrapped in their own narratives—felt like an echo of my own journey.

In this vibrant moment, surrounded by the sounds and smells of life, I began to imagine the possibility of moving forward, of shaping my destiny rather than letting it be shaped by others. Perhaps the storm I felt brewing inside could transform into a powerful force for change. Perhaps it was time to embrace the chaos, to step boldly into the light that awaited me.

With every sip of my mocha, I felt a renewed sense of purpose stirring in the depths of my being, igniting a warmth that spread through me like sunlight breaking through heavy clouds. I looked across the table at Mia, whose expression was a blend of concern and encouragement. The way her eyes glimmered, filled with unwavering support, made me believe that maybe I wasn't as alone in this chaotic whirlwind as I had felt moments before.

"Okay," I said, my voice steadier than it had been just minutes earlier. "What do you think I should do?" The question hung between us, a fragile thread woven into the fabric of our conversation, and I could sense the weight of it.

Mia leaned forward, her fingers curling around the rim of her cup. "You need to be honest with yourself first. What do you truly want? Not what you think you should want or what others expect you to want. What's in your heart?"

Her words hung in the air like the scent of fresh coffee, rich and intoxicating. I closed my eyes, letting her question settle in my mind, the chaos quieting as I turned inward. What did I want? I had been so busy accommodating Jake's desires and Leah's expectations that I'd lost sight of my own. The realization was like a cold splash of water, awakening something dormant within me.

"I want to feel free," I finally said, the words tumbling out, raw and unfiltered. "Free to make choices that resonate with who I am, without feeling like I have to apologize for them."

Mia smiled, her eyes sparkling with delight as if I had just revealed a hidden treasure. "That's a start! You need to communicate that with both of them. Set the stage for what you want your life to look like. Maybe it means redefining your relationships or even reevaluating what you're willing to accept from them."

Her insights sparked a cascade of thoughts, weaving a tapestry of possibilities that filled the space between us. I envisioned a world where I could stand firmly in my truth, unafraid of the ripples it might cause. I imagined telling Jake how I felt—the weight of my fears, the nagging doubts that clouded our connection, and how

I yearned for a partnership rooted in understanding rather than expectation. I saw Leah, too, standing before me, her laughter still a cherished melody but now underscored with honesty instead of tension.

"But what if they don't understand?" I asked, a flicker of doubt dancing in my chest.

"That's the risk you take," Mia replied, her tone unwavering. "But you have to ask yourself: what's worse? Living in the shadows of someone else's expectations or stepping into the light of your own truth, regardless of how they react? It's about your happiness, after all."

Her conviction struck a chord, resonating like a beautifully crafted symphony. I could feel the gears shifting in my mind, thoughts transitioning from fear to determination, each one snapping into place like pieces of a puzzle. It was as if the universe conspired around me, guiding me toward clarity, even in the midst of uncertainty.

A sudden gust of wind rattled the windowpanes, sending a shiver through the cozy space. Outside, the vibrant leaves danced in a swirl of red and gold, marking the arrival of autumn. It was a season of transformation, after all—a time when nature shed its layers to reveal something more authentic beneath. Maybe I needed to do the same.

"Okay," I said, a newfound resolve swelling within me. "I'll talk to them. But I don't know how to begin."

Mia's smile widened, and she leaned back, her fingers drumming lightly on the table, the rhythm of an upbeat tune. "Start with honesty. You don't have to have a script; just let them see your heart. You might be surprised at how they respond."

The idea settled comfortably within me, a spark igniting a fire of possibility. I imagined myself in that moment—sitting across from Jake, my voice steady as I bared my soul, and then confronting Leah with equal vulnerability. It was exhilarating and terrifying all at once, but for the first time in a long time, I felt ready to take that leap.

As we continued our conversation, I could feel the pulse of the coffee shop around us—the clattering of cups, the laughter echoing off the walls, and the comforting familiarity of shared stories. I noticed a couple at the next table, their heads bent together in shared secrets, the glow of intimacy casting a halo around them. It made me long for that kind of connection, one built on openness and understanding, where fear didn't serve as a barrier but rather a bridge to deeper intimacy.

"I can't thank you enough for this," I said, glancing at Mia, my heart swelling with gratitude. "You have this way of making everything seem possible."

She waved her hand dismissively, but her modesty only made me admire her more. "I'm just reminding you of what you already know deep down. You have the strength to face this. Trust yourself."

With each word exchanged, I felt a little more unshackled from the weight I had carried for so long. The world outside the coffee shop seemed brighter, the sky bluer, and even the cacophony of voices turned into a symphony of encouragement. Perhaps I had been too focused on the shadows of my choices, allowing them to loom large in my mind, when all along, I had the power to illuminate my own path.

When the barista called out for my order, it broke through my reverie, pulling me back into the present. I stood to grab my drink, a renewed energy bubbling within me. The rich mocha tasted sweeter than before, the perfect blend of chocolate and coffee, each sip a reminder of the fortitude I was beginning to reclaim.

As I returned to the table, I locked eyes with Mia, a smile spreading across my face. "You know what? I think I'll start with Jake tonight."

The confidence surged through me, like electricity coursing through my veins. I could already envision the conversation unfolding—the nerves, the hesitations, but ultimately, the clarity that would come from finally voicing my truth. This was my story, my journey, and it was time to step forward, to reclaim the narrative I had nearly lost amidst the chaos of others' expectations.

With that thought, I finished my drink, savoring the last bit of warmth before it vanished. I felt lighter, as though the weight of my choices had transformed into something tangible and beautiful—a canvas waiting for the strokes of my desires and dreams. Today, the light had broken through, and I was ready to embrace whatever lay ahead.

As I left the warm embrace of the coffee shop, the brisk autumn air nipped at my cheeks, invigorating me. Each breath filled my lungs with a newfound sense of purpose, crisp and refreshing, like biting into a tart apple. I walked briskly down the street, my mind dancing with possibilities. The world felt vibrant around me—cars honked impatiently, leaves crunched underfoot, and the laughter of children playing in a nearby park wove through the cool air. I was acutely aware of how every sound and color seemed heightened, as if the universe had aligned to remind me of the beauty nestled within the chaos of everyday life.

My destination loomed ahead, an unassuming brick building where I had spent countless hours pouring over textbooks, doodling in the margins, and dreaming of what lay beyond graduation. It felt surreal to be returning, my heart racing with the weight of anticipation. I had decided to confront Jake first, to untangle the mess that had become our relationship. As I approached, I could see him through the large windows, his familiar silhouette hunched over a table, focused intently on his laptop. The sight stirred a mixture of nostalgia and apprehension within me.

Taking a deep breath, I pushed open the door, the chime echoing a welcome. As I stepped inside, the aroma of freshly brewed coffee enveloped me like a warm blanket, and I spotted Jake immediately. He looked up, his eyes brightening at the sight of me, a smile spreading across his face that sent a flutter through my stomach. There was a comfort in his presence, a reminder of our shared history, but also an awareness that things had shifted beneath the surface.

"Hey! I didn't expect to see you here," he said, closing his laptop. His casual demeanor was disarming, but I could see the flicker of curiosity in his eyes.

"Yeah, I just had a meeting nearby," I replied, trying to keep my tone light as I approached. "Mind if I join you for a bit?"

"Of course, always," he replied, gesturing to the empty seat across from him.

As I settled in, I could feel the familiar warmth of his gaze, but beneath it lay a tension that mirrored my own. The words I had rehearsed in my head began to churn, battling against my nerves. I could no longer pretend that everything was fine, that our dynamic hadn't shifted. "Jake," I started, my voice trembling slightly, "there's something we need to talk about."

His expression shifted, concern etching lines across his forehead. "What's wrong? You seem serious."

I swallowed hard, gathering my thoughts like a patchwork quilt. "It's about us," I said finally, searching for the right way to articulate the storm brewing within me. "I've been feeling...lost. Like we've been drifting apart without even realizing it."

Jake's brows furrowed, and he leaned forward, his hands clasped tightly on the table. "I've felt that too. Things have felt off lately, but I didn't want to bring it up. I thought maybe it was just a phase."

A sense of relief washed over me, knowing that I wasn't the only one grappling with this uncertainty. "I don't want us to just drift," I continued, feeling emboldened by the honesty coursing through our conversation. "I want us to be real with each other. I want to explore what we both truly want, without fear or expectation."

He paused, his eyes searching mine. "I want that too. I've been scared to admit it because I care about you so much. I didn't want to ruin what we have."

"By pretending everything's okay?" I replied gently. "Maybe we need to redefine what we have. Explore whether we're meant to be more than just a comfort zone for each other."

The silence stretched between us, thick and charged, until a small smile broke through Jake's tension. "You know, I appreciate your courage in saying this. I think we owe it to ourselves to be brave. But what does 'more' look like?"

As I leaned back, contemplating his question, I was struck by the realization that the answers would be as unique as our relationship. "It means having those difficult conversations, creating space for vulnerability. It means understanding that it's okay to take risks with our hearts. It means being willing to put ourselves out there."

He nodded, a mix of admiration and uncertainty flickering across his face. "I want to do that. Let's figure this out together."

Our conversation flowed easily after that, as if a dam had broken and all the words we had kept bottled up began to spill forth. We laughed, reminiscing about old memories, and explored the depths of our feelings. With every exchange, the weight on my heart lightened, revealing a path forward where honesty and authenticity could flourish.

As the sun dipped lower in the sky, casting a warm golden hue over the café, I felt the last remnants of my anxiety dissipate. Jake and I had stepped into uncharted territory, but I felt invigorated, like a ship unfurling its sails to catch the wind.

After our conversation, I ventured into the cool evening, buoyed by the resolve we had reached. My next stop was Leah. The thought of confronting her tugged at my heartstrings, an amalgam of affection and fear. Our friendship had been a bedrock in my life, yet the uncertainty of her feelings loomed large.

As I walked toward the small bookstore where she often worked, I recalled our countless heart-to-heart talks over cups of tea, sharing dreams and secrets as though they were rare treasures. The door jingled as I entered, the familiar scent of old paper and fresh ink enveloping me, grounding me in nostalgia.

Leah was at the register, her auburn hair pulled back in a messy bun, eyes lighting up when she saw me. "Hey! It's so good to see you!" she exclaimed, her voice infused with genuine warmth.

"Hey! You too. Do you have a moment?" I asked, already knowing the answer but hoping for a brief respite before the conversation I needed to have.

"Of course! Just let me finish up here."

As she finished ringing up a customer, I paced slightly, glancing at the stacks of books that lined the shelves. Each title was a doorway to another world, another perspective, much like what I was hoping to find in our conversation.

Once the store quieted, Leah turned her attention fully to me, her brow furrowing slightly. "You look serious. What's going on?"

I took a deep breath, letting the comfort of familiarity wrap around me. "I've been doing a lot of thinking lately. About us."

"Us?" Her eyes narrowed in curiosity, and I could see the flicker of concern cross her face.

"Yeah, about our friendship. I love you like a sister, and that's why I need to be honest. I feel like something's shifted between us, and it's been bothering me."

Leah's expression softened, but I noticed the tension in her posture. "I've felt it too. It's like we're standing on opposite sides of a canyon and can't quite reach each other."

Her words struck a chord, resonating with my own feelings of isolation. "I don't want us to drift apart. I think we need to talk about how we've been feeling. We owe it to ourselves."

She nodded, her eyes glistening with unshed emotion. "You're right. I've been holding back because I didn't want to lose you. I've felt jealous and insecure about everything happening with you and Jake. I thought if I pulled away, it would hurt less."

"Leah," I said gently, "we've been through too much to let misunderstandings come between us. Your friendship is precious to me, and I don't want to lose that either."

We talked for what felt like hours, unraveling the threads of our friendship, stitching it back together with openness and understanding. The weight of unspoken truths lifted as we embraced our vulnerabilities, each revelation a step toward healing.

As I stepped out into the crisp night air, the stars twinkling above felt like a tapestry of possibilities woven into the fabric of my journey. I had faced the darkness and emerged stronger, the fears that had once paralyzed me now transformed into stepping stones. My heart felt lighter, filled with hope and the promise of new beginnings.

The path ahead was still shrouded in uncertainty, but I knew I had the strength to navigate it. With Jake and Leah beside me, ready to explore what lay ahead, I felt as if I could finally breathe, like the world had opened up and invited me to dance among the stars.

Chapter 28: The Breaking Point

The air inside The Willow clung to me like a fog, heavy with the scent of cedar and fresh-brewed coffee, as I pushed the door open. The bell chimed softly above my head, a reminder that I had entered a sanctuary that was both familiar and foreign. It was a small café tucked away on the edge of town, where the walls whispered stories of laughter, sorrow, and every human emotion in between. Mismatched chairs and tables adorned the worn wooden floors, each telling its own tale of a patron who lingered too long or left too soon. I spotted Jake and Leah immediately, their silhouettes framed by the sun streaming in through the window, casting long shadows on the ground that danced and flickered like the turmoil in my heart.

As I approached, I couldn't shake the feeling that I was intruding on something sacred. Their faces were taut with emotion; Leah's lips were pressed into a thin line, her eyes glimmering like stormy seas. Jake, on the other hand, appeared caught in a tempest of his own making. His brow furrowed as if he were wrestling with thoughts too heavy for his shoulders. The sight of them together ignited a fire in my chest, a simmering blend of jealousy and fear that I had tried so hard to suppress. With every step, I felt the weight of unresolved questions pressing down on me, demanding to be set free.

"Can we talk?" The words slipped from my lips before I could stop them, bold yet shaky, echoing through the small space and silencing the low hum of conversation around us. Their gazes snapped to mine, the tension in the air thickening as their moment shattered like glass.

"Hey," Jake said, his voice a soft balm to my frayed nerves. But there was a note of hesitation in his tone, as if he sensed the storm brewing within me. Leah shifted slightly in her chair, her posture rigid, and I could feel the walls of her fortifications rising, a barrier between us that felt insurmountable.

"Yeah, let's talk," Leah replied, her words laced with a steeliness that both intrigued and intimidated me. It was then that I realized the vulnerability I had kept hidden for so long was about to be laid bare, and I wasn't sure if I was ready for the consequences. But as I met Jake's gaze, I saw a flicker of understanding, an invitation to dive deeper into the uncharted waters of our complicated relationships.

I settled into the chair across from them, the wood cool against my skin, grounding me even as my heart raced. "I've been thinking…" I started, my voice faltering as I grasped for the right words to convey the chaos swirling in my mind. "About us. About everything."

The room was alive with the sounds of clinking mugs and distant laughter, yet it felt like we were in our own bubble, suspended in time. Jake leaned in, his brow lifting in curiosity. "What do you mean?" he asked, the warmth of his gaze washing over me like sunlight breaking through a cloudy sky.

I swallowed hard, the taste of trepidation bitter on my tongue. "I mean… the three of us. It feels like we're all dancing around something—like there's this unspoken tension that's been building, and I can't ignore it anymore." My pulse quickened, the weight of my words hanging in the air, begging for validation or rebuttal.

Leah crossed her arms defensively, her eyes narrowing slightly as if I had just poked at a wound she preferred to keep hidden. "You think it's just tension? You think that's all it is?" Her voice was laced with incredulity, and I could see the hurt flashing in her eyes, a flicker of vulnerability that contradicted her tough exterior. I could almost hear her walls creaking under the pressure.

"It's not just tension," I insisted, my voice rising with urgency. "It's fear. It's confusion. It's everything we've kept bottled up inside. I don't want to dance around it anymore." The words spilled out of me, each one heavier than the last, a tidal wave of raw emotion threatening to wash away the carefully constructed barriers we had all built.

Jake looked between us, his expression pained as if he were caught in a crossfire. "Maybe we should all just say what we're feeling. Lay it all out there, no more hiding." His voice was steady, yet the tremor in his eyes betrayed the turmoil roiling within him. I could feel the electricity crackling in the air, a charge that threatened to ignite everything.

Leah's jaw tightened as she drew a deep breath. "You want honesty? Fine. I'm tired of pretending that everything's okay. I'm tired of feeling like I have to compete for your attention." Her words cut through the tension like a knife, sharp and unyielding. "It's like you two are in your own world, and I'm just... here, waiting for a moment that may never come."

I felt my heart ache for her, for the girl who had stood beside me in countless moments of laughter and pain. She deserved so much more than to feel like an outsider in her own life. "Leah, it's not like that. I care about you—both of you. But I don't know how to navigate this. It feels like we're stuck in a maze, and I'm afraid of what I'll find at the end."

"Maybe we're afraid of what we'll find together," Jake murmured, a flicker of understanding crossing his features. "But isn't it worth the risk?"

His question lingered in the air, a silent challenge that beckoned us to confront the shadows lurking at the edges of our hearts. I could feel the weight of our unspoken truths pressing down on us, the stories we hadn't told, the fears we hadn't faced, all swirling like autumn leaves caught in a whirlwind. The café felt smaller somehow, the walls inching closer as if urging us to confront our realities.

I realized then that this moment was a crucible, a pivotal point that could either shatter our fragile connections or forge them anew in the fires of honesty. Each word that passed between us felt like an offering, a chance to redefine our tangled web of emotions, to untangle the threads binding us together. The realization was both exhilarating and terrifying, a leap into the unknown that would either liberate us or leave us splintered and broken.

In the midst of that electric silence, the world outside The Willow faded away, leaving only the three of us suspended in a delicate equilibrium of uncertainty and raw emotion. I could feel my pulse thrumming like a drumbeat in my ears, urging me to speak, to break through the unspoken barriers that had held us captive for too long. The café, with its cozy charm and flickering candles, felt more like a confessional than a place for coffee, as if it too recognized the gravity of our moment.

Leah's eyes narrowed, reflecting a tempest of feelings that flickered beneath the surface. "You say you care, but what does that even mean? Do you care about me, or is it just some vague notion of what we are together? Because right now, it feels like I'm on the outside looking in, and I don't know how to change that." Her voice, usually so full of life, trembled slightly, revealing the fear that lay just beneath her fiery exterior.

I could feel the weight of her words sinking into the space between us, heavy and unyielding. "I don't want you to feel that way. You're not just a footnote in my life; you're part of the story." Each word felt like a stepping stone, leading us away from the brink of misunderstanding. I searched for something profound to bridge the gap, something that would resonate with both of them.

Jake shifted in his seat, running a hand through his hair, a gesture so familiar it tugged at my heartstrings. "It's not easy to figure out how we fit together. I know we've all been dancing around it, but maybe we need to stop dancing and start talking." His tone was sincere, like a lifeline tossed into turbulent waters. The way he leaned forward, his gaze locked onto mine, gave me courage.

Leah huffed, her arms still crossed tightly, a fortress shielding her from the vulnerability that loomed like a shadow. "And how exactly do you propose we talk about this? Just spill everything? As if we haven't been tiptoeing around each other's feelings like they're made of glass?" There was a hint of sarcasm in her voice, a defense mechanism designed to mask her fear.

"Maybe we just need to embrace the messiness of it all," I replied, my heart racing. "We can't keep pretending everything's fine when it's clearly not." The truth of that statement hung in the air like a thick fog, suffocating yet oddly freeing. I could feel a shift in the room, a palpable energy that sparked with possibility, urging us to step into the unknown together.

"Fine, let's embrace the mess," Leah said, her voice softer now, almost contemplative. "But where do we even start?" She uncrossed her arms, and I saw a flicker of vulnerability in her expression that made my heart ache.

"How about with what scares us the most?" Jake suggested, his voice steady yet gentle, as if he were leading us on a tightrope walk above the abyss. "Let's each say one thing we're afraid to lose."

The proposal hung in the air, heavy with implications. I glanced at Leah, who was now fiddling with the bracelet on her wrist, her brow furrowed in thought. My heart raced as I considered my own fears—those gnawing insecurities that had nestled within me like unwelcome guests.

"Okay," I finally said, the word barely escaping my lips. "I'm afraid of losing the connection we have, of it becoming something awkward and forced. I don't want to lose you two because you both mean more to me than I can put into words." My voice was steady, but the raw honesty made my throat tighten.

Leah nodded, her expression softening. "I'm afraid of being alone in this. I've fought so hard to be a part of something real, and I'm terrified that if I open up, it'll all crumble." Her words hung in the air like a fragile thread, weaving us closer together even as we faced our fears head-on.

Jake took a deep breath, his gaze flickering between us, the weight of his own fear looming like a dark cloud. "I'm afraid of failing you both. I want to be the one who brings us together, but I worry that I'll mess everything up." The honesty in his voice echoed in the space around us, and I felt the urge to reach out, to touch his arm, to reassure him that we were in this together.

In that moment, the weight of unspoken fears transformed into a bond, a tapestry woven from threads of vulnerability and honesty. The warmth of the café enveloped us, a protective cocoon against the chaos outside. I felt a shift within me, as if the act of laying bare our fears had peeled away layers of uncertainty, revealing the raw truth of our connection.

"Let's promise each other something," I said, my voice steady with newfound determination. "Let's promise to keep this dialogue open. No more hiding. If something feels off, we address it, no matter how uncomfortable it might be. We owe it to ourselves." The words slipped from my lips, a gentle reminder of the commitment I was ready to make.

Leah met my gaze, her eyes glistening with an emotion I couldn't quite decipher—was it gratitude or fear? "Okay," she said softly, nodding in agreement. "I can do that. I think we all can."

Jake reached out, placing his hand over mine, an anchor in the swirling sea of emotion. "We'll figure this out together. No matter what, we're in this together."

The simple act of his touch ignited a warmth within me, a flicker of hope that had been dimmed by doubt. It was a promise—a thread tying our destinies together, a commitment to navigate the complexities of our entangled lives. As the conversations around us faded into a comforting murmur, I felt a weight lift off my shoulders, replaced by a sense of clarity and purpose.

Outside, the world continued its frenetic pace, but in that little café, we were crafting a story that was uniquely ours—one of courage, vulnerability, and an unwavering bond that refused to be broken. It was a beginning wrapped in the simplicity of truth, and in that moment, I knew we were ready to embrace whatever came next, together.

We sat in the warmth of The Willow, enveloped by the fragrant aromas of coffee and freshly baked pastries, yet the weight of our revelations hung in the air like a storm cloud ready to burst. Each breath felt like a prayer—a silent plea for understanding, connection, and the courage to traverse the murky waters we had just unearthed. The dim light cast a soft glow around our small table, making it feel more like an intimate confessional than a café. Outside, autumn leaves danced like fiery confetti, their rustling a faint reminder of the changing seasons—a metaphor I couldn't shake as I gazed at Jake and Leah, both radiant yet burdened.

"Can we really do this?" Leah's voice broke through the quiet, laced with uncertainty yet tinged with a glimmer of hope. I sensed a tremor beneath her bravado, the vulnerability that lay just beneath the surface waiting to be acknowledged.

"Yes," I replied firmly, emboldened by the momentum of our conversation. "We have to. If we don't talk about what we're feeling, we'll never move forward. I refuse to let fear dictate our connection." My heart raced, fueled by the resolve coursing through me like a shot of adrenaline.

Jake nodded, his expression softening. "We've been avoiding the deeper conversations for too long. I want us to be real with each other. No more games." His intensity pierced the veil of uncertainty that had cloaked our interactions, drawing me closer to him and to Leah, as if we were magnets suddenly charged with the same energy.

"What if we find out we're not who we thought we were?" Leah's voice was barely above a whisper, her eyes darting between us, reflecting her inner turmoil. "What if opening this door leads to something we can't come back from?"

"Then we face it together," I asserted, leaning forward, a surge of determination swelling within me. "We're stronger together than apart. Besides, how can we truly know ourselves if we don't allow ourselves to be seen?"

Leah inhaled deeply, her chest rising with the weight of her breath, and for a moment, I feared she might retreat into the safety of silence again. But then, the corner of her mouth lifted in a tentative smile, a flicker of bravery that ignited my own. "Okay, let's do this," she said, her voice steadier now, the barriers starting to crumble.

The café around us felt like a sanctuary as we began to peel back the layers of our complexities. Jake spoke first, his voice even yet revealing the cracks beneath. "I think what scares me the most is that I've spent so long trying to please everyone else, trying to be the perfect friend, that I've lost sight of who I am. I worry that if I show you my true self, it won't be enough." The vulnerability in his admission laid bare the weight he had been carrying, and I could feel the air shift as Leah and I absorbed his honesty.

"It's not about being perfect," Leah replied, her voice soothing yet firm. "We all have our flaws. I've made mistakes, too. I often worry that I'm too much or not enough—too loud, too opinionated, too demanding of attention. But those things don't define me; they are just parts of my story." The light in her eyes spoke of strength, and I admired her courage for bringing her own insecurities into the open.

"I think that's what makes us human," I added, feeling the warmth of our collective understanding wrap around us like a comforting embrace. "The messiness, the imperfections—it's what binds us. It's what makes our connection real."

We took turns revealing our fears and aspirations, the conversation ebbing and flowing like the tide, pushing us toward an understanding that felt both foreign and familiar. I recounted moments from my past, the lonely nights spent wondering if I would ever find a place where I truly belonged. I spoke of the walls I had built, brick by brick, to protect myself from hurt, and how they had isolated me even as they offered a false sense of security.

Jake and Leah listened intently, their expressions shifting from empathy to solidarity. "You're not alone in feeling that way," Jake said softly, his voice a gentle balm. "I think we've all built walls. Sometimes it feels like they're the only things holding us together."

With every revelation, I felt a weight lift, the burdens we carried no longer solitary but shared. I caught sight of the barista behind the counter, her hands expertly crafting intricate latte art, and it struck me that our lives, too, were a kind of art—a mosaic of experiences, colors, and textures that, when pieced together, formed a beautiful whole.

As the afternoon wore on, we shifted from our fears to our dreams, the air between us crackling with new possibilities. I confessed my desire to travel, to experience life beyond the small town that had cradled me for too long. "I want to see the world, to dive into different cultures, to lose myself in the beauty of unfamiliar places," I said, my voice laced with longing.

Leah's eyes sparkled with excitement. "Me too! There's so much out there waiting to be explored. I want to walk the streets of Paris, to see the Eiffel Tower lit up against the night sky." The image she painted was so vivid I could almost smell the fresh pastries and hear the soft murmur of French conversations around us.

Jake leaned back, a thoughtful expression on his face. "Maybe we should make a pact. A list of places we want to visit together—things we want to do before we get too caught up in life."

I could feel a sense of exhilaration building within me, the prospect of new adventures lighting a fire in my chest. "I love that idea! Let's make it a tradition—a bucket list that we keep adding to." The thought of crafting dreams together felt like a beautiful promise, a testament to the bond we were forging.

The hours slipped away unnoticed, and before we knew it, twilight descended, casting a warm golden hue over The Willow. The atmosphere was infused with a sense of renewal, our laughter mingling with the soft notes of music playing in the background, creating a symphony of hope that echoed through the café.

With the last of the sunlight filtering through the windows, illuminating our table with a golden glow, I knew we were embarking on something transformative. We were three flawed souls weaving together a narrative rich with promise and vulnerability, ready to face the world outside—together.

In that moment, I could see the threads of our connection strengthen, binding us not just through shared fears but through the intoxicating allure of shared dreams. And as the evening drew to a close, the air thick with unspoken promises and newfound intentions, I felt a profound sense of belonging wash over me, one that whispered of endless possibilities just waiting to be discovered.

Chapter 29: A New Dawn

The moon hung like a silver coin tossed into a velvet purse, its luminescence spilling over the patio like whispers of forgotten dreams. I could hear the soft rustling of the leaves in the breeze, an intimate conversation between the trees and the night, as Jake and I settled into the wooden swing that creaked gently beneath our weight. It was one of those nights where the air felt electric, saturated with a blend of lingering tension and the promise of uncharted possibilities. The stars overhead blinked knowingly, like cosmic spectators to our unfolding drama, and I could almost taste the bittersweet tang of nostalgia on my lips.

Jake's hand felt warm against mine, a gentle reminder that connection can exist even in the presence of ghosts. His thumb brushed over the knuckles of my fingers, an unconscious gesture that sent a shiver down my spine, igniting a flicker of hope amidst the fear clinging to my heart. The truth about Leah hung between us, palpable and heavy, and I could sense the conflict brewing inside him, a tempest of emotions swirling like autumn leaves caught in a gust of wind.

"I just don't want to forget her," he finally said, his voice barely above a whisper, as if he feared the very sound of his words would shatter the delicate night. "She was my anchor, you know? My mother... she was everything."

The vulnerability in his tone wrapped around me, tugging at the threads of empathy woven into my heart. I wanted to tell him that memories, however cherished, could be transformed, reshaped into something new. But the words danced on the tip of my tongue, caught between my desire to comfort him and my fear of pushing too hard. Instead, I squeezed his hand tighter, grounding us both in that moment—a silent pledge that we were in this together.

Looking up at the stars, I tried to weave a tapestry of courage from the shimmering constellations, their stories echoing the struggles of countless souls before us. Each twinkle seemed to echo the same sentiment: that life, in all its messiness, was a series of choices. I was beginning to understand that we stood at a precipice, teetering between the comfort of the past and the uncertainty of what lay ahead.

"Memories are tricky," I said finally, my voice softer, as if I were sharing a secret with the universe. "They can be our chains or our wings. It's all in how we choose to carry them."

He turned to me, searching my eyes for answers, and in that moment, I saw the conflict etched deep within him—the need to honor his mother while also yearning to live. It was a battle that many of us face, the desire to preserve the essence of those we've lost while forging ahead into the uncharted territories of our own lives. I understood all too well; the scars of grief were not easily washed away, nor were they meant to be. But I believed in the possibility of healing, even if it felt fragile and far away.

As the first hints of dawn began to stretch their fingers across the horizon, painting the world in shades of pink and gold, I drew in a deep breath, letting the crisp air fill my lungs with hope. There was something magical about dawn, a rebirth that whispered of second chances. It felt like a reminder that we are never truly alone in our journeys. The sun would rise again, just as we could find the strength to rise from the shadows of our pasts.

Jake's gaze drifted to the horizon, where the sky slowly surrendered to the sun's embrace. In that quiet moment, I saw the flicker of realization crossing his features, a tentative acceptance of the inevitability of change. His grip on my hand tightened, as if he were anchoring himself to me, to this moment of possibility.

"I don't want to lose her," he said again, but this time, there was a hint of determination in his voice, a growing understanding that letting go didn't mean forgetting.

The soft rustle of the grass beneath our feet felt like an invitation, a call to step into the unknown together. I leaned closer, feeling the warmth radiating off his skin, and whispered, "You won't lose her. You'll carry her with you, always. But you can also create new memories. We can, together."

As the sun peeked over the edge of the world, flooding us with light, I watched as Jake's expression shifted, the weight of uncertainty slowly lifting from his shoulders. The warmth of dawn spilled over us, casting away the chill of the night, and with it, I felt a flicker of hope igniting in my chest. We were embarking on a new journey—one defined not by what we had lost, but by what we still had to discover.

With that newfound clarity hanging in the air between us, I felt the ground beneath us shift, the world tilting toward a future ripe with possibilities. Our hands intertwined, I could sense the stirrings of a bond that transcended the pain of the past, a connection blooming in the light of a new dawn. And as the sun fully emerged, washing everything in golden hues, I understood that we were not merely survivors of our own stories; we were the authors, ready to pen the next chapters together.

The sun rose steadily, its warm glow sweeping across the landscape like a painter's brush, eager to splash vibrant colors across a canvas long shrouded in shadow. I could hear the distant chirping of birds welcoming the day, their songs weaving a melodious backdrop to the quiet rustle of the world waking up. Jake and I remained on the patio, our intertwined fingers a small oasis of warmth against the coolness of dawn.

The scent of fresh dew clung to the air, mingling with the fragrant hints of blooming honeysuckle that grew wild along the garden's edges. Each inhalation was a reminder that nature thrived even after the harshest storms, that life could renew itself in the most unexpected ways. It struck me then how much I longed for that renewal, not just for Jake but for myself, too—a shared journey toward a brighter horizon.

"Do you remember the first time we met?" I asked, turning my head slightly to catch his gaze. There was a glint of mischief in my tone, a playful attempt to lighten the weight we had been carrying.

Jake's lips curled into a smile, and for a moment, the shadows of the past faded, replaced by the memory of laughter. "I remember your questionable choice in footwear. What was that—some kind of rubber flip-flops? I thought they were going to be the end of you in that gravel driveway."

"Oh, come on!" I laughed, shaking my head at the recollection. "They were stylish! And a statement! Who knew gravel could be such a formidable foe?"

His laughter joined mine, ringing out like bells that shattered the morning stillness. It was refreshing to slip into the familiarity of those earlier days, before the weight of loss and longing had become so pronounced. In those moments, I could see the glimmers of the person he used to be—the carefree, charming guy who once seemed invincible.

As we reminisced, the air around us lightened, and I could feel the tether of fear loosening its grip, allowing the promise of something new to breathe. "I think we need a new adventure," I said, emboldened by the fleeting ease between us. "Something to remind us that life is still out there waiting for us to live it."

Jake turned to me, his brow furrowing in thought. "What did you have in mind? Bungee jumping? Skydiving? I could be convinced..."

"Maybe not quite that extreme," I said, feigning a contemplative look. "How about a road trip? Just the two of us, hitting the open road with no particular destination in mind. We could rediscover ourselves along the way."

The idea hung in the air, shimmering with potential. The corners of Jake's mouth turned up slightly, as if he were weighing the merit of my proposal. "You realize that means we'll have to stop for gas, right? I'm not sure my truck has survived more than a couple of trips to the grocery store in the last year."

I laughed again, the sound spilling over us like sunlight breaking through clouds. "I'll take that as a yes, then! We can make it a proper adventure—loud music, random roadside diners, maybe even a questionable hotel. I have a feeling we'd end up with some wild stories to tell."

His smile deepened, and I could see the tension in his shoulders beginning to ease, his expression softening with the possibilities. "Okay, I'm in. But only if you promise to bring those rubber flip-flops. They're practically legendary at this point."

"Deal!" I said, squeezing his hand in a moment of genuine excitement.

The prospect of escape, however temporary, felt like a breath of fresh air. It was as if we were shedding layers of ourselves, ready to expose the raw, unvarnished versions of who we were. Perhaps this adventure could help us navigate the labyrinth of our emotions, finding our way through the confusion of love and loss without the constraints of our past.

As we stood there, bathed in the golden light of morning, I couldn't help but envision the wide-open roads stretching before us, the hum of the engine harmonizing with the melody of our laughter. The world was vast and vibrant, filled with places waiting to be discovered, and I wanted to experience it all with him by my side.

The sun climbed higher, casting long shadows that danced playfully around us. I noticed the faint outlines of leaves shimmering like green jewels, the intricate patterns they created framing Jake's profile. He looked contemplative, as though he were mapping out the contours of a future that once felt lost.

"Do you really think it'll help?" he asked, his voice steady yet laced with an underlying fragility.

"I do," I replied, meeting his gaze with conviction. "Sometimes, the act of simply moving forward can shed light on what we're really holding on to. It's not about erasing the past but making space for new memories to coexist with the old ones."

He nodded slowly, processing my words as the sun continued its ascent, illuminating the world around us in warm hues. I could see the flicker of hope igniting within him, a spark kindling in the depths of his soul. It was a small, quiet moment, but it felt monumental, as if we had both taken the first step toward something monumental and life-altering.

Together, we sat in the sunlight, contemplating the endless possibilities that lay ahead. I could feel the magnetic pull of adventure, the intoxicating thrill of uncertainty that beckoned us to break free from the chains of our past. It was a delicate dance, one that required both courage and vulnerability, but with each passing second, I was reminded of the beauty in taking risks, in daring to step into the unknown.

As the sky transitioned from soft pastels to brilliant blues, I took a deep breath, allowing the weight of the world to shift from my shoulders. With Jake by my side, I felt emboldened to embrace whatever came next—an unwritten chapter bursting with promise, ready to be filled with laughter, tears, and the magic of rediscovery.

The day unfolded with the gentle insistence of spring, a promise wrapped in sunlight and a sky that seemed too vast to contain our hopes. Jake and I made plans, letting the excitement bubble between us like freshly uncorked champagne. The details were sketchy at first—a fleeting thought here, a whimsical idea there—until they coalesced into a tangible route on the map I unfurled on the kitchen table. Our journey would take us along winding country roads, through the very heart of America, where landscapes shifted from bustling towns to sleepy pastures.

With each pin I placed on the map, I imagined the sights we would see and the memories we would collect like souvenirs, each one a testament to our shared adventure. The rolling hills of Kentucky called to me, promising emerald pastures dotted with grazing horses, their sleek coats glistening in the sun like polished obsidian. I could picture us stopping at quaint roadside diners, where the smell of bacon and freshly brewed coffee wafted through the air, enticing us to linger over slices of homemade pie.

Jake leaned against the counter, arms crossed and a sly grin playing at the corners of his mouth. "I can already hear the country music twanging in the background. You know we're going to end up in a place that has a neon sign that reads 'Best Fried Chicken in Three Counties.'"

I laughed, envisioning the absurdity of it all. "As long as you're prepared for the questionable hygiene standards, I'm all in."

His chuckle was a balm, soothing the jagged edges of our earlier conversation. We were peeling away the layers of our pasts, embracing a future where laughter could drown out the ghosts that lingered just beyond our periphery. With every passing hour, the trip transformed from mere escapism into an opportunity for both of us to redefine who we were in the wake of our losses.

The morning passed in a flurry of preparation, punctuated by the hum of the radio, which provided a soundtrack of classic hits as we packed Jake's old pickup truck. The truck had seen better days, with its faded paint and mismatched upholstery, yet it held a certain charm that made it feel like a steadfast companion. I arranged our bags in the back, carefully selecting the essentials: a few worn novels, a cooler filled with snacks, and a playlist of songs we would sing off-key during long stretches of open road.

As we climbed into the cab, I caught a glimpse of the world beyond the windshield—the vast expanse of the sky painted in brilliant blues, dotted with fluffy white clouds that seemed to echo the rhythm of our hearts. With a turn of the key, the engine sputtered to life, and we were off, the road stretching before us like a promise waiting to be fulfilled.

The hum of tires on asphalt soon became a comforting white noise, allowing space for conversation to flow freely. We spoke about everything and nothing—the mundane details of our lives, the peculiar quirks of the towns we passed, and the dreams we had nurtured in silence. Each shared story felt like an unwrapping of layers, revealing the essence of who we were beneath the hurt and heartache.

It was in the soft glow of sunset that we made our first impromptu stop. We pulled over at a roadside vista, a sweeping view of golden fields and distant mountains basking in the evening light. The landscape glowed, as if the sun had dipped its brush in honey and painted the world in warm hues. We climbed out of the truck, our laughter spilling into the stillness of the evening, echoing against the mountains like a call to the wild.

Jake leaned against the hood, gazing out at the horizon. "You know," he began, "I've always thought there was something poetic about sunsets. They're beautiful, but they also mark the end of something. It's like saying goodbye to the day, even when it's been good."

"True," I replied, crossing my arms and leaning into the truck. "But isn't it also a reminder that a new day is just around the corner? It's cyclical—a natural rhythm."

He turned to me, his eyes reflecting the fiery hues of the setting sun, and for a moment, I thought I could see the gears in his mind turning. "You're right. It's almost comforting, in a way."

We stood there, enveloped in the tranquility of the moment, letting the weight of unspoken truths linger between us. The air grew cool as twilight approached, and I shivered slightly, pulling my cardigan tighter around my shoulders. Jake noticed and shrugged off his jacket, draping it over my shoulders with an easy familiarity that sent warmth flooding through me.

As darkness enveloped the landscape, we returned to the truck, our hearts lighter than when we had begun our journey. The road stretched ahead, illuminated by the glow of the headlights, guiding us into the unknown. It felt exhilarating, this new chapter filled with uncertainties and possibilities, as if we were driving straight into a canvas waiting to be painted.

The night unfolded with all the charm of a classic road trip: late-night diner stops, cups of coffee that felt like a warm hug, and the hum of laughter that filled the empty spaces between us. In those small moments, I felt the beginnings of something fragile yet beautiful taking shape. Each shared glance, each spontaneous joke, drew us closer, weaving a tapestry of connection that began to cover the scars left by our pasts.

By the time we settled into a small, quirky motel that night, I could feel the adrenaline of adventure coursing through my veins. The neon sign flickered above us, announcing the establishment's questionable reputation with a certain charm. I shared a knowing smile with Jake as we entered the cramped yet cozy room, its walls adorned with faded floral wallpaper and a mismatched collection of furniture.

"Welcome to the heart of America," I quipped, flopping down onto one of the beds, the springs creaking in protest.

Jake laughed, tossing his bag onto the other bed. "I think we've officially reached the apex of adventure."

And in that moment, as we sat surrounded by the absurdity of our surroundings, the laughter cascading between us felt like a promise—a pledge to move forward, together. The ghosts of our pasts lingered in the background, but they no longer held the same power. Instead, we were building new memories, fresh stories to layer over the old ones, creating a rich tapestry of experiences that would redefine our journey.

As we settled in for the night, the gentle buzz of the night's energy enveloped us. I glanced out the window at the moon hanging low in the sky, and for the first time in a long while, I felt a flicker of hope igniting within me. In the laughter, in the adventure, and in the uncharted territory of our hearts, I sensed the dawning of a new dawn—a shared path illuminated by possibilities, just waiting to be explored.